BY THE SWORD

ALISON STUART

The award-winning* first book in the GUARDIANS OF THE CROWN trilogy covering the turbulent years of the Interregnum... Three stories of men who would die for their King and honour, and the women who will do whatever it takes to protect those that they love.

England 1650: In the aftermath of the execution of the King, England totters once more on the brink of civil war. The country will be divided and lives lost as Charles II makes a last bid to regain his throne.

Kate Ashley finds her loyalty to the Parliamentary cause tested when she inherits responsibility for the estate of the Royalist Thornton family. To protect the people she cares about, she will need all her wits to restore its fortunes and fend off the ever-present threat of greedy neighbours.

Jonathan Thornton, exiled and hunted for his loyalty to the King's cause, now returns to England to garner support for the young King. Haunted by the demons of his past, Jonathan risks death at every turn and brings danger to those who love him. Finding Kate in his family home, he sees in her the hope for his future, and a chance at a life he doesn't deserve.

*Winner of the 2008 EPIC Award for Best Historical Romance

ABOUT THE AUTHOR

Alison Stuart writes historical romances and short stories set in England and Australia and across different periods of history. She is best known for her English Civil War stories and also THE POSTMISTRESS and THE GOLDMINER'S SISTER, stories set in the Victorian goldfields in the 1870s.

She also writes historical mysteries as A.M. Stuart and her popular Harriet Gordon mystery series is set in Singapore in 1910.

She lives in Melbourne, Australia with her husband and a geriatric cat. In a past life Alison worked as a lawyer across a variety of disciplines including the military and emergency services. She has lived in Africa and Singapore and, when circumstances permit, travels extensively - all for research of course!

To discover more about Alison Stuart visit her website or follow her on her social media accounts.

www.alisonstuart.com

BOOKS BY ALISON STUART

Australian Historical Romance

THE POSTMISTRESS (also in audio)

THE GOLDMINER'S SISTER (also in audio)

THE HOMECOMING (also in audio)

The Guardians of the Crown Series

BY THE SWORD

THE KING'S MAN

EXILE'S RETURN

GUARDIANS OF THE CROWN (BOX SET)

The Feathers in the Wind Collection

AND THEN MINE ENEMY

HER REBEL HEART

SECRETS IN TIME (also in audio)

FEATHERS IN THE WIND (BOX SET)

Regency/World War One

GATHER THE BONES (also in audio)

LORD SOMERTON'S HEIR

A CHRISTMAS LOVE REDEEMED (Novella)

(Writing as A.M. Stuart)

The Harriet Gordon Mysteries

SINGAPORE SAPPHIRE (Book 1)

REVENGE IN RUBIES (Book 2)

DEDICATION

This book is dedicated to the memory of my grandfather, ALST, who first took me to 'Seven Ways'

BY THE SWORD

GUARDIANS OF THE CROWN BOOK 1

ALISON STUART

OPORTET PUBLISHING

CHAPTER 1

BARTON, YORKSHIRE, FEBRUARY, 1650

*I*n the stone-walled garden of the little manor house at Barton, a fierce battle raged. Robert's well-aimed snowball caught his cousin Thomas Ashley squarely on the head, knocking off his hat. Unbalanced, Tom fell back into the snow and lay there, laughing while his three cousins stood around pelting him with snow. Tom recovered his feet and, brushing off the fine, powdery snow, he and Robert joined forces against the other two.

Watching the children from her chair by the window, Kate Ashley smiled. Although the same age as Robert, Tom stood nearly a head taller and his dark hair made him instantly recognisable amongst his red-headed cousins. Beyond the walls, a lowering sky threatened more snow and she opened the window, leaning out to call the children in.

'Look, Mother,' Tom called. 'Robert and I are General Fairfax and General Cromwell and Janet and Joseph are the King's men. We're winning of course.'

Kate sighed. How easily the games of adults could be mirrored in the innocent games of children, and war was all any of these children had known. They had been born into a country torn apart by a struggle between a King and his Parliament, leaving her son with the bitter legacy of a father he had never known.

'Kate.' Her sister's voice recalled her to the room. 'You're not listening. I asked what you intend to do about this letter?'

Kate looked around at Suzanne as she pulled the casement shut.

'I intend to do nothing,' she said. 'I will not go all the way to Worcestershire just so an old man can clear his conscience before he goes to the Lord.'

'Now, sister,' Suzanne scolded. 'The Lord teaches us to forgive.'

'I've nothing to forgive,' Kate said. 'As far as I am concerned the quarrel with the Thorntons died with Richard's father. It is nothing to do with me.'

'I think you should go,' her sister responded, 'Tom is his great-grandson. Doesn't the boy have the right to know his father's family?'

'Really, Suzanne.' Kate found it hard to keep the exasperation from her voice. 'It is thirty years since Elizabeth Thornton eloped with David. In all that time there has been not one word from the Thorntons. Whatever rights Francis Thornton had in respect of my son were long since forfeit.'

'I think you are unduly harsh, Kate.'

Kate shrugged. 'It's not a matter of being harsh. It is simply of no consequence to me. We don't need the Thorntons. We've never needed the Thorntons.' She turned back to look out of the window. 'Just look at that sky. It will snow again before nightfall.'

She rapped on the glass, summoning the reluctant children in from the cold. They tumbled into the warm parlour, leaving a trail of wet footprints on the well-polished floor. Kate's maid, Ellen, brought a tray of honey cakes, and with only the scantest regard for manners, the hungry children made short work of the food.

Kate sat back watching the scene with a fond smile. Tom's head bent close to that of his cousin and best friend, Robert, as they spoke in whispers. The two had been inseparable companions from birth, Tom being the older by only a few days. However, there the resemblance ended. In Robert's face and in his uncertain health was a fragility not found in his sturdy cousin or his siblings. The two sisters never spoke of it, but Kate, glancing up at Suzanne's impassive face, knew she feared her beloved child might not see manhood.

Suzanne packed away her sewing and stood, easing her aching back. Heavily pregnant with her sixth child, she found sitting difficult.

'Come, children,' she announced. 'We must be home before that snow.'

Ignoring the howls of disappointment, the children were bundled into cloaks, hoods and gloves and distributed between the various mounts they had brought with them. Suzanne and her husband, the sturdy William Rowe, lived at Barton Hall barely one mile distant. The children moved easily between the two houses and Kate did not begrudge Tom the company of his cousins. The life of an only child could be very solitary.

'Let me know what you decide,' Suzanne said, leaning down from where she sat pillion behind one of her grooms. 'I'm sure William will look after things for you, should you decide to go.'

'You needn't trouble William,' Kate replied. 'I have no intention of going.'

Suzanne glanced across at Tom, who stood stroking the nose of Robert's pony. 'Perhaps it is not a matter for you to decide alone,' she said. 'It seems to me that perhaps Tom should be consulted.'

Kate waved her sister off and stood in the shelter of the porch as the Rowe family turned out through the gates into the lane.

As Tom ran down to the gate to wave them off, Kate considered her sister's words. It seemed inappropriate to involve a child in such weighty decisions. He had never asked about his grandmother's family and Kate would not have known what answer to give if he had. She and Richard had only discussed the Thorntons on a couple of occasions, and in all the years she had shared a house with Richard's father, she had never heard David Ashley speak of them. Now he too was dead and there was nobody to ask.

How dare Richard's Thornton grandfather choose this moment to write.

She looked up as the first swirl of snowflakes drifted down from the bulging clouds. She let them fall onto her face, cold and stinging, and turned back to the warmth of the house.

'Did your grandfather ever talk to you of the Thorntons?' Kate ventured as she sat on the edge of her son's bed that night.

Tom regarded her from her under his heavy, dark fringe. 'No. Who are the Thorntons?'

'Well...' Kate took a deep breath and dredged her memory. 'Your grandmother, Elizabeth, was a Thornton.'

Tom yawned. 'Was she? Is this going to be a boring story, mother?'

Undeterred by her son's lack of interest, Kate continued. 'She married your grandfather against her father's wishes.'

'Really?' Curiosity sparked in Tom's eyes.

'Her father, Sir Francis Thornton, swore he would never have anything to do with her again.'

'So what happened then?'

'Well, as far as I know, the story, your grandmother died when your father was born. And we have heard nothing from the Thorntons before or since.'

Tom snorted. 'That's it?'

Kate bit her lip and considered leaving it at that, but Suzanne had been right. Tom deserved to know.

'I've had a letter from your great-grandfather, Sir Francis Thornton. He heard that your grandfather Ashley has died and he has invited us to visit.'

'Where does he live?' Tom's eyes were bright with interest now.

'At a house called Seven Ways in Worcestershire.' Kate replied.

'Worcestershire?' Tom's eyes widened. He had never been further than York. He frowned. 'Seven Ways is a funny name for a house.'

'I recall your father once told me it was called Seven Ways because one of your ancestors was told the King would be passing by and he constructed seven entrances to his property to make it easier for the King to find him.'

'And did he?' Tom asked.

Kate laughed and shook her head. 'I have no idea.'

'Seven Ways.' Tom tried the name out again. 'I suppose Sir Francis is very old?'

'I suppose he must be,' Kate agreed.

Tom pushed his thick hair out of his eyes and looked up at his mother. 'Do you think we should go, Mother?'

Kate thought for a long minute, remembering her conversation with Suzanne. 'I think, perhaps, if your grandfather were still alive he would want you to go. For all he never talked of them, I doubt he would prevent you from meeting them. It is your right.'

'What else do you know about them?' Tom hugged his knees.

She shook her head. 'I know nothing more than what I have told you.'

Tom looked up at her. 'Then I think we should go, Mother. Shall we? It will be an adventure.'

Every instinct within Kate screamed resistance. She had lived through a bitterly fought war and had no need for further adventures in her life.

She leaned over and kissed her son gently on the forehead. 'If that's what you want, Tom. I will see what can be arranged. Now sleep. You've had a busy day.'

Tom lay down and closed his eyes. 'Seven Ways,' he murmured drowsily. 'It is a funny name for a house.'

Kate drew the curtains around the boy's bed to keep out the cold draughts and crossed to the window. The snow had passed, obliterating the signs of the afternoon's battle and laying a fresh, white crust on the trees and the walls. She looked out across the garden, lit by the cold light of the winter moon, to the familiar dark shapes of the hills and woods beyond.

Seven Ways, she thought, echoing Tom's comment. It is indeed a very strange name for a house.

CHAPTER 2

SEVEN WAYS, WORCESTERSHIRE, MAY 1650

*A*n ache of homesickness, every bit as physical as her sore, weary muscles, clawed at Kate's heart as she looked from the long, low window of the pleasant bedchamber across the unfamiliar Worcestershire countryside. She thought longingly of her own parlour and the little garden bursting with spring life that she had left behind and fought back the tears that welled in her eyes.

The moment she had sent the letter to Sir Francis Thornton, accepting his invitation, she had regretted the decision. She had travelled little in her life, and the thought of making the long journey to Worcestershire filled her with dread. Using her sister's confinement as an excuse, she had delayed the journey as long as she could, but Suzanne had been safely delivered of another girl, the weather had improved and the promised visit could wait no longer.

Knowing she must feign some sort of cheerfulness while she prepared herself and her son for their first meeting with the mysterious Thorntons, none of whom had been at the door to greet them on arrival, she turned back to face her son. Tom turned an anxious face up towards his mother as Ellen, who had travelled with them, dragged a brush through his obstinate locks.

'Will they like me?' he asked.

'How can they not?' Kate smiled at him and planted a kiss on his forehead.

He cringed away from her.

'Please don't do that, Mother,' he protested.

She smiled with a little regret. Only a year ago her son would have covered her in kisses.

'Come, Tom. It is time to meet this mysterious family,' she said, opening the door to admit the elderly steward who had come to conduct the visitors to meet the residents of Seven Ways.

Their feet echoed on the polished boards of the ancient house as they followed the man. He stopped before a panelled door and knocked. Tom slipped his hand into his mother's and Kate squeezed it as the man opened the door admitting them into a bright, cheerful parlour.

The only occupant of the room, a young woman intent upon some intricate embroidery, sat perched on the broad windowsill of the long, low window. She set it down as Kate and her son entered and rose to her feet. Tom looked up at his mother, who released his hand and dropped a dutiful curtsy.

Before she could rise, the young woman had crossed the floor and embraced her.

'Mistress Ashley, I'm so pleased you have come.'

She released Kate, who, unbalanced by the effusive welcome, took a step backward to recover her composure. The woman turned to Tom, who bowed stiffly.

'And you must be Thomas. I am your cousin Eleanor.' The woman returned his bow with a low curtsey.

As she rose, she looked at Kate, a warm smile lighting the

pretty, heart-shaped face.

'Lady Eleanor Longley, but please call me Nell. We are kin after all. May I call you Katherine?'

Kate blinked. This lack of formality had caught her by surprise.

'K...Kate,' she stuttered.

'Kate it is then. Now, let me look at you, Tom.' Nell placed her hands on Tom's shoulders and appeared to study him intently. 'I do declare you are the image of my brother, Jonathan, at the same age. See, there behind you, Kate is a small portrait of my brothers done when Ned was about fifteen and Jonathan twelve or thirteen. I can't recall exactly, although I do remember Jonathan got into terrible trouble for turning up late.'

Kate turned to look at a charming head and shoulders study of two boys. The older one, whom she assumed to be 'Ned', shared his sister's golden hair and wide, sunny smile. The younger one, dark-haired Jonathan, glowered sulkily from the canvas. Even allowing for the sullen expression the resemblance to Tom was, as Nell had observed, striking.

'Nell, please forgive me. I'm afraid I know nothing of my husband's family,' Kate said. 'Will I have the pleasure of meeting your brothers?'

Nell's mouth drooped. 'Of course. I took it for granted that you would know of whom I spoke. We lost Ned at Edgehill, the first battle of the war, my father at Naseby and Jonathan...' She waved her hand, dismissing Jonathan's fate. 'We are a very sad family as you will come to see. My husband, Giles, is an exile in France and our home, Longley Abbey, is sequestered for his debts. If it were not for the generosity of my grandfather, my daughter and I would be quite homeless.'

'I'm sorry,' Kate said. The words seemed inadequate to cover the extent of this woman's loss. 'You have a daughter?'

Nell smiled, 'Ann. She's but three years old. You will meet her later.'

'Where's Sir Francis?' Tom asked, looking around the room as if he expected his great-grandfather to jump out from behind a chest.

'Grandfather is not in the best of health, Tom, but he will join us for supper tonight. He is very much looking forward to meeting you. Now would you like to see the house? It would be my greatest pleasure to show it to you.'

Following in her guide's wake, Kate concluded that Seven Ways had never been a grand house, but in its shabby gentility, it gave the sense of a much-loved home. The war had left physical scars: boarded windows, broken wainscoting — no doubt where axes had torn looking for hidden silver — and bare walls where once fine pictures or tapestries had hung. The furniture was ordinary, workaday stuff. Anything of value, including the better furniture, Nell told her in a matter-of-fact tone, had gone as plunder when the forces of Parliament had occupied the house at the end of the war.

'You cannot have failed to notice, Kate,' Nell said, her fingers twisting the gold chain around her neck, 'that this house is but a shadow of its former self. Our family has paid dearly for loyalty to the King.'

They finished the tour in the Great Hall, which occupied the centre of the house on the first floor. A fine chimney breast carved with the Thornton coat of arms — three golden leopards' heads on a crimson field — dominated the room and unlike the bare walls of the other rooms, a large family portrait still hung on one of the walls. Kate stood back to study it in greater detail, speculating on the identities of the stiff, formal group of people wearing the fashion of thirty years earlier.

'All gone save for me, Mistress Ashley.'

Kate turned and dropped a hasty curtsy. The frail, elderly man, stooped and leaning heavily on a cane, inclined his head.

'Grandfather,' Nell said. 'I thought you were resting?'

'There is plenty of time for rest, Nell. Mistress Ashley, welcome to Seven Ways. And unless I am gravely mistaken, this must be young Thomas?'

Tom stood very straight and gave his great-grandfather the benefit of his most formal bow.

'Sir,' he said, 'it is a great pleasure to make your acquaintance.'

Kate hid a smile at the gravity of her son's demeanour.

'And I yours, Master Ashley,' Sir Francis replied.

The trace of a smile twitched at the corners of his mouth and he indicated that the boy should come closer. With crabbed fingers, he tilted the boy's face towards him.

He frowned and addressed his granddaughter. 'Nell, is he not like Jonathan at the same age? The resemblance is quite remarkable.'

'I said as much myself,' Nell said. 'Let us hope, for his sake, that is where the similarity ends.'

Sir Frances turned back to Kate. 'You were admiring the portrait, Mistress Ashley? That is my family in happier days.'

Kate looked back at the family study. Sir Francis' younger self dominated it, tall, upright and imposing. Only the eyes and the rather long nose, now emphasised by old age, gave the clue to the identity of the sitter.

Sir Francis pointed with his cane. 'See there, my wife Anne, my son William and his wife Sarah and our beloved Ned as a baby.' The cane slowly lowered to the ground again. 'And of course, Bess.'

Kate looked at the first likeness she had ever seen of her husband's mother, the defiant Elizabeth who had eloped to York-shire with the love of her life, David Ashley. Elizabeth Thornton had been no classical beauty, but she had an arresting face and the hazel eyes, fixed forever on the father who had disowned her, revealed a determined and intelligent woman. She scanned the painted face, looking for some resemblance between this woman and her son, Kate's husband Richard. Perhaps she could see something about the nose and mouth? Or perhaps, Kate acknowledged bitterly, the memory of Richard had faded to a point where she could no longer recollect his features clearly.

'See, Tom,' she said indicating Elizabeth. 'There is your grandmother.'

Tom cocked his head to one side.

'It was painted the year Bess...' Sir Francis paused, then continued in a softer voice, '...the year she married David Ashley.'

He turned away from the painting. 'I'm pleased you have come, Mistress Ashley. I trust my granddaughter has seen you comfortably settled?'

'Indeed, thank you, Sir Francis. I have a delightful chamber and we have been made most welcome.'

'The gatehouse was Elizabeth's chamber. I thought you would appreciate it.' Moving with difficulty, he crossed the floor to seat himself in a chair beside the hearth.

He pointed his stick at the chair opposite him, and as Kate sat, he said, 'Tell me of the Ashleys. David Ashley never married again?'

She met his eyes and read the need for reassurance in them.

'No,' she said. 'For David Ashley, there was only ever one woman.'

He held her gaze then nodded slowly.

'And Richard? Your husband...' he paused, '...my grandson, he fought for Parliament, I believe?'

Kate nodded. 'He was a captain under Sir Thomas Fairfax.' She indicated her son. 'Thomas is named for him.'

Francis nodded thoughtfully. 'Indeed. I heard only good things of Fairfax. My grandson, Jonathan, had great respect for him. Now, if I recall Jonathan and Richard were much of an age. Jonathan was born to soldiering. His father's attempts to turn him into a scholar were sadly wasted. What was Richard's inclination?'

Kate smiled without humour. 'Richard was a scholar, not a soldier. He hated the war.'

She closed her eyes, remembering the bitterness in her husband's eyes as he told her of the deaths of the men under his command.

When she opened them again she found the old man's gaze resting on her face. 'Forgive me for dredging up painful memories, Mistress Ashley. It is to my sorrow that I do not even know how he died.'

The old, familiar pain clutched at her heart. It had been a great victory, the wounded had told her as they had trickled into the village after the battle at Marston Moor. Prince Rupert had been routed, the forces of the Parliament triumphant. Kate cared nothing for Parliament or victory. The broken man beneath her hands commanded all her attention that night.

'He died of the wounds he received at Marston Moor,' she said. 'His father brought him home after the battle. He took two days to die.'

Richard's grandfather shook his head. 'I'm sorry, my dear,' he said. 'The war has dealt ill with us all. Nell and her little Ann, you and Thomas are all that remains of this family and I am nearing the end of my allotted time on this earth. It is long past time to put away the differences born only of a stubborn man and his equally stubborn daughter.' He shook his head. 'Such a petty feud to cause all these years of division, and I regret every day that has passed. I hope, Mistress Ashley, and you Thomas, that your coming here is the start of a new chapter in the life of this family.'

CHAPTER 3

SEVEN WAYS, JUNE 1650

Despite the warmth of the sunny day, Kate found Sir Francis sitting in a chair by the window of his bedchamber overlooking the garden with a blanket over his shoulders and another around his knees. A book lay open but face down on the table beside him.

He looked up as she entered the room. 'I've been watching you, Kate. Your labours in the garden are to be commended.'

Kate self-consciously pushed back the loose strands of hair that strayed from beneath her cap and cursed the freckles that had appeared around her nose at the first touch of sun. She must look like a common kitchen maid, not the proper wife for this man's grandson.

'I've been tending the roses. Despite the lack of pruning, they promise a fine show. I thought you might like some to cheer the day.'

She shifted the book and placed the bowl of roses she carried on the small table at his elbow. The rich smell momentarily lifted the fug of the sickroom, and the long fingers of Sir Francis' right hand reached out to touch the blooms with a reverence that surprised her. For the first time, she noticed a heavy, gold signet ring loosely circling his skeletal index finger.

'I fear the garden is something of a lost cause,' he said.

Kate agreed but she disliked being idle. She had made the remains of the once fine, sunken rose garden her focus. Since her arrival, she had spent the afternoons clearing the beds of weeds and pruning back the wilder branches. The roses, responding quickly to the attention, bloomed prolifically in the warmth of early summer.

'Working in a garden is one of my pleasures in life,' she said

Sir Francis nodded. 'There is no room on this earth for idle people. As for the garden, it was one of the finest gardens in the county before several troops of Parliament horse trampled it in '45 looking for my scapegrace grandson. They cut down most of the orchard too.' His thin lips compressed. 'Since then I've had not the time or the money to rectify the damage.' He looked at her and nodded. 'It pleases me that there is someone to care for it again.'

Kate touched the soft petals of the roses. 'I have these same roses in my garden.' Looking up, she sought the old man's eyes, holding his gaze. 'Richard told me his mother had planted them from stock she brought from Seven Ways. Every year David would place the first blooms on her grave.' She hesitated before adding, 'I made sure that I remembered to do the same this year.'

The old man looked away. 'Bess would have only lived to see them bloom once. It is kind of you to remember.'

Kate took a breath. 'You must know, Sir Francis. David Ashley loved your daughter. He never stopped loving her,' she said, the words coming out in a rush.

He returned his gaze to her and nodded. 'Thank you, my dear. I know that. I have always known but it pleases me to hear it.' His thin shoulders straightened. 'Nell tells me that you plan on returning to Yorkshire shortly. Is that true?'

'In a few days,' she said. 'I have my own responsibilities I must return to.'

The door opened and Nell entered without knocking, holding a paper in her hand.

'Oh. Kate.' A flash of colour rose to her cheeks as she concealed the paper she carried in the folds of her skirt. 'I didn't expect you to be here.'

'Nell,' her grandfather greeted her. 'We were just discussing Kate's imminent departure. I was just going to say that I will miss the boy. I have enjoyed our chats.' His lips twisted in a rueful smile. 'I do believe he's not scared of me. Have I lost the power to intimidate, do you think?'

Nell smiled. 'Grandfather, St Peter himself will not dare refuse you entrance to heaven.' She looked at Kate. 'I have some business with my grandfather, Kate. Would you excuse us?'

Sir Francis smiled at Kate and gestured to the window. 'I suggest you return to your Herculean task in the rose garden while the weather stays fine.'

Kate smiled and with a brisk curtsy swept out of the room to return to the garden.

Nell joined her later, spreading a blanket beneath an oak tree where she sat and worked on her needlework while little Ann pottered after Kate, picking daisies in the overgrown lawn. As the afternoon wore on, Kate abandoned her task, dropping down on the blanket beside the younger woman. She wiped her face on her sleeve and surveyed the overgrown garden. Her poor efforts were a mere drop in a pond compared to the work the garden required, but it satisfied her needs both to be busy and to create some order from chaos.

Nell laid down her embroidery hoop and picked up the

flowers her daughter had brought her, weaving them into a chain. She placed the chain of flowers like a crown upon Ann's golden curls.

'Look, Mama. I'm a queen,' Ann declared and turned around on her toes, letting her skirts billow out.

'And a lovely queen too,' Nell agreed.

'I'm going to show Tommy.'

Ann had caught sight of her cousin in the company of his newfound friend, young Peter Knowles, son of the tenant of Home Farm. They were coming from the direction of the stables behind the house. The two women watched as Nan hurtled across the garden towards the boys.

'Tom is very patient with her.' Nell sighed as Tom stooped to pick up the flowery crown that had toppled from her head.

'He's used to small cousins. My sister has six children and, no doubt, more to come.' Kate laughed.

'You're so fortunate to be part of a large family,' Nell remarked wistfully. 'Ann and I will miss you sorely. Must you go quite so soon?'

A strange, unfamiliar feeling gripped Kate. In the month she had spent at Seven Ways she had grown to like Nell and to value their burgeoning friendship. They were two women from different backgrounds but the war had torn their families apart and left them alone and lonely. They found solace in each other's company.

'We must. I'm sorry. But perhaps you may come and visit me?'

'Perhaps,' Nell said without conviction, picking up her frame again.

Kate peered enviously at the fantastic beast conjured up beneath Nell's needle. She would describe herself as a competent, but unimaginative, needlewoman. Nothing she produced could match Nell's skill.

'Why do you stitch with wool and not silks?' she asked.

Nell did not look up. 'I can't afford silks, Kate.'

Kate cursed her insensitivity. With a husband in exile, her home sequestered, reliant on her grandfather's charity, there would be little money for fripperies such as embroidery silk.

'Where is Longley Abbey, Nell?' Kate asked.

Nell looked up and waved a slender hand in a northerly direction. 'Two miles beyond the woods. It is firmly in the possession of a poxy Roundhead Colonel by the name of Price.' She flushed and bit her lip. 'I do beg your pardon, Kate, I keep forgetting...'

'That I am a poxy Roundhead too?' Kate laughed. 'Nell, I hold no candle for either side but how can you endure it?'

Nell looked in the general direction of her home and shrugged. 'I don't allow myself to think of it,' she said. 'I live in the hope that Giles may make his peace with Parliament and come home but as we are...' She stopped and bent her head to her work again. 'He has his reasons not to,' she mumbled.

'I thought it was hard for us in the north in the early years,' Kate said, 'but I had no idea how much harder it must have been for families such as yours.'

Nell's lips tightened. 'No, I don't suppose you would.' She looked up again and smiled. 'Enough of such dismal talk. There is something I have been meaning to say to you all day. You should take better care of your skin. You are going quite brown and freckly. I have some excellent cream you may care to try. I make it myself.'

Kate laughed. 'Nell, I gave up on myself long ago. I just have to look at the sun and I go nut brown, and as for my hair...it simply won't do what it's told. My sister has tried but I'm afraid I'm a disaster.'

'Well, you will never catch another man unless you take better care of yourself,' Nell remarked. 'You're still young and you shouldn't stay a widow forever.'

'I've no wish to catch another man.' Kate declared.

'Why ever not? Has no other man shown an interest in you?'

An unfamiliar heat rose to Kate's face. 'I've had suitors,' she said.

Nell raised a teasing eyebrow. 'And what became of them?'

Kate smiled. 'If you had seen them, Nell, you would know what my answer was. No, I have loved only one man and I have no intention of supplanting his memory.'

'Were I ever to lose Giles,' Nell said, 'which God, in his mercy, will never let happen, I don't think I would stay a widow for long.' She sighed, 'Although with Giles so long gone, I sometimes wonder if being a widow wouldn't be preferable. At least I would have a chance to improve my lot.'

Kate stared at her. Nell lived in a nether world, neither wife nor widow. A woman in her position, alone, penniless and home-less, needed the protection of a man. Kate, on the other hand, had been left amply provided for and was beholden to no man. The difference was that her family had chosen the cause of the victors.

Nell smiled. 'Don't look so shocked, Kate. I adore my husband, but I cannot deny that Ann and I find ourselves in a parlous situation. When Sir Francis dies, who is to say what will happen to us?'

What indeed, Kate thought.

She looked up at the house, the red bricks glowing warmly in the afternoon sun, the sunlight catching on the diamond panes of the windows, and realised that the house, like its occupants, now occupied a place in her heart. The injustice and uncertainty of Nell's life mattered to her.

'What will happen to Seven Ways when Sir Francis dies?' she asked.

Nell hesitated for a fraction of a moment. 'Oh, I'm certain

Grandfather has made some arrangement. Besides,' she continued, returning to the original conversation, 'I think a woman needs a husband.'

'I don't need a husband,' Kate said. 'Richard and his father left me quite well provided for. I have my sister and her family to keep me company. What more do I need?'

Nell's mouth pinched in amusement. 'Men do have their uses, Kate.' It took a moment for Kate to discern her meaning and the glint in her friend's eyes.

Embarrassment heated her cheeks and she found herself rendered speechless for a moment. Nell laughed.

'Oh, Kate. Your face.'

Kate sniffed. 'Tell me about your wonderful Giles.'

Nell laid down her embroidery and a look of wistful longing crossed her face.

'Where do I start? He and Jonathan were of the same age and inseparable friends so Giles was here often. I think I loved him ever since I was very young and, happily for me, our families agreed we would be a good match. We were betrothed on my sixteenth birthday, just before the war.' Her face saddened. 'But it was another three years before we could wed. Ann was born in the spring of '47 and not long after her birth, Giles went into exile for his part in the second war. He's been on the continent these three years past.'

As if Nell had conjured her up, Ann ran across the garden towards them with cries of 'Mama, Mama.'

'Where is Tom?' Kate asked the child.

Ann looked at her. 'Tommy gave me this and told me to show you.' She opened a grubby paw to show them the sweetmeat Tom had used to bribe her.

'Look at that hand,' scolded her mother. 'Mistress Ann, you had best come with me and have a good wash.'

Picking up her work, she took her little imp by the offending hand and marched her firmly towards the house as Kate stood up and returned to the garden for one final assault before it would be time to go into the house.

~

'MOTHER!'

At the sound of her son's voice, Kate relinquished her battle with the weeds and sat back on her heels, shielding her eyes from the sun with her hand. She rose to her feet in alarm when she saw that Tom was borne on the shoulders of a tall, dark-haired man who strode down the path toward her.

Tom, wearing a wide-brimmed hat several sizes too large for him, waved.

As they neared, the man swung Tom down and carried him over to Nell's abandoned blanket, setting him down in the shade. He retrieved his hat from the boy's head and slapped it against his breeches, producing a cloud of dust.

Kate hurried over and knelt in front of the boy, inspecting his grubby face.

'Thomas. What have you been doing?' she scolded. 'Are you all right?

'I hurt my ankle a bit, Mother,' Tom said in a very small and, to Kate's ears, slightly guilty voice. 'But he' — he pointed at the man — 'says it's only a sprain.'

Kate rose to her feet and crossed her arms, looking from the boy to the stranger with narrowed eyes, suspecting some sort of collusion between the two. 'Exactly how did you come to sprain your ankle, Thomas?'

The man spoke. 'He had a fall, Mistress Ashley. I assure you nothing is broken.'

'What sort of fall?' she asked suspiciously.

Man and boy glanced at each other. The stranger coughed. 'He fell out of a tree. I happened to be passing by and came upon him.'

'That was fortunate, indeed,' Kate said, unconvinced by either her son's wide-eyed innocence or the stranger's disarming smile. 'Let me look at that ankle, Thomas.'

Tom submitted as his mother carried out her inspection of the injured ankle, confirming the diagnosis.

'It doesn't look too bad,' she said. 'Can you walk?'

With her help, Tom got to his feet and with much grimacing put his weight on his injured foot and limped around the tree.

'It feels much better already,' he said.

Kate studied her son, through narrowed, disbelieving eyes.

'Well, it seems that your guardian angel was watching over you once more, young man. You're lucky you didn't break your neck. However, I would like to know more about how you came to fall out of the tree.'

'It is a particularly fine tree for climbing,' the stranger said. 'I fear my appearance startled them.'

'Them? Were you and Peter Knowles up to mischief, Tom?'

Tom looked at his feet and swallowed. 'He was teaching me to use the slingshot, Mother.'

Kate raised her hands in exasperation. 'Enough. We will talk later. Now you have put this gentleman to a deal of trouble.' She turned to the boy's rescuer, who leaned against the tree, regarding them with amusement twinkling in his eyes. 'Thank you for returning my son to me, sir. The least I can do is offer you some refreshment up at the house.'

'No trouble.' The man's eyes creased in the corner as he smiled. 'As it is I am expected for supper, I believe.'

There had been no mention of guests from Nell.

'Expected?'

He straightened, all trace of humour gone.

'Ah, apparently not by you, it would seem. I must apologise, Mistress Ashley, for not introducing myself before.' He looked her squarely in the eye. 'I am your kinsman, Jonathan Thornton.'

Kate gave a sharp intake of breath. 'I'm sorry, sir. You did say Jonathan Thornton?'

He swept her a low courtly bow. 'Your servant, ma'am.'

A pair of bright hazel eyes, at once both green and then brown with flecks of gold, met hers as he straightened. Even if he had not told her his name she should have guessed this man was a Thornton.

He could have been Tom's father.

They shared the same light, graceful build, dark-brown hair and hazel eyes. His family had been right. The likeness even between man and boy was extraordinary.

Tom's eyes widened. 'Jonathan? You're Jonathan? Did you really take Horley Bridge with only five men?'

Jonathan looked puzzled then laughed. 'What tales has my grandfather been telling you?' He reached out and ruffled the boy's hair. 'Horley Bridge was a long, long time ago, Tom. Now, if you are up to it, how about you limp up to the house and tell my sister that I have arrived.'

'And Ellen must put some salve on your ankle,' Kate said. 'Go, Tom. Sir Francis will be anxious to know that your cousin is home.'

Tom's face fell. 'But I want to talk to Sir Jonathan...Colonel Thornton...' he corrected himself.

'There'll be time later,' Jonathan said. He bowed to his young cousin. 'It is a great pleasure to have made your acquaintance, Thomas Ashley.'

The boy flushed and broke into a halting run, his injured foot apparently forgotten.

Jonathan Thornton turned back to Kate, the smile fading from his face. 'You appear somewhat surprised by my arrival, Mistress Ashley?'

'I apologise, sir,' she said. 'I had been led to believe you were dead.'

He raised an eyebrow. 'Dead?'

'Well it's not as if I had been told you were dead,' Kate conceded, thinking about the few times Jonathan's name had arisen over the last weeks. 'It is just that your sister and your grandfather left me with the strong impression that you had not survived the troubles.'

Jonathan studied her for a long moment. 'I am no friend of Parliament, Mistress Ashley. Your family, the Ashleys, took Parliament's side in the late conflict and they may have felt it prudent to keep my continuing good health as one of the darker family secrets. My timing is a little unfortunate.'

He smiled but she did not see any humour reflected in his eyes.

'Did they think I not could be trusted?' she asked, unable to disguise the hurt in her voice.

Jonathan's hazel eyes scanned her face, 'Can you be trusted, Mistress Ashley?'

Kate straightened and looked him in the eye. 'I have told your sister that I hold no candle for either party, Sir Jonathan. Indeed it would be an abuse of your family's hospitality were I to go running to the authorities. Yes, I can be trusted.'

He rewarded her with an easy smile that lit his face. His gaze scanned her face and swept down her body. She self-consciously dusted her hands on her skirts and tried to restore her wayward hair to some order.

'I'm afraid you have caught me at a disadvantage,' she said. 'I'm not normally so dishevelled.'

He looked down at his dusty clothes. 'And neither am I. Having been nearly thrown from my horse, I am somewhat discomposed myself.'

'What did Tom really do?'

He hesitated. 'He has my word as a gentleman but rest easy, Mistress Ashley, it was not done deliberately and I think Tom got as much of a fright as my poor horse.'

Kate shook her head. 'It must be the slingshot. That child has a penchant for trouble.'

'Then he must be a true Thornton,' Jonathan said. 'We seem to attract trouble.'

'Really?'

'Well perhaps not all of us,' Jonathan conceded. 'My brother, Ned, was a paragon of virtue. You have only one child?'

Kate nodded. 'I was left a widow after Marston Moor and have not remarried.'

Jonathan Thornton visibly stiffened at the name of that terrible battle. 'Richard died at Marston Moor? I had heard he was dead but not how or when. I'm sorry.'

'Jonathan.' The sound of Nell calling her brother's name from the door to the house caused him to pause and he glanced at the house. Nell waved.

'Nell will be anxious for news of Giles, and my grandfather will want to see me,' he said. 'Please excuse me, Mistress Ashley.'

'Are you staying long?'

'Just tonight.'

Kate smiled. 'Then I shall see you at supper.'

He gave her a low courtly bow. 'Until supper, cousin…'

'Kate,' she said.

He inclined his head and gave her the benefit of another half smile. 'Kate.'

She leaned against the reassuring trunk of the oak tree and

watched him stride across the lawn toward the house, flicking his leg with the hat. He moved with a casual grace and an air of authority that she had not encountered in anyone before.

Supper, she thought, would be a meal worth looking forward to.

～

As Jonathan reached the terrace, Nell, abandoning all pretence of manners, threw her arms around his neck and kissed him on both cheeks.

'Jonathan, darling Jonathan. It's so wonderful to see you. What did Giles say? How is he? Are you carrying a letter from him?'

Jonathan disengaged himself from his sister's embrace and kissed the top of her head. 'Giles is well and I have letters and packets for you and the little lass.'

Nell looped her arm into her brother's as they walked back towards the house. 'We only received your note this morning. You can imagine what a shock it was, particularly with visitors in the house. What are you doing here?'

'Grandfather sent for me,' Jonathan replied. 'I'm not sure why. Do you?'

Nell shook her head. 'He doesn't confide in me. You know that. He has always thought me a scatterbrained addle-pate.'

'Nonsense. I am sure he thinks it is better for your safety that you don't know when I am likely to be around,' Jonathan pointed out.

'I wish he would confide in me more.' Nell sighed and squeezed his arm. 'I suppose I should know better than to ask how long you are staying?'

'Just the night, Nell.'

Her face fell.

'You know I dare not risk staying longer.'

'Well, I shall see that we eat well tonight then. You look as if you need feeding up. You're so thin,' she said.

Jonathan laughed. 'I manage, Nell. Don't fuss. Now, on the subject of your visitors, I've just met Mistress Ashley. She seemed to be under the impression I was dead.'

Nell bit her lip. 'I didn't actually tell her you were dead, but it seemed prudent not to say too much about you.' She smiled and slapped her brother's arm. 'Of course, I never actually expected you to turn up.'

'Who invited her?'

'Grandfather.'

Jonathan frowned. 'It is hardly a coincidence that Grandfather invites her to Seven Ways and then sends for me.' Realisation dawned on him. 'Of course. It's about the boy.'

'The boy?' Light dawned in Nell's eyes. 'Oh, of course, Thomas.'

'I can't think of any other reason Grandfather would have chosen this moment to make peace with the Ashleys, other than to secure Seven Ways.'

'Grandfather is dying. He needs an heir. It changes everything,' Nell said and added, 'I'm sorry, Jonathan.'

He squeezed her hand. 'Don't be. I set my own course a long time ago.'

She nodded and smiled. 'It is good to see you, Jon, whatever the reason. I've told Grandfather you are here and he said you were to go straight to him. Don't be shocked by the change in him, his time is coming fast.'

Jonathan knocked on the familiar door and admitted himself before the old man could answer. He paused on the threshold, momentarily overcome by the closeness of the room. Despite the warmth of the day, a new fire blazed in the hearth and the old man sat beside the fireplace, swaddled in blankets.

He looked up at his grandson and held out his hand.

'My dear boy. You came. Don't just stand there, come in and close the door. You're letting in draughts.'

Jonathan sighed inwardly. Only his grandfather would still call him a boy, a man nigh on thirty and a soldier for nearly ten years. He wondered if Sir Francis still thought of him as the impetuous youth who had stolen one of his best horses and ridden off to war.

'You sent for me, Grandfather,' he observed dryly. 'I came.'

He sat down opposite his grandfather. Despite Nell's warning, he found it hard to hide his shock at the old man's appearance. The pallid flesh on the old man's face had contracted back against the skull, giving him the appearance of a death's head. But the eyes that studied him were still as bright and shrewd as he remembered them. He opened his mouth to utter a platitude but a wave of the hand from the old man cut him short.

'Don't tell me I look well, boy,' Sir Francis said. 'I'm dying. However, the good Lord in his wisdom is giving me plenty of time to make my peace with him. He must think my sins worth a good deal of soul-searching.' He ended with a hollow cough. 'And you're right, I did send for you. Your timing is excellent.'

'Don't flatter yourself that I would come at your summons, sir. I have business in England that makes the risk worthwhile.'

The old man looked at him, the shrewd eyes scanning his face. 'Business? I know your sort of business. It only spells trouble.'

Jonathan flinched at the reproof in the old man's voice but he had long since abandoned any hope of ever winning his grandfather's approval. He turned a hot, angry gaze on his grandfather only to see the old man's colourless lips curled in a smile.

'We are too much alike,' his grandfather said. 'Were I your age,

I would be entwining myself in just such a web of deceit. Tell me, lad. What new misery is to afflict this land?'

'The King will be landing in Scotland shortly,' Jonathan said.

'The King in Scotland?' The old man shook his head and ran a hand over his eyes as he said, 'Does this mean war again, boy?'

'Yes,' Jonathan said, with a candour he reserved for his grandfather. 'It's just a question of what terms the King can reach with the Scots. God knows they want the earth and the heavens. However, I will say this for Charles, unlike his father, he's not above making agreements for the political expediency, however distasteful.'

The old man grasped the arms of his chair with skeletal hands and observed his grandson with his bright, astute eyes.

'Scotland is some way distant, lad, and Worcestershire is hardly on the route,' he observed. 'I take it you are up to your old tricks?'

Jonathan resisted the urge to laugh. His grandfather managed to make everything he did sound like the prank of a naughty child but Colonel Jonathan Thornton, King's Commissioner, did not indulge in tricks. His business was deadly serious. His natural ability as an actor had made him invaluable to the Royal cause long before the execution of Charles I when he had carried the coded messages of the imprisoned King to his exiled Queen.

Now, once again he found himself playing the role of the King's messenger.

'You mean am I here with the King's Commission to gather support for his cause? You know the answer to that question, Grandfather.'

The old man sighed. 'Where you go, inevitably trouble follows. And is there the support the King expects?'

Jonathan threw back his head. 'What do you think? Can you

spare any coin for the King's cause? I think not. You're no different from any other man who followed Charles' father.'

'So the cause is doomed before it has even begun?'

Jonathan said nothing. He looked at his grandfather and their eyes met in perfect understanding.

'So why did you send for me?' Jonathan changed the subject.

'I'm dying. I wanted to see you again.'

'You've been dying for the last three years,' Jonathan observed.

'The time has come for decisions. Have you met the boy?' Francis asked and Jonathan understood.

Unable to take the stuffiness of the room anymore, Jonathan stood up and walked over to one of the windows and opened it, breathing in the fresh air. Below, in the garden, Kate Ashley had returned to her battle with the weeds. Thick, honey-coloured hair tumbled down her slender back from beneath the brim of a battered straw hat. She had pushed up the sleeves of the blue gown, revealing strong brown arms. A woman of strength and determination, he thought, as he watched her hauling on a well-established dandelion.

He recalled the look of incredulity that had crossed the attractive, freckled face, and the concern in her grey eyes when she had realised the identity of her son's rescuer, and wondered if she suspected why Sir Francis had brought her to Seven Ways. She would need every ounce of strength and determination if Sir Frances got his way.

'Jonathan.' His grandfather rapped the cane on the floor 'Did you hear me?'

Jonathan turned back to face the old man again. 'Yes, I have met young Thomas Ashley,' he said, 'and I commend you on finding the solution to your problem.'

If his grandfather heard the irony in his voice, he gave no sign.

'I like the boy,' Sir Francis said, a note of petulance in his voice. 'He has the Thornton spirit.'

'And what is the Thornton spirit, Grandfather?' Jonathan turned back to the window again. 'If you mean using a slingshot and scaring horses then I would have to agree with you. He could have killed me.'

Sir Francis' laugh was a hoarse, dry sound.

'Did he, by God? Lucky for him that you are the horseman you are.' The old man added. The bantering went from his tone, 'I see a lot of you in him.'

'Well, God help him,' Jonathan leaned against the window casement and crossed his legs at the ankles. 'He's nine years old, Grandfather. Do they know the burden you intend to leave them?'

'Them?'

'Yes… them. It is, after all, his mother who will have to carry the burden until the boy is of age.'

'Ah, his mother.' Sir Francis smiled. 'What a fortunate woman his mother turned out to be. I couldn't have asked for better than the widow of a respected Parliamentary officer, an acquaintance of Sir Thomas Fairfax no less, and a thoroughly sensible young woman too. She's had the running of her husband's estates since Ashley died.'

'And she is a woman who has a right to know what you intend,' Jonathan said, making no attempt to disguise the exasperation in his voice.

'Of course she does, and I want you to tell her,' the old man said.

Jonathan straightened. 'Me?'

'Well it most closely affects you and,' the old man said with what was once a winning smile but now resembled a grimace, 'you have a better way with women than ever I had.'

Jonathan turned back to the window and sought out the

distant figure in the blue gown. He saw again the clear, level gaze of her grey eyes and wondered if Thomas owed the spirit his grandfather so admired to his mother rather than his father.

'There is no alternative, Jon. You know that. Without the boy, we lose Seven Ways.'

'No,' Jonathan said slowly. 'No, there is no other way. Very well, I'll speak with her tonight.'

The old man sat back in his chair, satisfied. 'Good. I am glad we had the chance to have this talk. Leave me now, boy. If we are to kill the fatted calf for your return tonight I had best get some rest.'

CHAPTER 4

*E*llen laid out the new dove-grey satin gown, made especially for this visit but as yet unworn and turned to Kate.

'If you ask me, it seems strange that they've said naught to you about him,' she said.

'I've no doubt they had their reasons,' Kate replied.

'Have you seen him, Ellen?' Tom said.

Kate cast a sideways glance at her son. He sat on the broad windowsill, swinging his legs and for once her son appeared clean and passably tidy, a feat normally only accomplished with prompting from herself or Ellen. However, the shiny face did not disguise the fact his collar looked as if it had been rolled in a ball and stomped on in muddy boots.

'Only in passing, Master Thomas.' Ellen laced Kate's bodice. 'The servants seem taken with him. Loyal lot in this house.'

'And so they should be. I would expect no less of my servants.' Kate gave her maid a sidelong glance.

Ellen's lips twitched.

'Ellen, did I tell you that the King knighted him after he took Horley Bridge with—'

'— only five men. I think you mentioned that, Tom,' Kate interrupted.

'You seem very well informed about your cousin, Master Tom,' Ellen observed.

'Oh, Grandfather's told me all about him. He stole a horse and rode away to join Prince Rupert and carried letters for the King when he was in prison. He's very brave and clever.'

'Indeed. Foolhardy may seem a better word,' Kate remarked more to herself than to Tom. 'Ellen, please take Tom back to his bedchamber and find a clean collar.'

Tom pulled a face. 'I washed my face,' he protested.

'Go.' Kate commanded. 'I'll finish my hair, Ellen.'

As Ellen and a grumbling Tom left the room they passed Nell in the doorway. Dressed in a gown of blue satin that set off the blue of her eyes, Nell wore her happiness like a bright, shining halo.

Kate's sharp eyes could not fail to notice that for all its lustre, Nell's gown was sadly outmoded, darned in places and worn at the hem.

Nell held out her right arm to Kate. 'Look what Giles has sent me,' she said.

Kate stooped to admire the exquisite, filigree gold bracelet that graced the young woman's slender wrist.

'It's quite lovely,' she agreed.

Nell touched the bracelet. 'Giles is so thoughtful,' she said with a wistful sigh.

Kate said nothing. She wondered how Giles Longley could afford such expensive presents while his wife lacked the means to purchase her embroidery silks or a new gown.

'Oh. Do stand up. Let me see your gown.' Nell circled Kate.

'Are the waists now worn that low?' she asked, putting her hands to her own, high-waisted bodice.

'I doubt my tailor in York is quite at the centre of fashion but he assured me this was the latest style,' Kate said with a smile.

Nell pleated the material of the skirt between her fingers. 'It's lovely but you always wear such sombre colours, Kate.'

'I am in mourning,' Kate replied, resuming her seat in front of the mirror. 'David Ashley has only been dead six months and since Richard's death I have not had the heart for bright gowns.'

Nell dismissed her long-dead cousin with a wave of her hand. 'You can't mourn forever, Kate. I think a gown of this colour...' — she held out her blue skirts — '...or a warm peach colour would become you very well.'

Nell seated herself on the edge of Kate's bed and fiddled with the hem of her skirt, trying to tuck its fraying ends away out of sight while Kate cursed her recalcitrant hair that steadfastly refused to stay where it was put.

Nell abandoned her skirts and looked up. 'I'm sorry if I misled you about Jonathan. In truth, I hadn't expected him to turn up while you were here, not when we haven't seen him in at least two years.'

'So why is here?' Kate asked.

Reflected in the mirror, Nell's gaze slid sideways, her mouth downcast. Kate sighed. Whatever had brought Jonathan Thornton to Seven Ways was none of her business.

'Let me do that.' Nell rose to her feet and took the comb from Kate's hand. 'I think Grandfather sent for him,' she said, twisting a handful of Kate's hair and pinning it firmly. 'Grandfather is dying and seems determined to put his affairs in order.' She stuck some hairpins in her mouth and tugged at the wayward locks. 'You must understand the terrible risk Jonathan takes in just being in England, let alone at Seven Ways.'

'What risk?'

Nell's hand stilled and she met her friend's eyes in the mirror. 'If he's caught, Kate, they will hang him.'

'Why? What has he done that is so much worse than others like him?' Kate twisted on her stool to look up at Nell.

Nell shrugged. 'He can tell you better than I.' Her face crumpled in concern. 'You wouldn't betray him would you, Kate?'

'Of course not,' Kate said. 'And it pains me that you should think that I would. I have told both you and your brother, I hold no candle for either King or Parliament. Whatever your brother's business here, it is none of mine.'

Nell's shoulders relaxed and she jabbed a pin into Kate's hair so hard that Kate winced as it grazed her scalp.

'Jonathan was a terrible trial when he was younger. Father sent him to London to learn the law but he wouldn't apply himself and there were awful rows. Then the war came. He defied Father and stole one of Grandfather's horses to join Prince Rupert. Oh and then there were the girls...' She sighed. 'Broken hearts everywhere. He was a complete disgrace. Mother used to despair of him.'

'And now?' Kate enquired stiffly.

Nell shrugged and resumed her task. 'The war or at least something, in particular, changed him. I've asked Giles, but if he knows he won't tell me. Of course, we can only imagine the things they saw.'

Or did, Kate thought. 'I don't have to imagine, Nell. I saw it with my own eyes when the wounded of Marston Moor came to my door, my husband among them.'

Nell's hand stilled and the two women's eyes met, reflected in the mirror.

'In what way did he change?' Kate asked.

Nell sighed. 'He been taken prisoner towards the end of the

war but he escaped and when we saw him again he had become so serious about everything. There was no more fun, no more girls. He played some very dangerous games. It was almost as if he didn't care about the risk he ran. Almost as if—'

'As if...?' Kate prompted.

'There. Much better.' Nell worked the last pin into Kate's hair.

Kate rose from the stool and Nell caught her hands.

'I do hope you like him, Kate,' she said. 'Despite everything, he's all that we have and we love him dearly.'

Kate smiled in response, 'I'm sure I will like him, Nell.' She squeezed Nell's hands, looking her directly in the eye. 'Please be assured, your secret is quite safe with me.'

THE TABLE in the Great Hall had been set for supper. Sir Francis had already taken his place in the large oak armchair by the fireplace, talking to his grandson who leaned with one arm against the chimney breast.

Jonathan looked around and smiled as the two women entered. Kate curtsied and he returned her greeting. A door slammed behind her as Tom, in a clean but crooked collar followed her in. He bowed correctly to his grandfather and the visitor.

Kate bit her lip, seeing the undisguised worship in her son's eyes as he looked up at Jonathan Thornton. Apparently, he had been well primed by Sir Francis about the daring exploits of this new-found cousin, and the reality had been no disappointment. Brought up by his mother and grandfather, Tom must have found his Uncle William and his Rowe cousins very dull, and even his dead father seemed an unsatisfactory hero, in comparison to Sir Jonathan Thornton of Horley Bridge.

The standard of the Seven Ways cook, a moody man with a liking for his wine jar, could be variable, but for once he excelled — indeed the whole atmosphere of the house seemed to have lifted with Jonathan's presence. Here, in the company of his family, he seemed able to relax and proved to be a wonderful raconteur.

He held them in rapt attention with a fund of stories about the court in exile for the duration of the meal. As he talked, Kate took the opportunity to study this prodigal son as closely as she dared without appearing rude.

Sir Francis had said Jonathan and Richard were much of the same age, which would make him not yet thirty. The dark-brown rough-cut hair barely reached his shoulders. Dressed in a plain suit of well-cut mulberry broadcloth, somewhat crumpled no doubt from being stuffed in a saddle bag, he hardly fitted the picture of a dashing cavalier, if indeed he had ever cut that image. She considered that the plain, sober cut of his clothes and hair seemed a natural affectation rather than a disguise.

No doubt there were plenty of women who would find his lean, well-proportioned face more attractive than boyish good looks. With his lively eyes and quick smile, he demanded attention and respect. Only in repose did she notice the deepening lines and the shadows about the eyes that spoke of the hardship of his life.

Throughout the meal Sir Francis' eyes hardly strayed from his grandson. However, the exertion of sitting at the table for a long meal proved too much for the old man. Several times Jonathan had glanced at his grandfather with great concern. Now as Sir Francis was overwhelmed by a coughing fit, Jonathan stood up.

'Come, Grandfather. I'll help you to your room.'

Sir Francis waved an apologetic hand at the assembly. 'Forgive me, ladies. I will return Jon to you shortly.'

Nell collected Ann, who had been allowed to stay up to see her uncle, and the company adjourned to the terrace to enjoy the last of the fine early summer day. Jonathan joined them, sitting beside his sister and Kate on the low wall where the women watched Tom throwing a ball with his small cousin.

Jonathan leaned his elbows on his knees and rested his chin on his hands. 'He doesn't have long, does he?'

Nell shook her head. 'I doubt he will live to see you again.' She reached out and touched his arm. 'Giles writes that the King will be landing in Scotland. Is that true?'

Jonathan nodded.

Kate shivered as if a cool breeze had blown across the garden. 'Will it all start again?' she asked, unable to hide the bitterness in her voice. 'Will this country never know peace?'

Jonathan looked from one woman to the other. 'You know the answer to that,' he said.

'So are you going north to join the King?' Nell demanded.

He smiled without humour. 'Of course I am, Nell.'

'One day, Jonathan Thornton, you will tempt fate once too often,' his sister said. 'And Giles...will Giles be in Scotland?'

When Jonathan nodded, Nell's eyes brightened.

'Then I must give you some letters to take to him.'

'Of course.'

'Do you suppose..?' Nell began and broke off, looking up at her brother.

Jonathan slipped an arm around his sister, drawing her close. 'Do I suppose Giles will come this way? I don't know Nell. We have the King's work to do. Write him your letters and I will carry them for you.'

'Uncle Jon. Story?' Ann tugged at his coat.

'About how you took Horley Bridge,' Tom put in.

Jonathan shook his head. 'I will save Horley Bridge for another day, Tom. How about a tale of King Arthur and his knights?'

The corners of Tom's mouth drooped but he brightened as Jonathan abandoned the women and sat down on the low step, his long legs crossed, with the children before him, looking up at him, their eyes wide, hanging on every word.

Kate exchanged a smile with Nell. For a soldier of fortune who carried the King's Commission on deadly and secret business, Jonathan Thornton had a natural rapport with children.

AS NELL HARRIED the children off to bed, Jonathan remained seated on the low step looking out over the garden, conscious that Kate lingered in the soft evening light.

The coward in him silently begged her to follow the others inside. He would be gone before daybreak and the first she would know of what his grandfather intended would be a letter on his death. Would warning her make any difference?

The rustle of skirts told him she had risen to her feet and he stood to face her.

'Mistress Ashley. Wait.'

She had started to walk toward the house but she stopped and glanced over her shoulder. 'Sir Jonathan?'

He flinched at the formality of her address but it was needed... for the moment.

He looked up at the soft pinks and greys of the gloaming and remembered how he had craved to be under an English sky once more.

'I have no great desire to leave this perfect evening. Unless you are anxious for your bed, would you do me the honour of walking with me a while?' he said, with what he hoped was an ingratiating smile.

They stood looking at each other for a long moment and indecision flashed across her face. She glanced up at the house and then back at him, no doubt considering the propriety of taking a stroll in a garden with a strange man.

'It would be churlish of me to refuse,' Kate replied with a smile, accepting the hand he held out to her.

As he helped her down the steps, he thought that she did not have the hands of a gentlewoman like Nell, used only to fine needlework. She still had the trace of dirt beneath her nails from her afternoon in the garden and strength in her grip. They were hands used to hard work.

They stepped out onto an overgrown pathway and Jonathan crooked his elbow. 'Will you take my arm?' he enquired.

Once again she hesitated and he looked down at her with an encouraging smile, finding her reticence refreshing. Most women of his acquaintance seemed only too pleased to be invited to a greater degree of intimacy, but to her, he was the enemy, a man whose very presence brought her closer to danger than any army.

The indecision in her face turned to resolution and she slipped her hand into the crook of his arm and they stepped out into the wild garden where the smell of the roses lingered on the soft evening air.

'Sir Francis told me the garden was ruined by Parliament horse,' Kate said, breaking the silence that strung between them.

'I suppose he told you that they were looking for me?' Jonathan said.

'He mentioned something about his scapegrace grandson,' Kate conceded.

Jonathan flinched. So often he had heard his father and grandfather describe him as the 'scapegrace' who bore the responsibility for all the trials that had befallen his family. 'They were disappointed, but they took their revenge on the house and the garden, as you can see. I am afraid you will have your work cut out trying to restore some order to this jungle. I hadn't realised how bad the damage and neglect has been,' he said.

'Alas, it is a task for someone other than I, Sir Jonathan. Tom and I are leaving on Friday.'

That was news. Despite her quiet demeanour, her presence and that of the boy had brought life and light to the house that it had not seen in many years.

'So soon? Nell will miss you.'

'And I will miss her but I have responsibilities at home that cannot wait any longer.'

They had reached the remains of a once intricate knot garden that had been his mother's pride and joy. Jonathan guided her to a lichened stone bench against a rose-bowered wall, dusted off the bench as best he could and indicated they should sit.

He stretched out his legs and looked up at the house. 'Home' had been nearly ten years of filthy inns on a good night or hedge rows on a bad night, and every time he saw Seven Ways he knew that this was where he wanted to be. Small wonder he stayed away when returning could be so painful.

'Tell me about your home,' he asked, curious to know more about this woman and to delay the difficult conversation to come. 'From memory, it's somewhere near York, isn't it?'

'Barton Manor, a few hours' ride west of York. My sister and her husband, William, live at Barton Hall, which is much grander than the Manor.' She smiled. 'My brother-in-law made a good fortune in the wool trade during the war years.'

'All those woollen uniforms,' he said without thinking.

Kate looked away and he regretted his remark, but it was true that the only victors in the war had been those able to turn the trouble to their advantage. No doubt this William had turned a healthy profit in selling stout woollen cloth to clothe the armies of both sides.

'And your parents?'

'Both dead. My father was a clothier in York and after his death, I went to live with my sister and her husband.'

'At Barton Hall?'

'Yes.'

'Hmm…and the Ashleys being neighbours, I presume that is how you met my cousin Richard?'

Kate nodded, a faint colour rising in her cheeks. 'I had a good dowry and Richard fair prospects.' She looked up at him, holding his eyes with her clear gaze. 'And we loved each other.'

Dear God, this bloody war, he thought.

'And if it were not for the war, you would be living in wedded bliss in Barton Manor, surrounded by a brood of children,' he said.

Kate swallowed and he knew his observation had hit home.

'I'm sorry, Kate, that was a thoughtless remark. From what I knew of Richard, he did not have the heart of a soldier.'

He knew more about Richard Ashley than he was prepared to reveal. A scholar, not a soldier. Richard should be at home at Barton Manor with this woman and their children. Not dead in the ground at the age of twenty-two.

Kate looked up at him, her brow creased in puzzlement, and he cursed himself for revealing too much.

'What could you possibly have known of him? The Thorntons have been estranged from the Ashleys for over thirty years.'

This time he held his tongue and she continued, 'To answer your question, Richard may not have gone willingly to the war but he followed Sir Thomas Fairfax into hell during those early years. Sir Thomas trusted him enough to keep him close as one of his staff.'

Jonathan nodded. 'Fairfax's men had it hard in those early years.' He paused. 'Was he with Fairfax that day at Marston Moor?'

'Of course,' Kate replied. She looked up at him, her grey eyes scanning his face, challenging him as she said, 'Were you there? Is it possible you faced Richard?'

Of course, Jonathan had been there with Prince Rupert's cavalry. It had been a bloodbath. Marston Moor had put in train a series of tragic events in his own life that had nothing to do with the battle.

He swallowed and gave a barely perceptible nod. 'I was on the other flank with Rupert.'

'What did it matter?' The colour rose in Kate's cheeks and her eyes flashed. 'You wouldn't have known Richard if you had met on the battlefield.'

Yes, I would, he thought.

'That is the tragedy of a civil war, Kate.'

She didn't seem to notice that he had used her given name. Her eyes blazed with anger and misery. 'They brought him home to die, a lingering, horrible death.' Her voice cracked.

She lowered her head and took several deep shuddering breaths that wracked her body.

Without thinking, Jonathan lifted his hand to her face, tilting her chin so she looked at him. Her eyes swam with unshed tears. Tears he had caused.

'So many deaths. Too many, Kate. Believe me, it's not always easy to be a survivor. I may not be dead but I have lost all that is important to me. It's a hollow victory over death.'

So many deaths...Marston Moor and afterwards, Oxford. He

had run at life, stumbled into the path of innocent people, and he had survived while they had died.

'Jonathan?' She touched his hand. The merest brush but she may as well have branded him with fire.

He forced himself back to the present and dropped his hand, turning his gaze back toward the house, which glowed serenely in the setting sun.

Time to stop dwelling in the past and concentrate on the present.

'Must you leave so soon?' Kate asked.

He shook his head. 'I only bring danger to my family, Kate.'

'What did you do to earn the sentence of death?' she asked.

That was an easy question to answer. 'I've done a lot of things, Kate. I carried letters for the late King and I killed someone who deserved to die.' He looked at her with a wry smile. 'I'm no saint, Kate Ashley.'

'Were you ever?' Her mouth lifted in a smile that lightened her face.

He smiled in response, 'So you were not entirely ignorant of my existence. Have my family apprised you of my wayward youth?'

She shrugged. 'You are no longer a youth, Sir Jonathan.'

'No, I'm not,' he agreed, 'but I still carry letters for my King and I face the hangman's noose if I am caught.'

'And you bring the threat of war with you,' she said.

'This is our last chance to return the country to its lawful King.' He sighed. 'Providing, however, that the King agrees to the Scots' terms and the English come to the King's support.'

'And will they?'

'Honestly?' He shook his head. 'You are correct. England is tired of war, Kate. Even the King's most ardent supporters are reluctant to commit themselves to what they rightly see as a doomed cause. Like this family.' He waved a hand towards the house and could not hide the bitterness in his voice as he said, 'The price for supporting the losing side has been enormous, and few are willing to risk what they have left.'

'Is that what you're doing in England?'

He nodded. 'I've been sent to seek out support for the King among his old friends. He has friends aplenty but little of what he needs: arms, men and money.'

Despite the comparative warmth of the evening, beside him Kate shivered, wrapping her arms around herself.

'So there will be war again. More deaths.'

He leaned his elbows on his knees and buried his head in his hands. She had been right in her supposition. It would all begin again. More wives would lose their husbands, mothers their sons. Would he even survive what was to come?

'But Sir Francis has not long to live,' Kate said. 'You are his heir. Surely it is time to make your peace and come back to England. You don't have to fight another war.'

She had come straight to the point of this long and difficult conversation.

He ran his fingers through his hair as he straightened. 'I can't return, Kate, even if I wished to. I have a price on my head too dear for this family to pay.'

'Others have made their peace with Parliament. It may mean more fines but there's always a way. I heard David Ashley and his friends talking of compounding and the like.'

Jonathan shook his head. 'There is no compromise for me. If I return, not only do I risk death or at best imprisonment, but all my estate is forfeit.'

Kate stared at him and her eyes narrowed, as the import of his words sunk in.

'Then who will inherit Seven Ways? Nell?'

He shook his head. 'Not Nell,' he said. 'The Longleys are Catholic.'

Kate stared at him. 'Nell is a Catholic?'

Something else she didn't know? He cursed his close-mouthed family.

'She took Giles' religion when she married him. And even were she not a Catholic, she is not up to such a huge responsibility. Nell is happiest with a needle in her hand and a child at her knee.'

Kate rose to her feet and turned to face him, looking down at him. Had the colour leached from her face, or was it a trick of the dusk?

'There's no one else, is there, except my Thomas?'

His silence gave her the answer.

Kate turned away, her hand going to her throat.

'That's why he sent for us,' she said, her voice cracking with anger. 'Sir Francis will not see out the year. All his protestations about making peace with Ashleys had only one end and that was to find an heir for Seven Ways.' She whirled around, looking at him with bright, hot eyes. ' I see it all now. You're his lawful heir. This is your responsibility but instead, it is being passed to a child... to me!'

Jonathan stood up and walked away from her, running his fingers through his hair as he composed a response to her justifiable fury.

'Kate,' he said, turning back to her. 'This is not my decision but it is my doing and there is nothing I can do to change it. If I inherit Seven Ways, it is lost. I still get the title, for what it's worth, and there are some lands in Warwickshire, which are entailed. I will get those...briefly, but Seven Ways...' He spread his arms, encompassing the garden and the house. 'This part of the estate is not entailed and Grandfather is free to do with it as he likes. Thomas is Elizabeth Thornton's grandson. You can't deny your son his heritage, and neither can you deny Francis the right to leave the estate where he feels it will be best served.'

He turned away from her to look at the house, now a dark shadow in the evening gloom. Seven Ways… home. The thought tore at his heart.

'Ten years ago there was something worth inheriting. I don't blame you for not wanting anything to do with this ruin of a house… and family,' he said

They stood an arm's length apart, faces now shadowed and unreadable. He was glad he did not have to see the anger in her eyes again. Yet when she spoke her voice held no anger, only resignation.

'Forgive me, Jonathan. I didn't mean to sound so harsh but you know it's not Thomas who will have the responsibility for this house and family, it will be me. There is no one else.'

He straightened and looked at her, taking her hand in his. Where before he had thought it strong and capable, now the bones seemed to have no more substance than those of a bird. Such a huge responsibility for such a small hand.

'Grandfather knows that, Kate. He has every confidence in you.'

She pulled her hand free and turned away. 'Does he understand what he's asking of me?'

Of course, his grandfather knew exactly what he was doing. His body may be dying but his mind had lost none of its acuity.

When he didn't reply, Kate turned back to look at him.

'He's no fool, is he?' she said with a shadow of bitterness in her tone. 'There's more to it than the simple question of finding an heir. Despite what you said about Nell, she could still have taken on the inheritance. I'm an Ashley; my son is an Ashley — good, respectable Parliamentarian stock. Seven Ways will be safe with me. Tell me, Sir Jonathan, if the King returns, are we expected to hand the estate back to you, its rightful owner?'

Jonathan shook his head. 'No. Seven Ways will always be Tom's.' He placed his hands on her shoulders, forcing her to look up into his face, seeking to give her the assurance she needed. 'If he didn't trust you, Kate, he wouldn't do it, and my grandfather is not a man who gives his love or his trust easily.'

She shook her head. 'He's dying, Jonathan. It seems to me he has few options.'

'He's never wrong in his assessment of people, Kate, and for what it's worth, I think he is right about you.'

'The widow of a man who fought for Parliament?' Kate said, her mouth twisting in a bitter, humourless smile.

'A sensible, capable, intelligent woman, Kate. A worthy guardian for your son.'

A sensible, capable, intelligent woman? That seemed an inadequate description for this woman he had only known a few hours. Even in the gloom, he could feel her eyes on his face, wanting to trust him.

His fingers tightened on her shoulders, drawing her closer. She leaned into him and as she lowered her head, he breathed in the faintest scent of rosemary over the headier scent of the roses. Rosemary for remembrance he thought, resisting the urge to bury his face in her hair.

To hold her closer would be a mistake. He would be bound to her.

He released her and took a step back, looking up at the darkening sky. 'I think it's time we went in, Kate. I have an early start in the morning.'

They walked in silence through the gathering gloom of the peaceful garden. As they approached the house, Kate stopped and turned to him.

'Do you mind?' she asked.

'Mind what?'

'Losing Seven Ways.'

'Kate, I knew long ago that losing Seven Ways was the price to be paid for the trouble I've brought this family. I've no right to complain. It might have been my father who made the decision. It was he who committed Seven Ways to the King's cause, but I am the one who survived the war and I bear the price of that decision. That's enough.'

'I don't understand…' Kate began, but he shook his head.

'There are things about me you don't need to know, Kate. Leave it at that.'

A long silence stretched between them.

'Will I see you again?' she asked at last.

He glanced down at her. Every sensible intention would dictate he should never see her again, but then he had never been known to be sensible.

Instead, he smiled. 'As my family will tell you, I turn up when least expected. Perhaps I may have cause to come and visit you in Yorkshire. Would I be assured of a safe place in my cousin's house?'

'A safe place? I think Tom would enjoy the adventure of hiding so dangerous a fugitive. He thinks highly of you.'

'And I of him. Now I must go and say my farewells to grandfather. I think it will be the last time we meet on this earth.'

He looked back at the garden, drawing in a deep breath, willing the memory of the lovely evening to remain with him for the long months to come.

As they parted at the door, he took her hand, lifting it to his lips. 'Farewell, Mistress Ashley. Thank you for your company tonight. Please say goodbye to Tom for me.'

He turned away and did not look back.

CHAPTER 5

*I*n the days following Jonathan's departure, Sir Francis took a turn for the worse.

Kate found him propped up in his bed, wasted and faded like the last of his spring roses. Resisting the urge to gag at the closeness of the invalid's room, she forced herself to smile as she set the tray with his evening meal on the table and drew a chair up to the bed.

The corners of his mouth twitched in the semblance of a smile, which seemed an echo of his grandson's easy smile.

'You've been avoiding me.' He looked at her with his bright, shrewd eyes. 'When are you leaving?'

'Tomorrow,' Kate said. 'While the weather continues fair.'

She picked up the bowl and walked over to his bed. Too weak to feed himself, he allowed Kate to feed him the invalid gruel like a small child.

'My grandson says he told you of my plans for the boy to inherit Seven Ways,' Sir Francis said at last.

She paused, the spoon halfway to his mouth. Whatever the

state of his body, his mind was still sharp and the subject needed to be broached.

'He did.' She set the spoon back in the bowl and folded her hands in her lap.

'I hope you don't think to change my mind,' he said. 'The papers are drawn and I can now die in peace.'

'I did not presume to think I could change your mind, Sir Francis. I know better than that. Thomas is your great-grandson and you have every right to provide for him as you think fit,' she replied, with a serenity she did not feel.

'You're not pleased?'

Kate met his eyes without blinking. 'No,' she said with what her sister would call Yorkshire bluntness. 'Why should I be? Neither Thomas nor I need Seven Ways. Thomas is already well provided for by his Ashley grandfather. Leaving my son a penniless estate, burdened by fines, is hardly bestowing honour upon him.'

'You're right, of course.' The old man's faded eyes did not leave Kate's face. 'But what else could I have done?'

'There are always choices.'

'No.' The old man's hands tightened on the bedclothes. 'There were no choices. I'll have no half measures. Dearly though I love my grandson, if he cannot inherit the estate in his own right he'll not have it by other means. It is his folly that has brought Seven Ways to its present state.'

'Nonsense,' Kate said. 'It is the folly of all of you. You, firstly, for providing finance to the King's cause, and your son for raising a regiment to fight for the King. Jonathan's only folly was to be the one who survived the war to become the family scapegoat.'

To her horror, Francis started to laugh. The effort brought on a coughing fit. She steadied him, holding a beaker of small ale to his lips and only after he lay back on his pillow did he look at her and smile.

'Forgive my laughter, my dear,' he said and the corners of his mouth drooped. 'You are quite correct Jonathan is a convenient scapegoat for the family fortunes. He deserves better and he has a good advocate in you.' His faded eyes narrowed. 'I'm fully conscious that it is an imposition upon you and an onerous task, but it is seldom that I have met a woman who I felt more capable of the responsibility. I see in you, my dear, the best hope that this family has had for many years. Richard did well in his choice of a bride.' He paused, catching his breath. 'Ultimately, of course, it will be your decision as to what becomes of Seven Ways. I'll not fetter that freedom. You're free to sell the estate, although for what little it will fetch, I doubt that you'll see its true value realised. That b— Colonel Price over at Longley Abbey would have it off you for the cost of a lamb.'

He coughed again and Kate waited until he continued. 'Although my motives may appear purely personal, my primary concern is not so much for what happens to the last of the Thorntons but for the people dependent upon my family. By that I mean my servants and my tenants who have served this family faithfully for generations. I owe them a debt to them far greater than that which I owe to this Parliament. It is my responsibility to ensure there is enough to eat for the winter and none of them lacks for clothes or shoes. So far I have succeeded in that end but at a terrible cost to my estate and myself. When you make your decision, my dear, think about them.'

Kate sighed and looked at the dying man lying in the bed. She thought of the tenants whose farms she and Nell had visited during the weeks she had been at Seven Ways— the women, the children, the old and the sick— and knew that he was right.

Whatever became of the last of the Thorntons, the tenants needed care.

'I am sorry that it had to be like this, Katherine,' Sir Francis said, his voice no more than a hoarse whisper. 'I have lived more than eighty years and have few regrets. My greatest sorrow is that I let my daughter go in a fit of petulance that cut me off from her family for so long. I speak in all honesty when I say my intention in bringing you here was not just to test young Thomas' suitability to be my heir, but to make amends for thirty years of my own stupidity.'

Looking into the faded eyes, Kate saw that he spoke the truth. She laid her hand over his frail hand and nodded. There seemed nothing more to be said, and she sat with him until he slept.

CHAPTER 6

'*I*s it much further, Mother?'

Tom's fretful whine set Kate's teeth on edge.

Ignoring her son, Kate stared resolutely into the gathering gloom as her weary horse picked up one hoof then another only to set them down again into the thick, gluey mud of the road. She didn't need Tom to remind her that England's notoriously fickle weather made travel a nightmare.

The rain had set in on the second day after they had left Seven Ways and now three days later they were all tired, wet and muddy.

'I see a light ahead.' Ellen's nephew Dickon, riding ahead with Ellen on the pillion saddle of the sturdy cob, rose in his stirrup and pointed ahead at the tiny glimmer of light in the gloaming.

'Pray God it's an inn,' Kate muttered between clenched teeth.

Her prayer answered, they turned into the lonely travellers' inn. The lights from the windows beckoned and the prospect of a dry bed and some warm food immediately cheered the party.

Kate left the horses in Dickon's care and swept into the inn with what dignity she could muster in her damp, mud-spattered clothes and asked for the best room and hot water. The accommodation she was offered was clean and comfortable and the landlord set a fire going in the hearth and promised hot food would be coming.

As Ellen fussed over Tom, pulling off his muddy boots and setting them to dry in front of the fire, a maid knocked on the door and entered, bearing a bowl and jug of warm water.

'I have a message for thee, madam.'

The girl handed Kate a small square of folded paper. Kate took the paper and unfolded it, peering at the unfamiliar scrawl.

Mistress Ashley. I would esteem it an honour if you would dine with me tonight. We are, I believe, old acquaintances. Yr servant, J. Miller.

'Who is this Master Miller?' Kate asked the girl.

The girl shrugged. 'A traveller like yourself, madam. Arrived not long afore you. Said you would find him in the parlour.'

'For the life of me I can recall no man by the name of Miller,' Kate said to Ellen, as the girl closed the door behind her.

'You're surely not going to meet him?' Ellen protested. 'It wouldn't be proper. Should I come with you?'

Kate shrugged. 'Believe me, I want nothing more than a hot meal and a warm bed, Ellen, but I'm curious. I'll present myself and then retire gracefully. Find me some clean petticoats. You stay here with Tom.'

Ellen dug clean petticoats and a bodice out of the luggage, crumpled but a definite improvement on her mud-spattered travelling clothes. Kate straightened her collar in front of an old, smoky and speckled mirror and kissed her son, who was too intent on the rabbit pie he had ordered for his dinner to pay her much attention.

Few travellers braved the road in this weather and apart from a table of local men, to judge by their rough clothes, the parlour seemed quiet. Kate peered into the gloom of the cosy room, lit only by a single brace of candles. A lone man sat beside the fire, his legs propped on a firedog, spectacles pushed to the end of his long nose, too deeply absorbed by his book to notice her entrance.

'Master Miller?'

He jumped up from his seat, hastily removing the spectacles. 'Mistress Ashley. I'm delighted you could join me.'

She took a breath as she recognised the tall figure. 'Jon —' she began, but he interrupted her, holding out his hand.

'John Miller, indeed the same. I was a friend of your husband's, you may recall? It has been some years, I realise, but as soon as I saw you arrive I thought I should make myself known. Come and sit by the fire. This weather is the very devil. You would think it mid-winter, not mid-summer.'

She took the seat he indicated sending a maid for glasses and a bottle of the house's best Rhenish.

'Take that look off your face, Kate.' Jonathan Thornton leaned forward and lowered his voice. 'I assure you I'm real enough.'

'How do you come to be here?' Kate found her voice at last.

He shrugged. 'I'm travelling in the same direction as you.'

'How is it we have not seen you on the road?' Kate challenged.

A smile twitched the corners of his mouth. 'I passed you when Tom's horse cast a shoe this morning and you were at the blacksmith's. I had to see someone this afternoon and hazarded a guess that this would be your stopping place for the night.'

The maid reappeared with a jug of wine and two glasses. Jonathan took them from her and poured the wine, handing a glass to Kate.

'So who is John Miller?' Kate settled back in the chair, the welcome glass in her hand.

'John Miller is a bookseller from London, travelling to York to purchase a rare volume of Spenser.'

'He is an old friend?' Kate observed.

'A very old friend.' Jonathan smiled. 'Ah, here is the landlord with food. I took the liberty of ordering for you. Come and dine, you must be famished.'

They adjourned to the table and sat in silence as their supper was served.

'I have a favour to ask of you,' Jonathan said as soon as they were alone again.

Kate paused in cutting her meat and looked up at him. 'A favour?'

'As you may have noticed the roads are busy with troops.'

Kate nodded. They had been passed several times by red-coated soldiers heading northwards.

'A man travelling alone is instantly suspect, no matter how good his papers. A man travelling with a woman and child excites less interest. Would you object to my riding with you as far as York?'

Kate's breath caught in her throat. 'Do you know how dangerous that would be for us?'

He laid his hand on hers. 'I wouldn't ask if I thought it would bring danger to you. I assure you my papers are quite in order and the reason for my journey quite plausible.'

Kate looked down at the strong hand that covered hers. The simple gesture stirred something deep within her; a forgotten memory of a man's touch on her skin. It had been so long since a man had touched her... held her.

Propriety wrestled with curiosity. If she were honest with herself, she had thought about this man a great deal over the last few days and the thought of his company for the few days they had left on their journey intrigued her.

She withdrew her hand and smiled. 'I've no objection, and Tom would relish your company. He has had enough of mine for the last few days.'

'Good.' Jonathan sat back. 'It's settled. Your cousin, John Miller, will join you tomorrow.' He frowned. 'Can your servants be trusted? They both know who I am.'

Kate stiffened. 'Ellen and Dickon are trustworthy,' she said. 'Ellen has been with me since I was a girl. Dickon's her nephew.' A moment of doubt nagged at her. 'How much is your head worth?'

'Enough to keep the likes of Dickon in comfort for a year or too,' Jonathan said.

'Well, if you want to travel with us, you will have no choice but to trust them,' Kate observed.

'True.' Jonathan poured himself another glass of wine. 'So, home to Barton, Mistress Ashley, home to peace, away from the Thorntons and their terrible impositions.' He raised his glass to her and smiled.

'For the moment anyway,' Kate said.

The further she travelled from Seven Ways, the angrier and more resentful she had become. How dare Sir Francis think to impose this burden on her shoulders at a time when the Thornton fortunes were at their lowest. In the good times, there had been no generosity of spirit to his abandoned daughter and her family to warrant any magnanimity on her part. She could, she had reflected several times, snap her fingers at the whole shipload of Thorntons and leave them to drown in the tempest of their own choosing.

She could if it were not for one thing. She liked them.

Sir Francis' days were numbered but he had been right. What would happen to the tenants and Nell and little Ann if she were to desert them? Could she, in all conscience, see them driven from

Seven Ways to face an uncertain future dependent on the charity of friends and relatives even worse off than they?

'What shall I do, Jonathan?' She looked up at him as if expecting him to have read her thoughts.

For a moment their eyes met and she knew he understood exactly what she had been thinking.

He shook his head. 'I can't answer that question. Your best hope is to pray that the King will prevail in the coming conflict and I am returned to my inheritance before my grandfather dies.'

She sat in glum silence for a moment. 'It seems a slender thread of hope,' she said at last.

Jonathan shook his head. 'It is. I wish to God that I could change the past, but I can't. Kate?' He caught the yawn that Kate tried to stifle. 'You're exhausted. Might I suggest you retire? We have another long, damp ride again tomorrow.'

Kate pulled a face and reluctantly stood to leave.

'I will excuse myself,' she said. 'Good night, John Miller.'

Jonathan rose and his eyes smiled at her again as he inclined his head. 'Good night, Mistress Ashley. Thank you for your company.'

Ellen dozed by the fire in their room, waiting for Kate. She started up when Kate closed the door and made Kate sit on the stool while she unpinned her hair. Behind her, Thomas slept curled up in the bed with a beatific smile on his face.

'So, who was your mysterious Master Miller?' Ellen asked.

'Jonathan Thornton,' Kate replied.

Ellen's hand paused in the brushing. 'Not that 'un. Now what mischief is he playing at?'

'He'll be travelling with us to York, Ellen, in the guise of my cousin John Miller, a bookseller from London,' Kate said.

'Will he now?' Ellen's lips pursed.

'Don't give me that look.' Kate knew her maid well. 'There is naught but the need for company...and the need for secrecy.'

Ellen glared at her mistress in the mirror's reflection. 'His secret's safe enough with Dickon and me,' she said. 'You've my word on that, mistress. It's more a question of whether we'll be safe with 'im. Seems to me that lad's trouble.'

'We'll be fine, Ellen. Anyway,' she added brightly, 'it will be good to have another man travelling with us. Much safer.'

'If you say so,' Ellen said.

As they gathered in the inn courtyard early the next morning, Jonathan cast a disapproving eye over Tom's pony.

'No wonder your progress is so slow,' Jonathan remarked.

'I keep telling Mother I need a bigger horse,' Tom said.

Kate stiffened. 'You are only nine. Holly does you well enough,' she said.

Jonathan exchanged a deeply sympathetic look with his young cousin. It had gladdened his heart to see young Tom, and he had every confidence that the boy understood the need for the subterfuge.

Too much like me at that age, he thought.

Ellen glared at him, and the young groom, Dickon, inclined his head with suitable respect. He knew his very presence brought them all into danger but as long as they played their parts, they would be safe. For a couple of days at least, he could enjoy the tedious journey north and it gave him the time and leisure to get to know the intriguing Mistress Ashley.

His grey mare, Amber, nudged him and he gave her a piece of carrot before swinging easily into the saddle.

'Would booksellers normally ride quite so obvious a horse?' Kate inquired once they were on the road.

'They would if they liked horses.' Jonathan patted his handsome mare on the neck.

'Where did you get her?' Kate asked.

He smiled at her. 'I won her at cards.'

'Is cards one of your vices?'

'Not generally. I lack Giles' ability to cheat convincingly,' he replied. 'My vices are the love of good horses, good wine and attractive women.'

'So I hear.' Kate said with a tight little smile.

He gave her a sideways glance. He did not doubt that Nell had embroidered his faults as skilfully as she did her needlework.

'You shouldn't believe all you hear about me.'

Kate turned her level gaze on him. 'I don't. I prefer to make my own judgments about people.'

'And what have you concluded about me?' he ventured.

Her cheeks coloured and she fixed her gaze on the road ahead. 'I don't think that you fit the description of the Jonathan Thornton of family legend, the scapegrace grandson.'

His heart jumped. Could it be possible that this woman was prepared to look past the persona he had carefully cultivated? He had never thought of himself as lonely but if loneliness meant not having anyone in your life who truly understood you, then the void seemed dark and impenetrable.

'There are things about me even my family do not know,' he ventured, but when she cast him a curious glance, he chose not to elaborate. Not now, not here, not yet.

'And what about you, Mistress Ashley? What sort of person are you?'

'You tell me,' she challenged him.

He looked at her thoughtfully. 'It seems to me that either there is a lot of Puritan in you or you have forgotten what it is to have fun. You have a tendency, Mistress Ashley, to view life far too seriously.'

Kate laughed. 'Maybe a little bit of both. My mother came from Puritan stock, and as I was left a widow with a son at the age of twenty with the responsibility of running an estate, it is most probable that I have forgotten what it is to have fun.'

Before Jonathan could respond, Tom came barrelling up between them. He pointed up the road. 'What's that?'

Kate reined in her horse and they paused in the road, looking at the grim silhouette against the grey sky.

'It's a gibbet,' Jonathan said.

He could see the decomposing remains of a man, swinging from the hastily constructed scaffold that had been placed at the crossroads as a warning. It could not be avoided.

As they rode past he looked at the crudely painted sign that hung from the man's neck. Kate looked away, pressing her gloved hand to her nose but Tom stared with ghoulish fascination.

'What does the sign say, Jonathan?' Tom asked.

'*Murder, rapine and brigandry*,' Jonathan read. 'This man was a footpad.'

'Well I hope it serves as a warning to those who would follow, and that there are no more on this road,' Kate said with a cough.

Jonathan looked at her. 'Sadly the country is rife with such brigands. The legacy of war, Kate. Men with no homes to return to or men who think a better living is to be made on the roads.' He paused and dropped his voice so she alone could hear him. 'In a way, I'm only one step removed from them.'

'At least you're not a danger to innocent travellers,' Kate replied.

He looked at her. 'Who is to say I'm not? Believe me, Kate, if a man is hungry and desperate enough...' He left the sentence unfinished. There had indeed been the odd occasion when he had resorted to holding up a wealthy coach for the chance of a little gold that would mean the difference between a bed and a meal or a hedgerow and hunger.

From the shocked glance that Kate shot him, she could not be sure if he teased her or if Jonathan Thornton had resorted to such methods for his survival. He returned the glance with an enigmatic shrug.

Long after they had ridden past the gibbet with its grim warning, the sickly smell of the decomposing remains seemed to cling to them.

CHAPTER 7

*K*ate looked up at the clearing sky and her spirits lifted as the first warm rays of sun broke through the clouds. Despite the state of the road, with continuing good weather they would be in Selby in time for lunch and York on the morrow.

'Mistress.' At Dickon's shout, she twisted in her saddle to see a large body of cavalry riding hard up behind them.

As the jink of harness and the reverberation of hooves grew nearer, she glanced at the man who rode beside her.

'Jonathan, what do we do?'

'There is nothing to fear, Kate. Just let them pass,' Jonathan said with calm confidence.

Kate wished she shared that confidence. A woman and child in the company of a notorious malignant...she would hang for certes.

'Make way there,' the officer at the front shouted, and the travellers pressed back against the hedge to let the soldiers pass.

Her heart sank as the officer reined in beside them. His eyes flicked across the small party. 'Where are you bound?'

Kate opened her mouth to speak but Jonathan pre-empted her.

'York,' he said. 'My cousin has been visiting with my mother and, as I've business in York, I'm accompanying her.'

'Papers?' The man demanded.

Obediently Kate produced the papers that the local magistrate had issued her before the start of her journey and Jonathan fished his out from inside his jacket. The officer scanned them.

'Bookseller, eh?' The officer said, looking up at Jonathan.

Jonathan returned the suspicious look with an air of innocent confidence.

'A hard trade to make a living in these days, captain,' he said as the officer returned the papers.

'We have encountered a great many soldiers travelling north. Is there trouble brewing?' Jonathan remarked.

'Scotland,' the man replied. 'Word is Charles Stuart has landed there.'

'Really?' Jonathan raised an eyebrow and shook his head in apparent disbelief. 'Is Fairfax going to invade Scotland?'

'Nay, Fairfax would have no part of it. He's resigned command. Cromwell's now Commander-in-Chief,' the soldier replied.

Jonathan's face betrayed nothing. 'Well, my friend, God speed your cause and may you deal swiftly with the scurvy Scots and their so-called King.'

The man nodded and, with a quick inclination of his head in Kate's direction, turned his horse's head and rode off to catch up with his men. Kate stared after the man, her heart hammering beneath her bodice.

'Don't look like that, Kate,' Jonathan reproved. 'You have a face that can be read like a book, and if I'm to be betrayed it will be your doing, not mine.'

Kate had not even been aware she had been holding her breath. She now expelled the air from her lungs. 'How can you lie like that?'

'Years of practice.' Jonathan sounded terse and she suspected he was cross with her.

THE ENCOUNTER with the soldiers gave Jonathan cause for thought as they rode on. Kate rode beside him in silence and only when he glanced at her did he notice the downcast corners of her mouth. Was it possible she thought he was displeased with her?

She had no reason to think that. She had held her nerve but he was conscious of the danger he had placed her in and felt the need to make amends.

The spire of a sizeable town loomed on the horizon and a motley assortment of tents and stalls had been set up on the commons outside the town.

'What town is this?' Jonathan asked.

'Selby,' she replied. 'It must be market day.'

Tom rode up beside them. 'Can we stop for a little while, Mother?'

'Why not?' agreed Jonathan. 'It seems an excellent place to find something for lunch.' His stomach growled in response to the suggestion.

They found a place to leave the horses and Kate gave Ellen some coins along with an order to watch Tom like a hawk. Ellen in her turn told Dickon to stay away from the ale and he followed his aunt with a sulky caste to his face.

'It's not quite the fairs of my childhood,' Kate said. 'Then there were jugglers and dancing and music.'

'For that, we can thank your friends in Whitehall,' Jonathan remarked. 'Would you care to take my arm, Mistress Ashley?'

As they strolled towards the centre of the activity, Kate said, 'I owe you an apology for my behaviour this morning.'

'What behaviour?'

'I thought I might give you away.'

He sighed. 'It's a very dangerous game, with a hangman's noose at the end if I forget the rules. No harm was done and contrary to what you might think, I gained considerable information from our encounter with the Roundhead. I now know the high command of the army is divided. Scotland will be invaded and Cromwell is taking his best troops with him.'

Kate shivered and looked up at the spire of the church looming above the roofs of the little town.

'It will be a hard fight?'

Jonathan nodded. 'And Cromwell is taking it to us. My only consolation is that Scotland is such a God-forsaken place, his English troops may well tire of it before the Scots capitulate. Let's not talk of war anymore. It is a beautiful day and I can smell roast meat. If I don't eat soon I will fade away.'

After they had eaten, they strolled among the stalls until Kate's eye was drawn to a vendor selling bolts of material. She turned over the cloth with what Jonathan took to be the expert eye of a clothier's daughter. As she hesitated between a grey and a russet he felt compelled to intervene.

'Those colours make you look like a Puritan goodwife. Why not this? It will suit you much better.'

He drew a bolt of sky blue fine woollen cloth from the table. She stared at him. 'But...' she began to protest.

'Now have you any lawn?' he asked the merchant before she could finish.

The merchant produced a small bolt of fine white linen. Jonathan cocked an inquiring eyebrow at Kate. 'Well, Mistress Ashley?'

She stared back at him. 'I suppose...' She smiled. 'Why not indeed?'

'I am not a Puritan goodwife,' she muttered as Jonathan picked up her parcels.

'Good,' he said and strode towards a stall selling lace. With the deliberation of a cook selecting the finest apples, he pulled a pretty, narrow needlepoint from the pile.

'This will do for edging the collar and cuffs,' he said.

'Jonathan, I...'

He just looked at her.

Kate reached for her coins, but he laid a hand over hers.

'No, this will be my present for you,' he said. 'A gift for allowing me the pleasure of your company over the last two days.'

'You can't afford it,' she blurted out.

He dismissed her protests and her thanks with a wave of his hand and handed her the parcel with a mock bow.

It would probably mean an enormous difference to his lodgings in Scotland unless he supplemented his income with a little highway robbery, but it felt like a small gesture for this woman who had already given so much and who, thanks to him, now faced an uncertain future.

'Can you see Tom?' Kate said, looking around the crowded market.

'I think I see him over yonder. He's admiring pigs,' Jonathan said. He looked up at the clock on the church tower. 'Mistress Ashley, as I would like to be in York by tomorrow night, perhaps we should retrieve your son from the pigs and be away.'

~

THEY REACHED the town of Cawood by evening and, as she changed into what passed for a clean and tidy gown for supper that night, Kate struggled with her conflicting emotions. This would be her last night on the road with Jonathan, and she had to admit that for all the danger he presented to them, she did not want it to end. He made her laugh. He reminded her that she was still young and that life, however difficult, could be lived to the fullest.

She had not been without suitors over the years of her widowhood; colleagues of her sister's husband, William, or other local gentry. Young, old, handsome or otherwise, none of them had touched the place in her heart that she had thought would be forever Richard's. Now she had to admit to a stirring of emotions she had thought never to experience again; the flutter in the pit of her stomach when Jonathan was near, the gladdening of her heart when he smiled at her, the desolation of imminent parting.

She looked hard at her reflection in the chipped and stippled mirror provided by the inn and saw the brightness in her eye, the flush of colour in her cheek. She tightened her lips and took a deep breath. She could not, would not, permit herself these feelings.

Jonathan would leave her tomorrow and she might never see him again. For the sake of her own peace of mind, she could not afford herself the luxury of... she expelled her breath in a deep, shuddering sigh... of falling in love.

They had taken a private parlour for their supper and, having sent Tom to an early bed, they would dine alone. As Kate entered the room she saw Jonathan standing by the window, gazing out at the last of the summer evening.

For a brief moment, time stood still as she caught his profile against the light.

'Richard.'

Jonathan turned and looked at her, an eyebrow raised in query.

'Kate?'

She gasped, her hand flying to her mouth. She had not meant to say the name aloud. How could she have mistaken Richard's cousin, so much taller and darker than her husband?

'Are you all right?'

She heard the concern in his voice and nodded, lowering her hand and making a pretence of smoothing her cuffs.

Unable to look him in the eyes, she said, 'I apologise, Jonathan. A foolish notion. I'd never thought that you and Richard had much of a likeness, even for cousins. But just for a moment…'

He turned to face her, his face unreadable.

'Not such a foolish notion,' he said. 'If you had ever seen us together you wouldn't have doubted that we were related.'

She frowned trying to make sense of what he had just said. When had he ever come face to face with his cousin?

'You told me you'd never met.'

He waved a hand at the table. 'As you can see, supper is served. Come and sit down and I will tell you about Richard.'

She took the seat he held out for her and accepted a glass of wine. Jonathan sat down across from her and picked up his glass. He gazed into its blood-red depths for a long moment before he then looked up, a rueful smile curling the corners of his lips.

'Another, not quite truth, Kate. I did know Richard. We were at Oxford at the same time. Not at the same college and he was older and far more sensible than I, but our paths crossed on more than one occasion. It may not surprise you to know that we didn't get on very well. Blood does not always spell kinship, even without the added complications of longstanding family estrangement. We were probably about as different as two young men could be. Richard, as you well know, was a scholar. I was...' He shrugged. 'However, the one thing we were both determined upon was an end to Grandfather's pointless feud.' He set the glass down and cut his capon. 'I once took him to Seven Ways to see Grandfather.'

Kate shook her head in disbelief. 'Richard never told me any of this... nor your grandfather.'

'And that surprises you?' Jonathan looked up at her. 'Grandfather refused to see him and Richard quite rightly saw no point in remaining where he was not welcome, so he returned to Oxford.'

'Did you see Richard again?' she asked.

He nodded. 'From time to time, but we never sought each other out. Once he left Oxford we had no cause to communicate. Then, of course, the war came and the Ashleys sided with Parliament and the rift deepened.' He met her gaze with a fierce intensity. 'I told the truth, Kate when I said I didn't know the circumstances of Richard's death.'

Kate sat quite still, trying to imagine her beloved Richard and this man as young men together in Oxford, united only by one goal: to end the rift between the two families. Two more different men she could not imagine. She looked away to hide the pricking of tears behind her eyes.

'Richard...' she began, swallowing hard on the threatening tears. 'Richard lacked the heart for the fight. He would have been happier with his books.'

Jonathan nodded. 'That I could imagine,' he said. 'He was the scholar I could never hope to be.'

She brought her gaze back to him. 'It took courage on both your parts to face Sir Francis. In the circumstances, I can imagine that it would not have pleased your family, or his, to even pretend an acquaintance with an Ashley.'

Jonathan grimaced. 'My father was furious, and Ned sided with him as he always did. It was just another transgression to add to the ledger.'

Kate caught the edge of bitterness in his voice.

'If Richard still lived, would Sir Francis have named him his heir instead of Thomas?' she asked.

Jonathan nodded. 'I think so. Time has softened his anger and I believe Grandfather quite genuinely regrets the estrangement, Kate. Yes, I believe he would have made peace with Richard.'

'Then why not with his father? Richard was dead but David Ashley has only been dead this year past.'

Jonathan shrugged. 'I can't answer for my grandfather. It's my observation, no more, that the King's execution marked the final resistance for Sir Francis. Nothing else seemed to matter if they could kill a king with such impunity.'

Kate looked down at the cooling food on her plate. When she looked up again she hoped that the deepening shadows in the room would disguise the yearning she felt in her heart.

'Do you have to leave us at York? Could you perhaps come on to Barton? I'm sure Tom would love to have you to himself for a few more days.'

He shook his head. 'I can't dally, Kate. The King is in Scotland and will be waiting on me and the letters I carry.'

Kate reached out and put her hand on his. 'I fear this venture will not end well. Please don't go, Jonathan.'

He looked down at her hand and before she could withdraw it, curled his fingers around hers. Heat rushed to her face and she pulled her hand back, burying it within the folds of her skirt as if it had been burnt. She had never behaved so wantonly in all her life. How could she be beseeching a man she barely knew to stay by her side? Stay safe...

Without looking at him, she sensed him watching her.

'I appreciate your concern, Kate,' he said at last, 'but I am bound to the King. I must go to Scotland.'

'And what awaits you in Scotland?' she asked without looking up, her heart tight within her bodice.

'I hope for a regiment of horse but,' he said with a shrug, 'with the Scots calling the tune I may well be doing nothing. That is the soldier's lot.' He paused. 'Please, believe me, Kate. If I could dally I would. I can think of nothing I want more than time...'

He didn't finish the sentence and when Kate dared to meet his eyes again, she found him watching her.

'You will be careful?' was all she could say.

He smiled, a humourless smile not echoed by his eyes. 'There is no one who knows better than I how to look after myself. I have managed remarkably well up to this point in time.'

Kate shivered. 'As your sister said, you may well tempt fate once too often, Jonathan.'

He looked at her, the hazel eyes searching her face, a slight frown puckering his brow. 'And that worries you, Kate?'

'Yes,' she admitted. 'As the fate of any *friend* would concern me,' she added.

'Friend,' Jonathan echoed the word and raised his glass. 'Then let us drink to friendship, Mistress Ashley. A valuable commodity in these times.'

She raised her glass in answer. 'Friendship.'

CHAPTER 8

'Jonathan. You're not listening,' Tom grumbled

'Sorry, Tom. What did you say?' Jonathan replied.

They had entered York, and a multitude of thoughts had been running through Jonathan's mind as he contemplated the impending farewell and the long, hard ride north to an uncertain future awaiting him in Scotland.

'I asked if you were going to stay at Uncle William's with us.' Tom's raised voice broke Jonathan's reverie and he shot Kate a glance.

'Uncle William?' he asked.

Kate smiled. 'William Rowe, my sister's husband. His house is just down this street, yonder.' Kate indicated the direction. 'He's been seeing to the wool sales, and the plan is that Tom and I will travel back to Barton with him on the morrow. You would be welcome to stay.' Kate looked up at Jonathan. 'William is a generous host.'

William the wool merchant, Jonathan recalled. A house built on the profits from war, he thought, as he considered the pleasant half-timbered house. Could he sacrifice his principles for a few more hours of Kate's company, a comfortable bed and free lodgings?

'If your brother-in-law has no objection, I would be honoured,' he replied.

The smile lit up Kate's face. 'Oh no, I'm sure William won't mind.'

'I have some business that I must transact first, Kate. If I could leave my horse, I'll go on foot.'

'Of course. There are stables at the rear of the house. Dickon will see to Amber. Shall we expect you for supper?'

Jonathan shook his head. 'I've no idea how long my business will take. Don't expect me.'

The disappointment on Kate's face was plain to see. Jonathan resisted the temptation to reach out a finger and raise her face to look into her eyes... to kiss her. That had been a temptation he had been resisting for some days, conscious that Kate would return his advances with a glad heart.

He took a steadying breath and cursed himself for forgetting, just for a moment, that his life allowed for no such distractions, beyond passing dalliances. Yet he had let his guard down with this woman, and had, unforgivably, let her form an attachment that, whatever he wished, could never have a future.

Still, one more night could make no difference.

He left them at the house of William Rowe and set out on foot to the home of a wealthy merchant, not unlike William Rowe, who lived across the river. The rain had stopped and broken sunlight dappled the narrow, muddy streets.

After the long days in the saddle, Jonathan relished the chance to stretch his legs. He had been to York before and had a lingering affection for the ancient town with its magnificent Minster, mercifully spared the ravages of a victorious Parliamentary army by its commander, Sir Thomas Fairfax.

A real bookseller with a tempting table of books caught his eye. It was no coincidence that he took the persona of a bookseller in his travels. He loved books, and over the years had compensated for his indolent years at Oxford by becoming a voracious reader.

To his delight, he saw a copy of Shakespeare's sonnets in pristine condition. He picked the book up and turned it over in his hands, gently flicking through the pages, handling it with the same care he would show a beautiful piece of glass. He wondered if Kate cared for the sonnets and in a brief flash of romantic fantasy, imagined himself reading them to her in a peaceful time that he knew did not exist.

A shadow fell across the table. Assuming it to be the bookseller, without looking up Jonathan said, 'I'll take this volume —'

'Thornton.' The name fell onto the table like a fist.

At the sound of the familiar voice, Jonathan looked up into the cold, blue eyes of a man he knew too well, a man he had once called a friend, and his blood froze in his veins. The book dropped from his nerveless fingers back onto the table.

The stocky man in the uniform of a Parliamentary officer smiled without humour or warmth.

'God is with me this day,' Stephen Prescott said as he reached for the pistol he carried in his belt.

In that moment of hesitation, Jonathan threw the table over in one swift movement and took off down the street crowded with the afternoon shoppers. Behind him, he heard his name bellowed as Prescott gathered his men for the chase. Heavy feet trampled the slimy cobbles and loud voices shouted exhortations for someone to stop the fugitive.

No one paid them any heed. The shoppers simply parted

before the running figure and despite the urging of the soldiers, none made to catch him. Twisting and turning down the narrow streets, Jonathan found himself unable to shed his pursuers. His heavy boots slipped on the wet, mired streets and made running hard. Almost spent, he heard Prescott behind him, urging his men on, knowing that the man would not let up with his long-sought quarry in such plain view.

The man thought he had God on his side.

Jonathan turned sharply down a street he knew led to one of the gates but was brought up short by a heavy ox cart, laden down with wool bales, taking the width of the passageway.

'Cornered, Thornton. Turn around and face me like a man.' Prescott's breathless voice came from behind him and he turned slowly to face his pursuers.

There was no mistaking the look of malicious triumph on Stephen Prescott's face. He had seen it before in a town square in Devon six years ago. Nothing but Jonathan Thornton's death would give this man rest.

'WHILE I LIVE I HOPE,' the late King had said, and Jonathan had escaped Stephen Prescott before. He raised his hands away from the hilt of his sword. At least with so public an apprehension, there might be some hope of a fair trial, if not immediate escape.

A fascinated crowd pressed back against the shops as Prescott swaggered towards him. The man stopped some fifteen yards from Jonathan, breathing heavily, savouring the moment. Jonathan held the man with a cold, hard gaze, determined that Prescott would see no fear in his eyes.

'No escape this time, Thornton. You stand tried and convicted.'

Prescott straightened and raised his heavy pistol in a slow

deliberate movement. In the brief moment before the report of the pistol echoed from the houses, Jonathan saw his death written in the man's eyes.

Surely it would be better to die now than at the end of a rope?

The watching crowd gasped as the pistol ball smashed into his shoulder. The force knocked him backwards, and he fell to his knees in the mud.

He looked up and saw Prescott accepting a second pistol from one of his soldiers. He would not remain here waiting to be shot like a dog in the streets of York with Stephen Prescott his judge, jury and executioner.

'Scurvy Roundhead.' An angry voice broke the silence.

'Kill a man in cold blood?' Another voice cried out.

'We'll not have that. Not here…'

From somewhere in the crowd a missile flew through the air, striking the Roundhead officer squarely on the chest. Prescott staggered, dropping the pistol.

'Who threw that?' he demanded.

'Murderer.'

The rest of the crowd joined in the fray, hurling whatever missile came to hand at the unpopular troopers. Forced to defend themselves, the troopers retreated from the fury of the crowd that now interposed itself between Prescott and the fallen man.

Jonathan mustered his scattered thoughts. He had been given the chance and he took it. There had been no time for pain and, heedless of his injury, he rolled under the cart, scrambling away from the growing melee. On the other side of the cart, he rose to his feet. The world roaring in his ears, he stumbled forward, to be caught by a pair of strong hands.

'This way,' a man's voice hissed in his ear.

Reality blurred and faded as his rescuer half-carried and half-dragged him down narrow streets, pushing him through a dark shop entrance and bundling him into a space that seemed no bigger than a large cupboard. The door shut and he heard furniture being moved in front of it.

Alone in the pitiless dark, his heart thumping behind his ribcage, Jonathan took a long, slow, shuddering breath and bit his lip against the sudden fierce and terrible pain in his left shoulder. One sound and he would betray not only himself but the stranger who had rescued him.

He put a shaking hand to the injury, his fingers feeling the warm stickiness of blood. Clutching his left arm to his chest, he closed his eyes, trying to control the pain and nausea and muster his thoughts but the walls of the dark cupboard closed in on him and he slipped into blessed unconsciousness.

He came back to his senses, lying on a none-too-clean floor. Above him, the carcass of a pig swayed from a hook and he smelled blood and offal. The blood could be his but the other noxious odours were those of the Shambles. A bearded face came into view and strong hands hauled him into a sitting position.

'Ye can't stay here,' the man said. 'The soldiers have already been and I've a wife and bairns upstairs. Have ye friends in York?'

Jonathan found his voice. 'Petergate. The house of...' The instinct of his profession overcame his fuddled senses. 'Just get me as far as Petergate.'

The bearded face nodded. 'Aye, I can do that for 'ee. It's gone dark so we'll be safe enough. Now on your feet.'

Despite being a good head shorter than Jonathan, his saviour was solid and took Jonathan's weight with ease. Winding their way through the backways and alleys of the city, they made faltering progress to Petergate.

'Just around the corner is the Minster. I'll leave you 'ere,' the man said. 'The wife'll be wondering where I've gone.'

'Thank you,' Jonathan muttered, struggling to keep a grip on consciousness. 'I owe you my life.'

'Aye, well I've no love for them troopers, particularly not when they take to shootin' unarmed men in't street.'

He melted away into the dark. Jonathan leaned against the wall, breathing heavily and determined not to faint. It was just a little way to the tenuous safety of William Rowe's house.

KATE SAT BACK in her chair and smiled affectionately at her brother-in-law as William Rowe poured another glass of wine and belched with satisfaction.

'Damned good meal,' he said. 'Made all the better for your company, my dear.'

Kate laughed. 'Don't tell me that. I know you relish escaping from Suzanne for a few days. I've probably ruined your plans for a game of cards tonight.'

'Aye well, mayhap you have,' William agreed. 'But the truth is we've all missed you, my dear. The farm's doing well. Young Phillip's done you proud.' He looked at the dark sky outside the window. 'Now when's this cousin of Richard's turning up? Lookin' forward to meeting him. Does he play cards?'

'He does and rather better than you I suspect, William.'

'Never. Don't 'ee durst tell thy sister but I'm a dab hand at cards.'

Kate smiled and William continued. 'So these Thornton relatives of yourn have been hard done by?'

Kate shook her head. 'They've nothing left but a run-down estate and their pride. The price for supporting the King has been heavy.'

William nodded. 'Aye, well, they're not alone there, lass.

There's many here in Yorkshire that have suffered the same fate. What is it, Mistress Gates?'

William's housekeeper hovered in the doorway.

'Please, sir. I'd not disturb you but there's a man in my kitchen asking for Mistress Ashley.' Indignation flashed into the woman's face. 'Bleedin' all over my clean floor he is.'

Even as William rose to his feet, Kate had already left the room, running down the corridor and the stairs to the kitchen.

Her heart stopped at the sight of Jonathan. He stood by the door to the courtyard, or rather leaned against the wall, holding his left arm, his face ashen and, as Mistress Gates had observed, dripping blood from his left hand onto the immaculate floor.

'Kate. I'm so sorry...' he began but did not finish as he slid down the wall to the floor, leaving a trail of blood against the whitewashed wall.

Her hands flew to her mouth and she stifled a scream.

'Is he dead?' Mistress Gates enquired.

Her voice jerked Kate out of her state of immobility and she knelt beside Jonathan, her hands hovering helplessly over his shoulder where the jacket was blackened and sodden with blood.

'Good God, lass. Who's this?' William, puffing heavily, had followed Kate into the kitchen.

'Jonathan Thornton,' she replied without looking around. As she put a hand to Jonathan's icy forehead, his eyes flickered open and he grimaced.

'Jon, what happened?'

'I was recognised.'

He groaned as Kate fumbled with his jacket as gently as she could, peeling it back to reveal the injury. Her stomach lurched as she took in the extent of the damage, and she gave an inadvertent gasp.

'It's all right, Kate. It's not fatal,' Jonathan muttered, his right hand closing on hers. 'I should be grateful for inaccurate cavalry pistols.'

'It may not be fatal but it looks bad enough,' Kate observed. 'Gates, don't just stand there. Give me a cloth.'

Mistress Gates, keeping her distance and wearing an expression of distaste, handed Kate a clean cloth.

Kate held it to the wound, trying to staunch the bleeding as William bent over them.

'Who did this, lad?'

'Prescott...' he began, frowning as he looked up at the faces around him. 'He'll turn the town upside down...I'm putting you all in danger...'

He tried to rise to his feet but Kate pushed him back down again.

William looked down at the wounded man. 'Prescott? You mean Major Prescott.'

But William's question went unanswered. Jonathan's eyes had closed, his breathing ragged.

'Do you know this man?' Kate demanded.

William nodded. 'Aye. It pays to know the men in power, lass. As for you Thornton, I won't ask why, for its none of my concern, but if you're kin of Kate and young Tom, then you're safe enough here.'

Kate looked up at her brother-in-law. 'He needs a chirrurgeon, William.'

'Aye, well, that's obvious,' William agreed. 'Mistress Gates —'

Jonathan raised his right hand in protest. 'No. He knows I'm hurt. There'll be men watching the surgeons.'

Kate rose to her feet. 'Ellen will know what to do. She's nursed wounded before. I'll fetch her.'

Ellen had earned a formidable reputation among the wounded that had come to Barton after the battle that had taken Richard

Ashley's life. There may have been nothing she could do for Richard, but there were plenty of others who owed their lives to her practical and skilled hands.

Kate left Jonathan in the care of a reluctant, and squeamish, Mistress Gates and went to fetch Ellen, who would be waiting in the bedchamber for Kate to adjourn. She reached the top stairs and stopped, at the sound of an authoritative knocking on the door.

Her hand froze on the banister, her heart beating behind her bodice, as William himself answered the door, opening the door to an officer, distinguishable by the gorget around his neck, and behind him two troopers in heavy helmets.

Kate took the last few steps to the gallery, drawing into the shadows. The officer removed his hat revealing a thinning pate of fair hair.

'Major Prescott,' William said. 'What brings you here at this hour of the night? We were just retiring.'

A cold hand clawed at Kate's heart. Major Prescott. Stephen Prescott? The man who had shot Jonathan?

'I'm sorry to disturb you, Master Rowe.' The officer sounded suitably deferential. William, after all, enjoyed a respectable reputation. 'I came to warn you that there is a notorious delinquent loose in the town and a curfew has been declared until we apprehend him. Would you please ensure neither you nor your household goes abroad tonight?'

'Is this man dangerous?' William asked.

'Any desperate man is dangerous,' Prescott replied. 'Have no fear. I have sealed the gates and I have reason to believe he has been badly wounded. He won't get away.'

Prescott looked around the hallway, raising his gaze to the gallery where Kate stood in the shadows. He frowned as if trying to bring her into sharper focus.

'Thank you for your trouble, Major,' William said, pointedly moving to the door.

With his eyes still fixed on Kate, Prescott said. 'I'll bid you goodnight, Master Rowe...Mistress.'

He gave a cursory bow and turned on his heel, the two troopers following.

William shut the door behind them and bolted it. He looked up at Kate, and she read the concern in his usually bluff, cheerful face.

CHAPTER 9

Kate set down the tray she carried and crossed to the bed where Ellen leaned over the wounded man who muttered and tossed in a restless, feverish sleep.

'Mary!'

The name was uttered with such anguish that both women took a step backward. Jonathan's eyes opened wide but unfocussed as he struggled to sit up. Ellen gently eased him back against the bolsters. He turned his head from side to side, muttering incoherently.

'I wonder who Mary is,' Kate remarked more to herself than Ellen.

Ellen laid a damp cloth on Jonathan's forehead and shook her head. 'Whoever she is, I don't think that they're happy memories.'

Jonathan knocked the cloth aside and his eyes flickered open, this time with the light of lucidity.

'Kate?' He frowned in an effort to concentrate and reached up to touch her face. His fingers brushed her mouth and she caught his hand and held it fast. 'I found a copy of Shakespeare's sonnets. I…I must have dropped it.'

'Another time, Jonathan.' She pressed his hand to her breast and bit back the threatening tears. Exhaustion, that was all.

'Are you crying?' he asked.

'Of course not,' she snapped. 'We've stopped the bleeding and Ellen has patched you up as well as any doctor. Now we need you to get some sleep.'

Ellen hovered at her elbow with a beaker.

'Drink this,' Kate said. 'We found some laudanum. It will help.'

Kate raised his head and held the cup to his lips. He drank the liquid and she laid him back on the bolsters.

She stroked the back of his hand. 'Try and sleep now. We will need you in the morning if we're to get you away from York.'

Jonathan's fingers tightened on hers. 'I'll be fine in the morning, you'll see,' he muttered as his eyes closed.

LONG AFTER MIDNIGHT, Kate paced the downstairs parlour.

'What are we to do, William? We must get him away from York. You saw that man Prescott. If he even begins to suspect…' Her voice tailed off and she turned to traverse the length of the room again.

William rose to his feet and put a hand on her arm to still her. He handed her a glass of his best Canary and she drank the sweet wine almost in one gulp, feeling her taut nerves begin to loosen.

'Prescott'll have the gates well guarded,' William said. 'I don't see as how it will be easy to get a wounded man past 'em.' He sat in his chair and toyed with the wine. 'Now I brought the wool clip in on a wagon that's got to go back to Barton. If we were to leave the city with it…'

Kate looked up at him. 'What do you have in mind?'

William's eyes twinkled mischievously. 'As long as your lad, Tom, can play along, I've a thought or two that might work...'

Together they conceived a fragile plan and at dawn, Kate slipped into the small bedchamber where they had put Jonathan for the night. Ellen sat beside him, dozing in her chair. She looked up as Kate entered and stood, easing her back.

'How is he?' Kate asked.

Ellen looked down at her patient. 'Well as can be expected.'

'He has to do better than that.' Kate said with determination. She leaned over the bed. 'Jonathan. Wake up.'

He opened his eyes, still hazy with the after-effect of the laudanum.

'Jesus wept,' he swore, as he tried to move.

'Listen to me.' Kate waited until his eyes had focused on her face. 'Do you think you can stand?'

He gave her a rueful smile. 'Mistress Ashley, I'll do whatever you tell me.'

'Good. Ellen, get him dressed and pack. We leave within the hour.'

'Leave?' Ellen looked surprised. 'It'll be a miracle if he gets on his own two feet. He'll nowt sit a horse.'

'We'll be using a wagon.'

'E'en so...' Ellen protested.

'We can't stay here, Ellen. It's too dangerous.' She smiled at her maid with more reassurance than she felt. 'It will be all right. We have a plan. Jon, listen to me.'

Kate explained the plan she and William had concocted to both Ellen and Jonathan.

Ellen sucked her breath in through her teeth and shook her head. 'I don't know...'

'It's the best we can do.

Ellen nodded. 'Aye well, tha's as well as maybe.'

Jonathan closed his eyes. 'We will make it work. If there were any other way that didn't involve you—'

'There is none.'

Ellen nodded. 'Come on lad let's get 'ee on thy feet if we're to leave within the hour.'

They gathered in the hallway. One glance at Jonathan's ashen, unshaven face and a wave of panic passed over Kate. She needed him to have his wits about him, and he would have to endure the pain until she could get him back to Barton — if he ever reached Barton. She pushed that thought to the back of her mind.

William clapped a hand on his nephew's shoulder. 'So, young Tom. You've heard the plan. Are you up to a spot o' play actin'?'

'I'm much better at pretending than Mother,' Tom pointed out. He looked up at Jonathan. 'Are you going to be all right?'

Jonathan managed a watery smile. 'Just fine,' he said. 'You'll see.'

'WHAT'S THIS?' William inquired of the guard at the city gates. 'I've not been stopped afore.'

The man put his fingers to the brim of his hat. 'We've orders to search every wagon leaving the city,' he said. 'There's a notorious delinquent on the loose.' The soldier lowered his voice. 'There's talk of witchcraft. Those that saw him says he just vanished into thin air.'

'Your name, sir?' The other guard enquired of William.

'William Rowe of Barton Hall.' He indicated Kate and Jonathan who sat hunched between them on the bench, his hat pulled down as low as possible. 'My sister, her husband and my nephew.' He jerked his head in the direction of the back of the cart where Tom sat among the piles of empty sacking munching on an apple. 'We're returning home from the wool sales.'

'I've orders to search the cart, sir,' the guard said.

'Search away,' Kate said assuming a tone of petulance in her voice. 'You'll find naught. We sold our wool and I swear my husband has drunk all the money away in celebrating.'

'*Here dwells a pretty maid whose name is Sis...*' A slurred rendition of the popular drinking song issued from underneath Jonathan's hat.

'*You may come in and kiss...*' The song tailed off as Kate elbowed him in the ribs, her lips set in a hard, tight line.

The guard grinned. 'I can smell the ale fumes from here, mistress,' he said. 'I'll warrant he'll have a sore head tomorrow.'

A sore head would be the least of Jonathan's problems, Kate thought, as her heart hammered beneath her bodice. She had never told a lie in her life.

The guards gave the back of the wagon a peremptory search.

'On your way then, Master Rowe,' the first guard said, giving the rump of the horse a firm slap. 'With this rain, it'll be a slow road home today I wager.'

'*Her whole, her whole, her whole estate is seventeen pence a year...*' Jonathan concluded drunkenly.

Behind them, the guards laughed.

The breath returned to Kate's lungs.

'Well done,' William said. 'Keep it up till we're out of sight and then we'll put the lad in the back.'

Jonathan groaned and leaned his head on Kate's shoulder.

'*Here dwells a pretty maid...*' he muttered.

'That song is quite disgusting,' Kate said.

'But it did the trick,' Jonathan muttered.

~

'KATE, WE'RE HOME.'

From where she sat in the back of the wagon, Kate raised her head and looked up at William's sodden back. The rain dripped off her hat into her eyes. Jonathan lay on the floor of the wagon, covered by sacking to protect him from the rain while she supported his head in her lap to try and minimise the jolting of the cart on his injured shoulder. Tom, with the carefree abandon of youth, slept curled up beside her. They were all soaked to the bone and exhausted by the strain of the long and trying day.

'I've never been so glad to see Barton's gates in my life,' William observed as he turned the wagon through the gates into the courtyard of Barton Manor.

Suzanne stood on the porch of the house, a shawl clutched around her shoulders.

'I'd not expected you home until the morrow,' she said.

'What are you doing here, lass?' William asked.

'I got Kate's message from Selby and came to see the house was in order before they returned. I thought they would be with you?'

'We're here, Suzanne,' Kate spoke up from the back of the wagon.

'What's going on?'

Suzanne pulled the shawl over her head and picked her way across the muddy yard to the wagon. She stood staring at the trio huddled beneath the wool sacks.

Kate shifted Jonathan's unconscious weight and stretched her stiff, cold limbs as Tom sat up, rubbing his eyes.

'What do you mean by this? Who is this man, Kate?' she demanded, indicating Jonathan. 'Thoroughly sotted by the smell of him. William, what were you thinking..?'

'Oh for the good Lord's sake, Suzanne,' Kate blasphemed. 'We doused him in ale as a ruse to get us past the gates.' She stopped herself from saying that part of the plan had been William's idea. 'He's not drunk. He has a pistol ball in the shoulder and he's lost a lot of blood. Today's soaking won't have helped.'

'Shot?' Suzanne stared in disbelief at her sister. 'Who? Why? And how do you come to have him with you?'

'Later, my dear.' William came around to the back of the wagon and took charge. 'Give me a hand here, Dickon. Take his legs. That's right.'

Dickon and Ellen had, by agreement left York well after the others, but they had caught up with the lumbering wagon a few miles out of York and travelled on together.

Not without some difficulty, the two men managed to carry the barely conscious Jonathan up the stairs to the guest bedchamber. They deposited the injured man on the bed, and William looked around at his wife and her sister.

'Well, Kate, now what?' he asked.

'You take Thomas and go home, William,' Suzanne replied, already unbuttoning her collar and cuffs. 'I'll stay and help with... who is this man, Kate?'

Kate turned a pale, strained face to her sister. 'Richard's cousin, Jonathan Thornton.'

Suzanne opened her mouth to say something but seeing her sister's face, a look of concern creased her brow. 'Kate, what is it?'

Whether it was exhaustion or strain or something else, Kate's hands shook and her heart felt as if it would leap straight out of her chest. It was happening all over again: The same room, the scent of blood... of death.

The memory of Richard's last horrific days overwhelmed her.

'I can't... Suzanne, I can't...' She began to back away.

Suzanne put a sisterly hand on Kate's arm. 'Go to your room, Kate. I'll send the maid to light the fire and bring you some supper. Ellen and I will do what must be done.'

Kate turned and as she fled she heard her sister say to her husband, 'You great fool, don't look like that. This is the room Richard died in, or have you forgotten?'

～

IT SEEMED a long time before Suzanne found Kate, hunched in front of the fire in her bed-chamber, her arms wrapped around her knees.

'You silly girl,' she chided, looking down at her sister and the tray still laden with the cold, congealing meal beside her. 'You've not changed out of your damp clothes, nor eaten...'

Kate looked up at her sister, flinching at the blood smear on her sister's cheek. Suzanne knelt beside her and took her in her arms as the tears that were the result of the strain of the last twenty-four hours finally came flooding out.

'Kate,' Suzanne stroked her hair as she had done when Kate had been a child, 'he's not Richard. His wound is bad but with Ellen's care and God willing, he'll live.'

Kate managed a small watery smile and grasped her sister's hand. 'Thank you,' she whispered.

'Now,' said Suzanne in her normal, brisk fashion, 'perhaps you can tell me what this is about, Kate? Who is this Jonathan Thornton.'

'Richard's cousin. He... he travelled with us some of the way from Worcestershire.' She stopped and took a deep breath, 'I... we...oh, Suzanne, that awful man shot him.'

'What awful man and why would he shoot Jonathan?'

'Jonathan is a fugitive; there is a price on his head.'

'I suppose that would be a good reason for someone to try and shoot him,' Suzanne observed in her practical fashion. 'What on earth were you thinking involving yourself in his business?' She narrowed her eyes and looked at her sister. 'Kate, you're surely not in love with this man?'

Kate looked away from her sister's appraising gaze. 'Of course not,' she said. 'It's just the shock...' To her mortification, the tears began again.

Suzanne waited patiently, holding her close, until the tears subsided into dry sobs and Kate sat up, frantically dabbing at her eyes with a sodden kerchief.

'Enough of this wallowing.' Suzanne stood up. 'I've sent Thomas home to the Hall with William and I'll stay and see to this dangerous fugitive for however long I am needed. You, my dear, are going to bed.'

Kate smiled faintly. 'I will, I promise, but first I must see him.'

At the door to the bedchamber, she hesitated. The memories of Richard's broken body and agonising death, which had driven her away before, were suddenly as sharp and clear as they had been seven years before.

This isn't Richard, she told herself. *It isn't happening again.*

She took a breath and opened the door.

Ellen sat by the fire, asleep, her mouth open, snoring gently. She'd sat with Jonathan most of the previous night and it had been as long a day for her as it had been for all of them. She was no longer a young woman and Kate realised, with a guilty pang, that Ellen must be exhausted.

She crossed to the bed and stood looking down at the man she had risked her life for that day. His right arm lay outside the bed covers. The other arm had been strapped uncompromisingly to his chest with fresh bandages, the shoulder heavy with padding and bandages, through which a bright star of fresh blood still managed to seep. She could not tell whether he was unconscious or asleep and only the slight rise and fall of his chest gave any indication that he still lived.

Kate picked up his right hand, noting the silver line of an old scar snaking its way down his forearm. The heavy gold signet ring he wore glinted in the candlelight and she turned it towards the light. Although well worn, she could still make out the leopard's head of the Thornton crest. She frowned, recognising it as the ring Sir Francis had worn.

His fingers tightened on hers and life flickered back into his pale face. The hazel eyes, foggy with opium and pain, sought her out.

'Kate,' he whispered.

She laid his hand back on the covers. 'It's late, Jonathan. I just came to say good night.' She forced herself to smile. 'Promise me you'll still be here in the morning?'

He grimaced and closed his eyes. 'I don't think I am going anywhere for a little while,' he said. Then with sudden urgency, he tried to raise himself on his right elbow. 'My letters?'

Kate turned to the table where his sword and baldric had been laid and picked up a pile of letters tied together with a ribbon. They were stained dark in the corners. Jonathan's blood. If the King ever got these letters he would know the price that had been paid for them.

'They will have to wait,' she said quietly as she opened the heavy oak chest that stood at the foot of the bed and placed the letters inside.

CHAPTER 10

*J*onathan raised his head from the book he had found in David Ashley's modest library to breathe in the scent of roses mingled with the cool breeze from the moor. He was seated on a well-cushioned stone bench with his back against a wall, warmed by the summer sun, his feet crossed at the ankles.

A few yards away Kate looked up from her gardening and pushed a stray lock of hair behind her ear.

'What are you reading?' She asked.

He looked at the little book. Reading with the use of only one hand had precluded any of the larger tomes.

'Donne,' he replied. 'Do you know his work?'

Kate nodded. 'That was one of David Ashley's favourite books.

'He had excellent taste.'

Jonathan set the book down and eased his shoulder. It would be weeks before he would be strong enough to resume his journey north. He thought of the letters that the King waited on. Nothing he could do about it. He could just as easily have died in that street in York and Prescott would have some interesting intelligence for his masters in London. That was the fate of war.

'They're particularly fine roses,' he said.

Kate sat back on her heels. 'Elizabeth's legacy,' she said. 'David lavished such care on them that I am afraid they will die in my hands.'

'Mother. I'm home.' The crash of a door heralded the arrival of Tom, accompanied by another boy.

Kate stood up, smoothing her skirts. Suzanne Rowe followed the boys out into the garden. The two women kissed, and Suzanne turned to face Jonathan, her hands on her hips.

'Should you be out of bed?' she demanded.

Jonathan looked up at her, shielding his eyes against the sun. 'Stay inside on a day like today?' he said.

'I brought you some broadsheets.' Suzanne laid the papers on the bench next to him.

'Who's this?' Jonathan looked at the other boy, who smiled shyly. The child had a pale, thin face and dark circles around his eyes.

Suzanne laid a maternal hand on the boy's shoulder. 'My son, Robert,' she said.

Robert bowed, coughing as he straightened. He whispered something in his cousin's ear.

'You ask him.' Tom responded, but Robert shuffled his feet and turned a bright shade of pink.

'What does he want to know?' Jonathan asked.

'He wants to know if it hurts being shot?' Tom said.

Jonathan's mouth twitched in wry amusement.

'Yes,' he said, 'it does.'

Robert whispered in Tom's ear again.

'He wants to know if you really knew Prince Rupert,' Tom interpreted again.

'I knew him well,' Jonathan replied.

Suzanne made a disapproving click of her tongue but, catching Jonathan's quick glance, she kept her peace.

'We have something to show you,' Tom said with a conspiratorial glance at his cousin, and both boys raced inside the house.

'They're quite different,' Jonathan said.

'Aye, as were you and your cousin, no doubt,' Suzanne responded.

'True, but Richard and I were not the boon companions those two are.'

'Robert is older by two months,' Kate said.

'Really?' Jonathan raised an eyebrow. 'I'd have never guessed.'

'Robert has always been…' — Suzanne cleared her throat — '… a little less robust than Thomas.'

Jonathan glanced at Kate. Her downcast mouth and lowered eyes gave him the answer he sought. Robert Rowe would not make old bones.

The boys returned with a squirming bundle held tightly in Tom's arms.

'What have you got there?' Kate asked.

Tom looked up at his aunt, who had the grace to look shamefaced.

'William's best bitch whelped recently and he promised Tom one of the pups,' Suzanne said. 'I should have mentioned it earlier, but,' she cast a significant glance at Jonathan, 'you have been a little preoccupied.'

Tom set the puppy down on the grass. It wagged its tail, the entire rear end going into spasm as it let out small, delighted baby yaps. Kate crouched down and held out her hand. The little animal bounded over to her, covering her fingers with doggy kisses. She looked up at the company and laughed.

'Well he knows the way to a woman's heart,' she said. 'What are you going to call him, Tom?'

'Rupert,' Tom said.

Jonathan gave a snort of laughter that he immediately regretted. The slightest movement jolted the barely knit bones in his shoulder.

'The Prince had a dog,' he said to distract himself. 'He called him Boy and he followed him into battle.' He refrained from adding that Boy had several other tricks taught to him by the Prince, such as peeing on the mention of the name of the King's bitter enemy 'Pym'.

Suzanne gave him a disdainful glance. 'You are not a good influence on this household, Jonathan Thornton.'

Jonathan returned her look with equanimity. 'Alas, Mistress Rowe, I fear I am never a good influence.'

Suzanne nodded at the broadsheets. 'I read there's a handsome reward for the capture of a notorious delinquent, recently escaped from York,' she said.

Jonathan raised an eyebrow. 'Indeed? Tempted?'

Suzanne sniffed. 'I have too much of an investment in seeing a certain notorious delinquent stays in good health,' she said. 'Robert, it's time to go.'

'Mama,' Robert protested.

'He can stay, Suzanne,' Kate said.

'Be home by supper,' Suzanne chided her son. 'Sir Jonathan.' She dropped Jonathan a curtsy with a mocking twinkle in her eye.

'Mistress Rowe.' He inclined his head.

KATE WALKED her sister to the front gate.

'Your patient is looking much improved,' Suzanne observed.

'Irritable and bored,' Kate said with a smile.

'A true convalescing male,' Suzanne replied. 'I swear when William broke his leg, I considered administration of something more powerful than laudanum.' Her eyes narrowed with the memory. 'Anyway, dearest, bring him to dine with us on Saturday, if he is well enough of course.'

'I have never met anyone more determined to be well,' Kate said, keeping unvoiced her belief that Jonathan would be away to his king in Scotland as soon as he could sit on a horse.

She kissed her sister and returned to the garden, where Jonathan had the boys enthralled in another of his fund of stories of Arthur and his knights. While the puppy gambolled around her, she returned to her roses, with half an ear on the tale of magic and enchantment.

When the story was done and the boys, accompanied by the excited puppy, had left to see Robert off to Barton Hall, Kate returned to Jonathan. He sat back against the wall, his long legs stretched out in front of him and his right hand resting on the little volume of Donne. His eyes, still circled with dark smudges, were closed.

'You're tired,' she observed.

He opened his eyes and smiled. 'Leave your labours, Mistress Ashley, and come and sit down for a little.'

She wiped her hands on her apron and sat beside him. 'What are you thinking?' she asked.

He turned his head to look at her. 'Why do women always ask that?' he asked. 'Since you are so interested, I was thinking about young Robert.'

'Ah.' Kate looked down at her hands. 'William calls him the "runt of the litter". I fear his health is deteriorating.'

She looked up and met Jonathan's gaze.

Kate looked away and picked up the volume of verse. 'Which is your favourite?' she asked.

'*True Plaine Heartes,*' he replied without hesitation.

She flicked through the well-thumbed pages and read:

> *My face in thine eye, thine in mine appeares,*
> *And true plaine heartes doe in the faces rest,*
> *Where can we finde two better hemispheares*
> *Without sharpe North, without declining West?*
> *What ever dyes, was not mixt equally;*
> *If our two loves be one, or, thou and I*
> *Love so alike, that none doe slacken, none can die...*

She trailed off. 'That's beautiful,' she said.

Jonathan looked out beyond the walls of the garden to the blue of the sky above the moors where a pair of hawks danced.

'I taught someone else to love Donne,' he said softly.

'Mary?' she asked, conscious of a harsh edge to her voice.

He looked back at her, his eyes hard and cold. 'How do you..?'

'Your fever,' she said.

His eyes took on a shadowed, haunted cast. 'Ahh...what did I say?'

Flustered, Kate stammered, 'Nothing...just called her name...I thought you must,' her voice caught in her throat, 'you must love her...'

'She's dead, Kate,' he said in a hard, flat voice. Without meeting her eyes, he rose to his feet. 'You're right, I'm tired. Please excuse me.'

She watched him walk toward the house and picked up the book he had abandoned.

If our two loves be one, or, thou and I

Love so alike, that none doe slacken, none can die...

Had Mary been, for Jonathan, that love so alike that even death could not part them?

~

Upstairs in the bedchamber, Jonathan paced the floor. By the bed, he stopped and leaned his head against the bedpost.

'You fool,' he said out aloud.

You fool, he said to himself and closed his eyes.

He had seen the hurt in Kate's eyes but knew there was nothing he could do to prevent it. Mary's reproachful ghost haunted his nightmares and would always be there, standing between him and any hope of another life, another love. How could he have begun to even think there could be another life or another love?

This should never have happened. He should never have let Kate Ashley come so close.

No, that was wrong.

He should never have let himself come so close. The scent of roses and the smell of rosemary in her hair in the garden at Seven Ways had quickened his blood in a way he had not felt for a long time — had never thought to feel again.

He sat on the edge of the bed and sighed. He had to get away from Barton, get away from her before they both did something they would regret.

A knock at the door made him start.

'What?' he snapped.

'It's me, Jonathan.' Tom peered around the door. 'I...I wondered if you would like to play chess? But if you're tired...'

The boy carried a wooden board under his arm and a box in his hand.

'Sorry, Tom, I didn't mean to sound so cross,' Jonathan said.

'If your shoulder is sore, we can play again another day..'

'It's fine,' he lied. 'Set the pieces out and we'll play.'

Tom chattered as he set up the board. 'This was Grandfather's board. He was teaching me to play when... when he died. Mother said she would play but she is always too busy.'

'What about Robert?'

'He plays sometimes, but he's not very good and it's not much fun to keep beating him all the time. Sam and Phillip play with me sometimes too, but they're away at school.'

'Sam and Phillip?'

'Robert's older brothers. There's Joseph too, but he'd rather go hunting.'

'How many cousins do you have?'

Tom stopped to consider for a moment. 'Six, counting the baby,' he said.

That explained Suzanne Rowe's matronly figure and bossy ways, Jonathan thought to himself.

'Where's Rupert?'

Tom pulled a face. 'Mother said he had to stay in the stable until he is older,' he said. He looked up at Jonathan and his eyes sparkled. 'But I'll smuggle him into the house when she's not looking.'

Jonathan suppressed a smile. The more he had to do with the boy, the more he saw himself as a lad.

They played in silence for several moves. Jonathan moved Tom's king into check.

Tom frowned as he contemplated his next move.

'Jonathan...' Tom began.

'Tom?'

'Are you married?' the boy asked.

'No,' Jonathan said.

Tom looked up. 'Ever?'

'Not ever.'

'So you don't have any children?'

'No,' Jonathan replied. 'You're asking a lot of questions, Tom, you need to concentrate.'

'I was just wondering,' Tom said in a tone that was far too casual.

'Why?'

Two innocent hazel eyes met his own. 'No reason,' he said.

CHAPTER 11

Suzanne and her family waited for their guests in the great hall of the pleasant and prosperous manor house. A handsomely carved mantle dominated the room, and the table had been set with the best linen. The Rowes, Jonathan concluded, had done well with the wool trade and their support of the Parliamentary cause.

He took Suzanne's hand and kissed it with all the grace of the most accomplished court gallant.

'Mistress Rowe,' he said. 'You look charming. The colour of that gown is perfection.'

A blush spread across Suzanne's cheekbones and she smiled as she said, 'Your charm is wasted on me, Sir Jonathan, but you're welcome to Barton Hall. Indeed it's a pleasure to see you so much recovered.'

'A tribute to your patient care,' he replied.

'I'm not sure if you remember my husband, William.' Suzanne turned to the portly, good-natured man by her side.

'Sir Jonathan, it's a pleasure to have you with us. Looking a damn sight better than when last we met.' William declared, clapping Jonathan heartily on the left shoulder.

Jonathan subsided onto the nearest chair, biting his tongue against the profanity that sprang to his lips. It took a few minutes to recover while William, apologising profusely, produced a glass of the best brandy Jonathan had tasted for a long time.

It was hard not to like the bluff, cheerful Yorkshireman, and once Jonathan's good humour had recovered, they introduced the children. The eldest son, Phillip, a sturdy young man of about twenty, was a carbon copy of his father. Sam and Joseph, it was explained, were absent at school. Then there were the girls, Janet and the baby, Elizabeth.

Tom had already told him that Robert had been ill and the boy sat huddled by the fireplace, his thin face pale and drawn, coughing spasmodically. Tom sat beside him, playing with the ears of one of the several large dogs sprawled in front of the hearth.

Jonathan crouched down beside the boy's chair. 'So, Robert. What's this? I thought I'd not seen you in the past week. Are you better?'

Robert smiled, a wan little smile. 'I'm much better. Mama said I should keep to my bed but I wanted to see you tonight.' He cast a reproachful glance at his mother.

'What's this?' Jonathan reached behind the boy's ear and produced a shiny groat. He dropped it into the hand of the astonished boy. The other children laughed and clapped.

'Do another one,' Janet demanded.

Jonathan smiled and produced another groat. He held it in the palm of his hand for all the children to see then closed his fingers over it.

'Now.' He addressed Janet. 'You must tap my hand three times and say the magic words.'

'What magic words?'

Jonathan raised his eyebrows. 'You don't know any magic words?' Janet shook her head, her eyes round with concern. 'Well, try saying "*Tush, hush by the fairy's ear, make my coin disappear*".'

Solemnly Janet complied with the instructions. When she had completed the task, Jonathan uncurled his fingers. A collective sigh went up from the children as his palm was revealed to be empty.

'Where'd it go?' Janet wailed.

'Why here, pretty maid.' Jonathan put his hand up to her head and produced the coin from behind her ear.

Suzanne took his arm as they sat down for the meal. 'You have a very fine way with children.' She gave him a direct look that was so like Kate's, except Suzanne's eyes were brown. 'Do you, by chance, have any of your own?'

'I have neither wife nor child,' Jonathan replied with a smile that he knew was not echoed in his eyes. 'My life has not lent itself to such commitments of home and hearth.'

'Well that, sir, is your loss,' William said. 'Home and hearth, wife and bairns. Nothing like it, in my opinion. Come, Sir Jonathan, take a seat. We have one of the finest cooks in the county and I do believe there is beef on the menu. Suzanne thinks you need feeding up and I have to agree with her. Too thin, man, too thin.' William slapped his well-fed stomach that strained against the fastenings of his jacket.

The rowdy, joyful meal was quite unlike the painfully formal occasions Jonathan remembered enduring as a boy. The walk from the manor had given him an appetite and the table groaned with food. For a penniless exile living a hand-to-mouth existence during the best of times, it was probably more food than Jonathan had seen in the last year. Little wonder William considered him thin.

The afternoon wore on and darkness closed in. It had been agreed that the visitors would spend the night, a decision for which Jonathan was profoundly grateful. With the combined effects of the brandy and William's excellent wine, he seriously doubted if he could have staggered beyond the front door.

The children were harried off to bed and Suzanne and Kate left the men to their pipes in front of the fireplace. William propped his feet on one of the dogs, who shifted slightly but did not complain.

'Have some more brandy, lad.' He refilled Jonathan's glass. 'Eh, you've got a bit of colour, now. That's grand to see. Have you a mind to share a pipe of tobacco?'

Tobacco being a luxury Jonathan rarely indulged in, he lit the pipe William loaned him and drew in, deeply and thankfully, savouring the indulgence. William did likewise and they sat in companionable, masculine silence for a while before William took the pipe from his mouth.

'Suzanne and I, we worry about young Kate.'

'In what way?'

'Too set in her ways. A lass like that should not spend her life fretting away over a husband seven years in his grave. Don't you agree, lad?'

Jonathan spluttered an incoherent response.

'Young Richard was a good lad, but he was too interested in books. Could never get him out with the hounds. Do you hunt, lad?'

'I used to, years ago, before the war of course,' Jonathan said, grateful that the conversation had turned away from the uncomfortable subject of Kate Ashley.

'Good hunting down your way?' William inquired.

Jonathan shook his head. 'Not anymore. The forests have been cleared for wood and the wildlife decimated.'

'Aye, much the same round here,' William agreed with a tone of regret. 'I suppose you've naught much time for my sort?'

'What sort is that?' inquired Jonathan, thinking his words sounded a little slurred.

'Those of us who had naught to do with fighting,' said William.

'You had your reasons, I suppose,' Jonathan mused, holding out his glass gratefully as William slopped more brandy into it.

'Aye, and I was right glad I'd no sons old enough to fight. Old David Ashley, he tried to get me to come along with him but I have a gammy leg, from a hunting accident ye know.' He took another sip of his brandy. 'I'll not hide it from you, lad. Parliament had my money when they asked.' He looked across at Jonathan. 'I thought I should tell you, just so's you know how I stand.'

Jonathan shook his head. 'I like to think I'm a better judge of a man than that, Rowe.'

Whatever political difference stood between them, Jonathan owed this man his life. Rowe could have simply turned him over to Prescott but he had chosen to risk his own life in getting him away from York.

William nodded and took a deep drag on his pipe. He scrutinised Jonathan with brandy-bleared eyes. 'He was a good lad, Richard. You've quite a bit of the look of your cousin about you, for all he was as fair as ye're dark.'

Jonathan sighed. No one in his entire life had ever described him as a 'good lad'.

Like his brother, Ned, he doubted he could never live up to the ghost of this paragon. Dead heroes would forever haunt him.

William stretched his legs out, disturbing the dogs, one of which gave an indignant woof before settling into a new position. 'Now that's a fine grey mare you have. My man brought her in from York for ye. She's in my stable.'

'Thank you, I have been intending to ask what became of her.

She's the only thing of value I own.' He set his pipe down. 'I want you to know I'm grateful for everything you've done for me. I don't know how to repay you.'

William took the pipe from his mouth. 'It was done for Kate,' he said. 'She seems to have become a might attached to ye and I'd have hated for her to mourn another man.'

'What do you mean?' Jonathan suddenly felt cold and sober.

'I mean, lad, that the heart's not always summat that can be governed by the head. She— and ye— will deny to my face that there's aught between you, but I'm no fool, lad. I saw her face that night you collapsed in my kitchen. All I'm saying is don't ye dare break her heart or ye'll have me to answer for.'

Jonathan tapped the pipe on the heel of his shoe. 'I will be gone soon,' he said. 'She'll forget me.'

'Aye, and my name's Oliver Cromwell,' William scoffed. 'I'll say no more on't subject. Here, lad, your glass is empty…'

They talked amiably about hunting, hounds and horses, and the brandy bottle slowly emptied as the night drifted by. When Jonathan came to stand the room tipped and swayed. He hadn't been this drunk in years. He staggered and caught the back of the chair. William, a little more steady on his feet, caught him.

'Time we were abed,' he grumbled. 'There'll be hell to pay if I fall asleep during Parson's sermon tomorrow.'

'Sermons,' sympathised Jonathan, throwing his good arm companionably across William's shoulders. 'Do you suppose God has to listen to sermons? I tell you, Rowe, the bloody Scots are good for an interminable sermon. They think they have the monopoly on God.'

'Aye, well, perhaps they do,' William remarked as they wove across the room in the direction of the door.

'I think,' Jonathan philosophised drunkenly, 'that God has a better sense of humour than the Scots give him credit for.'

Finding the door, they staggered and lurched up the stairs. William deposited his guest on his bed and mumbled goodnight. Jonathan could hear him pitching down the corridor singing brokenly. For some time he lay flat on his back, looking up at the bed hangings that pitched and swayed like a boat until he decided he really should get undressed.

Sober and single-handed, the fastenings on David Ashley's old-fashioned jacket were difficult; drunk, they were impossible. He swore and decided he needed someone to help him.

He tried the door catch of the room opposite and stumbled into the chamber, tripping on a carpet. He cursed and tried to make out the bed in the dim light. He heard the rattle of bed hangings, and to his relief, Kate's voice in the dark.

'Jonathan. What are you doing?'

He put his finger on his lips. 'Shh. You'll wake the whole house.'

He staggered towards her and sat down with a bump on the edge of her bed. 'It's all right, Kate. I am not after your virtue. I can't get out of this damned jacket.'

She gave a splutter of laughter.

'What's so funny?' he demanded.

'You are,' she replied.

'I'm not funny,' he said indignantly. 'Normally I am a very serious drunk.'

'I am glad it will not be your head on my shoulders in the morning. Come here.'

He edged over towards her. She knelt up on the bed and undid the fastenings. She helped him out of the jacket and unlaced his shirt.

'Thank you,' he said. 'You did that very well. Christ, my shoulder hurts.'

'Don't blaspheme,' Kate said primly. 'You don't get any

sympathy from me. To smell you, I suspect you have drunk enough brandy to deaden the pain for a week.'

'Don't be such a Puritan,' he said. 'By the way, I like your brother-in-law. He has excellent brandy.'

He looked across at her, just making out her features in the dim light. Suddenly sober, he reached out to touch her face. She did not draw back.

'You're very beautiful,' he said. 'Has anyone ever told you that?'

'Many times,' Kate replied. 'I am not without suitors, you know.'

'Really? Is there someone special?'

He held his breath in the pause before she replied.

'No,' she said. 'Now go to bed.'

'Yes, bed,' he said, looking doubtfully towards the door. 'I don't think I can make it.'

'You are not staying here. My reputation is probably in tatters as it is.'

Kate slipped off the bed and hauled him to his feet. Putting his good arm across her shoulders, they staggered back to his bed-chamber. She pulled off his boots and rolled him still half dressed under the covers. Jonathan heard the door close behind her and lay for a moment while the world spun dizzily around him.

'Kate. Kate Ashley, I love you,' he whispered to the dark.

Words he could never say to her face.

KATE LOOKED up from her book as Jonathan collapsed into a chair by the window.

'You and my husband make a fine pair,' Suzanne remarked through tight lips. 'You should both be ashamed of yourselves,' she continued. 'On the Lord's day as well.'

William managed a weak grimace of indignation. 'Yon lad didn't have to endure Parson's sermon this morning.'

'Did I miss much?' asked Jonathan with a sideways glance at his fellow sufferer.

A grunt was all the reply he got. William sat in a large chair, his hands folded across his stomach and his eyes firmly closed.

Jonathan closed his eyes as well and let the warmth of the sun wash over him.

Kate looked at her sister and her slumbering spouse and set down her book. 'Suzanne, I think I should take Jonathan for a walk. He seems in need of fresh air,' she said.

Jonathan opened his eyes and sighed. 'Kate, have some pity on a man barely out of his sick bed.'

Kate snorted and held out her hand. 'If you were well enough to indulge in a drinking session with William, you are well enough for a stroll in the garden, Jonathan Thornton. It is a beautiful day and the Barton garden is a particularly fine one.'

'I think your sister disapproves of me,' Jonathan said once they were clear of the house.

Kate smiled. 'Small wonder. You and William drank yourself into quite a state last night. But don't take it to heart. William has a very comfortable approach to religion which does not always accord with the Puritan sensibilities in poor Suzanne. She loves him too much to stay angry.'

'And how are your Puritan sensibilities? Mortally offended by my improper behaviour last night?' he asked with a grimace.

Kate glanced up at him, wondering if he remembered anything of their conversation. She had lain awake for a long time, remembering the touch of his hand on her face and his words. She had lied. No one, since Richard, had told her she was beautiful. Her suitors were far more interested in her land and her inheritance than in her.

She sniffed. 'I'm surprised you can remember last night.' She gave him an impish look. 'How is your shoulder this morning?'

Jonathan shrugged his good shoulder. 'Tolerable. William says he has Amber in his stables. Can we walk around to check on her?'

Kate nodded and they strolled across an elegant expanse of lawn toward a high, stone wall.

'It's a lovely view,' Jonathan observed, pausing to look down the slope of the garden to the rolling lands beyond the wall. 'You must have known a very happy childhood here, Kate.'

'My mother died when I was seven and my father when I was nine, Jonathan. Suzanne was just eighteen and a new bride when I came to live here. William is a dear man, and he was as good as a father to me, but I don't think one ever really recovers from the early death of one's parents. What about you? You never talk about your parents or your brother,' she observed.

Jonathan stopped to pick up a stick. He flicked at the bracken with it as he said, 'What is there to say? My parents were blessed with the perfect son in Ned. He was charming, intelligent, handsome, loyal and courteous. They adored him.'

'And you?'

'I tried hard but I was everything Ned was not. I seemed to be continually in trouble and I was well beaten for it.' He paused, adding with a trace of bitterness in his voice, 'Until I got taller than Father, then we just used to quarrel.'

'Your grandfather did not seem to think so badly of you,' Kate observed.

He smiled. 'No, I suspect Grandfather saw himself in me and, as he was not my father, he could afford to be indulgent. Indeed if it had not been for my grandparents I think my childhood would have been considerably more miserable.'

'It is never easy being a parent,' Kate commented.

Jonathan smiled bitterly. 'I don't blame them. I know I was not an easy son. My parents thought I should go into the church of all things.' He laughed and stopped in the path, holding out his good arm as if inviting Kate to look at him. 'Can you seriously see me as a bishop?'

Kate smiled and shook her head, Jonathan continued. 'After they had abandoned their notions about the church as an appropriate calling for their second son, they sent me off to my uncle in London, to learn to be a lawyer.'

'I can no more see you as a lawyer,' Kate put in.

'Well, in truth, I did not learn much law.' Jonathan laughed. 'I spent all my spare time training with the London militia. It is the ultimate irony that they should so skilfully defend London in the name of Parliament. I must have done a good job. When the war came, it was heaven-sent for the likes of I. Father raised a regiment and assumed command of it with good old Ned as his second-in-command. I pointed out, with a lamentable lack of tact, that I was the only one in the family who knew anything about the martial arts. I had a terrible quarrel with my father and in the end, I refused to have anything to do with him and went off to join Prince Rupert and the cavalry.'

He frowned and leaned against a tree, grimacing as his hand went to his bad shoulder. Kate started forward but he held up his hand, keeping her at a distance. 'It's fine.'

'And Ned died at Edgehill?' she asked

'A musket ball straight between the eyes.' Jonathan flinched at the memory. 'He would never have known what hit him. Father was devastated, of course, and I don't think my mother ever really recovered.' He paused. 'I think if it had been me, their grief would not have been quite so overwhelming.'

Kate saw the old hurt in the set line of his jaw.

'Jon, how can you say that about your parents?' she asked. 'As a parent, I am sure that could not have been how they felt.'

'It's the truth,' he replied. 'The family would have seen it as my well-earned fate. After Ned's death, Father did try to make peace with me but it was too late. The last time I saw him was just before Naseby, and as usual, we quarrelled. He wanted me to ride by his side under the Thornton colours, and I refused.' He paused, squinting into the distance. 'I often think that if I had gone with him, maybe I could have saved him.'

Kate closed the gap between them and this time he took her hand, twining his fingers in hers.

'And maybe,' she said, willing him to look at her, 'you would both have died.'

'Maybe.' He looked down at her and his fingers tightened on hers. 'Perhaps I should have died that day.'

Kate disengaged her hand and stepped back. 'Why would you think something like that?'

'Because of what happened later...after Naseby.'

He seemed to look at a point beyond her shoulder, to the events of the past, and for a fleeting moment, Kate sensed she had come close to the key to this man — the woman, Mary, and the enmity with Stephen Prescott — did these lie in the events that had occurred after Naseby?

'What happened...after Naseby?' she asked softly.

He looked down at her, his eyes returning to the present, and shook his head. 'It's all in the past, Kate.'

She resisted the urge to hit him, to protest that it was not in the past but a very real part of his present, provoke a reaction in him, but he had shut the door again. The moment had passed. He pushed himself away from the tree and strode towards the stables with Kate hurrying to catch up with him.

CHAPTER 12

*J*onathan leaned against the door to Kate's bedchamber, slowly pulling off his gloves. Kate knelt on the hearth, where she had been drying her hair in front of the fire, humming to herself. She looked for all the world like a wild, untamed thing and he thought he had never seen anything so beautiful. With difficulty, he fought back the rising desire to take her in his arms and press his lips to hers.

He swallowed and straightened, holding out the papers he fished from inside his jacket.

'Your sister sent you those recipes you wanted.'

She started to her feet, throwing back the mane of hair. 'I didn't hear you at the door.'

He apologised and she took the papers he held out without looking at them, her eyes studying his face. He ran the fingers of his right hand through his windswept hair as he struggled to find the words that had to be said.

'Kate, I have something to tell you...' he began

'You're going to tell me you're leaving,' she cut across him.

He swallowed, the pretty speech he had been rehearsing forgotten.

'How did you know?'

'It's in your eyes. I've known for days that I could no longer hold you here.'

Over the past weeks, he had pushed himself to the limit of his endurance as he had ruthlessly forced his arm back into use. His tenacity had paid off and although he would probably never again have the full use of it, and it still hurt like the devil, he considered himself functional. It was a tribute to the long-suffering and sharp-tongued Ellen that the damage was nowhere near as bad as it could have been.

However, if he was honest with himself, it still needed time — but time was something Jonathan did not have.

'Is there nothing I can say to keep you here?' she asked.

He shook his head. 'I must go, Kate. You know that.'

'Even though you know it to be a lost cause?'

'My obligation is to the King. That is never a lost cause,' he replied, forcing a conviction he did not feel into his voice. 'I'll leave in the morning.'

She bit her lip, an unconscious gesture he had observed in the past weeks when something worried her. He found the gesture particularly endearing.

'Will you tell Tom?' she asked.

He nodded and turned away, closing the door behind him. He could not bear the pain in her eyes but he knew there was nothing he could say to make amends. He could not dally any longer and he dreaded the long, bleak ride to Scotland hampered by a bad shoulder.

He quickened his step, reminding himself that whatever his feelings for this woman, he owed a duty to the young King biding his time in Scotland and he was too long overdue.

He found Tom in the parlour wrestling with Latin conjugations set by his tutor. Jonathan pulled up a chair and sat down opposite him.

'I don't see why I have to learn Latin. No one ever speaks it anymore,' Tom grumbled.

'But you will be able to read all the great classics,' Jonathan pointed out.

'Why would I want to do that?' Tom inquired. 'When I am grown up I want to go to the New World and be an explorer. Latin won't be much good then.' He cocked his head. 'What languages do you speak, Jonathan?'

Jonathan dismissed the picture of Thomas Ashley, explorer, encountering a tribe of Latin-speaking natives that had sprung to his mind.

'By necessity, I speak French, Dutch, a little Spanish and a little German.'

Tom looked impressed. 'Now they are useful languages. Can you teach me?'

Jonathan looked down at the well-polished table and, steeling his resolve, he looked up at the boy again. 'Perhaps one day, but not now. I'm leaving tomorrow, Tom, if the weather stays fine.'

Tom's face fell. 'I thought you were going to stay...I thought you were going to marry Mother.'

'What made you think that?' Jonathan asked, genuinely surprised.

Tom shrugged. 'Janet said that you and Mother were in love...'

'And what does a twelve-year-old girl know about love?'

'She said she heard Aunt Suzanne talking to Uncle William.' Tom sighed and looked down at his work. He had not been watching his pen and it had left a large blot on the page.

Jonathan tapped the table with the fingers of his right hand.

'Tom,' he said quietly, 'there is nothing I would like more in this world than to stay, but I'm a soldier. I have sworn loyalty to my King. I have to go.'

A curtain of hair obscured the boy's face and to Jonathan's distress, a large tear dissipated the blot of ink.

'Don't get killed,' Tom said softly, his voice choked. 'Mother thinks I'm too young to remember but I do. I saw him, all covered with blood, and Mother was crying and crying.'

'Your father?' Jonathan asked, his chest tightening at the thought of what this child had witnessed.

The boy nodded and looked up at him with brimming eyes. 'I thought you were going to die too but you didn't and I thought that meant you would stay.'

The agony in the boy's voice pierced Jonathan's heart. A man of less honour would stay here in this comfortable home with the woman whom he had come to love and this boy he cared for as deeply as he would his own son. The knowledge that the King's cause was doomed even before it began just made the decision harder. He may not even survive the months to come, his very life wasted in a lost cause.

But, as he had told Kate, it was not the King's cause that held his loyalty but the King himself, and Jonathan had given him his word.

KATE CLOSED the door to Jonathan's bedchamber behind her and stood with her back to it, trembling from cold and nerves. The only light in the room came from a single flickering candle and the dying fire. Next to a half-empty bottle of wine, Jonathan's sword lay on the table, polished and sharpened and ready to do battle. The man himself leaned against the chimney mantel, his coat unbuttoned. The glow from the fire cast his face into deep shadows as he looked up at her, his gaze raking her with the intensity of a first meeting.

The silence stretched between them.

'Jonathan?' Her voice shook and she bit her lip.

'Kate, you're shivering. Come by the fire.'

Frightened by her audacity and unsure of what she should do or say, she moved towards the fire.

'I came to see if you had all you need for the journey,' she lied, trying to keep her voice light and conversational.

'I have all I need, thank you,' he replied, and a smile twitched at the corners of his lips.

Did he know why she had really come?

He placed his hands on her shoulders, turning her to face him. The hunger in his eyes reflected the yearning in her own. Yes, he knew why she had come.

His long, strong fingers ran across her shoulders and lingered at the soft skin of her throat. Involuntarily she quivered as sensations, long forgotten, pulsed through her body.

'I've been waiting for you,' he said. 'It had to be on your terms, not mine, Mistress Ashley.'

Her heart beat a rapid tattoo as she struggled to control her breathing. 'I've been a faithful wife and a virtuous widow for a long time, Jon.' She looked up at him, her eyes holding his. 'You will be gone tomorrow. I know I may never see you again and I do not want to spend the rest of my life wondering what might have been.'

Whatever the consequences, she thought.

He bent his head and his forehead rested against hers. She closed her eyes, breathing in the scent of him, revelling in the touch of his skin against hers.

'Kate,' he whispered, 'I want you to be sure of one thing and that is my feelings for you. Would that our lives were different —'

'Wishing doesn't change anything, Jon. We only have now, here... tonight.'

'If this is what you want?' He straightened, searching her face. She nodded. 'It is.'

He ran his hands along her shoulders and up her neck, twisting his fingers in the soft hair, pulling at the pins that held it in place. It tumbled down about her shoulders and she heard the ping of the hairpins hitting the hearth.

He tilted her face up towards him, and she closed her eyes and parted her lips, surrendering herself to the moment.

They kissed hungrily and passionately, the pent-up emotions of the past month, if not the lonely years, surging through them. His fingers traced the line of her throat and the tilt of her nose as if he were in some way imprinting the memory of her.

He kissed her hair. 'Rosemary,' he whispered. 'The scent of rosemary will always make me think of you. That first night in the garden at Seven Ways...' He groaned and pressed her to him.

Kate melted against him, willing her body to become one with his. She hardly noticed as his hand slid down her shoulder again, searching unsuccessfully for the lacings of her bodice.

'Damn,' he muttered, releasing her. 'I'm out of practice.'

Kate laughed and obliged him by unlacing the bodice of her gown. He drew her towards him and kissed her again. In a moment of panic, she stiffened and drew back.

'I...' she started to speak but he silenced her, drawing her closer and kissing away her fears. Entwined, they stumbled over towards the bed, leaving a trail of clothing in their wake.

Kate lay back on the bed, and he leaned over her, stroking her cheek as he studied her face in the soft light.

A smile lifted the corners of his mouth. 'Relax,' he said, 'you look like a virgin on her wedding night, not a widow with a nine-year-old son.'

Kate felt a rush of heat rise to her cheeks.

'I...I'm not that experienced,' she said, hearing the fear in her voice. 'Richard and I were both so young and...' She took a shaky breath. 'We were only married months before the war came. Then I was pregnant...'

'Trust me, Kate.' His soft voice became a low purr and he bent his head, kissing her mouth as his hand moved slowly down her body. Kate shivered under his gentle touch.

'You're quite lovely, my dearest Kate,' he whispered.

Made bold by his loving patience, she reached out and ran her hands through the dark hair on his chest, her fingers lightly tracing the ugly, barely healed scar which disfigured his shoulder before moving downward, wanting to remember every part of him. Slowly, as if they had all the time in the world and not just one night, they explored each other with fingers and lips, until long-suppressed passion and desire overcame them.

A lifetime ago she had come eagerly to her marriage bed, a virgin wedded to a virgin. That happy but inept coupling bore no comparison to the skill that now allowed her to soar to unimagined heights. Kate wondered firstly how many other women Jonathan had known and secondly if she was being somehow unfaithful to Richard's memory. Both thoughts flickered momentarily and were extinguished as she allowed herself to be led to a world she did not know existed.

CHAPTER 13

PERTH, SCOTLAND SEPTEMBER, 1650

The cold, grey and cheerless town of Perth resembled every other Scottish town Jonathan had passed through. There had been moments in the past two weeks when he had despaired of reaching this far north. Several close encounters with the soldiers of Cromwell's army had forced him to sidetrack. Inevitably he had lost his way and found himself in the sullen, unfriendly little hamlets of the Scottish low country with no money and no friends and barely able to make himself understood.

He had found the King's Lifeguard at Kinross but Giles was not among them, and after enquiries he discovered the King himself was now in Perth. Jonathan, with his letters to deliver, had pushed northwards. The weather had closed in on him the further north he had gone, and he could feel the heavy hand of the fever recurring. If he did not find shelter and rest soon, he had no doubt that he would be in for a relapse.

Amber hung her head, her own weariness reflecting his. All that drove him on was the thought of a dry bed and some food. At the cheerless, grey stone inn where he had been told Giles Longley lodged, he saw Amber stabled, fed and groomed before making terse enquiries of the tapster as to which chamber his friend occupied.

He opened the door the tapster indicated. Two men sat at a rickety table playing cards; Giles Longley and another English officer of Jonathan's acquaintance, Kit Lovell. A half-dressed drab, no doubt picked out of the gutters of Perth, leaned on Lovell's shoulder, apparently engaged in nibbling his ear. Another girl sprawled on Giles' lap, twirling a lock of his hair in her fingers.

Giles had his back to the door so it was Kit who looked up, his eyes widening.

'Jesus Christ!' he swore.

Jonathan forced a wry smile. 'Not quite.'

Hearing Jonathan's voice, Giles leaped to his feet, letting the woman fall in an ungainly heap on the floor. He whirled on his heel, scattering cards in his haste.

'We'd given you up for dead,' Giles said.

'Believe me, Giles, there have been times in the past few months when I have as well,' Jonathan observed, heaving himself away from the doorjamb.

Lovell rose more slowly to his feet. 'You look bloody awful,' he observed.

Jonathan cast a glance at the two women. 'Get rid of them,' he said.

Giles tossed the woman on the floor a coin and indicated for her to leave, which she did, muttering unintelligible Scottish curses in the direction of Jonathan as she pushed past him. Lovell put his arm across the shoulder of the girl who had been paying him attention.

'I'll leave you,' he said. 'Maggie and I have some unfinished business. I'll hear your news tomorrow, Thornton.'

The ill-fitting door slammed shut behind Lovell and his doxy. Fumbling at the cord on his cloak, Jonathan stumbled towards the fire, where he collapsed into a chair.

His forehead puckered with concern, Giles knelt down and hauled Jonathan's mired riding boots off.

'Lovell's right, you look terrible,' he said.

'Nothing a few days rest won't fix,' Jonathan said, his voice muzzy with exhaustion. 'Cromwell must have most of his army between here and Yorkshire.'

He stared into the fire, feeling its warmth steal into his chilled bones, and gratefully accepted the cup of wine Giles had poured for him.

'Sorry to disturb your sport,' Jonathan said in a voice heavy with sarcasm.

Giles wiped the traces of the whore's paint from his face and straightened his crooked collar. 'There's precious little else to do here. May as well have some fun when I can.'

'God's death, Giles, do you not spare a thought for your wife?' Jonathan had little patience with Giles' philandering ways and routine unfaithfulness to Nell.

Giles looked offended. 'Of course I do. I think of her continually but thinking of her is hardly solace to the urgency of the moment and anyway,' he added, 'what right do you have to start preaching at me about such matters? You're hardly a saint.'

Jonathan looked at his friend. 'I do not have a wife and what's more your wife is my sister,' he reminded him. He ran a hand through his hair. 'I'm sorry. I'm bone tired and my patience is short.'

Giles shrugged as if to indicate no offence had been taken and, pouring himself a cup of wine, he sat down opposite his friend.

'On the subject of my wife, did you see Nell?'

Jonathan nodded and fumbled in his jacket for the bundle of letters. Those for the King had waited this long; a few more hours would not hurt. The letter from Nell to her husband could not wait.

Giles took it and held it up between thumb and forefinger, his eyes widening. He glanced at Jonathan.

'Blood?'

'Mine,' Jonathan said. 'I was recognised in York. Our old friend Prescott.'

Giles lifted an eyebrow at the name. 'Ahh,' he said slowly.

'He put a ball through my shoulder,' Jonathan continued, rubbing his aching shoulder. 'I'm afraid all my correspondence is similarly stained.'

'How —'

A knock at the door interrupted Giles. The surly innkeeper entered with the tray Giles had been expecting. Giles paid him and served up some of the gelatinous stew that was the best on offer. It was as good a meal as Jonathan could have hoped for, and he ate gratefully.

Revived by the warmth and the food, Jonathan looked up at his friend as he pushed the empty platter to one side.

'So, what's happening here?'

'Precious little,' replied Giles, pulling a face. 'David Leslie is playing catch-as-can with Cromwell and we're here, twiddling our thumbs and being forced to listen to endless sermons from these bloody Covenanters. Sweet Jesu, Jonathan, even at dinners they carry on as if they were in the pulpit. The food is appalling when hot and inedible cold.' He used his knife to push aside a gristly piece of unidentified meat on his platter. 'The King will want to see you. His spirits are very low.'

'I doubt that anything I can say to him will improve them,' Jonathan remarked bleakly.

He sat drowsing in the chair by the fire as Giles read through the pages that Nell had written to him.

Giles laid down Nell's letter and prodded Jonathan with the toe of his boot. 'Who is this Kate Ashley that Nell writes so affectionately of?'

'My cousin Richard Ashley's widow,' Jonathan replied, schooling his face to reveal nothing. 'You may recall she has a son? Grandfather has named him his heir.'

'Has he indeed. So Seven Ways stays in the family? Clever Sir Francis.' Giles chuckled. 'And you, my friend? I take it you've not been lying untended in the streets of York for the last two months. What fair creature took you in to bind your wounds and stroke your fevered brow?'

Jonathan scowled. He was in no mood for Giles' teasing and his few weeks with Kate were still too precious to share with the world at large.

'Another time, Giles.'

Giles' face sobered. 'You're dead on your feet, Thornton. Take the bed. We'll talk more in the morning.'

Jonathan nodded and without bothering to undress, he was asleep almost before his head hit the pillow.

CHARLES STUART, erstwhile King of England and newly crowned King of Scotland, stood by a window, staring out at the interminable drizzle of the bleak Scottish autumn. He did not even bother to look around as Giles and Jonathan entered the room.

Lord Wilmot, the King's friend and adviser, stood by the table with a couple of others Jonathan recognised, poring over a map. In a chair by the fireplace, George Villiers, Duke of Buckingham, played Patience with a stained and battered pack of cards, his handsome face petulant with boredom.

He looked up and, seeing Jonathan, a malicious smile flickered across his lips. 'Well, well, look who it is. Thornton. Returned from the dead, it would seem to look at you.'

Jonathan swept the Duke a bow more notable in its contempt than respect.

'My Lord Buckingham, I trust you are well?'

The King turned on his heel to face the room, a smile breaking the swarthy face when he saw Jonathan.

'Sir Jonathan. We truly thought you dead or, as George has suggested more than once' — he gave Buckingham a significant look — 'deserted. But I can see from your face that it is not either. I'm pleased to have you by my side again.'

Jonathan bowed low over the King's proffered hand. 'Your Majesty, it is my pleasure to be here and to see you once more on your own soil.'

The King sighed deeply. 'Ah, hardly "my soil" yet. Do you have dispatches for me?'

Jonathan handed the stained documents over, a flush of embarrassment rising to his face as the King raised an eyebrow as he turned the documents over.

'Am I right in assuming that you encountered some difficulty in bringing these to me?'

'I had the great misfortune to be recognised, Your Majesty. Regrettably a pistol ball in the shoulder slowed me down.'

'As I imagine it would. That explains your absence. I trust that you are recovered? Do you wish Dr Fraser to see to your shoulder?'

Jonathan shook his head. 'It has been well tended. Time and rest will set it fully to rights.'

'Well you should have ample amounts of both,' the King

remarked, the tone of his voice bitter. 'Has Longley told you what has befallen us since I landed?'

Jonathan nodded and said slowly. 'He's apprised me of how things have gone with you and the Scots.'

The King sat down heavily, his hands hanging between his knees, his shoulders slumped. He was barely twenty but in that moment looked like a man twice his age.

He took a deep breath and gazed around the gloomy room. 'They promised me an army. They promised to make me King. What they didn't tell me was what it would cost me.'

Jonathan said nothing. The King needed to talk. He needed a friendly shoulder on which to lay his troubles. Charles rose, walked over to the fire and kicked a log back into place. It sputtered angrily, shooting a tongue of bright red flame up the chimney.

'Well, I paid the price they asked. I have sworn their Solemn League and Covenant. I have publicly renounced all that I believe in, everything my father died for.' He turned to look at Jonathan, his eyes hot with anger and perhaps even unshed tears. 'Even that was not enough. They have now demanded I renounce my parents.'

Jonathan shook his head in disbelief. 'And the army they promised?'

Wilmot gave a snort of laughter. 'Oh they provided an army but only after the bloody Covenanters had purged it of its best commanders.'

Jonathan turned to look at Wilmot.

'General Leslie?'

'Leslie survived the purge, but he will have to do the best with what he has got. Don't hope for a command, Thornton. If they won't have their own, they certainly do not want Englishmen.'

'So what do we do?'

'We sit here, we listen to sermons, we drink too much and when the Scots aren't looking, we whore too much.' George Villiers held up his glass, swilling the wine as he did so. 'And we play cards, don't we, Longley?'

Giles shrugged, and Lord Wilmot cast the Duke a look of pure dislike.

'Our only consolation is the weather,' Wilmot said as he walked over to the window and gazed out at the rain. 'This lovely Scottish weather has dispirited the English troops. Their morale is low and Leslie is fighting on his own ground. Despite his problems, I believe he has the advantage.' Wilmot turned back to the table. 'See, Thornton.' He jabbed a finger at the map. 'Even now, Leslie has Cromwell trapped between the land and the sea at Dunbar. Leslie holds the high ground. I do not see how he can lose.'

'Do not underestimate Cromwell,' Jonathan warned. 'With Fairfax tending roses in Yorkshire, I fear we will see exactly what Oliver Cromwell is really capable of.'

The King joined them at the table. 'I would almost like to see him prevail if only to teach these damned Covenanters the price they pay for my humiliation is a high one.'

George Villiers stood up and stretched like a cat.

'You've read Thornton's letters, Your Majesty? What news?'

Charles threw the letters down on the table and looked at Jonathan. 'You know what they say?'

Jonathan nodded. 'Yes, Your Majesty. You will find they are professions of love and loyalty but no promises of troops or arms or money.'

'You nearly lost your life to bring me this ill news,' the King observed.

'I did the task you asked of me, your Majesty.'

Charles smiled grimly. 'I know. You have served me as loyally as you did my father, Thornton. I'll not forget that.'

Villiers clapped Jonathan on his bad shoulder. Jonathan swore, apologised and glared at the Duke, who gazed back with a look of utter innocence.

'Your injured shoulder? I do apologise, Thornton. Now tell us of the wench who cared for you in your agony. There had to be a wench. No woman can resist a wounded hero.'

'The wench of your imagination, George, was a raw-boned Yorkshire woman who should be properly hung as a witch for all the vile potions she made me swallow,' Jonathan snarled.

Buckingham pouted. 'Oh you disappoint me, Thornton. I imagined at least some young nubile squire's daughter with pert breasts and a sweet —'

'Take your fetid imagination, back to the gutter where it belongs,' Jonathan snapped, his hand flying to the hilt of his sword.

Buckingham raised his hands. 'Now, now, where is your humour, Thornton? I fear I must have touched a nerve.'

Jonathan relaxed his hand and an urgent knocking on the door broke the tense atmosphere of the room. At Wilmot's command a breathless and mud-stained messenger entered and, ignoring the company, he fell at the King's feet.

'You bring me news of Leslie's army?' Charles' eyes were alight with anticipation of good news.

The man rose to his feet. 'I do, Your Majesty. They are defeated.'

Lord Wilmot broke the dreadful silence that followed this news. 'Defeated?' he croaked. 'How can this be? Leslie had the English troops cornered.'

'Cromwell attacked at night. He took the Scots by surprise. It was done in no time.'

All eyes in the room turned to the King to gauge his reaction. The Scots had been defeated. Their great army, the fetter by which they held their young King, had been destroyed in one bold, unpredicted move.

Charles Stuart threw back his head and laughed.

CHAPTER 14

BARTON, YORKSHIRE MARCH, 1651

*W*illiam set Nell's letter down on the table beside him. He laced his fingers over his ample stomach and regarded his sister-in-law thoughtfully.

'So, lass, the old man's dead.'

Kate turned a strained face towards him. 'You know what it means, don't you?'

'Aye. I've eyes in my head, I can read between the lines right enough. The old man has named Thomas as his heir. Where does that leave your Jonathan?'

Kate smiled bitterly. The family had developed the annoying habit of referring to the absent Jonathan Thornton as 'your Jonathan'. 'Jonathan Thornton is an outlaw in this country. He knew the old man's intentions.' She sighed heavily. 'I wish it could have been some other way, William.'

'Well if it's my advice you're after, Kate,' William tapped a second letter that lay beside Nell's on the table, 'you're better off without the place. If what yon lawyer says, the whole estate's in financial ruin.'

'You are right.' She bit her lip and sighed. 'But there are people involved, William. People I care about.'

'They're not your responsibility, Kate,' interposed Suzanne who had been listening to the conversation.

'Aye. Leave 'em to make their own way in't world,' agreed William. 'The Lord alone knows they've been precious little help to you and yours over the years.'

Suzanne, more perceptive than her husband, leaned toward her sister and spoke in a gentler tone of voice. 'You have to leave your heart out of this, Kate. You cannot take responsibility for Jonathan Thornton's life, no matter what your feelings for him.'

'Aye, Suzanne's right,' William said. 'He's a good lad but if he's not prepared to make his peace and settle down, that's his lookout.'

'It wasn't Jonathan I was thinking of.' Kate said sharply.

She stood up and walked over to the window, pressing her forehead against the cool glass. The snow had gone at last and there was the faintest breath of spring in the air. Suzanne joined her, putting her arms around her sister.

'Don't leave us, Kate. Particularly not now,' she said.

Kate turned to her sister, seeing the dark circles under her eyes and the lines of strain at her sister's mouth.

Robert was dying. The doctor had given him only days to live and Suzanne needed her sister. Kate squeezed her sister's hand.

'Of course, I won't leave you,' she reassured Suzanne.

From behind her, William spoke up again. 'Apart from naught else, lass, you've done a grand job of running the Ashley lands. But an estate like Seven Ways, well that's a man's job.'

Kate stiffened and shook off her sister's hand as she turned on her brother-in-law. 'Queen Elizabeth reigned over England for forty years, William. I am sure I, a mere woman, am equal to managing an estate. Even one like Seven Ways.'

Suzanne glared at her husband.

'I'll thank you to keep your opinions to yourself, William Rowe,' his wife snapped. She turned back to Kate. 'Have you considered, Tom? You would be taking him away from all that he knows.'

Kate picked up her lawyer's letter. 'You are right to suggest this should be a business decision with Tom's best interests in heart. If I were to sell Seven Ways now, I would never recover its full worth.' She looked up at them both. 'You cannot seriously tell me that it is in Tom's interests to squander his inheritance in such a manner?'

Suzanne and William looked at each other. That had not been what they had meant.

'All right,' said Suzanne. 'Keep Seven Ways but put a steward in to manage it. There is no need for you to go there.'

Kate nodded. 'I have considered that,' she acknowledged.

Suzanne visibly relaxed. She picked Nell's letter up from the table and scanned the contents again.

'What have you told Tom?' she asked.

'I have told him Sir Francis is dead. Nothing more,' Kate replied. Her voice softened and almost broke, as she said, 'You know as well as I that now is not a good time.'

As Robert's health failed, Tom spent every waking moment with him and had to be prised away from his cousin's bedside at night so that both children could rest. Tom could not accept that his dearest friend, who was as close to him as any brother could be, lacked his own robust good health and would not recover.

Tom would have given his own life to prevent what was coming.

Kate looked from her sister to her husband. 'This is not the right time to concern either of you with my problems.' She managed a weak smile. 'I will pray and I am sure God will show me the way to resolve these difficulties.'

'Aye well. You've more faith in him than I,' William said pragmatically.

~

ROBERT DIED early in the evening of the following day. Tom stood by the bed with his cousins, dry-eyed while they wept. Kate could do nothing, knowing that Tom's grief went too deep for tears.

On a mild March day, they laid the small coffin to rest in the cold ground of the little church at Barton where Kate's own Richard and his parents lay. The faintest breath of wind from the moors Robert had so loved bowed the heads of the daffodils and stirred the women's skirts as they stood in the churchyard. There being nothing more Kate could do for her sister, she returned home with Tom riding silently beside her.

For two days Tom sat in the parlour, working at his books or staring out of the window as if he expected Robert to come riding up on his fat little pony. If Kate tried to hold him, he stiffened and turned away. It frightened her that she could not reach him and she watched him in agony, her grief not so much for Robert, who was beyond mortal pain, but for this silent, suffering child of hers.

'It's not natural,' Ellen remarked to Kate as another half-touched plate of food was set aside. 'The lad'll fade away himself if he keeps this up.'

The mild weather did not last. It broke in a fierce storm, lashing the trees and subjugating the new growth in the walled garden. Kate lay in her bed, listening to the beating of the rain on the windows and thinking, as she often did, of Jonathan. The nagging ache of loneliness was as painful as a physical hurt.

She turned over as a sudden draught blew through the door

and Tom climbed into her bed, putting his cold feet against her. She took him into her arms and held him close as she had done when he was a baby.

'Surely not frightened of the storm?' she asked softly.

He shook his head. 'Mother,' he said, his voice muffled against her body. 'I want to go to Seven Ways.'

Kate hid her surprise. 'Why?'

In the dark, Tom sniffed. 'I won't miss Robert so much if I go away.' The tears came in full flood now. 'And I do — I miss him so much, Mother.'

Tears starting in her own eyes, Kate stroked the dark head. 'Running away is not the answer, Tom,' she said. 'The pain does get better and soon you won't miss him so much. It just takes a little time.'

'It didn't when Father died,' Tom said, with a perception that made Kate's heart miss a beat. 'I used to hear you crying at night when I was in bed.' He paused. 'You don't cry anymore. Not for Father.' Tom gave a great shuddering sigh. 'I miss Jonathan too.'

Kate had no platitudes for that pain. She felt it too keenly herself. She held her son closer as the last of his tears resolved into hiccups. Stroking his hair, she waited until the sounds subsided.

'Do you really want to go to Seven Ways, Tom?'

'Yes.'

'We will talk about it in the morning.'

Long after Tom finally fell asleep in her arms, Kate lay awake staring into the unrelenting blackness of her bed canopy. The wakeful minutes dragged by, turning into long hours. The wind tore at the house, loosening a shutter on the window in her bedchamber. Kate listened to it swing loose and bang against the wall for a long time before she laid her son to one side and tore herself from the warm bed to secure it.

As she reached out into the dark, wild night to draw the shutter back, she thought she saw movement on the road. She looked again and her eyes did not deceive her. A dark horse with a rider crouched low against the rain turned off the road and came through the open gates into the courtyard. She closed her eyes and drew a quick breath, hardly daring to hope.

Stopping only to slip on some shoes and grab her cloak, Kate ran down the stairs and out into the night, heedless of the rain and the cold. The heavily cloaked rider had dismounted from the soaked horse that stood with its sides heaving and its head drooping with exhaustion.

'Jonathan.'

The rider turned and held out a gloved hand. Kate fell into his arms, entwined in his embrace, afraid that if she let go he would vanish into the night.

'It's you? It's really you? You're not some phantom of the night?' She found herself babbling as the rain tore through her inadequate cloak, plastering her hair to her skull. Her simple shift clung to her like a second skin.

'Kate, enough. You're soaked.' Jonathan said at last.

'I don't care,' she said, the edge of tears in her voice.

A light appeared in the stable and Dickon, half-dressed and bleary-eyed, held up a lantern and peered out of the door. His jaw dropped open in surprise.

'Dickon. See to the horse.' Jonathan handed over the reins and turned to Kate. 'Now, you foolish wench, I'll not be responsible for you dying of lung fever. Inside, now.'

He picked her up as if she weighed no more than a child and carried her into the house.

In the kitchen, Jonathan stoked up the fire while Kate wrapped herself in a blanket and tried to dry her hair that now hung in damp rat's tails around her face. Her gaze did not move from him, even as he raided the larder for the last of the rabbit pie and a mug of ale. If she looked away he might vanish.

'God's death, how I've craved some decent food,' Jonathan announced as he bit into the pie.

'I can't believe you're here. I'm going to wake in a minute and find it is all a dream.' Kate pulled her frozen feet up onto the oak settle and hugged her knees, her happiness radiating from her.

Jonathan smiled. 'A fleeting visit only, Kate. I must be gone tomorrow.'

The smile faded from her face. 'So soon?'

He nodded. 'I should not even be here now.'

'What are you doing ?'

He shrugged. 'Need you ask?'

She knew better than to ask him more.

Jonathan brushed the last of the crumbs from his damp jacket. 'What news is there here, Kate? Have you heard anything from Seven Ways? How is Grandfather?'

Kate stared at him. He didn't know; how could he know?

'Sir Francis died six weeks ago,' she said.

His face betrayed no emotion but he looked away, staring at the glowing coals of the kitchen fire.

'So there are decisions to be made. Or have you already decided, Kate?'

'No,' she admitted. 'I've made no decisions. My nephew, Robert, also died barely a week ago and that is a greater grief for me than the death of an old man I hardly knew.'

He swung his gaze around to look at her, his expression stricken.

'Robert is dead?'

The grief he had not shown for his grandfather was written on his face.

'Tom?'

Kate felt her eyes fill with tears, as they did whenever she thought of Robert.

'Tom is heartbroken.' She wiped her eyes and summoned a smile. 'But this dismal talk can wait. How are you? Your shoulder?'

'I'm fine. The shoulder... does me well enough.'

'And Scotland?'

Jonathan rolled his eyes heavenward. 'Scotland is unspeakable. The Scots have dealt very ill with the King.'

'And you?'

'And all of us, or those of us who have refused the Solemn Oath and Covenant. I am not the most God-fearing of men, Kate, but to take that Oath defies everything I have ever believed in. The King must have done it with his fingers crossed behind his back.'

'We heard there was a battle. Were you there?'

'No. Thank the Lord. I only arrived in Perth on the day the King received the news of the defeat.'

He stood up, stretching like a cat, easing his stiffening muscles.

'Kate, I've been on the road all day and I'm exhausted. At this moment I want nothing more than to fall into a warm bed, preferably with you in my arms.'

Kate smiled and felt herself blush as he raised a quizzical eyebrow at her.

'Tom is in my bed. Will you settle for a cold bed in the guest chamber? It is kept made up.'

'As long as you are there as well, I could sleep on the floor.'

With their arms around each other, they climbed the stairs to the familiar room where Jonathan had spent so many weeks. They slid between the icy sheets and both still damp from the rain, curled into each other's arms as naturally as if they had been made to suit.

'How I have missed you,' Jonathan whispered.

Kate stroked his damp hair. 'And I you. Jonathan…?'

'Hmm?' he whispered sleepily.

'Jonathan. I need to know…I mean I don't mind…I would understand.'

'What are you talking about?'

'Other women?' she said in a small, tight voice.

In the dark, she could not see his face.

He pulled her closer. 'Why do you ask?'

She sighed. 'Nell says Giles is unfaithful.'

'Regularly,' agreed Jonathan. 'Kate, how little you understand men. A man may love a woman to the ends of the earth, and the act of taking another woman to his bed will not alter that. For some men, it is no different from eating or sleeping. It is a need of the moment that has nothing to do with his heart, and that is how it is with Giles.' She stiffened and he laid a finger on her lips. 'I'm not Giles. Did you ever doubt Richard's fidelity?'

'No.'

'Then why doubt me?'

'I know your reputation.'

'And you should also know I have only ever loved one other woman in my entire life, Kate. She is many years in the grave and while I have not been a monk, I have never told another woman that I loved her…until you.' He kissed her gently. 'Kate, you have my word that I have lived a life as chaste as that of a priest. Indeed my less charitable comrades in arms have remarked upon my apparent lack of interest in the fairer sex on many an occasion in the last few months.'

'And what did you tell them?'

'I told them that Scottish women held no more allure for me than their particular hairy breed of cattle.'

'Jonathan.'

''Tis true, Kate. Hairy and dirty and no bedfellow for me. Now you, on the other hand, are worth the wait.'

As he talked his hand strayed across her shoulder, his touch sending shafts of fire through her body.

'I thought you were tired?' Kate remarked.

'Licence my roving hands, and let them go, Before, behind, between, above, below...' Jonathan quoted, *illustrating his words as he spoke.*

'Don't quote Donne at me. I've read all his poems.' Kate giggled as she wrestled with the roving hands. 'Jonathan..' She broke away and looked at him. 'You haven't told me.'

'Told you what?'

'That you loved me.'

He paused and frowned as if the words that followed were the hardest words he had ever had to say. 'I love you, Kate Ashley.' He took a deep breath.

'Thou art my life, my love, my heart,

The very eyes of me:

And hast command of every part

To live and die for thee.'

'Donne again?' she asked in a hoarse whisper.

'Herrick.'

Outside the storm began to abate, while in the guest chamber the bed rapidly warmed as two people lay entwined in each other's arms, sated with love.

JONATHAN SAT on the low stone wall overlooking the brook that ran behind the house, tossing pebbles into the water. Beside him, Tom watched the stones fall into the swiftly flowing water, swollen by the recent rain.

'I'm sorry about Robert,' Jonathan said at last.

'Mother says it gets better and that I'll stop feeling sad.'

'It does, Tom. The pain will get better but you never forget the person who is gone. Do you remember how you felt when your grandfather Ashley died?'

'Yes, but that was different. He was old, like Sir Francis.' The boy looked up at him. 'Will you miss Sir Francis?'

Jonathan nodded. 'I'll miss him very much. He was the one person in the world I could rely on to give me sound advice.' He paused. 'Has your mother told you about Seven Ways?'

'What about Seven Ways?'

'That Sir Francis named you his heir?'

Tom's eyes widened in evident surprise and Jonathan quietly cursed himself. Kate must have had her reasons for not telling the boy. He had no right to interfere.

'You mean Seven Ways belongs to me?'

'Strictly speaking not until you're twenty-one,' Jonathan said, 'but, yes.'

'But what about you?' Tom asked. 'Aren't you his heir?'

Jonathan threw a large pebble into the water and it landed with a thunk as it sunk.

'What would I do with Seven Ways? I get the title though.' He smiled at the boy. 'I'm the third baronet now.'

'That sounds very grand,' Tom said. He frowned. 'If I own Seven Ways does that mean I can go and live there?'

'That's up to your mother. You wouldn't want to leave your home and your friends would you?'

Tom's face took on a pinched look and he mumbled, 'I don't have any friends, not now Robert is dead.'

'Of course, you do,' Jonathan stood up. 'I cannot dally any longer. Dickon should have Amber ready for me by now.'

'Must you go?'

Jonathan nodded. 'Yes.'

The boy looked up at him. 'When will I see you again?'

A shaft of almost physical pain cut through Jonathan's heart. Both mother and son were his world now and he hated to leave them.

'I don't know.'

Jonathan put his arm across the boy's shoulders as they walked back to the house where Kate waited with a parcel of food and a flask of ale.

She said nothing and he silently thanked her for knowing better than to ask him to stay. Her very silence was harder to bear than if she had screamed and begged. At the end of the lane, he looked back to see her standing by the gate, with the letters from Giles he had left for her to forward to Nell pressed to her breast.

He raised his hand and turned away. He could not look back again.

CHAPTER 15

*R*elieved that it had fallen to Jonathan to tell Tom about Seven Ways, Kate still hesitated on a decision. Following Jonathan's fleeting visit, she had sent Giles' letters on to Nell with a brief letter of her own, explaining the situation with Robert's death and her sister's need for her.

On receiving Nell's reply, and realising the importance of what it contained, Kate immediately rode over to consult with William and Suzanne.

In the warm, familiar parlour of Barton Hall, Kate read Nell's letter aloud.

Dearest Kate, My heart bleeds for your sister over the loss of her son, so I do understand your delay. Oh but, Kate, what am I to do? We had barely buried Sir Francis before Colonel Price and his bullies from the County Committee were at our door. We explained that the property was now Thomas's but they would not believe me. Price wants the Thornton land so badly, that he will not leave us in peace, and every day one or more of

*his men are seen on our land. I have no one else to turn to. Please come
soon. Yr loving Nell.*

Kate laid the letter down and met her sister's hot, angry eyes.

'You're surely not going.' Suzanne exclaimed.

'I've no choice, Suzanne,' she said. 'Firstly, I have a duty to see
that Tom's inheritance is secure from the grasp of men like Price,
and secondly, Nell is my friend and she needs me.'

'I am your sister,' Suzanne's said in a harsh, flat voice that cut
to the bone. 'I need you.'

Kate steeled her resolve. 'You have William. You have your
children. Nell has no one. She is utterly alone, trying to run a
house and an estate that is not her responsibility. Whatever my
feelings on the subject, I'm sorry, Suzanne. I must go.'

'I wish I'd never advised you to go to Seven Ways in the first
place,' Suzanne said bitterly. 'The devil take the Thorntons. All of
them.'

'Suzanne.' Kate took a step toward her sister, who shrugged off
her hand and walked over to the window where she stood with her
back to the room, her arms wrapped defensively around her body.

Kate turned back to William. 'You understand don't you,
William?' she asked in an uncertain voice. The vehemence of her
sister's response had shaken her.

'Aye, lass. You and Thomas have to be seen to take possession
of Seven Ways. I've no love for these damned Committees. Too
quick to feather their own nests, most of them, and this Price
sounds no better than any. I think mayhap I should come with
you and deal with the man myself.'

Kate hesitated. It would be so easy to allow William to take
control and deal with the likes of Colonel Price in his forthright
Yorkshire manner. Perhaps William had been right when he said

Seven Ways was a man's job. However it was not his fight, and Sir Francis and Jonathan both had confidence in her ability. She did not want to betray that confidence to them or to herself. She glanced at her sister's stiff back and slowly she shook her head.

'No, William. You're needed here. I must go alone,' she said.

William frowned. 'Is there no one you can call on for help? Surely you cannot be the last living relative of the Thorntons.'

Kate frowned. 'There is an uncle in London.' She grappled for the name, wondering now if Jonathan had ever told her. 'A lawyer.'

'Nathaniel Freeman?' William sat up in his chair.

Kate shook her head. 'I can't remember.'

William slapped his knee. 'It can be no other. That's how David Ashley met Elizabeth Thornton. Nathaniel Freeman. He had just wed a Thornton. When David sat in the Parliament, he would stay with Freeman and his wife. Ah, lass, you don't know it, but you've a powerful ally there. Freeman has done well for himself under this rule.'

'You mean he took Parliament's side?'

William nodded. 'Lost a boy in one of the early battles if I remember rightly.'

Kate shook her head. 'I don't recall David ever mentioned him.'

William shrugged. 'They'd not have met since the last Parliament was dismissed in '41. It's none of my business, but you ask this lass, Nell, to write to her uncle and ask him to come to Seven Ways to meet with you and between the two of you, you'll set this man Price on his ear.'

Kate stood up. 'I'll do that.' As she passed her sister, she laid a hand on Suzanne's stiff unresponsive shoulder. 'I won't be gone long, Suzanne. I plan to see the estate settled. The bailiff at Seven Ways is a good man. I trust him. I will shut up the house and bring

Nell and the bairn back here.'

'A papist in Barton?' Suzanne said, without moving.

Kate took a steadying breath, regretting that particular confidence she had shared with her sister. 'Jonathan's sister. Tom's cousin…a woman who needs help, Suzanne.' She turned back to William. 'I'll take Ellen and Dickon with me again if they'll come, and if I need anything I'll send for it. We will leave by week's end.'

Suzanne gave a strangled cry and ran from the room. William watched the door as it slammed shut behind his wife.

'You'll have your work cut out for you but you've a good head on your shoulders.' He paused. 'And don't you fret for Suzanne. She'll come round, you'll see.'

That night Kate sat in her parlour and penned a letter to Nell, assuring her that she and Thomas could be expected within the next few weeks, depending on how long it took to arrange her affairs in Yorkshire and the state of the roads. Kate also asked Nell to send for her uncle as William suggested. She sanded the letter and sealed it neatly.

She stood and walked over to the window. The window faced north… north to Scotland. A cold shiver ran down her spine and she wrapped her arms around herself and closed her eyes, willing her mind to reach out to Jonathan, wondering if he had returned. She had been lonely after Richard's death but the loneliness of this uncertainty was worse, far worse.

She turned her thoughts to the journey she and Tom would make. Strangely, now the decision was made, she had no regrets. It was as if she had cast herself off from her old, familiar, safe life and was sailing like a Drake or a Raleigh into strange waters. She felt no fear, only a sense of exhilaration and freedom that had nothing to do with the Ashleys or the Thorntons but came entirely from within herself.

CHAPTER 16

SEVEN WAYS, WORCESTERSHIRE JUNE, 1651

*N*ell all but flew out of the front door and hardly waited for Kate to dismount before she threw her arms around her neck, half-sobbing.

'Kate, Kate, I am so glad you've come.'

Kate gently disengaged her friend and took a step backwards. Nell seemed a shadow of the bright, lively young woman of a year ago. Her black dress and plain white collar accentuated her pallor and her fair hair, drawn back severely from her pale face, had lost all its lustre.

Nell put her hand to her mouth to stifle a sob. 'I've had no one to turn to. All my life there has been someone to turn to but since grandfather's last illness, I've been so alone.'

'I'm so sorry, Nell,' Kate said, 'I had no idea how hard it's been for you.'

Kate slipped her arm into Nell's and walked her into the house and to the upstairs parlour, where Nell subsided onto a chair.

'It's all such a mess,' Nell said, the tears bright in her eyes. 'I just didn't know what to do.'

'I'm sure things can be put to rights,' Kate said in a tone she normally reserved for one of her wayward nieces or nephews,

Nell looked up at her. 'No, it is worse than you can imagine,' she said. 'You don't know everything about us... me. I can only compromise you.'

'What do you mean?'

Tears started trickling down Nell's face. 'You have to know. I profess the Catholic faith.'

'I know that,' Kate said.

Nell sniffed. 'You do?'

'Jonathan told me. It makes no difference to me, Nell. You're still welcome here. This is your home. Now, tell me everything that has happened.'

Drawing in a great, shuddering breath, Nell began, 'Sir Francis was barely cold when Price came with three others of the County Committee. They had a paper with them, an order to sequester the house. I refused to admit them. I told them that they were mistaken and that according to my father's will the estate was now the property of one Master Thomas Ashley of Barton in Yorkshire.'

Nell allowed herself a small smile. 'I told them to verify my story with the family lawyer in Worcester and ascertain the truth of the situation before making such wild assumptions.'

'And did they?'

'Oh yes, but Price returned a couple of days later.' Her face darkened. 'He threatened to burn the house down over our heads and that this Thomas Ashley would regret the day he inherited Seven Ways.'

'Did you write to your uncle as I asked?'

Nell nodded. 'And he wrote such a kind letter in reply. He cannot get away from London but he has written a letter, verifying Thomas' claim on the estate and threatening Price with action should he pursue any claim for sequestration. He's a powerful man in London these days, Kate. I don't know why I never thought of turning to him before.'

'You had no reason to.'

Nell shrugged. 'I suppose so, but the real reason is that Uncle Nathaniel, like David Ashley, sided with Parliament. None of us would have had contact with him these ten years past.' She buried her head in her hands. 'Kate, I'm so very tired of this war and these estrangements.'

Kate held her close. 'The gaps are closing, Nell. Now, I plan to settle matters here and take you and Ann back to Barton with me.'

Nell's eyes widened. 'You'd do that?'

'You've nowhere else to go and I'm not leaving you alone in this big house to be prey to Price and his ilk.'

'You wouldn't stay?'

'Barton is my home, Nell.'

'I understand,' Nell said. 'I always thought of Seven Ways as my home but now I feel I don't belong anywhere.'

Kate stood up and walked over to the window. The green fields, the Thornton lands, rolled away, fringed by the woods. How could it all seem so peaceful?

Without William or Suzanne to turn to, and no hope of Jonathan re-entering her life, Kate had never felt so utterly alone in her life.

OBEDIENT TO HER REQUEST, the following morning Kate found Jacob Howell, the bailiff of the Seven Ways estate, waiting in the downstairs parlour with the estate books tucked under his arm. His father and his father before him had been a bailiff for the Thorntons, and Sir Francis had relied heavily on Jacob in the last few years. Kate knew he was well liked and well respected by the tenants. In short, he was a good bailiff and a fair man.

Kate smiled at him as she swept into the parlour. She had met him once on her last visit and then only fleetingly. She recalled the quiet, almost taciturn man with a long, mournful face who regarded her now with an unreadable countenance. Nell had warned her that he could be reticent in his dealings with women and despite Sir Francis's recommendation he viewed the new mistress of the house with the greatest suspicion.

'Master Howell, good morning,' she said, indicating a seat at the table. 'Please sit. Are those the books?'

He set the books on the table and sat down. She pulled her chair up next to him and opened the first volume.

It was early afternoon before Kate laid down her pen and leaned back in her chair. Due mainly to Sir Francis' careful management over the last few years, the estate was not as badly off as it could have been. The fines, which had been massive, had mostly been met by the sale of lands not connected with Seven Ways itself, and while it was by no means wealthy, the estate had begun to pay its way again.

However, the figures revealed a couple of matters of immediate concern.

'Why the low price for the stock sold at market?' she asked. 'In Yorkshire, fat sheep would be fetching twice that amount.'

Jacob, hastily swallowing the last of the pie supplied for his lunch, said, 'That's Price's doing. We're forced to sell to him. No one else durst go over him for fear he will turn on them. It's no secret that he covets this land for himself and he hopes to beggar us by buying our stock at below cost.'

Kate frowned. The necessity for an interview with Price had become urgent. She did not relish the prospect.

'What about the reports that his men have been trespassing on our land?' she asked.

'Aye. They've been harrying the tenants and there have been a few unexplained fires and stock losses.' Jacob scowled. 'Nothing we can prove. Anyway, even if we could, Price is the local magistrate.'

Kate set aside the problem of Colonel Price for the moment and turned back to her tenants.

'What about the Barlows?' Kate tapped the cover of the second volume. 'They're months behind in their rent.'

Jacob nodded slowly. 'I'll admit I've done naught about them,' he replied. 'Jem Barlow took a bad knock on the head during the war and has been addled ever since. He's good for naught. His wife Susan and their boy have tried their best but truth is, Mistress, I've no heart to chase them.'

Kate looked at him. 'What do you suggest?'

'Well, Mistress, rightly speaking you should turn them out.' Jacob left an unspoken 'but' at the end of his sentence.

Kate sighed. 'We'll ride over and see them tomorrow,' she said, 'but first I think a visit to Colonel Price is called for.'

'We? Do you want me to come?' Jacob asked.

Kate smiled. 'Jacob, you're an old soldier, surely you have faced worse in the field?'

Jacob sighed, 'Aye, Mistress, but I were better armed. Yon Colonel Price, he holds the whole armoury.'

Kate stood up and handed the estate books back to her bailiff. 'Tomorrow morning, Jacob, please.'

CHAPTER 17

*C*olonel John Price stumped into the parlour of Longley Abbey where his man had shown Kate and Jacob Howell. Kate curtsied politely and he returned the greeting with a curt nod of his head.

As she rose to face him Kate summed up the small, portly man with a receding hairline, unsuccessfully disguised by brushing his hair over his pate. His florid, self-important face told her all she needed to know about the sort of man she had to deal with.

She, in turn, had dressed carefully for the interview in a plain gown of black wool, relieved only by a spotless white collar with the narrowest lace edge, matched by the white linen matron's cap. Mindful of Jonathan's lessons on the subject of disguise and subterfuge, she hoped that she presented as the picture of a godly widow.

'You have business with me, madam?'

Kate smiled and inclined her head towards a straight-backed chair. 'May I sit?'

He waved his hand at the chair. 'Of course. Err.. umm... you have the advantage of me, Mistress...?'

'Ashley... of Seven Ways.'

Price's eyebrows rose at the name.

'Ah, of course... Seven Ways.' He sat down with a thump on another seat. 'Your, er, husband is not with you?'

'My husband is dead,' Kate replied.

Price frowned. 'Then who is this Thomas Ashley, who is said to have come into the Seven Ways estate?'

'My son.'

Price blinked.

'Your son? But surely you are not old enough...'

'My son is nine years old. I am the guardian of his estate.'

'You're a woman.'

'So I am.' Kate gave him the benefit of a charming smile. 'And as your new neighbour, Colonel, I thought it incumbent upon me to make your acquaintance. You know my bailiff, of course?'

She indicated Jacob, who lurked in the shadows of the room. Price cursorily acknowledged his presence.

She could almost see the coils of the man's mind working as he tried to decipher Kate's relationship with the Thorntons.

'It's my understanding that Sir Francis had only one surviving grandson,' he said.

She affected a moue of disapproval. 'You refer to the notorious delinquent, Jonathan Thornton? From what I hear tell of his exploits, he should be damned for all eternity.' Kate said a silent apology to her lover. 'My late husband, Captain David Ashley of Sir Thomas Fairfax's Regiment, was also a grandson of Sir Francis and by his will, Sir Francis has left Seven Ways to my son, his last surviving male heir.'

Price blinked. 'Your husband fought for Parliament?' She hoped he could see all his careful plans for the acquisition of

Seven Ways unravelling in the light of this new, unwelcome, information.

Kate nodded. 'Indeed, his father was a member of both Parliaments and,' she added for good measure, 'a personal friend of the Fairfaxes.'

Price rose to his feet. 'Madam, you must be aware that I hold an order to sequester Seven Ways and the Thornton land.'

Kate pulled out Nathaniel Freeman's letter. 'And I have a letter under the seal of the Council of State, verifying Thomas Ashley's claim to Seven Ways and countermanding the sequestration order.'

Price took the letter and turned it over in his hands as if it burned him. He opened it and scanned the contents. His lips tightened as he sank back on the chair.

'That appears to be in order,' he said.

'I should hope it is,' Kate replied.

Price grappled to regain some lost ground. 'You're aware, madam that you are harbouring a nest of papists?'

Kate pursed her lips. 'A nest? You refer, I presume, to Lady Longley and her daughter? In the name of Christian charity, I can scarcely turn them out.' She looked around the pleasant parlour that should, by rights, have been Nell's. 'As you are well aware, they have nowhere else to go as their own home is in your possession.'

She was rewarded by the darkening colour in the man's already ruddy cheeks and Price leaned forward in his chair. His smile revealed a row of uneven yellow teeth.

Bluster having failed, he tried charm. 'Mistress Ashley. You are obviously a woman of undoubted good sense; perhaps we could discuss the possibility of my taking Seven Ways off your hands. The estate requires a man's hand to bring it to rights again.'

She smiled. 'That is a very kind offer but you see I am merely trustee for my son, and Thomas, young as he is, has formed a great attachment to Seven Ways. I feel honour-bound to respect Sir Francis's wishes in this matter.'

She stood up, forcing Price to scrabble to his feet.

'Thank you for your time, Colonel, but Master Howell and I have a busy afternoon planned. There is much work to be done so I will take my leave of you.'

'Think on my offer, Mistress Ashley,' he said. 'I am sure you will find you have set yourself a major undertaking. The Seven Ways estate is in a parlous condition.'

She nodded. 'Thank you, Colonel. I will see what needs to be done.'

Kate held out her hand, and Price bowed over it. 'Madam. It only remains for me to bid you welcome and ask if I can be of any service.'

As Kate pulled on her gloves, she said, 'Well there is one small matter, which you as a Justice of the Peace may be able to assist me with. My tenants are being harassed by men who claim, wrongly I am certain, to be acting on your orders.'

Price blustered, his face going a pleasing shade of puce. 'That is outrageous, madam. I shall make immediate investigations and such ruffians will be sternly dealt with.'

Liar, Kate thought, but she smiled sweetly. 'Thank you, for your time. I hope we may meet again soon.'

'My wife is presently visiting family but when she returns you must dine with us, Mistress Ashley.'

'I would be delighted, Colonel.' She swept past him, with Jacob trailing in her wake.

Their horses, held by a groom, waited on the gravelled fore-court of the handsome late Elizabethan house. This should be Nell's house, Kate thought again, looking up at the mullioned windows and curling chimneys. Nell would be happy here.

She hoped Jacob didn't notice her hand shake as she took the reins of her horse from him.

'Did you mean what you said about Sir Jonathan?' Jacob asked boldly as they rode away.

'Which part?'

'You said he should be damned.'

'No, Howell, of course I did not mean what I said. I have met Sir Jonathan and I have high regard for him.'

Jacob gave her a quick sideways glance but said nothing. She wondered if any servants' gossip about her relationship with Jonathan had permeated the walls of Seven Ways.

Kate smiled to herself and thought how Jonathan would have enjoyed being a witness to that interview. She had learned a great deal from him in their short acquaintance.

'I think that went well, don't you? I have certainly left him with something to ponder and I doubt our tenants will be harassed again.'

Jacob Howell. 'Aye, Mistress. You've certainly given him pause. I liked the part about your family's friendship with Sir Thomas Fairfax. Is that true?'

Kate cast him a sharp glance. 'Perfectly true, Howell. Lady Anne sends me her best Crab Apple Jelly every Christmas.'

IN SOME WAYS, the next interview would prove to be more difficult, and Kate's heart sank as they turned into the yard of the Barlow's farm. She caught Jacob's sharp eyes on her, waiting for her reaction. It had all the look of neglect she had expected. The roof sagged and a few skinny chickens pecked around the churned dirt of the yard.

A thin, harried woman waited by the door, her hands twisting in a not-too-clean apron.

As Jacob helped Kate dismount, the woman smoothed the crumpled folds of the apron and curtsied.

'You're welcome, my lady,' she said. 'I'm Susan Barlow. Would you care for some refreshment?'

Susan held open the door of her house with such a look of hope and anxiety on her face that Kate thought better of correcting the woman on the use of the correct mode of address.

Instead, she smiled and thanked her and followed her into the dark house.

It took a few minutes for Kate's eyes to accustom themselves to the gloom of the kitchen. Like the farm, it bore the discernible signs of neglect, with dust and cobwebs where there should be none and mud on the stone pavers that covered the floor. She fought against the overwhelming stench of stale bodies, boiled cabbage and mould.

A man sat by the fire, staring at nothing in particular. He looked up and when he saw Kate he began to twitch and jerk, uttering unintelligible sounds.

Susan Barlow went to his side, calming him as she would a small child. 'Don't fret, Jem. 'Tis just my lady come to pay a call.' She looked up at Kate. 'Don't you mind my Jem, my lady. He don't mean no harm.' She paused, looking sadly at the man, who had resumed staring into the coals of the fire. 'He's not been quite right since the war.'

My husband is dead, but that is nothing compared with this living death, Kate thought.

Mistress Barlow indicated a chair at the table, and while she busied herself with whatever was cooking over the fire, Kate exchanged a knowing glance with Jacob Howell. Small wonder the bailiff had no heart to turn this family out.

A tall, lanky boy of about fifteen stomped in from outside. 'What's to eat, Ma?' he demanded.

'Now, Sam, mind your manners. My lady and Master Howell have come to visit,' Susan Barlow said with an apologetic hitch of her shoulders in Kate's direction.

The boy, to his credit, whipped off his hat and apologised. Kate smiled at him and he took a seat at the other end of the table, as his mother set out bowls of a thin gruel and a hard, almost inedible bread, made from the poorest grinding.

The boy hunched over his bowl, occasionally casting Kate furtive glances. Did he suspect the reason for her visit?

Kate finished the food she had been provided with and brushing the last crumbs from her skirt, she folded her hands on the table. 'Mistress Barlow,' she began. 'You must know why we have come.'

The woman looked at her with wide, frightened eyes. 'Aye, my lady. It's about the rent. It's just with only the boy and me' — she cast a glance in the direction of her husband — 'we just can't seem to make ends meet.'

'Have you no one else to help?' Kate asked.

She shook her head. 'I've put five children in their graves, my lady, and my brother was lost in the war. I've no one but Sam and my girl Essie, who works up at the hall.'

Kate stood up and wandered around the room, looking for inspiration. She stopped to inspect the work on a loom that stood beneath a paneless window. She had been the daughter of a clothier and knew enough of the weaver's art to recognize quality.

'Did you weave this?' she asked Susan.

'Aye, my lady. I do a bit of weaving for the extra money it brings in.'

'It's good work,' Kate observed. She looked at Jacob. 'Master Howell, I believe there is a vacant cottage in the village?'

Jacob scratched his head. 'Aye. Old widow Read's place. It needs a mite of fixing up though.'

Kate looked back at Susan, seeing the small glimmer of hope begin to flicker in the woman's eyes.

'Mistress Barlow, it is plain that you cannot cope with the farm and the responsibility of caring for your husband. You must understand I have no choice but to turn you out of the farm.' The boy jumped to his feet but before he could protest, Kate raised a hand. 'Hear me out. If I were to offer you the cottage instead, as a grace and favour for the service your husband did for the Thorntons during the war, you could work full time on your weaving and earn an income doing what you're good at. Would that be acceptable to you?'

'And me?' Sam glared at her.

'There's paid work for you on the other farms,' Jacob Howell said. 'Keep your peace, boy.'

The woman's face broke into wreaths of smiles and she grabbed her son's hand. 'Oh, my lady, would you do that for me... for us?'

With Susan Barlow's effusive gratitude ringing in her ears, Kate left the sad little farm. 'Have we anyone to put into the farm?' she asked Jacob.

Jacob thought a minute then nodded slowly. 'Aye, Jeremiah Knowles' eldest boy has just taken a wife. They're an honest, hard-working family. They'll soon put the farm to rights.' He paused, before clearing his throat and saying gruffly, 'You've done well, Mistress Ashley.'

Kate drew a deep breath. She could understand any reticence on the part of the tenants and villagers. Not only was she a foreigner but a 'Roundhead' as well, but if she had won Jacob Howell over, she hoped that general acceptance of herself and Thomas would follow.

As the days passed, it became obvious that she had underestimated the weariness of the Seven Ways tenantry. Of course, Jacob told her, they would have preferred to see Jonathan Thornton take his rightful place, but they had known that were that to happen the land would be immediately sequestered and some crony of Colonel Price's assume the position. They had lived with penury and uncertainty for so long that Kate's coming proved to be a relief.

Given a choice between that possibility and a boy of good Thornton blood, loyalty to Kate and Tom seemed assured. Respect still had to be won, but Kate's fair treatment of the Barlows had been well received and Ellen reported the kitchen gossip that Susan Barlow had become Kate's staunchest defender to any doubters remaining in the village.

The full impact of Kate's influence came at the first market at Kidderminster following her arrival. For the first time in years, the Seven Ways tenantry received the full price for their stock. Kate attended in person and Colonel Price greeted the new mistress of Seven Ways with a polite doffing of his hat and a bow. For the time being, anyway, it seemed he was not willing to earn the enmity of a personal friend of the Fairfaxes.

The months began to roll into each other as Kate grew in confidence and asserted control over the estate. There always seemed to be some new problem, some knot to unravel, and some plausible reason to stay on a few more weeks.

Conscious of her promise to her sister, Kate wrote to Suzanne and told her that while she still planned to return to Yorkshire before winter, she could see no way to come earlier as there was too much to do before she would be content to leave Seven Ways in Jacob's capable hands.

CHAPTER 18

$\mathcal{A}$s summer drifted into a fine, hot August, Jacob Howell sought Kate out to discuss the matter of the harvest with her. The crops were ready and it seemed foolish not to make the most of the fine weather. To Nell's horror, Kate insisted that every member of the household assist with the harvest.

'Kate, I simply can't,' Nell protested. 'It will ruin my hands.'

Kate had no sympathy to spare. 'I'm sorry, Nell,' she said. 'Everyone is to help, and that includes us. There are simply not enough hands for this task.'

Dressed in an old gown and a wide-brimmed straw hat, Nell made a grudging appearance the next morning. She scowled at the summer sun, already fierce and promising a warm day.

'This will be death to my complexion,' she complained. 'Are you sure I can't help with the food?'

'No,' said Kate. 'That is a job for the old and infirm. We need every able-bodied person out here if we are to get the harvest in while the weather is fine.'

As she trailed after the rest of the party, Nell's appearance at the first field created some amusement among the tenants and villagers who had gathered to help. Nell smiled as graciously as she could, and casting a last despairing look at Kate's implacable face, she followed the reapers into the field, their allocated task being the gathering of the straw into stooks.

After two days of handling the coarse straw, Kate's hands were raw and her face and arms pink from the sun. On the third day, they had reached the fields closest to the hall and as the sun moved toward midday, Kate straightened and eased her aching back, grateful for the sight of the party coming from the direction of the hall with baskets of food and jugs of cold ale.

Nell subsided to the ground in the shade of a tree, fanning her face with her hat. Kate handed her a beaker of ale and a hunk of bread and cheese and sat down beside her.

Young Sam Barlow stood a little way off, chatting to Master Knowles' pretty daughter. He broke off and turned to Kate, his eyes wide.

'Troopers, Mistress. Yon.'

His announcement provoked a murmur of disquiet from the other tenants and workers. Troopers were an unpleasant memory from the past and meant only one thing: trouble.

Kate stood up and squinted into the sun. Sam's sharp eyes were not wrong. A body of about fifteen horsemen was riding up the lane towards the house, the sun glinting off breastplates and helmets.

Nell came up beside her, her face puckered with concern. 'Is it Price?' she asked.

Kate shook her head. 'They're not parliament troops.' She squinted into the sun. 'I've never seen such a raggle-taggle collection of horsemen.'

She drew a sharp breath as she recognised a familiar grey horse at the head of the troop.

'Nell,' she said 'I think it may be Jonathan.'

The small band of mounted troops stopped in the forecourt to the house, and old Joseph came out of the gateway to meet them. Jonathan leaned down from his horse to talk to the steward. Joseph pointed toward the fields and Jonathan straightened, and he and another rider broke away, cantering toward the field where the two women waited.

Beneath her sunburn, Nell paled. 'Oh no. It's Giles.' She looked at Kate and held out her dusty skirts and ruined hands. 'Oh, Kate, how could you? This is not how I imagined greeting my husband after four years,' she wailed.

But Kate had eyes only for one man and she didn't care how she looked.

Conscious of the eyes on her, she walked forward to greet the riders, Nell trailing in her wake. As they drew closer she could see both men were dressed in well-worn buff coats and red sashes. Jonathan wore the familiar, low-crowned hat pulled well down as always. His companion sported a more fashionable tall crowned hat with a jaunty red feather beneath which his light brown hair curled to his shoulder.

Jonathan drew rein and Kate placed her hand lightly on Amber's bridle. A cheer went up from the tenantry behind her and Jonathan's name was called as people came forward to greet him.

'Sir Jonathan,' Kate said, conscious of being the centre of attention, 'what brings you to Seven Ways?'

Jonathan bowed from the saddle. He looked tired and thin, but she caught the familiar sparkle in his eye. Her heart leapt in response.

'Mistress Ashley, please pardon this intrusion,' he said. 'We were hoping for some provisions and a bed for the night for some weary soldiers.'

She looked across to the troopers, waiting patiently in the hot sun on the forecourt. She indicated the building they called Long Barn, which had once been the original manor house but was now used to store the hay and was resident to nothing more than bats, rats and owls.

'Tell your men they can rest in the barn. With plenty of new hay, they should be able to make themselves comfortable.'

'Thank you,' Jonathan said. 'It will only be for tonight, you have my word.'

Disappointment tugged at her. Only one night? Another snatched moment in time?

'This I take it is the incomparable Mistress Ashley, of whom I only hear high praise,' Jonathan's companion interposed.

Jonathan looked around and inclined his head.

'My apologies,' he said. 'Mistress Katherine Ashley, Giles, Lord Longley.'

Kate curtsied and Giles inclined his head but his eyes were only for his wife who had hung back while Kate greeted the riders.

'Is that you, Nell?' Giles pushed his hat back. 'Here I was thinking that there was a pretty maid and damn me she turns out to be my wife.'

He dismounted easily from his horse and took Nell in his arms, kissing her with a passion that drew whoops and cheers from the onlookers. There could be no such reunion between Kate and Jonathan. They would have to wait for the privacy of the house.

Jacob Howell, arriving late on the scene from the other fields, greeted Jonathan warmly. Barely raising his quiet voice, he ordered everyone back to work. The reapers turned and trailed back to the fields with dragging feet, whispering among themselves.

Jonathan looked down at Kate. 'I must see to my men.'

She nodded. They both had duties to be seen to before there would be time for them.

Jonathan turned his horse, cantering back to his men. Giles followed on foot, the reins of his horse looped around one arm and his other arm around his wife.

Kate turned to Jacob Howell.

'Jacob, see this field is finished, and then everyone can take a break,' Kate said. 'I must return to the house and see there are supplies for Sir Jonathan and his men.'

He nodded. 'Of course, Mistress Ashley,' he replied.

Kate walked slowly back to the house, composing herself and rehearsing the words she longed to say to the man she loved... her secret lover.

Jonathan's troopers had dismounted and were leading their horses toward Long Barn. Any impression of military might proved to be an illusion. To a man, the troopers looked tired and dirty. They wore an assortment of uniforms, carried some decidedly antique weapons and rode every description of nag. They were, as she had observed, a raggle-taggle collection.

In the kitchen, Kate paused to discuss dinner for the family with the cook. Tonight, she decided, they would kill the fatted calf. The prodigals had returned.

Upstairs there was no sign of Nell and Giles and she assumed they had withdrawn to Nell's apartment for some privacy. However, she found Jonathan in the parlour, seated in one of the large, well-cushioned oak chairs, a draught of ale in his hand provided by the faithful Joseph, who hovered at the door with a smile on his face. Tom sat on a stool at Jonathan's feet, hanging on every word as Jonathan recounted the long march south from Scotland.

He broke off and looked up at her entrance.

'Go on,' she said

Kate leaned against the wall by the door and listened. For now, she was content just to observe, take in every detail of his face, still dusty from the road. Her turn would come.

'So where is the King now?' Tom asked.

'Ten miles away, no more. He expects to enter Worcester tomorrow,' Jonathan said casually as if such an occurrence was commonplace.

'Will there be a battle?' Tom asked.

'Yes,' Jonathan said, 'there will be a battle, Tom.'

'Will you win?' The boy's eyes shone in anticipation.

Only Kate, knowing Jonathan so well, detected the momentary hesitation before he replied with a smile, 'God willing, Tom.'

He placed the empty mug down on the table and rose to his feet. 'Now, if you will excuse me, Tom. I have some business to discuss with your mother before we all gather for supper.'

He took Kate by the arm and guided her out of the room, across the hall to the study where he shut the door, locking it behind him. His face gave away nothing but his eyes were bright with suppressed laughter.

Kate stood in the middle of the room and crossed her arms. 'And what business, pray, do you have to discuss with me that requires the door to be locked?'

'This business.'

He drew her into his arms and kissed her with a passion that was only met by her own.

'Are we doomed forever to meet like this? Hurried kisses behind closed doors?' he whispered when they drew apart.

'It seems so.'

Kate held him closer, breathing in the scent of man and horse and the reassuring pulse of his heart beneath her cheek. There was so much to say and this might well be their only chance of privacy, but reluctantly she laid her hands on his chest and took a step back.

'What are you really doing here, Jon?' she asked.

He turned away from her and crossed to the window where he stood looking out at the newly mown fields. 'You heard me tell Tom, the King entered England with a Scottish army about a month ago. Giles and I have come on ahead to try and raise some support for the cause.' He shook his head and his tone was bitter as he continued, 'To little avail. Unless the Welsh can join us at Worcester, this is a battle that will be lost before it is even begun.'

'How many men do you have?' Kate asked.

He turned to face her, leaning back on the window sill. The grim line of Jonathan's mouth spoke more eloquently than his words. 'Barely thirteen thousand to Cromwell's thirty thousand.'

'Why Worcester?'

'It's strategic to Wales and London and well protected by the Severn and the Teme.' He shrugged. 'It's as good a place as any.' He expelled a head sigh. 'The Scots are fighting among themselves. Charles' great childhood friend, the Duke of Buckingham, is behaving like a sulky child because Charles, quite rightly, has refused him the supreme command. And as I predicted, the English are tired of war. Few have flocked to the King's standard and in the middle of this petty squabbling the King tries to remain optimistic, but he is young and buffeted this way and that by his advisers.'

Kate had no comfort to give and none was expected. She cared nothing for the King, the Duke of Buckingham or the Scots. Her only concern was that amidst the conflict to come, he would die. She would lose him, just as she had lost Richard. She wanted to rail against him, hold him here in this locked room where he would be safe, but she knew that those words had to lie unspoken.

'And you? Are you well, Jon?' she asked, changing the subject.

'Well enough,' he said, his hand going to his bad shoulder with a grimace. 'How goes it here, Mistress Ashley? It cannot be easy for you.'

Kate could take some pride in her achievements and she allowed herself a smile. 'Not as bad as I feared, Jon. Thanks to the intervention of your uncle, Nathaniel Freeman, Colonel Price has caused us no trouble and our harvest looks good. We should survive into next year unless of course, you plan to abscond with our winter supplies?'

He shook his head and smiled. 'No, we paid our first call on Longley Abbey and found Colonel Price away from home. We divested Longley Abbey of ample supplies that are now on their way to meet up with the main party. Giles took particular pleasure in relieving the wine cellar of some of its best.'

Despite herself, Kate laughed at the thought of Giles calmly reclaiming his own wine from under the indignant and ruddy nose of Colonel Price. But her humour faded with the realisation that she would be the one that had to face Price's anger and humiliation.

'What have you done? Price will be furious.'

He had the grace to look shamefaced. 'I wish I could say it was all Giles' idea.'

'About Giles. I am looking forward to getting to know him after all I have heard from Nell,' Kate said. 'Does he know about us?'

Jonathan shook his head. 'I haven't told him, or at least not in so many words, but Giles knows me as well as anyone living so I can't answer for what he may have surmised. Kate, enough talk, come here and kiss me again.'

He caught her hand and pulled her toward him. His eyes, smoky with desire, narrowed and he bent his head to kiss her.

A knock on the door and Ellen's voice interrupted them. 'Cook needs you in the kitchen.'

Kate leaned her head against his chest. 'I must go. I fear I am making loaves and fishes to feed the five thousand this evening. I want this meal to be special. We have had so little cause for celebration in the last months.'

Jonathan bowed. 'Then on no account, delay, Mistress Ashley. I am ravenous.'

Unlocking the door, he stood aside to let Kate pass.

FROM HIS SEAT at the head of the table, Jonathan sat back, a glass of Colonel Price's excellent wine in his hand, and surveyed the people gathered around him. Just for a night, they could forget the world that gathered outside the door. Just for the night, they could be young and carefree without trouble or care.

Giles, as always, was the centre of attention with his fund of stories; Tom had been laughing so hard there were tears in his eyes; Nell, so willing to forgive her philandering husband, sat with one hand on his arm as if she feared he would vanish any moment. and Kate...

His eyes lingered on her serene oval face. She wore a gown fashioned from the sky blue fabric they had purchased at the Selby fair, a long year ago. Her thick honey-coloured hair fell around her face in soft ringlets and every time she glanced at him she radiated happiness.

He longed to reach down the length of the table and gather her in his arms. He ached for this one night together but there was a cost. She had come willingly to his bed and he had taken what she offered without thought of consequence.

A dark memory speared his consciousness. He, more than

anyone, understood those consequences. What if he died in the coming conflict, leaving her with a bastard child? Another life destroyed?

'Jonathan?' Kate's voice cut through his maudlin thoughts.

He forced a smile.

'Music, Giles,' he said. 'Nell, oblige us?'

Nell sat down at the ancient and tuneless virginals that gathered dust in a corner of the hall and opened the lid. She looked across at her brother.

'Only if you sing, Jon,' she said.

Jonathan's set down his wine glass and feigning horror, he said, 'Me? My dear sister, you know perfectly well I cannot hold a tune.'

'Liar,' interjected Giles, draining the last bottle of wine into his glass. 'Kate, he regularly serenades the lovely demoiselles.'

'And look at the result,' pointed out Jonathan. 'When they have stopped laughing, some other man has whisked them away.'

Kate smiled. 'I would have to agree,' she said. 'I've only heard him sing once and 'twas not a pretty sound. You and Giles give us a song, Nell.'

The Longleys obliged with a charming duet, remembered from happier days, and Jonathan stood next to Kate, catching her hand and entwining their fingers in the hidden folds of her skirts.

As it grew late Tom struggled to keep his eyes open and, without much prodding from his mother, made his way to bed. Giles leaned over the virginals and whispered in Nell's ear. A high colour rose in her cheeks and with her husband's arm over her shoulders they wandered slowly out of the room.

Kate and Jonathan were alone. He laid his hand on her shoulder and turned her around to face him. He cupped her face in his hands and kissed her gently on the forehead.

'And is it time for us?' Her voice sounded tight, her eyes bright.

'If that is what you wish.'

She nodded. 'You will be gone tomorrow.' The unspoken fear radiated from her.

'Go ahead,' he said. 'I will be with you presently.'

Jonathan checked on his men, made sure the guard had been set for the night and wrote a dispatch.

Outside the door to Kate's bedchamber, he hesitated. Another stolen night, a brief respite from the troubles that lay ahead. Once again he wrestled with his conscience, wondering after all if it would be better to seek his own bed but the thought lingered only a moment and he put his hand to the door catch.

Kate waited for him, curled up in a chair by the open window, wearing nothing but a soft linen shift, her hair loose around her shoulders. The soft summer night stole into the room and as he entered she looked around at him, her eyes shining in the candlelight.

'All done for the night?' she asked.

He nodded. 'The world is at peace, for the moment.'

He crossed over to her and she rose from her chair to face him.

'Kate,' he said, 'I wanted to give you something.'

He took her hand and dropped the heavy gold signet ring Sir Francis had given him on the last visit into her palm, closing her fingers over it.

He smiled apologetically. 'I'm sorry I have nothing else. All the family jewellery is long gone. Look after it for me. I hope when I come to claim it I may be able to exchange it for one more fitting your hand.'

She opened the small, carved box that sat on her dressing table and selected a gold chain. Slipping the ring onto it, she returned to him and he fastened it around her neck.

'I will wear it next to my heart,' she said.

He took her in his arms and carried her over to her bed. 'One night, my dearest love,' he whispered as he buried his face in her hair. 'It seems that once again, that is all we have.'

'Then let's not waste it,' she replied, wrapping her arms around his neck and smiling into his eyes.

CHAPTER 19

*A*t first light, Kate and Nell, still in their nightgowns, stood by the window of Kate's chamber watching the men assemble on the forecourt. Kate had seen this sight before... soldiers preparing for battle, silent except for the chink of harness and the nickering of horses.

Jonathan had decided to leave Amber and taken one of the older horses from the stable. As he swung into the saddle, he looked up at the window where the women watched and raised a hand. He flicked his fingers to the brim of his hat before turning away. Giles, in characteristic style, swept them a low, courtly bow from his saddle, with a flourish of his feathered hat and then they were gone.

The two women stood in silence, watching until the last of the troopers had rounded the bend and disappeared from view and the sun had risen on another hot day. They did not need to speak. Their thoughts were the same as those of so many women who had watched their men ride away to battle.

When, if ever, would they see them again?

Kate turned away from the window as dull, empty loneliness settled on her. She sat down on the edge of the bed, trying to summon the energy to dress and face the day.

Nell sat down beside her and took her hand. 'Kate, why didn't you tell me about you and Jonathan?' she asked.

Kate started as if Nell had hit her. She thought they had maintained an excellent pretence of mere acquaintance. The heat rose in her cheeks and she swallowed.

'How did you know?'

Nell smiled. 'Well, my virtuous widow Ashley, it is plain that two people have slept in this bed and besides, Giles told me. Even if he hadn't I would have guessed. Kate, I have never, and I repeat never, seen my brother look at a woman the way he does at you.'

Relief washed over Kate. Like a young girl with her first love, she now had someone with whom she could share the confidence. Only she wasn't a young girl and her lover was riding away to possible death.

'In truth, Nell,' she admitted, 'I think I loved him from our first meeting.'

Nell smiled. 'You are well suited.' The smile vanished and she frowned. 'But are you wise to take him to your bed? Were I to be with child, there would be no questions, but you...we rely on you and your virtue. A Thornton bastard would not sit well with the likes of Colonel Price.'

Kate bit her lip. The same fear had crossed her mind. Common sense told her that she had been a fool to allow Jonathan into her bed, but she found when she was with him, common sense evaporated.

She yearned to feel his hard body against her and to experience the intimacy only two people in love can ever really know - something she had never thought to find again. Her hand moved to her belly. What if she was with child?

She hungered for a child— Jonathan's child— but Nell was right, no one would believe an immaculate conception had occurred.

She straightened her shoulders.

'I intend to shut up Seven Ways and return to Yorkshire by Christmas. If, and God willing it will not come to anything, then no one here needs ever know.'

Now she had Nell's confidence she could ask the question that still nagged at her and that she had not broached with Jonathan since that first night.

'Nell, what do you know of a woman called Mary?'

'Mary?'

'She had some connection with Jonathan, a long time ago.'

'Oh, that Mary.' Nell frowned. 'That was years ago, before the war, when he was at Oxford. He came home one day and told Father he intended to marry this girl. She was, I think, the daughter of one of the dons. I remember now. Her father was a Puritan. Zounds, Father was furious. He forbade the union. There was the most terrible row, but then most discussions with Jonathan and Father always ended in a terrible row.'

'Was that it?'

'As far as I know,' Nell said. 'It was all over long before the war. He's not still pining for her, is he?'

'She's dead,' Kate said.

Nell shrugged. 'Well then, she is hardly a rival for his affections now.'

'No,' Kate agreed, although some instinct told her that while Mary might not be a rival for his affections, she still lingered as a ghost in his memory.

The King's headquarters had been at Oxford; perhaps the friendship had been reignited during the war years? Whatever part Mary had played in his life, it went beyond a mere youthful infatuation.

'Jonathan does not give his heart easily, Kate. It may well be that this Mary and you are the only women he has ever loved. There are some men, like Giles, who love women and there are some, like Jonathan, who are loved by women. That is just the way of the world and for what it's worth, I think it's wonderful. Will you marry him? If you do, we'll be sisters.'

'Nell.' Kate raised a protesting hand and glanced at the window. 'Jonathan has just ridden away to fight a lost cause. We have no future to contemplate and if I allow myself to believe there is such a future, I will only end up like you, pining for a man I cannot have. I am a fool for even letting Jonathan into my heart.'

And into my bed.

Nell's mouth drooped, and Kate instantly regretted her thoughtless words. 'I'm sorry, Nell. I did not mean that to sound the way it did.'

Nell looked away with tears glistening on her lashes. 'No, you're right. Unless they prevail, there is not much future for any of us, is there?'

CHAPTER 20

Jonathan caught up with the King's forces only a couple of miles from Worcester. As he and Giles approached the King, the Duke of Buckingham waylaid them.

'Where have you been?' snarled Buckingham. 'His Majesty thought you had deserted.'

'I doubt that,' said Jonathan under his breath. 'Did you not get the supplies we sent on, kindly donated by the good man in occupation of Longley Abbey?'

'That did not answer my question,' Buckingham responded.

'We spent the night with our family,' Jonathan answered quietly.

Buckingham's lip curled into a sneer and he shifted his gaze to Giles. 'A night with the good lady wife, Longley? That should put you in good stead for the next few days. You had best hope you've not given her the pox.'

Giles's characteristic good humour evaporated and he lunged

forward, his hand on the hilt of his sword, the colour high in his cheeks. Only Jonathan's restraining hand on the bridle of his horse stopped him from running Buckingham through.

'He's not worth it,' Jonathan said.

Buckingham turned his sharp eyes on Jonathan. 'And you, Thornton? Who keeps your bed warm at night? Rumour would have it that you no longer find women to your favour?'

Jonathan's eyes narrowed. 'Perhaps, my lord, I am somewhat particular about what I share my bed with. I am certainly not so desperate as to take anything as ill-favoured as that which you made your bed mate in Perth.'

This time Buckingham's hand shot to his sword but a low chuckle behind him stayed him.

'Well said, Thornton.'

The King rode towards them, looking every inch a monarch, splendidly dressed with the Order of St George hanging around his neck. He smiled broadly, evidently in good spirits and jubilant at the thought of his entry into the loyal city whose gates stood open before them. He had borne so much in his short life that sometimes it was easy to forget that this princeling was only twenty-one. At that age there is still hope, Jonathan thought.

'It's a fine morning, gentlemen,' he said, 'and Worcester awaits us.' He pointed south to where the square turret of the mighty cathedral rose from the surrounding landscape.

'It is indeed, Your Majesty.' Jonathan bowed from the saddle.

'This is your country, Thornton, is it not?' The King looked around the pleasant, rolling countryside and took a deep breath as if English air was the sweetest scent on earth.

'It is, Your Majesty. Longley and I come from near Kidderminster and I confess we took the opportunity to visit with family last night.'

'As is your right,' the King said. 'Would we have the same joy to anticipate, but—'

Jonathan sensed the man's pain. Charles carried deep grief from the death of his sister Elizabeth, who had died a prisoner in Carisbrooke Castle only a year earlier.

He recovered himself and, raising himself in his stirrups, pushed his hat to the back of his head and addressed the assembled troops. 'On to Worcester. Where we will rest and await our loyal subjects.'

'Or Cromwell. Whoever reaches us first,' Giles muttered under his breath to Jonathan as the King cantered forward with Buckingham trailing in his wake.

The gates of Worcester stood wide and the townspeople turned out in force to welcome home their King. Fine words were spoken by the mayor, and the King, for one brief moment, lived out the sad parody of his birthright.

ONCE THE ROYALIST forces were in occupation, work began immediately in re-fortifying the city. The bridges to the south were destroyed, denying access to the city from the east. The earthworks, thrown up during the earlier conflict, were re-dug and the walls reinforced. Jonathan busied himself where he could with organising the strengthening of Fort Royal, a former stronghold that had fallen into ruin in the intervening years of quasi-peace.

Despite the King's tireless optimism, there was no disguising the utter weariness of the largely Scots army and the dispirited and desperate air of its commanders. The news came that the Earl of Derby, landing from the continent with badly needed troops, had encountered Parliamentarian forces in a battle outside

Wigan. He barely escaped with his life, let alone any men to rein-
force the forces waiting at Worcester.

In worse news, Cromwell, who had followed the Scots Army
south, had met up with Lambert and they were closing in on the
city from the south. Despite the best efforts of the Royalists, the
bridge at Upton had not been completely destroyed and Lambert
took Upton without difficulty, pushing back the Scots and giving
his troops free access to the west bank of the Severn.

The King decreed that all loyal subjects were to gather at a
field called Pitchencroft just outside the city on the 26th of
August. Barely a soul came to the assembly and that night the
King sat in the large, pleasant house on the outskirts of the town,
ironically named 'The Commandery', sunk in the harsh realiza-
tion that his only resource remained the Scots. The English had
abandoned him to his fate.

He attended the meetings at the Commandery and concluded
the house had been wrongly named. He saw precious little
evidence of command taking place within its walls. In the endless
councils that took place in the hall, the young King found himself
assailed from all sides by conflicting advice. One man suggested
that they attempt to break out and make for London, another that
a foray for new supplies should be made.

Jonathan sat back and listened to the exchange, his long
fingers beating an impatient tattoo on the arm of his chair. He
had been a soldier long enough to recognise the virtue of a
strategic withdrawal. In Wales, they stood a chance of bolstering
their forces and drawing Cromwell to a fight on unfamiliar terri-
tory, although that particular tactic had not worked well in Scotland. When pressed for input, his suggestion that they abandon
their position and make for Wales was howled down and he
found himself accused of cowardice.

While Cromwell with his thirty thousand troops came closer

every day, the interminable, inconclusive councils went on. August turned to September and Cromwell now had the city under bombardment from guns positioned to the east at Red Hill. The general himself sat at Evesham, waiting.

CHAPTER 21

*A*nother evening at the Commandery had ended in bickering and Jonathan trudged wearily back up Friers Street to his billet. Tomorrow would be the third of September, exactly one year since Dunbar. Cromwell was known to be a superstitious man and his incredible deliverance at Dunbar would point auspiciously to another success if the battle were to be brought on the same day.

In the downstairs parlour of the large, half-timbered house, Giles played cards with Kit Lovell, who had recently rejoined them. They were both fiendish card players, with a tendency to cheat, and Jonathan declined their invitation to join them.

He left orders with his orderly that he was only to be disturbed if Cromwell attacked, undid his sword belt, took off his boots and fell still fully clothed onto his bed. Despite his utter weariness, sleep did not come easily as he played out the events of the morrow. The outcome of the battle seemed a foregone conclusion and death— his death— seemed inevitable.

He had not been deliberately careless of his life in the past, but he had known that while his family would grieve, his death would have been viewed without surprise. Now there were people in his life who would mourn him and he knew with utter certainty that he did not want to die.

When sleep came he dreamed of Kate in deepest mourning, weeping. He woke with a start and lay awake staring at the dusty bed hanging above him, the sweat prickling his forehead and his breath coming in short gasps as if he had been running.

For the first time in his life, Jonathan Thornton admitted to himself that he was afraid.

He rose and pulled his boots back on. Downstairs in the parlour, Giles and Kit Lovell still played cards. Jonathan pulled up a chair, and Giles dealt him a hand.

'Can't sleep?' Giles asked.

'No.' Jonathan scowled at the cards. 'Christ, Lovell, did you deliberately deal me this hand or are you determined to take every last coin I own?'

Kit Lovell placed a hand over his heart. 'Thornton, you wound me. You take the cards as they are dealt.'

So true, Jonathan thought as he set out his wager.

'Can I join you?'

The men looked up at the youngster who had entered the room. He could not have been more than seventeen or eighteen and wore an unlaced buff leather coat that had been made for a much larger man and seen considerable wear.

'Only if you have a large purse and a resignation to losing,' Jonathan said. 'These two are notorious at cards.'

The boy pulled up a stool beside Lovell.

'I thought I told you to get some sleep,' Lovell said tersely, addressing the boy, without looking at him.

'Belong to you, does he?' Giles said.

'My brother, Daniel,' Lovell waved a hand at Giles and Jonathan. 'Viscount Longley, Colonel Thornton.'

Giles rolled his eyes. 'What in God's name did you bring him for, Lovell?' he said.

Lovell cast his brother a glance that was at once both reproving and affectionate.

'He followed me,' Lovell replied. 'His mother will hold me responsible if anything happens to him and, God knows, I fear her wrath more than Cromwell, but what could I do?'

'This may be my last chance,' the boy said returning his brother's look with a furrowed brow.

'Your last chance for what?' Giles asked. 'Getting yourself killed?'

'My last chance to return the King to the throne where he belongs,' Daniel's eyes shone with an idealism that had long since escaped Jonathan.

Lovell laid his cards down and fixed his brother with a hard look. 'You don't see do you?' he said. 'You're the last of us with any hope. Look at us...' He waved his hand at the men seated around the table. 'If we lose this battle, what future do we have? But you... you can still make something of your life.'

Daniel looked from one to the other. 'You were my age when you went to war, all of you.'

'True,' Giles conceded.

'But we had hope,' Jonathan said.

'We're not going to lose.' Daniel declared. 'We are the guardians of the crown. We'll fight for the King and glory and honour,' he continued, oblivious to the cynical silence of his audience.

Jonathan considered the boy for a moment, seeing himself in the youthful romanticism of a cause in which he had believed so passionately, but wanting desperately to prevent the futile loss of another life.

'Daniel, war has nothing to do with glory and honour,' he said and leaned forward, fixing the boy with a hard gaze. 'Have you ever smelt the stench of death? Have you ever seen a man with his guts hanging out and still living or a man with his face shot away? Have you watched a friend die of gangrene?'

Jonathan knew his words were brutal, and Daniel paled and swallowed. But he met Jonathan's gaze.

'I was there when they took and burned our home,' the young man said. 'I saw men die. I saw my father killed.' He glanced at his brother. 'He died in Kit's arms. So, yes, I have seen death.'

Lovell laid down his cards and put a hand on his brother's shoulder. He said in a gentle tone, 'Dan, there'll be a battle tomorrow and you'll be more use to us well rested. Go upstairs and see what sleep you can get. I'll not be long.'

The boy set his hand of cards down on the table. 'Tomorrow?'

'For certes,' Giles said without raising his eyes from his cards.

Daniel looked at his brother who nodded. 'Tomorrow,' Lovell repeated.

'Then you're right I should try and rest, but I don't think I will sleep,' Daniel said. He stood and bowed.

'Do that, lad,' Giles said. 'Tomorrow is going to be a busy day.'

CHAPTER 22

SEPTEMBER 3 1651, WORCESTER

*J*onathan awoke to the sound of bombardment from Cromwell's guns. With practice born of long experience, he was dressed and ready and halfway down the stairs as Giles emerged still half asleep.

They encountered Kit Lovell, fully dressed and armed, at the door. Beside him, his brother, Daniel, looked impossibly young in his borrowed buff coat and unfamiliar breastplate and helmet, but he had colour in his face and his eyes gleamed with excitement. He smiled broadly at Jonathan's peremptory greeting.

Guardians of the crown indeed, Jonathan thought.

'The word is that Cromwell is throwing bridges of boats across the Teme and the Severn,' Lovell said. 'He's going to split his force.'

Jonathan nodded. He understood what that meant. They would be attacked from two sides and they did not have the strength to repel such an attack.

He clapped the boy on the shoulder. 'Ready, lad?'

Daniel nodded, his helmet slipping down into his eyes.

Jonathan glanced at Kit Lovell and saw the moment of unguarded desperation in his friend's face. Kit Lovell would have given anything to have the boy as far from the battle as he could. But this was not the time for sentimentality. Daniel Lovell had made his choice, just as his brother had ten years earlier.

'This is it, gentlemen.' Lovell loosened his sword and stepped into the street. He looked back at them and tipped his fingers to his hat in salute. 'God be with us all this day.'

As soldiers dashed to their positions, the Scots' guns on Fort Royal answered Cromwell's guns on Red Hill. Jonathan and Giles strode off down Friers Street in the direction of the cathedral where the King would have taken up his position.

They found the King very much awake and eager for the fray. He leaned on the wall of the cathedral tower with a telescope trained on the action well to the south of the city. From this vantage point, he had a clear view of all points of the compass.

He handed Jonathan the telescope but even without it, Jonathan could see that, as Lovell had said, Cromwell had divided his forces; a manoeuvre that went against every precept of war. Half the troops had been set to cross the river and were engaged in constructing the bridge of boats to the south of the city. The other half waited on the heights of Perry Wood to the east of the city.

Jonathan scanned the fields for the King's forces. He could see part of the Scots army to the south, strongly positioned behind hedgerows, apparently waiting for the boat bridges to be completed and the army of Parliament to cross. The bulk of the King's forces remained within the city walls.

'What do you think?' the King asked.

Jonathan looked around at the surly faces of those older and more experienced than he. 'I think,' he said slowly, 'that Cromwell is at his most vulnerable whilst he is crossing those bridges. Attack now and attack fast and we could push them back.'

'Your Majesty is advised to wait,' the thick Scottish burr of General Leslie interposed. 'My men will hold them back at the hedges.'

Other voices chimed in with more suggestions, and with dull resignation, Jonathan retreated to where Giles propped against the wall, enjoying a rough breakfast of bread and cheese.

'The day is lost even before it has begun,' Jonathan said in a low voice, accepting the food Giles handed him. For once Giles did not have a sharp rejoinder. His eyes met Jonathan's in silent agreement.

Cromwell crossed the river without interference and by early afternoon all the Parliament forces had completed the crossing. Incredibly they were able to muster themselves for the first attack without hindrance from the King's forces who watched on as the enemy gathered against them.

When the attack came, to their credit, the Scots resisted stoutly, forcing Cromwell to deploy more of his men to assist in the fighting, depleting his force to the east. A cheer went up from the watchers on the cathedral as they saw the Parliamentary troops begin to waver.

'Your Majesty now is your chance.' The Earl of Derby leaned forward. 'If we could sally out and take the guns on Red Hill, this battle could yet turn to our advantage.'

The King looked from one of his advisors to the other and for once they were all in agreement.

'I will lead the men myself,' the King declared. 'Horse or foot?'

'Foot will be more effective.' Derby's response was assented to with a nod of heads.

The King turned to the Scottish general. 'Leslie, keep your horse in reserve and press home the advantage.'

'As Your Majesty orders.' Leslie bowed low and was gone, his boots clattering on the tower's stone steps.

Looking around his assembled officers Charles squared his shoulders. 'Well, gentlemen, to the fray.'

As is always the way with war, the inactivity in the city gave way to frantic commotion as the King's men flooded out of Sidbury Gate. Covered by the Royalist guns on Fort Royal they charged, on foot, up Red Hill towards the Parliamentary guns.

All that long, hot afternoon the Royalists pushed onwards; pike against pike, muskets used as clubs. Jonathan and Giles stayed with the King and his officers in the thick of the charge and it seemed that the objective would be in reach.

Honed by the years of combat, they formed a familiar partnership. They had fought at each other's shoulders and knew the nuances of battle. Once the action began there was no time for fear or any thought except survival and the need to trust the man beside you.

The Lovell brothers, on their left, likewise fought side by side. Despite Kit's misgivings, Daniel, now bareheaded and bleeding from a cut beneath his right eye, acquitted himself with all the skill of a man who had seen battle before. His sword flashed in the hot sun, his face streaked with blood, dirt and sweat.

By late afternoon, Cromwell and his cavalry recrossed the river to attack the defenders on the hill in the flank. Cromwell's superb cavalry hit fast and brutally. The exhausted and insufficiently armed Royalists were no match against the heavily armed and highly efficient cavalry. The King called for Leslie's horse but none came. Leslie, it seemed, had failed his King completely.

As any hope of the King rallying his men disappeared in the face of Cromwell's horsemen. As the full force of the cavalry broke the royalist lines, Jonathan found himself alone on the battlefield.

The King's safety became paramount, and he scoured the faces around him looking for the King.

'Daniel!'

Hearing Kit Lovell's voice, Jonathan turned and saw his friend standing in the path of a Parliament trooper who bore down on him from behind with his sword upraised. Of Lovell's brother, there was no sign.

Summoning all his energy, Jonathan managed to reach Lovell and push him aside just as the trooper slashed down with his sword. The razor-sharp blade caught Jonathan across the back of his hand, slashing through the heavy leather of his glove.

Lovell regained his feet and clutched at Jonathan's sleeve.

'I can't find Daniel.'

Before Jonathan could respond, the same trooper turned, pulling his pistol from his belt. He fired and Kit crumpled to the ground

Seizing a primed pistol from a dead Scot at his feet, Jonathan fired. The trooper's face exploded in a mass of blood and the man toppled, screaming, from his horse.

Jonathan stooped down to see to Lovell, who had taken the pistol ball in the leg and now lay helpless on the trampled grass, his face a rictus of agony.

'Go!' Lovell said. 'Don't worry about me. Save the King. If you find Daniel—'

Giles grabbed Jonathan's arm and pulled him away from the fallen man.

'Thornton, there's no time. We must find the King and get back to the city,' Giles yelled above the noise.

Abandoning Kit Lovell to his fate, they forced their way through the heaviest of the fighting to the centre of the fray where the King still tried to rally his men.

'It's hopeless, Your Majesty. We must flee,' Giles said.

Charles looked from one to the other, reading his defeat in their faces. He glanced toward the illusory safety of the city walls and nodded.

They ran, tumbling down the hill with Cromwell's troopers bearing down relentlessly upon them.

His breath searing in his throat, Jonathan ran with the others. The guns on Fort Royal thundered impotently as the scattered remains of the King's Army converged on Sidbury Gate through which they had left in such high hopes only a few hours earlier.

The Parliament guns had been brought to bear on the gate, turning the retreat into wholesale slaughter. Amidst the screaming of man and beast, the carnage of blood and guts and shots pounding into the walls and the city, the King managed to get back through the gate. Jonathan followed through the confusion, scrambling over an overturned oxen cart to reach his King.

Charles called for a horse and, stripping off his amour, rode among his panicking men, urging them on. He was an inspirational sight but it was too late. The Duke of Hamilton's men had nothing left and Leslie had failed them completely. Behind them, Fort Royal fell and the victorious Parliamentarians turned their guns on the city.

Cromwell's exultant troops were at the gates and the King's men could not even be rallied to shut the gate against the invaders.

Jonathan and Giles fought shoulder to shoulder, protecting their King, but after a hard day, they were exhausted. Lord Wilmot, one of the King's closest advisers, hatless and dirty, tugged at Jonathan's sleeve.

'Thornton.' Wilmot shouted above the noise, his voice dry and hoarse. 'You know this country; we have to get the King away.'

'Go, Jon,' Giles rasped. 'I'll cover your retreat.'

As much as he hated leaving Giles, the King was the priority and Jonathan turned and ran after Wilmot who was almost lost in the fleeing men who converged on Friers Street. He took only one look back to see Giles, fighting like a virago, a small defence against the mass of red-coated soldiers who now flooded into the city from all gates except one: St Martin's Gate stood close by the King's lodging and remained as yet unbreached. The only chance for escape would be through that gate.

They found the King within his lodgings, watching uncomprehendingly as Buckingham burned papers on a hastily lit fire.

'We must go, Your Majesty,' Wilmot said.

The King looked up at his old friend and advisor. 'Leslie will come,' he insisted. 'We will rally again.'

'No, Your Majesty,' Buckingham spoke. 'It's too late. Leslie has failed us, Hamilton is fallen. We must away while we still have breath in our bodies.'

The noise of the fighting, drawing closer up the street, brought the King to his feet. With the Parliament's soldiers at the front door of the house, the King and his party left by the back.

Taking the nearest horses they fled, at a hard gallop, through St Martin's Gate, the gate that led the way to the north.

CHAPTER 23

Kate threw open her window to let the morning air into her chamber. It promised to be a humid and oppressive day and she stood at her window looking out over the newly mown fields while she turned her mind to the tasks of the day. She had slept badly and a crushing sense of impending doom, which she attributed to the weather, weighed on her.

As she turned away from the window, a distant sound like a roll of thunder carried on the still air, causing the breath to stop in her throat. She knew that sound. She had heard it before, seven years ago, when the King and Parliament had met at Marston Moor, barely a few miles from Barton.

Guns.

Her mouth dry, she closed the window and leaned against the wall beside it, tears pricking at the back of her eyes.

As the day wore on Kate failed to settle into any task. It was as if, with each beat of the guns, a thunderstorm hung over the house, ominous and brooding and full of threat but yet to break.

By afternoon she sought out Nell, who had pleaded a headache brought on by the warm weather and kept to her chamber.

Nell sat by the open window, gazing out, her lips moving, her hands moving across the beads of a rosary.

Nell looked up quickly and her hands fell still. 'There, did you hear? Is that guns? It seems to have been going all day.'

Kate nodded. 'Yes. Once you hear that sound you never forget it.'

'You've heard it before?'

'Marston Moor,' Kate replied. 'Richard…' Her mouth went dry at the memory of that awful day. 'David Ashley brought Richard home that night.'

Nell placed her hand on Kate's in empathy. 'Perhaps if we pray?' she suggested.

Kate nodded and they clasped each other's hands in silent prayer. Catholic or Protestant, it made no difference. It seemed such a small, ineffectual gesture but it brought some measure of comfort.

Anxious to distract herself, Kate picked up the rosary beads, weighing them in her hands. 'I know nothing about the Catholic faith,' she admitted.

Nell allowed herself to smile. 'Except that we should be banished or burned?'

Kate shook her head. 'No, I believe everyone has a right to practice whatever faith they profess,' she said.

'Well that's very liberal-minded of you, Kate, but you belong to a perfect world that does not exist.' Nell could not conceal the trace of bitterness in her voice. 'Did you know the Thorntons maintained their Catholicism until Sir Francis' grandfather considered it politically expedient to be otherwise?'

'Ah, the first baronet,' mused Kate, who had become well

schooled in the Thornton family history. 'Darling of Queen Bess. Maybe he grew weary of concealing the priests?'

Nell's eyebrows rose in surprise. 'Do you know about the priest holes?'

Kate nodded. 'Tom made it his business to find them. He showed me four of them. Is that a sufficient number for one priest?'

The priest holes, Kate had discovered, were ingenious but uncomfortable hiding places. Two of them were barely large enough for Tom. One, from the closet in what had been Sir Francis' room and was now Tom's room, formed part of the kitchen chimney and must have got rather warm for the poor priest. As he faced a fiercer fire if he was discovered, the discomfort must have been worth it. However the fourth, in the room she used as a study, seemed to be slightly larger and better concealed than the others; it would certainly fit a grown man with more ease and a modicum of comfort. She wondered with a shiver whether her sudden thought of the priest holes presaged a need for them.

The guns boomed again. The cold memories clawed at her heart, and tears welled in her eyes. She turned away from Nell to hide her distress. The memory of Richard's broken body had now become intrinsically tied up with the present, and in her imagination, she now saw Jonathan, dead or dying, among the carnage of the battlefield. Unlike Nell, she knew the cost of a battle and the terrible injuries that could kill a man.

Even as darkness fell, the echo of the guns still came faintly through the open casements.

As the women sat for their supper, Nell, ever optimistic, said, 'Perhaps there is victory?'

'If there is it will not be the King's.'

'Is that what Jonathan thought?' Nell asked, and Kate nodded.

Nell sighed. 'I did hope…I have prayed that there may be a chance…' Her voice choked on the words.

Kate took her friend's hand. 'No, Nell, this was the very last chance they had and it was such a slender one. There will be no King on the throne of England tonight.'

Nell stood up. 'I think I will see to Ann,' she said, her voice catching as tears trickled down her cheek.

Kate went in search of Tom, whom she had last seen working on his lessons in the library. She found him in his room, the same chamber that had been his grandfather's. All trace of its previous occupant had been replaced by Tom's childish muddle. Like Nell he sat by the open window, leaning on the sill, his chin on his folded arms.

'That's guns, isn't it, Mother?' he asked rhetorically.

She nodded and he looked up at her

'Will they be all right?'

'I don't know,' she replied, trying to keep her voice calm and neutral. 'Their fate is in God's hands. Come, it's time for bed.'

Even after the rest of the household was in bed, Kate retired to the study. She told herself that she would know if Jonathan were dead, that she would sense it, but her ruthless logic dismissed that notion as folly. She had not 'known' about Richard. Why would it be any different now?

To distract herself, she turned to study the figures for the harvest, but the numbers wavered and tears blurred her eyes. She dried her tears like a child on the sleeves of her dress and forced herself back to the books.

Through the open window, the silence of the night was broken by the distant, unmistakable beat of horses' hoof beats on the Kidderminster road. She sprang to the window, as the hooves skittered on the gravel of the forecourt.

Her heart jumped at the sound of men's voices and she stood

unable to move, facing the study door, following the sound of heavy boots on the stairs and the corridor. She held her breath as the door opened, expelling it in a choking sob as Jonathan stood framed in the doorway, unshaven and dirty, his buff coat streaked and stained. The unmistakable smell of powder and sweat drifted across the few feet of floor that stood between them.

She fell into his arms, pressing her face against the leather of his coat, her fingers meshing in his dark hair, damp with sweat from the hard day's work. They kissed with desperation and relief.

Jonathan pulled away from her. 'My darling girl, I've no time,' he said. 'The King and some of his men are in the kitchen.'

She stared at him. 'The King? The KING? Jonathan, you fool. Why bring him here? This will be the first house they will search.'

Irritation flashed back from his bloodshot eyes. 'Kate, I do not have time for any lectures from you. We will be gone within the hour but we need a respite. We fought and lost and it has been a long and brutal day. Few of us have had any sleep in twenty-four hours. Give us time to gather our thoughts and make some plans.' He held the door open for her. 'Now come and tend to your guests.'

This was an order. The man who stood before her now was not her lover but a soldier giving a command.

He caught her arm as she passed him, and the expression on his face softened. 'Dear heart, I would not have brought danger to this house if it could be helped but the King has fought bravely today and is weary beyond measure. He is young and afraid.'

She looked up at him. 'Giles?'

His face creased in pain. 'I don't know, Kate. Giles stayed to cover our escape. We can only pray that he is a canny enough soldier to look after himself.'

A suppressed gasp came from the stairwell. Nell, dressed in

her nightdress stood in the shadows, her hand over her mouth. She must have heard the last of the exchange. Jonathan took her gently by the shoulders and held her in his arms.

'Nell, I'm sure Giles will be fine.'

She looked up at him, her eyes full of tears. 'But you can't be sure, can you?'

He shook his head and put his arm around her shoulders. 'Go and find some clothes, Nell. We have a kitchen full of tired, hungry men who need the sight of a pretty face to cheer them.'

She turned back up the stairs to her chamber. Seeing the bloodstained remnants of a scarf tied around Jonathan's left hand, Kate caught his hand in hers.

'You're hurt,' she said.

He looked down at his hand as if noticing it for the first time. 'Just a cut, nothing serious,' he said. 'Ellen will be able to patch it in a moment. Come, Kate, we have tarried too long.'

At least a dozen red eyes, filthy men slumped on the benches or leaned against the wall in the kitchen. Roused by the noise, the cook and the kitchen scullions already circulated amongst them with cold pie, bread and cheese and ale while Ellen tended the assorted cuts and scratches.

A tall, dark young man, his face already old beyond his years, stood by the fire, staring into its depths. From his clothes and his demeanour and the deference shown to him by his companions, he could only be the King.

Jonathan presented Kate and she sank into a deep curtsey.

'Mistress Ashley.' A smile lit the King's saturnine face as he held out his hand to raise her as if he were at court and she was a fine lady in a beautiful dress, instead of a plain, ordinary house-wife in a faded russet gown. 'I am grateful for your hospitality. Sir Jonathan has been singing your praises since we so unceremoniously departed the fair city of Worcester.'

As Kate looked into his eyes she knew why these men had been so willing to lay down their lives for this man. They were dark and hooded and they compelled her to meet his gaze as if he searched her soul and had heard her terse words only minutes earlier.

Other introductions were made. Buckingham, Derby, Lauderdale, Wilmot — the names all merged among the faces.

As Ellen seemed preoccupied with more serious wounds, Kate sat down with Jonathan and gently unwound the bloodstained cloth. It may not have been serious but it was still an awkward, nasty cut and would take time to heal.

While she dressed it Jonathan bent his head towards the little man who had been introduced as Lord Wilmot. They talked hurriedly in whispers and Kate made no effort to listen in. It was not in her interest to know their plans.

Someone tugged on her sleeve and she turned to see Tom, half-dressed, with his nightshirt, tucked into his breeches and his hair tousled from the bed.

'Mother, what's happening? Who are these men?' Recognising Jonathan, his face lit up. 'Jonathan!' Tom looked down at Jonathan's bandaged hand. 'Are you hurt again?'

Jonathan laughed and rumpled the boy's hair. 'It's an occupational hazard, Tom. If you've finished, Kate, the boy must meet his King.'

Tom bowed deeply and gravely when he was introduced to the young man by the fire. From somewhere the King produced a smile and took off the Order of St George from around his neck.

'Master Ashley,' he said, 'can you find somewhere in your house where this will be safe until I have need of it?'

Tom flushed red to the roots of his hair and he hugged the precious George against his chest. 'Oh yes, Your Majesty. I'll keep it quite safe. I promise.'

His wound dressed, Jonathan became the commander again. He ordered the others to divest themselves of their heavy armour, which they did, leaving a large pile of metal in the middle of the kitchen.

Jonathan turned to Kate. 'When we are gone, drop all this into the moat and you will never know we have been here.'

IT WAS AGREED that the rescue party would disperse. The King left with Wilmot and several others for a loyal house to the north. The fewer who knew what plans were made for the King's escape the better. Even Buckingham begged the King not to tell them.

One by one they slipped away and now all Kate could do was watch on as Jonathan left her once more. He went to an uncertain fate and she wanted to remonstrate with him, beg him to stay by her side, pleading with him to surrender — anything as long as she knew where he was and that he was alive, but the words would not come out.

Instead, she had to content herself with a last, brief, loving kiss before the night swallowed him up and she and Nell were left alone in the empty courtyard.

They had work to do and after the last helmet and breastplate lay at the bottom of the moat, the two women sat in the kitchen absorbed in their thoughts and too tired to talk. Kate had not seen Tom since the men had left and she assumed he had gone back to bed but as she rose, at last, to go to her bed, he came in from the kitchen yard dirty and smelly and wearing a huge grin on his face.

She looked at him, wrinkling her nose with distaste. 'Tom, where have you been?'

'Hiding the King's medal, as I promised,' he said triumphantly. 'I've put it in a place where they'll never look.'

'Where?' asked Nell.

Kate's nose wrinkled. 'I can guess,' she said. 'You've hidden it in the refuse heap.'

The boy nodded and the women laughed in the knowledge that it would be the last time they would have cause to laugh for many days to come.

CHAPTER 24

*J*onathan decided to head south again, back into the countryside he knew and where he could be assured of loyal friends and in the cold, dark hour before dawn, he led his horse across the deserted stable yard of the Black Cross inn at Bromsgrove.

Jonathan knew this hostelry well. He and Giles had spent many evenings in the congenial warmth of the front parlour under the watchful eye of the innkeeper, Joseph Bramble. Old Joseph had been dead some years now but his son, Harry, still ran the inn and Jonathan trusted Harry with his life.

The stable door opened on well-oiled hinges and he led his weary horse into the stable, securing it in the furthest stall, well concealed by the shadows. The other horses stirred and nickered but did not wake the stable lad, whose stentorian, drunken snoring came from one of the stalls.

He unsaddled the beast and checked it had food and water before looking around for a suitable place of concealment. The beams in the roof were strong enough to provide him with reasonable support if somewhat lacking in comfort. He climbed up one of the stalls and swung himself into the beams. Slats had been laid between the beams to provide some extra storage for hay and he took up a position where he could see the main door of the stable. Well concealed from a casual eye, he allowed himself the luxury of his first real sleep for days.

At daybreak, the stable boy came to life, waking Jonathan. The boy retched into the filthy straw and staggered out into the courtyard. Jonathan heard water being pumped and the sound of splashing before the boy began his morning chores. The presence of an extra horse did not seem to unduly alarm him and Jonathan's faithful mount shared the morning's rations.

As the horses below him munched their straw, Jonathan's stomach rumbled, reminding him that he'd not eaten in over twenty-four hours. He gritted his teeth and set himself to wait. It was well into mid-morning before a familiar face appeared at the stable door looking for the errant stable hand, who had fallen asleep again.

Harry's sister, Sally, had been a cheerful, pretty girl with flaming red hair. If she liked a man she had been more than happy to share her considerable favours and Jonathan had been sixteen when Sally had cast her eyes in his direction. He had been only too happy to follow where she had led.

But those days were long gone. Although she was only a few years older than Jonathan, time had not dealt kindly with her, and he struggled to see a trace of the girl in the large, frowzy woman who stood in the doorway. Sally Bramble now had five children, all with different fathers, and presided over her brother's taproom — a loud, cheerful and formidable presence.

'Sal,' he called down from the rafters in a low voice, not wanting to rouse the sleeping stable boy.

She started and looked up, reaching for a nearby pitchfork.

'Who's there?'

Her concern turned to a grin of delight as Jonathan slid off the rafters and landed ungracefully in the hay below. He stood up and brushed the straw from his clothes, shaking out his cramped limbs.

'I'm getting old, Sal,' he said ruefully.

Sal dropped the pitchfork. 'We all are, love, but I'm right glad to see you.' She threw her arms around him and hugged him tightly.

Jonathan suffered her embrace. For all her faults she had a heart of gold, and he still had an enormous affection for her.

'I need your help, Sal,' he said.

'Aye, I guessed that. I doubt that 'ee would be hiding in my roof in the hope that it was my body you were after,' she said. 'This wouldn't have anything to do with that scrap at Worcester the whole county's in a tizz about?'

He nodded.

'Well, you've picked a fine time to be skulking in my stable. I've a troop of Parliament horse in the front room,' Sal said, looking around as if she expected them to appear. 'You need to stay put until it's a little quieter. I'll send my boy John out to you with something to eat and drink.'

As Jonathan looked up at his perch in the rafters, a movement in the hay made them both start. His hand went to the hilt of his sword and he swung around on his heel, brandishing the weapon. The stable boy, roused by their voices, cowered in alarm at the sword.

Sal laid her hand on his sword arm, forcing him to lower the weapon. 'Don't you mind Abel,' she said and tapped her head. 'He's a bit daft but he'll not give you away. Will you?' She directed the last at the boy, who shook his head. 'Now get back up where you came from and bide your time. That your horse in the far stall?'

Jonathan nodded.

'See to him, Abel. Looks like he needs a good grooming and those cuts seeing to.'

In the daylight, Jonathan could see that the animal he had purloined in the dark was indeed a thoroughbred but there were open cuts on its flanks and legs. The poor beast had been through the battle.

He had no choice but to return to his perch in the roof and wait.

True to her word, John Bramble, a solid lad of about thirteen, arrived with bread, cheese and a jug of ale and kept watch while Jonathan wolfed down the food. Without any great enthusiasm, Jonathan resumed his lofty perch and waited. It proved to be a long day and a longer evening. Twice, soldiers searched the stable giving the place a cursory glance and prodding half-heartedly at the larger piles of hay with the pitchfork. Jonathan held his breath and prayed they did not think to look upwards.

It must have been past midnight before Sal appeared at the door of the stable with a lantern. Stiff, cold and ravenously hungry, Jonathan stumbled into the large, warm kitchen of the inn where Harry Bramble, as large and cheerful as his sister, waited for him.

'It's good to see you safe, Sir Jonathan,' he said. 'Parliament soldiers aren't leaving a stick unturned anywhere in the county. Gave us a few hairy moments today, didn't they, Sal? Anyway, we thought it best to wait until they were long gone afore fetchin' you in.'

'I owe you both a debt of gratitude,' Jonathan said humbly. God alone knew what fate would befall the Brambles if he had been discovered in the stables. 'Just give me something to eat and I'll be gone within the hour.'

Well, you're going to get nowhere looking like that.' Harry cast a critical eye over Jonathan's unmistakably military appearance.

Sally picked up a wicked-looking pair of shears.

'We'll start with your hair,' she said. 'Needs roughenin' up a bit.'

With no great skill but plenty of enthusiasm, she wielded her shears. Jonathan's clothes were replaced with an old brown doublet of Harry's father's, a little short but large enough, and a greasy leather jerkin and his boots with a serviceable but uncomfortable pair of shoes.

'And that.' Sal pointed to Jonathan's sword and baldric.

Reluctantly he added his only means of defence to the discarded pile of clothes.

'What do you want us to do with the horse?' Harry asked.

'When the hue and cry have died down can you take it and my belongings to Seven Ways?'

'Is that safe? I heard there's a new Mistress at Seven Ways and her sympathies may not be with your King's cause,' Sal said doubtfully.

Jonathan nodded. 'She can be trusted, Sal.'

She cast him a knowing glance and bundled the clothes and the sword into Jonathan's cloak. 'If you say so.'

Harry lit a pipe and contemplated Jonathan's transformation. 'Not bad. What do you think, Sal?'

Sal laughed. 'If your mother could see you now, I swear she'd not recognize you. Now I reckon you'll be needing this.'

She completed the picture by clapping Jonathan's own, now somewhat battered hat onto his head, pulling it down over his ears.

Harry leaned forward and pointed the long stem of his pipe at

Jonathan. 'Tomorrow I'll be taking a wagon of ale to my cousin in Ludlow. You can ride along with me. It may take us a couple of days and there'll be troops on the road, but I'm willing to wager you'd pass without trouble. You know how to play a part.'

'Harry, please don't take this risk for me.'

Harry shrugged. 'I only wish I could take you further, Sir Jonathan.'

His mind raced ahead. From Ludlow, he should be able to find a way into Wales, where a boat could be found for Ireland. That would do. The way north would be heavily patrolled, as would the road to London and the roads south through Gloucestershire.

He looked at the two familiar friendly faces and smiled. 'I cannot thank you both enough.'

'Aye well, there'll be time enough for thanks later,' Harry said. 'You can doss down on that mattress there and we'll be off at daybreak.'

CHAPTER 25

$\mathcal{T}$he full wrath of the victorious Parliamentary army, led by Colonel Price, descended on Seven Ways. Kate had expected that Price, angered by the sacking of his own home by Jonathan and Giles, would find an opportunity to revenge himself on the woman who had cheated him of Seven Ways and he wasted no time.

On his orders, the household was ordered to assemble in the great hall while from all over the house came the sound of furniture being upended, beds scraping and splintering wood.

Price himself entered the hall and stood with his hands on his hips surveying the Seven Ways household, with a tight smile of malicious triumph.

The pristine condition of his military uniform and his generally well-rested demeanour indicated he had seen precious little of the previous day's fighting if any.

'What is the meaning of this outrage, Colonel?' Kate demanded.

He rubbed his hands together. 'Surely you know why I'm here, Mistress Ashley.'

'No? Tell me.' Kate's voice was cold.

'We're seeking traitors, escaped from the battle which the Lord in his mercy gave to us.' Price turned his eyes heavenwards.

'Well you'll find none here, save old men, women and children,' Kate replied, indicating her household.

'Come, Mistress Ashley.' The gleeful smile widened. 'It's common knowledge that those two malignants, Giles Longley and Jonathan Thornton, were here before the battle.'

'I'll not deny that they were here,' Kate said. 'They, like you, came with armed men, and while I can hardly prevent Lord Longley from visiting his wife or Thornton his sister' — she cast a sidelong look of feigned displeasure in Nell's direction — 'I made it abundantly plain to that ungodly man that this house is no longer his and he is not welcome. Any of my household can bear witness to that conversation.'

To her gratification, a low murmur of assent from the assembled household, accompanied by nodding heads, bore out the apparent truth of her words. The Thornton household had, by dint of long practice, become accomplished dissemblers.

Price covered his annoyance with bluster but before he could complete his invective on the character of Jonathan Thornton, the door of the great hall opened and another officer entered. He joined Price and surveyed the assembled household with a cold, unsympathetic eye.

The newcomer was a man in his mid-thirties, fair-haired and not ill-looking, despite a thinning pate. His eyes, red-rimmed with exhaustion, rested on Kate's face. Her breath caught and for the first time since Price had arrived, a wave of genuine fear clutched her heart.

The house in York had been dark and she had carried no light.

Surely he would not have been able to see anything more of her than a shadowy figure in the gloom but she did not doubt the identity of the man who now stood appraising her with cold, blue eyes.

Jonathan's nemesis, Stephen Prescott, had come to Seven Ways.

To her relief, she saw no recognition in Prescott's haggard, battle-stained face.

'Ah, Prescott.' Price turned to greet him. 'Any success?'

Prescott shook his head. 'No sign of the traitors, but we did find these.'

He flung Nell's crucifix and rosary and her devotional missal to the floor in front of the women. Nell gave a sharp cry of distress.

'We seem to have unearthed a little nest of papists, Colonel,' Prescott remarked.

Colonel Price indicated Nell. 'Indeed, Major. The papist is this lady— Lady Eleanor Longley, whose husband was with the traitor Charles Stuart and who is sister to Thornton. However this lady' — he indicated Kate — 'is Mistress Katherine Ashley. Mistress Ashley is the widow of a Captain Richard Ashley of Fairfax's Regiment who, I am told, perished at Marston Moor. We have no reason to believe that Mistress Ashley is anything but loyal to our cause, despite having given food and lodging to the traitors.' He took a step towards Kate. 'I will ask you again, madam. Have you seen either Giles Longley or Jonathan Thornton since the battle?'

Kate met his eye. 'No, I have not seen either man since the battle. They know better than to come again to this house. It was enough that they saw fit to billet themselves here before the battle. I assure you I would have sent word to you as soon as they set foot here again.'

Price gave a snort of exasperation. 'If you have finished,

Prescott, we will leave Mistress Ashley in peace for now.' He turned on his heel then, as if struck by a thought, turned back to her. 'However, I have every reason to believe Longley or Thornton will try to make their way here. They have nowhere else to go. We will return, Mistress Ashley.'

'I have no doubt you will, Colonel,' said Kate, fighting to keep her voice even despite the terror that clutched her heart, 'but it will avail you nothing. I will have no traitors in my house and you have my assurance that I will contrive to send you word if they arrive on my doorstep.'

The door slammed shut behind the two men and Price could be heard barking orders to depart.

Kate let out a breath and ordered the servants to return to their duties and restore order to the house.

As Nell dropped to her knees, gathering the small icons of her faith in her hands, Kate walked over to the window. She took a deep breath and grasped the window ledge to stop her hands from shaking as she looked down into the courtyard.

Prescott strode out of the door and as he swung himself into the saddle, he looked up at the house. She saw the wolfish malevolence in his face that went beyond an enmity born of differing allegiances and a cold chill ran down her spine. Price wanted Seven Ways and Jonathan Thornton had all but opened the door to him.

Clutching her crucifix and missal to her chest, Nell joined her at the window. 'I'm sorry, Kate. I told you I would bring nothing but trouble.'

Without looking at her she said, 'Before I met Jonathan Thornton I had never told a lie in my life. Now all I seem to do is lie, and so much seems to depend on how good a liar I can be.'

'I don't understand,' Nell said.

Kate glanced at her friend's innocent face. Nell might have known nothing about Prescott and whatever feud lay between him and her brother. Now was not the time to make a confidante of Nell, so she kept her peace. Major Prescott's interest in this house and its inhabitants would have to remain her burden to carry alone.

It took the rest of the day to restore the house to order. No chest had been left unemptied and no piece of furniture unmoved. The search had been thorough and destructive, but mercifully nothing seemed to have been plundered — not that there was much of value. It gave her some comfort that Price did not dare push her too far.

As evening drew on Kate sat in the parlour sorting through the pile of torn linen that would now require mending. She scarcely heard the timid knock at the door. When it came again she looked up with a start and saw Essie Barlow standing in the doorway.

'Beg pardon, my lady,' Essie began.

'What is it, Essie?'

'My brother Sam's here to see you. Says he's got a message for ye.'

Kate's heart skipped a beat. 'Send him in, Essie.'

Sam stumbled through the door and stood shifting from one foot to the other, nervously twisting his hat in his hands. He waited until Essie left, closing the door behind her.

Kate smiled encouragingly at the boy. 'You have a message for me, Sam?'

He looked around as if he expected a Roundhead trooper to materialise from the gloom and swallowed nervously.

'There's a man, my lady. I was bringin' a cart of hay from Knowles' farm to the Long Barn when I found him in a ditch. He's all done in. Those soldiers were everywhere so I hid him under the hay in the cart. The easiest thing to do was to take him up to Long Barn.'

'Do you know him, Sam?' Kate asked, her mouth dry.

'Aye.' Sam nodded. 'I believe he's Lady Longley's man. I seen him here with Sir Jonathan the other day.'

Giles was alive.

Relief flooded over Kate. She rose to her feet and walked over to the window. It would be dark within the hour. She dared not risk going to him now, not with Prescott and Price still in the area. Giles would have to wait until nightfall.

'You've done well, Sam,' she said and turned back to face him. 'Can you go back and tell him we will come for him after nightfall.'

The boy paled. 'You mean go back to Long Barn?' He swallowed as Kate nodded. 'It's near dark and I don't like that place, my lady.'

'You don't have to stay. Just tell him I'll be there.' The boy turned to go and Kate called him back. 'Sam, go by the kitchen and get something for him to eat and drink.'

Sam bowed and left the room. Kate paced the room, her thoughts racing. If she told Nell, Nell would hitch her skirts and run to Long Barn. The present situation required the utmost prudence and she wanted to be sure it was Giles before she alerted Nell.

She choked down a hasty supper with Nell and Tom. After the events of the last few days, they were all tired and if Nell found Kate a silent and pre-occupied companion, she did not comment. She was too lost in her own misery to notice anything untoward amiss with Kate.

Only when Kate was certain that the household was settled for the night did she go in search of a lantern and a tinderbox. She alerted Ellen and Jacob Howell to the mission and the two women slipped out of the house and into the night, meeting up with Howell along the way.

Long Barn stood about half a mile from the house. During the day she found it a gloomy and oppressive place; at night it loomed out of the dark and she quite believed Nell's tales of ghosts. She did not blame Sam for not wanting to go there after dark.

Taking a deep breath, she pushed the heavy door open and knelt on the packed earth to light the lantern. As it flickered into life she raised it to her face.

'Giles?' she whispered into the dark.

'Kate. Thank God.' The voice came from the shadows.

She held up the lantern and peered into the shadows seeking out the direction of the voice. There was movement in the straw and Giles stumbled out into the light, leaning heavily against one of the solid oak posts that held up the roof.

He raised a tired, unshaven and still powder-blackened face to her. This was not the Giles with the jaunty red feather in his hat. Even in the poor light of the lantern she could see he was exhausted, his hair devoid of all curl hung in lank strands around his face.

'Giles, it is I who should thank God you are safe,' she said. 'When Jonathan said you had stayed behind, we feared the worst.'

His face creased in pain and he lowered himself painfully to the ground with his back against the post, his right leg stretched out on the straw.

'Jonathan was here?' Giles' gaze flicked to Howell and Ellen.

'Yes but long gone. Where are you hurt?' she asked

He indicated his right leg and rubbed the knee. 'My horse died under me, halfway here. I didn't get my foot free of the stirrup fast enough and seem to have done something to my knee. It hurts like hell and it's devilish inconvenient.'

Ellen knelt beside him. 'That knee is badly swollen. Ye'll have to come to the house,' she said. 'There's naught I can do for 'ee here.'

'Is it safe?' he asked.

Kate nodded. 'For the moment. The soldiers came today, but they left without posting any watch on the house. I'm afraid they will be back, though. Price is in a vile mood.'

Giles studied her face for a moment. 'I'm sorry, Kate. I didn't know where else to go. I'll not stay to be a danger to you. Just patch me up and send me on my way,' he said.

He groaned as Jacob Howell hauled him to his feet, supporting his weight.

'What news of the King?' he asked between gritted teeth. 'Did he get away?'

'Yes,' Kate said, judging it wiser not to enter into a conversation about the King's whereabouts.

Giles closed his eyes. 'Thank God they got him away safely,' he said with heartfelt relief. 'How's Nell?'

'She'll be better for knowing you're alive,' Kate replied. 'Now let's get you back to the house. Can you manage, Jacob?'

Jacob Howell grunted and they made slow, painful progress back to the house. After the visitors of the last twenty-four hours, one more hungry, exhausted, filthy soldier made no difference to Ellen. Back at the house, she installed Giles in a chair by the fire in the kitchen with his injured leg propped up in front of him.

He grumbled and swore as Ellen examined the knee. When she had finished she stood up and looked from Kate to Giles with a shake of her head.

'That knee's not taking you anywhere for a while, my lord.' She turned to Kate. 'What are we to do with him, mistress?'

Kate shook her head. 'Let's start by giving him some food and I'll fetch his wife to hold his hand while you do what you need to do.'

Nell cried out and fell on her husband, wrapping her arms around his neck and kissing him.

Giles gently disengaged her. 'Time for reunions later, Nell.'

While Ellen poulticed and bound his knee, Giles recounted the details of the battle, pausing only when he got to the retreat through Sidbury Gate. There he stumbled in his narrative, running a hand over his eyes. He looked spent, drained of all his liveliness and humour.

'Sorry,' he said. 'I can't go on.'

'Was it so awful?' Nell asked.

He put his hands over his face and said, 'Nell, it was a slaughter.'

Nell grimaced and closed her eyes.

Kate laid a hand on his shoulder. 'You're tired, Giles. I think we've heard enough.'

Nell looked up at Kate. 'We'll have to hide him. The soldiers will be back again. Price and that Major Prescott have already made that much clear.'

'Prescott?' Giles stiffened, all exhaustion gone from his face. 'Prescott was here?'

'Do you know him?' Nell asked.

Giles' eyes met Kate's and flickered away. Kate caught the meaning. Giles not only knew Prescott, he knew the danger he posed, but there would be time to press Giles later. For now, they had the problem of concealing one crippled Royalist from the prying eyes of Cromwell's men.

'We'll have to put you in one of the priest holes,' Kate said.

Beneath the grime, Giles paled. 'I'd rather hand myself over now,' he said. 'Jonathan locked me in one of those rat holes when I was eight years old and I cannot abide small spaces since.'

'There's no choice, Giles,' Nell said, her tone softening as she saw the look on her husband's face. 'It will not be forever. The soldiers may come but they won't stay. We'll be left alone soon enough.'

Kate rose to her feet. 'Nell, we'll use the priest hole in the study. It's the largest. Ellen, can you find a mattress and the other things he'll need?'

'You won't shut me in there until you need to, will you?' Giles pleaded.

Kate shook her head. 'We have no choice but I promise, we will leave the entrance open until we need to secure it.'

Not without difficulty, they managed to manoeuvre Giles up the stairs and installed him on a straw mattress in the priest hole. It was entered through a cupboard and concealed behind sliding panelling that could only be accessed by swinging the beam out of the wall behind. Kate felt quietly confident that Giles would be quite secure there until the danger passed.

Fortunately, Giles was too weary to argue about the accommodation and he was asleep before she closed the door to the study. She left Nell sitting in the cramped space beside him, her arms wrapped around her knees, lost in exhaustion and confusion.

CHAPTER 26

Stephen Prescott laid his hat and gloves on the table of the lower parlour and smiled at Kate. Washed and rested, he presented a less threatening presence than he had the previous day, and she could almost believe that his smile held some warmth.

Kate did not return the smile. 'Are you here to turn my house upside down again?'

'No. I don't think that will be necessary, Mistress Ashley, do you?' He raised an enquiring eyebrow at her.

'You have my word that no errant royalists have come this way since your last visit, Major.'

His gaze scanned the room before returning to her. 'I'm pleased to hear it. No, I have come in the hope you may be able to assist me with another problem. Mistress Ashley, we probably have some weeks of work ahead of us, rounding up the stragglers from the battle. Colonel Price has suggested that given your obvious and declared loyalty to the Commonwealth, you would be amenable to some of my men being billeted with you.'

It was not a question. Kate felt the colour drain from her face.

Your face is a book, Jonathan had told her.

She covered her panic with bluster. 'I am most certainly not amenable to any such suggestion. There is no man in this house, and I do not wish to have my household subjected to the moral danger of having soldiers inflicted upon them.'

Prescott looked down at his gloves on the table. A vein twitched in his temple and she wondered for a horrible moment if she had said too much. However, he maintained his smile as he looked up at her.

'I regret it's not something over which you have much say, Mistress Ashley.' His tone remained even, but his eyes had lost their warmth. 'While I appreciate your sensibilities on the matter, perhaps you could view it as being a matter of your household's protection? You surely would not wish to have any desperate men forcing their way in on you. I'm sure such a risk would present considerably more moral danger to your loyal household than my godly soldiers.'

She looked at him, defeated by her own logic. 'How many men do you propose to billet on me, Major Prescott?'

'No more than thirty.'

'And yourself?' she asked, her voice tight with anxiety, trying to imagine how she could keep up the pretence with this man under her roof.

'Of course. We'll not trouble you unduly, Mistress Ashley. We have the Lord's work to perform in rounding up the traitors and that will keep us much occupied for some days to come.'

'And who is to feed them? We have barely enough for this household let alone another thirty mouths.'

His face revealed nothing and his tone was icy as he replied. 'Then you should reacquaint yourself with the gospel of St John 6 beginning at verse 1.'

The gospel of the loaves and fishes.

'I am quite well aware of the verses to which you refer, Major,' she snapped.

She folded her arms and walked over to the window. Looking across the courtyard to the unused wing of the house, a sudden thought came to her.

'As it seems I have no say in this matter and you have my assurance of loyal adherence to your cause, Major Prescott, may I suggest you and your men take the north wing? It is presently shut up, and there you can come and go without disturbance to my household,' she said.

He joined her at the window and, following her gaze to the north wing, nodded in agreement. 'That sounds entirely reasonable, Mistress Ashley. Your co-operation is greatly appreciated. It is refreshing to come across a sympathetic household amid such disloyalty.'

Kate did not look at him and chose to say nothing.

'I will bid you a good day, Mistress Ashley.'

She turned as he picked up his hat and gloves and bowed politely to her, before leaving her to contemplate whatever would come next.

'What did he want?'

She turned and saw Tom standing at the door to the library. His hair fell over his eyes, barely concealing a deep frown of disapproval. He crossed to where she stood by the window, and Kate put her hand on his shoulder.

'I don't like that man,' Tom said. 'He has horrible eyes.'

Kate sighed. 'You're right, Tom. He is not a man we should trust. He must never know that Jonathan and the King were here.'

Tom looked up at her. His eyes held the ghost of his father in them. 'I'd never tell him, Mother.'

'Has he gone?' Nell peered around the other door. She looked tired and strained. 'Are we not to be searched again?'

'Not for the present, Nell, but he is coming back and we are to have a troop of his horse billeted on us.'

'Oh, sweet Mary.' Nell crossed herself, one of the few times Kate had seen her demonstrate her faith. 'What are we to do, Kate? We can't leave Giles shut in a priest hole indefinitely.'

'No,' Kate agreed. 'We'll just have to take a risk, Nell. I've told him that the soldiers can have free run of the north wing. They should not bother us unduly over there and we can move Giles to your room when things are a little calmer.'

'Lord Longley is here?' Tom looked from one woman to the other and Kate cursed herself. The less Tom knew the better but she had inadvertently said too much and now he had to know the whole story.

'We have him hidden in one of the priest holes. Tom —'

'I won't tell anyone. Not even if they torture me,' Tom said with a frown of indignation. 'But what about Ann? She is such a prattle tale. She could tell them about Lord Longley, without knowing it.'

Kate looked at Nell. They hadn't thought about the child.

'I'll send her to the Knowles,' Nell said. 'Betty Knowles can look after her while the soldiers are here.'

'Are you sure, Nell?' Kate asked.

Nell's mouth set in a hard, grim line. 'It will break my heart, Kate, but then so would losing my husband.'

Later that night, when the house was quiet, the women extricated Giles from the priest hole. He looked at them with bright, feverish eyes. 'I could not have borne another minute in there,' he declared with a shudder.

'Well, I hope there'll be no need for you to go back,' said Kate, 'but it may be necessary. Prescott is billeting a troop of horse on us.'

Giles ran a hand through his hair. 'Prescott will not rest until we are all behind bars. I'm only putting you in terrible danger, Kate,' he said. 'Do the right thing and hand me over.'

'No.' Kate and Nell chorused together.

'I would no more turn you in than I would Jonathan,' Kate said. 'As long as Prescott and Price think I'm sympathetic and the troopers keep to the north wing, there'll not be too much danger. As for the rest of the household, we have spun the tale that Nell is unwell and that Ellen is tending to her. That has justified us sending Ann to the Knowles' farm. It means Nell stays with you and the only person who needs to attend to her is Ellen.'

The women managed to haul Giles up the stairs to Nell's bedchamber where he was put to bed. He fell back on the pillows with a heartfelt sigh of relief and looked up at his wife.

'Sweeting, I must speak with Kate alone for a few minutes.'

'Surely there is nothing you have to say to Kate that I cannot be privy to?'

'Please,' Giles said. 'It concerns Jonathan and is a matter for Kate's ears alone.'

'But— ' Nell looked from one to the other. 'Oh, very well. Keep your secrets.'

She flounced from the room and Giles patted the edge of the bed. 'Sit down.'

She obliged and he took her hand in his.

'Kate, be very careful,' he said. 'Prescott is a dangerous man.'

'I know. He is the man who shot Jonathan in York. I saw him there.'

'Do you know what lies between Jonathan and Prescott?' Giles asked.

'No,' Kate said. 'Jonathan wouldn't tell me. Can you?'

Giles shook his head. 'It's not for me to tell you. All I can do is warn you that Stephen Prescott will stop at nothing to avenge himself on Jonathan. Whatever he might tell you, he is here for one reason alone and that is because he thought to snare Jonathan.'

Kate looked at Giles' grim face, startled by the difference from the man she had first met only a few short weeks ago.

'Why can't you tell me?' she demanded. 'I'm so tired of these hints and half-truths.'

Giles grimaced. 'Because I don't know the whole story,' he said.

'Has it got anything to do with Mary?'

Giles looked startled. 'Mary? What has he told you about Mary?'

'I know Mary is the only woman he ever loved. I know she is dead. That is all.'

Giles looked away, and she saw the indecision on his face. He looked back at her and said quietly. 'Her name was Mary Prescott.'

'Prescott's sister?'

'His wife.'

Kate swallowed. 'His wife?

'I'm sorry, Kate. That's all I can tell you. I honestly know no more. Only Jonathan and Prescott can tell you what lies between them, but perhaps you can surmise?'

Kate took a shuddering breath. Prescott's wife... a lost love... yes, she could surmise what enmity lay between the two men.

'I'm very glad you're here, Giles,' she said with heartfelt honesty.

'I'm not good for very much, Kate.' A ghost of his old smile crossed his ashen face.

'You're a friend,' she said, 'and more importantly a friend who understands about Stephen Prescott.'

Giles chuckled. 'It must have come as something of a shock to him to find you, instead of Jonathan.'

She stood up to leave.

'I'm sure it did, but he frightens me, Giles.'

Giles caught her hand. 'You have reason to be afraid. Kate, be careful. Prescott is no fool. If he even suspects there is anything between you and Jonathan he will use that against you.'

Kate sighed heavily. 'I will be careful, Giles. The Lord alone knows how careful I must be. Now I'll leave you to get some rest and organise our guests' accommodation. I would like them to be sufficiently comfortable to keep to their quarters.'

Giles released her hand and shook his head. 'You're a remarkable woman, Kate Ashley.'

~

As HE HAD PROMISED, Prescott returned in the afternoon with his men. He and his officers seemed satisfied with the arrangements she had made. So they should be, thought Kate. They were no doubt considerably better billets than they were used to.

Mindful of the part she must play, Kate asked the officers to join her for dinner. They accepted with an alacrity that surprised her and presented at the appointed time, well scrubbed and tidy. Nell had her part to play too and while they might view her papist beliefs with horror, she had a pretty face and a cheerful disposition and she knew how to play on those charms.

Prescott introduced his men: Captain Bennett, Lieutenants Fairbairn and Butters, and a young Cornet whose name Kate didn't quite catch. Lieutenant Fairbairn said a very long-winded grace over the cooling food, during which a few suspicious glances were directed at Nell but she ignored their curiosity.

As the soup was served Prescott shook out his napkin.

'Your husband fought with Fairfax, I believe?' Prescott asked.

Kate nodded, adding for good measure that the Fairfax family were indeed close friends and allies of the Ashley family.

Prescott's eyes narrowed. 'But your husband was a Thornton, Mistress Ashley?'

'His mother was a Thornton,' Kate replied. 'Richard was a first cousin of Jonathan Thornton, but the family had been long estranged by more than just politics. And what of you, Major?' Kate deliberately steered the conversation onto the risky ground. She wanted to understand this man better. 'Have you a wife and family?'

Prescott shook his head. 'Sadly my wife died some six years ago and we were not blessed with a child,' he said. 'I've not remarried. My life is the army and my master is our Lord God.'

His face told her nothing and Kate had no reason to believe that he told her anything except what he truly believed.

During the meal she watched him as he ate, noting the way his eyes glanced around the room as if taking in every detail. If he had thought to find Jonathan Thornton here, her presence must have proved a grave disappointment.

CHAPTER 27

*J*onathan wrapped his cloak tighter around himself and sniffed as a drop of rain dripped from his hat onto his nose. The tree under which he crouched provided poor shelter from the rain that had fallen continually since he had left Worcestershire. He thought knew the Marches reasonably well but in evading the omnipresent soldiers he had lost all sense of direction and had to admit that he was lost.

He considered his situation. He still had sufficient coin, he hoped, to secure a passage to Ireland, but it left nothing over for the necessities such as food or a bed. Despite careful rationing, the small parcel of food that Harry's cousin's wife had provided him with had long since gone. Furthermore, he had been walking for two days and his feet hurt in the ill-fitting shoes.

The rain stopped and the sun appeared to mock the sodden fugitive. Jonathan stood up and shook out his cold, cramped limbs. It still lacked a few hours until nightfall and he needed to get some sense of direction or he would just end up walking in circles for days.

Distantly he could see the spire of a church. The rain had mired the roads but at least the sun had broken through with enough warmth to dry his damp clothes. He put his head down and set his teeth to endure the last mile or so to the village.

On the outskirts, Jonathan leaned wearily against a tree and observed the tranquil scene. It seemed impossible to believe that any place in England could still be this peaceful and seemingly oblivious to the turmoil that beset the entire nation.

In the late afternoon sun, a group of women gossiped by a door. A small knot of men finished with their daily chores, gathered at the inn door, mugs of ale in their hands, talking and laughing.

A sizeable stream ran through the village, widening into a deep, still millpond just beyond the inn. Beside the pond, a small group of boys played with rough boats of their own construction. A boy of about Tom's age leaned over with a long stick to retrieve his fragile craft that drifted out into the centre of the pond.

The little boat floated tantalisingly out of reach and the child overreached himself, toppling into the pond with a loud splash. A strong current, running beneath the still waters in the direction of the mill wheel, quickly pulled him out of the reach of his friends' grasping hands.

From his wild splashing, he plainly could not swim, and his cries of distress alerted the men at the inn door and a woman screamed.

Without stopping to think, Jonathan ran to the edge of the pond where he divested himself of shoes, hat and the threadbare cloak. He threw himself into the cold, dark water without hesitation. It took him a while to find the boy, who had gone under as his struggles had become weaker. The child made no resistance as Jonathan dragged him out of the pond and laid him on the ground.

As one of the village men tended to the child, Jonathan sat back on the grass and ran his hand through his wet hair. The boy spluttered and coughed, spewing out a stream of water and the remains of his last meal. Another man hauled Jonathan to his feet, slapping him on the shoulders as another threw his abandoned cloak across his wet shoulders. A murmur of appreciation grew around him as the crowd escorted him to the inn. He looked around for the child and was relieved to see him being carried off by his mother, shivering and tearful but alive.

Inside the inn, a cheerful fire burned in the hearth. The innkeeper's wife produced food and promised while looking doubtfully at Jonathan, who towered nearly a head taller than most of the men in the room, to look for some dry clothes that might fit.

A mug of ale was pressed into his hand and the room was made by the fire. Steam rose from Jonathan's clothes as he sat in front of it, trying to get some warmth into his chilled bones and he took the platter of stew with thanks.

"Ere, slow down,' the goodwife said as Jonathan shovelled the food into his mouth. 'Anyone would think you'd not eaten for a week.'

If only she knew, he thought, wondering where his next meal would come from.

'Where are you from?' someone asked.

Jonathan paused. 'Near London,' he said, slipping an appropriately colloquial accent. 'Come west looking for work.'

'Harvest's near done,' one man said, 'but I daresay we can find work for you.'

Jonathan mumbled his thanks.

'Do you have news of the battle at Worcester?' another man asked.

Jonathan shook his head. 'Bin on the road. I've heard nothing.'

'Soldiers were here a day or so ago. They reckon there's Scots and the like on the loose and that we're all to lock our doors.'

'Aye, they say Charles Stuart's on the run and all.'

Suddenly amidst the chatter, a woman's voice rose shrilly. 'What did those soldiers say?' Silence fell on the gathering as she continued. 'A dark man over two yards high? Look at his hands, he ain't no labourer.'

Jonathan's sharp mind, dulled by the events of the past week, failed him and before he could react his arms were seized and pinioned. A dark man over two yards high? He fitted that description and the mood of the crowd swung.

Two men hauled him to his feet, sending the empty platter clattering to the stone floor. Another grabbed his hands, holding them out for inspection. He flinched as they twisted his injured hand with the filthy bandage. Despite the long years as a soldier, there was no disguising the swordsman's hands. Calloused though they were by long hours holding reins, they were not the hands of a common labourer.

'What did they say the reward was?' someone else shouted.

'One thousand pounds,' came the answer.

One thousand pounds for the King — a fortune to these people. Jonathan's heart sank. An ignominious end to his freedom, he thought.

A bearded face thrust itself into Jonathan's. 'Be you Charles Stuart?'

'I am not,' he protested. 'Lost everything in the war and I'm just looking for work to keep body and soul together.'

All memory of Jonathan's selfless act of courage had been forgotten and despite his protestations of innocence, all they could see was the rich reward. His denial fell on deaf ears.

They dispatched someone called Ezra to fetch the soldiers from the nearest garrison, and Jonathan's eyes flicked around the now hostile faces, looking for an escape. The grip on his arms had slackened in the general excitement and he seized his chance.

Throwing off his captors, he dived into a gap in the crowd only to be brought up short in the door of the inn by a solid man in a leather apron, clearly the blacksmith come late upon the scene. Before he could dodge, a mighty fist flashed out, catching him squarely under the left eye. The last thing he saw before the world went black was the blacksmith's grimy face.

HE CAME BACK to his senses with a raging thirst, matched only by a thudding headache. He lay face down on a cold, slimy stone floor. No chances had been taken; his hands and feet had been firmly and securely tied and it took an effort to manoeuvre himself into a sitting position with his back against some barrels of wine.

A low evening light filtered through a small window, high up in the wall, and illuminated his prison which he judged, by the barrels and the sacks against which he sat, to be the cellar of the inn. Well-trodden stone steps led up to the stout oak door that he supposed would be firmly barred on the outside.

He licked his dry lips and thought longingly of the wine in the barrels. With grim humour, he told himself this must be some sort of hell where one could die of thirst in a cellar of wine barrels. He called out but his shouts went unheeded. He concluded the inn's occupants must be toasting their success and dividing the reward between themselves.

If 'Ezra' had ridden for the soldiers, he probably only had a couple of hours before they showed up to take him away. His only consolation in the whole sorry affair was that the ungrateful villagers would not receive a thousand pounds once his true identity had been ascertained.

He allowed himself some ungracious thoughts about his captors as he shivered in his damp clothes. With his arms twisted behind his back, his fingers had begun to lose feeling and the muscles cramped. His shoulder hurt like the devil and from the ache above his cheekbone, his eye would be blackened and closed by morning. As the last streaks of light faded from the small window he shut his eyes against the thumping pain in his head and shoulder and drifted into an uncomfortable and fitful doze.

He woke with a start and strained his eyes against the uncompromising blackness of the cellar. A scrabbling noise came from behind a pile of barrels in the corner of the cellar. It seemed to be made by an animal, but something considerably larger than a rat.

He strained his ears but silence descended and he thought he must have imagined it.

As he allowed himself to relax, the scrabbling noise came again, only this time a small, wavering light could be seen above the barrels and a young girl of about seven or eight, holding a small lantern, crawled out from behind the debris at the very back of the cellar.

She stood and held up the lantern, illuminating a thin, pointed face. For a brief moment, Jonathan wondered if he was conjuring up delirious visions of the fairy folk. Seeing him, she crept across the floor and crouched in front of him.

'I've come to rescue you,' she said with such gravity that Jonathan almost laughed at the idea of this tiny child rescuing him from his present predicament.

However, the girl had access to his prison from somewhere above the ground and that gave him hope.

'What's your name?' he asked.

'Sarah Morgan,' she said. 'It was my brother, Hew, you saved today.' She paused and held up the lantern, examining his face with open curiosity, her eyes as round as plates in her small face.

'Are you the King?' she asked.

Jonathan shook his head. 'No, Sarah, I'm not the King.'

She sighed. 'Mother said you weren't. She said you were too old.' Then her face brightened. 'But are you an escaped Royalist?'

There seemed no point denying it and he nodded.

'What's your name?' she asked.

'Jon,' he said simply. It would be better for the child not to know his full name.

She held the lantern up again and touched his bruised face, screwing her own up in response. 'That looks sore. Father didn't know about Hew,' she said. 'Mother threw a trencher at him when he told her what he'd done.'

'Is your father the blacksmith?'

Sarah nodded. It seemed incredible that such a burly man could produce such an elfin creature.

It occurred to Jonathan that time was being wasted in idle conversation. He twisted so his back was to Sarah.

'Can you undo these ropes?' he asked.

Obediently she set to work but her small fingers were no match for the tight knots. Jonathan felt his small glimmer of hope beginning to evaporate. Every moment they delayed the soldiers would be coming closer.

A loud rustling from the direction Sarah had entered made them both start. An older boy of about twelve appeared from behind the boxes.

'Hurry up, Sarah,' he said in a low urgent voice.

'Owen,' she wailed. 'They've tied him up and I can't undo the knots.'

'Here, let me.'

Owen crossed the floor towards them and set to work on the

knots. His stronger, more skilful fingers made quick work and Jonathan sighed with relief as he shook out his cramped arms, trying to get some feeling back into the numb fingers.

'This way, sir,' Owen urged him, indicating the back of the cellar from where he had come. 'There's a tunnel from here to the churchyard. It's very old and I don't think many people know about it. It's only 'cause ma was born in the inn that she knew about it.'

Behind the boxes, Jonathan saw a small opening at ground level. He recoiled. His height gave him an illusion of being slight, but he knew he carried some breadth across the shoulders and the size of the opening gave him pause as he weighed up the potential threat of death by slow suffocation in a tunnel against his fate at the hands of the soldiers.

'You'll fit,' Owen opined with considerable more confidence than Jonathan felt.

The tunnel indeed proved a tight squeeze in parts and Jonathan began to have some sympathy with Giles and his fear of tight, dark spaces. When they eventually emerged from beneath the church into the churchyard, he breathed the cool fresh air with gratitude, offering silent thanks to God for his deliverance from the tunnel.

'Sir, this way.'

A woman stood in the shadow of a large yew tree, holding the reins of a small horse.

'This is Mother,' said Sarah, and by way of explanation added for her mother's benefit, 'He's not the King. His name is John.'

'There I told you, silly,' her mother said, her soft voice betraying a Welsh accent. She held the lantern up to him. 'Oh, your poor face,' she said, reaching up to touch the bruising. Jonathan flinched away from her touch. 'I was so cross with

Morgan. When I told him that you had saved Hew he was proper sorry for hitting you.'

'Do you have anything to drink with you?' Jonathan asked.

She produced a flask of small ale and he drank greedily.

Owen, who had taken up the watch at the church gate, ran towards them. 'I can hear horses,' he said.

'There's food in the saddle bag,' the woman said. 'You must hurry. The soldiers will be here within minutes. The horse is for you. Morgan says it is the least he can do.'

She handed him the reins of the horse. Sarah handed him his hat and cloak, which she had retrieved from the floor of the cellar, as he swung himself into the saddle.

He leaned from the saddle and kissed the woman's hand.

'Thank you, Mistress Morgan. I'll not forget this kindness.'

'You owe us nothing, sir,' she said. 'We will have Hew to remind us of our debt to you.'

A loud clamour from the direction of the inn proclaimed that 'Charles Stuart's escape from the cellar had been discovered. With a backward wave at the two children, Jonathan kicked the horse into a canter and rode away from the village as fast as the horse would take him.

CHAPTER 28

The walls of the lower parlour closed in on Kate as the full import of the piece of paper she held in her hand hit her. She looked from the smug, self-satisfied face of Colonel Price, dressed for the occasion in buff coat and a sash with gold fringing, to the implacable, unreadable face of Major Prescott, who leaned against the fireplace idly stoking the logs.

'The order is quite clear, my dear Mistress Ashley,' Price repeated. 'The Committee has ordered that you surrender to me the livestock and produce listed as compensation for the losses I incurred at the hands of Charles Stuart's followers.'

'These are our winter stores. We'll starve. What gives the Committee the right to make this order? It was not me who took your stores and livestock.' Kate tried to keep the panic out of her voice.

Price smirked. 'Someone must pay for the ravishing of my home by Longley and Thornton. May I remind you, madam, that regardless of the present ownership this estate is still subject to considerable debts owing for the participation by its occupants in the late troubles.'

'Surely those debts died with Sir Francis.' Kate grew desperate. She turned to Prescott. 'Major Prescott, surely this cannot be right?'

Stephen Prescott shrugged. 'The charge is on the land, regardless of ownership. I am sorry, Mistress Ashley, the order is correct.'

He cast a look of distaste in the direction of the portly colonel and for a brief moment, Kate almost liked him.

'I'm not the fool you take me for, Colonel. You think by this action you will beggar this estate into a position where we must sell?' Kate glared at him. 'In that, you are mistaken. I shall be writing to Master Freeman.'

'It will avail you nothing, Mistress Ashley. Even Master Freeman lacks the power to overturn this order.'

Kate cast the man as cold and venal a look as she could muster, and with the two men following her, she swept from the room to issue the order to Jacob Howell. She could do nothing but watch as the hard-won sacks of grain were loaded onto carts and her sheep and cattle were driven away by ten of Prescott's men.

'What about the horses?' Price demanded.

To Kate's surprise, Prescott stood firm, barring the door to the stables. 'I'm sorry, Price, but the order is satisfied without any necessity to take the horses. Unless you want to bring Whitehall down on your head, you would be advised not to provoke the situation any further.'

Price's face turned scarlet, but the threat of London reminded him that the widow Ashley did indeed have some powerful friends. He drew his cloak around him and without acknowledging her presence mounted his horse. Prescott gave Kate a curt nod of the head and followed.

As the last of the soldiers rode off, Kate remained standing in the courtyard as the chill autumn wind whipped unheeded around her ankles. Jacob stood beside her in silent sympathy.

'Mistress Ashley,' he said, 'it's not all bad. I had some word of the Colonel's intentions, so we managed to hide the best of the horses and some of the livestock in the quarry.'

She smiled sadly at him. 'Thank you, Jacob, but I don't think that will be enough to get us through the winter.'

'What will you do, Mistress?'

She shivered as the wind gusted around them.

'I don't know, Jacob,' she said and, gathering her skirts in her hand, she walked slowly back into the house.

Once inside her misery gave way to a wave of rare and sudden anger. Without knocking, she burst into Nell's room. Nell sat by the fire, apparently alone.

'Have they gone?' she asked. 'Kate? What's wrong?'

'Where's Giles?'

'In the priest hole,' Nell said. 'We saw Price and thought it prudent.'

Without waiting for her friend, Kate swept down to the study and opened the priest hole.

'Out!' She ordered.

Grimacing, Giles eased himself out. 'Kate, what's happened?'

'You!' Kate jabbed an accusing finger at him. 'This is all your fault.'

Nell had followed Kate into the study and went to her husband's assistance as he rose uncertainly to his feet.

'What do you mean?' he asked.

'Price and his bullies have just stripped this manor bare of its winter supplies because you decided to liberate the wine cellar at Longley Abbey. Your actions have ensured we may well starve this winter.'

Nell gasped and looked at her husband.

Giles, to his credit, looked appalled. 'Kate, I'm truly sorry. It never occurred to me that he would take his revenge on you. If I had it in my power to make amends I would here and now.'

The anger ebbed and Kate sat on the nearest chair and looked down at her hands.

'What am I going to do?' she asked no one in particular.

Nell sat down next to her. 'Could we not borrow the money?'

She looked up. 'From whom?'

'Your family?' Nell ventured.

Anger surfaced again, and Kate glared at her. 'My family? Why should my family lend us the money? They counselled me not to take on this venture. They warned me that I would be dealing with trouble and now I have it, enough for a lifetime of misery.'

She stood up and stormed out of the room, slamming the door to her bedchamber behind her. She stood for a moment, her breath coming in short, sharp gasps that gave way to despair as the enormity of the situation closed in on her.

This is what comes of throwing your lot in with Jonathan Thornton, she railed into the bolsters of her bed.

Where is he now? Where is he when I need him?

CHAPTER 29

W hat made the life of a fugitive unbearable, Jonathan reflected, was not so much the discomfort, the lack of sleep, the rain or the cold. It was hunger. At least the horse could eat grass, but for over two days Jonathan had little except a rabbit he had caught and cooked on a fire and what wild berries he could find.

His purse had been taken by the ungrateful villagers before they had thrown him into the cellar. The little mare, which he had named Morgan in gratitude to his liberators, was the only thing of value he now possessed, and although he could have sold the horse for a good price, he remained wary, skirting the towns and villages. Conscious now of his distinctive looks, not improved by the black eye and days of beard growth, he travelled mostly at night, resting during the day in whatever shelter the woods and coppices could provide.

Hunger gnawed at him and he knew that unless he ate soon, he would not have the strength to go much further. With that in mind, he had been watching an isolated manor house for most of the day, wondering about the wisdom of begging some food from the kitchen. The lonely house clung to a riverbank, its solid grey stone walls stout defence against weather and marauders.

As he watched a woman came out of a side door holding a basket. She knelt beside one of the vegetable beds and began to pull up carrots. Jonathan's stomach knotted. Aware of the alarming appearance he presented he brushed the worst of the grass and dust from his clothes but nothing he could do could lessen his ruffianly appearance.

Looping the reins of his horse over his arm he limped down the hill toward the house. The woman looked up at his approach, her eyes widening in alarm. She jumped to her feet and began backing away, holding up the garden fork as if it would provide her with some protection.

'Get away.' she said. 'Before I summon my man.'

He held out his hands to show he was unarmed. 'I'm sorry to startle you, Mistress. I mean no harm. I just wondered if you could spare some bread.' He made no pretence of his accent. He was beyond that.

Something in his voice and bearing must have allayed her fears, for her face softened. Jonathan could see how very young she was, and from the quality of her clothes, he concluded that he had stumbled upon the daughter of the house. She lowered the garden fork, and even in his exhausted state, Jonathan could appreciate a pretty face when he saw it.

'When did you last eat?' she asked.

'Two, three days ago.'

Jonathan took a step towards her, but to his mortification, the world began to spin and ten days of near starvation and fatigue caught up with him. He slid to the ground in a graceless heap.

When he came round, the girl knelt over him, her face full of concern.

'Sir,' she said, 'are you hurt?' She reached out to touch his eye.

He winced at her touch and struggled into a seated position, trying to regain a modicum of dignity.

'Thank you, Mistress,' he said. 'I'm not hurt, just damnably hungry.'

'Are you... are you an escaped Royalist?' she asked, her eyes wide.

He surveyed her with narrowed eyes, looking for some indication of her loyalties. As if reading his thoughts, she added, 'You're quite safe in this house. My husband's son was killed fighting for the King.' She frowned. 'Are you one of the Scots?'

He shook his head. 'English.'

'Good,' she said, 'I'm not so sure about the Scots. I've heard terrible stories of them. Come to the house, sir, and I shall see to some food. Can you stand?'

He nodded and she helped him to his feet. He collected up the reins of his horse and followed her to the house. She called for a boy who came out and took the horse, his eyes wide with curiosity but he asked no questions.

Throwing open a door she ushered him into the kitchen and saw him seated at a table. An older woman stood by the kitchen range, wiping her hands on her apron and glowering at the filthy, ragged stranger.

'The household is busy with the harvest,' the girl said. 'It's just Maggie and I and the lad in the stable. Maggie, fetch this man some of that stew.'

So not the daughter of the house... the mistress. Jonathan's spine tingled a warning but he was beyond caring.

Maggie deposited a large bowl of hot stew, accompanied by bread and ale, in front of him. Without the slightest recourse to manners he downed the stew, and at a nod from her mistress, Maggie refilled the bowl.

'What day is it?' he asked when he had eaten his fill.

'Friday,' she replied.

'Where am I?'

She smiled. 'Just south of the Forest of Dean,' she said.

Herefordshire?

Jonathan laid his hands on the table and looked down at his fingers. Ten days since Worcester and he seemed no closer to freedom.

The girl reached over and took his left hand.

'You're hurt,' the girl exclaimed.

With all his other difficulties, the savage cut across the back of his hand had just been another inconvenience and he had hardly thought of it, but the girl seemed concerned and bustled around finding bandages and salves.

The tattered, filthy bandage Kate had tied so many days ago had become well adhered to the wound and the young woman had to soak it off. Despite the ill-treatment, the wound seemed to be healing without putrefaction.

She salved and redressed the wound and when she had finished her ministrations, Jonathan rose to his feet. He inclined his head. 'Thank you for the food and the care, mistress. I must be on my way.'

'Elizabeth Griffith,' she said, placing herself in front of him. 'My name is Elizabeth Griffith. Please, there is no need to leave yet. As I said, you're quite safe here.' This last was addressed more to Maggie than to Jonathan. 'You must surely be desperate for a night's rest and,' she added, pulling a face, 'a bath would not go amiss.'

He hesitated. He knew he stank to high heaven. A wash would have been pleasant and a bath even better. And the prospect of a night in a bed could not be so easily dismissed. He looked at the girl's pretty face and the not unsympathetic face of the maid behind her and decided that it was a risk worth taking.

~

JONATHAN WOKE from a deep dreamless sleep with a start. For a few moments, he had no sense of time or place and only the bright day beyond the unfamiliar window told him he had slept too long. He lay with his right arm behind his head, relishing the sensation of being clean and lying between fresh sweet-smelling sheets and giving silent thanks that young Mistress Griffith had not betrayed him — not yet.

The click of the door latch caused him to turn his head as Elizabeth Griffith, carrying a pile of clothes in her arms, entered the room. He cast a glance around the room but saw no sign of his own ragged, filthy garments. She laid the clothes on the bed and smiled at him.

'I thought you would sleep forever,' she said. 'It's nearly midday.'

Jonathan sat up, pushing the dark, tangled hair from his eyes. She sat down on the bed beside him and her eyes flicked over his naked chest with a bold gaze that caused Jonathan to pull the bedclothes a little higher. Her lips parted and Jonathan found his own eyes resting on the inviting swell of her breasts beneath the fine lawn of her collar.

'What did you do to your shoulder?' she asked, reaching out to touch the ugly scar that marred his left shoulder.

He shivered against her light touch, and grasped her wrist, drawing her closer. A sweet scent, redolent of jasmine enveloped him and he wondered if she had dabbed on a perfume. 'It's nothing,' he said, his voice husky with desire. 'Just an old wound.'

'It doesn't look all that old.' She looked at him from under her long lashes. 'My husband has gone to London. I don't expect him back for some considerable time. You could stay here for a little longer. Regain your strength.'

The smoky look in her eyes and the gentle pout of luscious, red lips made her meaning clear. She leaned towards him, with her eyes half shut and he drew her closer. An hour or so lost in the pleasures she was so blatantly offering him would be a salve to his bruised and battered soul.

As he felt the touch of her lips on his, the heady scent repulsed him and he thought with longing of another, softer scent...that of rosemary. He dropped her wrist and gently pushed her away.

It was not the thought of cuckolding the absent husband or enjoying the company of another lonely wife to his list of crimes — he could not be unfaithful to Kate, no matter how great the temptation.

She sat back, her eyes brimming with tears. He reached out and brushed them away and she leaned against his hand.

'You're very lovely, Elizabeth,' he said softly.

'Why don't you want me?' Her voice trembled.

'Because we both know it would not be right. You have a husband, and for my part, I have a wife and two children,' he lied.

Her eyes widened.

'You must love your wife very much,' she said in a flat voice.

Jonathan nodded.

'And your children?' she asked. 'Tell me about them?'

'A boy aged nine and a girl of four.'

'Do they look like you?'

'The boy does, the girl is like her mother,' Jonathan replied, drawing on Thomas and Ann for inspiration.

The girl looked down at her hands. 'I wish I had children,' she said. 'That would please my husband. He wants a son to replace Matthew.'

'Is that why he married you?' Jonathan asked gently.

She nodded, and a tear dropped onto her hands. 'But I have not conceived and now I do not think he even notices me,' she said.

Jonathan tucked a curl of fair hair behind her ear. 'Then he is a fool,' he said.

He could see her situation only too clearly. This woman, so young he had taken her to be the daughter of the house, had been tied to an ageing widower who saw her only as the brood mare to replace the son he had lost. Trapped in a loveless and lonely marriage, it came as a small surprise that she turned to the first attractive man who crossed her path.

As he stroked her hair she looked up at him and smiled a wan little smile. The boldness had quite gone from her eye.

'Thank you, sir, you are very kind. Your wife is a fortunate lady to have such an honourable man as you for her spouse.'

'And I, her,' Jonathan said. 'Now, Mistress Elizabeth, I really must be gone. My clothes?'

She stood up. 'We burnt your clothes, they were quite beyond salvation.'

Jonathan tried unsuccessfully to suppress his irritation. She caught his expression, and her chin rose as she faced him.

'If you are to wander the country in disguise, you make a poor beggar. Even in rags, any fool could see you were a gentleman. If you still intend a disguise then disguise yourself as a gentleman.'

She had brought with her an old-fashioned doublet and breeches of dark grey wool, a clean shirt and stockings and a serviceable cloak.

'These were all Matthew's,' she said. 'He was quite tall, so they should fit. See, I even have shoes.' She held them up for his inspection.

'A mirror and razor would not go astray,' Jonathan said, ruefully rubbing the ten days of growth on his chin.

The clothes were an excellent fit and by the time he had shaved, he felt quite presentable. The mirror had confirmed his worst fears. Even without the villainous growth of stubble, his face looked pinched and drawn. His left eye was surrounded by a lurid combination of blues, purples and greens but at least the swelling had gone down. He wondered, as he scrutinised his face in the mirror, what Mistress Elizabeth could possibly have found attractive in his current appearance.

He found her in the kitchen, engaged in sorting herbs with Maggie. She clapped her hands in delight when she saw him.

'There, Maggie,' she exclaimed. 'You would not think this was the same person.'

Maggie smiled. 'Quite an 'andsome gentleman under all that dirt. There you go, sir,' she said, setting a meal down on the table.

After he had eaten Elizabeth set to work on tidying his hair in a more expert fashion than that displayed by Sal and her shears. When she had finished she had one last surprise for Jonathan. With something of a flourish, she produced his beloved hat, which had miraculously survived the worst of his adventures. It had been steamed and cleaned and looked almost respectable.

Morgan too looked fed, clean and rested. She chewed contentedly as Jonathan cast an expert eye over her, checking hooves and fetlocks. When he finished he patted her neck. She had done well for a little pony.

'She's a little small,' observed Elizabeth. 'I'm surprised your feet don't drag on the ground.'

Jonathan shrugged. 'Beggars, Mistress Elizabeth, cannot be choosers.'

'There is one last thing,' she said. 'You need money.'

Jonathan opened his mouth but before he could speak she pressed a bag of coins into his hand

'Take it. I was saving up for a new gown. It can wait.'

Jonathan hesitated only for a moment before stowing the purse in his jacket. Beggars could not be choosers.

'Thank you,' Jonathan said. 'Your generosity has been over-whelming. Now I would be grateful for directions towards the coast.'

She shook her head. 'South to the Severn estuary but from what I hear tell, every port is guarded, sir.'

Jonathan ran a hand down Morgan's neck while he considered his position. Disguise yourself as a gentleman, she had said. If he was to hide in plain sight, perhaps the answer was to go where you were least expected.

He would turn back in the direction of Worcester and then strike out for London. It sounded, even to his tired mind, a desperate and reckless plan, but it was the only one he had for the moment. Surely no one would expect a desperate fleeing Royalist to return to the field of battle.

She looked up at him and Jonathan put a hand on the girl's shoulder, drawing her closer. He took her in his arms and kissed her, a proper lingering, kiss of gratitude. She tasted sweet but she was not Kate. Kate, who waited for him at Seven Ways, not knowing if he was alive or dead.

'It is strange, sir,' she said as they drew apart, 'but I never knew your name.'

He gave her the benefit of what he knew was his most disarming smile. 'Perhaps, Mistress Elizabeth, we will leave it at that.'

CHAPTER 30

*A*t the sight of Stephen Prescott coming down the garden path towards her, Kate straightened her back and sighed. She could not complain about his conduct towards her. He treated her with courtesy and deference, and had they met in other circumstances she may even have liked him.

Until she looked into the depths of his cold, blue eyes and remembered York.

'Major Prescott,' she said. 'What can I do for you?'

He coughed. 'Forgive my intrusion. I am conscious that the last few days have been difficult for you.' He looked around at the snaggled garden beds and overgrown paths. 'You have set yourself a challenge, Mistress Ashley. I believe this was once a very fine garden.'

She forced a smile. 'And do you like gardens, Major?'

Something that might have been a smile twitched at the corners of his mouth. 'I have lived all my life in a town, Mistress Ashley, and have little appreciation of gardens. Perhaps if you have a few moments you could show it to me?'

She could hardly refuse this pleasant overture. She took him up and down the paths, boring him with her plans for the reconstruction of the garden's lost glories.

'These are fine roses,' he said pausing to smell the last of the blooms. 'My wife was very partial to roses. Her father had a garden in Oxford that was much admired.'

Oxford...Mary...her heart skipped. Perhaps she could glean something of the story from this man, if not from Jonathan.

'Are you from Oxford yourself, Major Prescott?'

'Yes. I had a law practice there before the war,' he replied.

'And do you intend to return to the law?'

He shook his head. 'No, after my wife's death I have had little heart to return to Oxford. The Army is my life now. Although, God willing, the day will come soon when my usefulness will have been exhausted. Then I may consider marriage and a small estate in the country. I have a reasonable private income, certainly sufficient to support a family.' He cast her a sideways glance. 'Do you have a mind to marry again, Mistress Ashley?'

Kate shook her head. 'I cherish my independence and the memory of my husband, Major Prescott.'

'I see,' he said and added. 'Tell me, is that your husband's ring you wear around your neck?' He leaned forward and lifted the chain. 'It's the Thornton device unless I am mistaken?'

Kate's heart skipped a beat and her hand flew to the chain on her neck. It must have come free of her bodice while she worked.

Prescott continued to smile. 'Did I tell you I was acquainted with Jonathan Thornton in the days before the war?'

Panic coursed through her veins.

'No,' Kate said, 'no, you didn't mention it. My husband was a Thornton too, Major. He treasured this ring greatly. I took it from his finger when he died.'

'I recall you telling me your husband's family and the Thorntons were estranged. Why then would he wear a ring with the Thornton coat of arms?'

She felt the betraying heat rising to her cheeks and turned away to look up at the house. 'It was all he had of his mother.'

Prescott followed the line of her gaze. 'It's growing late, Mistress Ashley, and I have kept you from your work.' He smiled and bowed. 'Guard that ring well, Mistress Ashley. Who knows what stories it could tell?'

She watched Stephen Prescott walk away, her heart hammering beneath her bodice. So much depended on him believing her to be loyal to the Parliamentary cause. Her courage drained from her and her hand closed on the incriminating ring. It seemed to burn like a brand.

CHAPTER 31

The imposing tower of the Worcester Cathedral rose from the surrounding countryside just as it had done barely a few weeks earlier. From a distance, it seemed nothing could have occurred to disturb the serene vista of cathedral and town, but the air of tranquillity proved superficial. The traveller did not have to look far to see the broken earthworks and the churned fields or smell the unmistakable stench of death rising from the mass graves Jonathan passed on his way into town.

Mistress Elizabeth must have been saving for an exotic gown, as the money she had given him proved sufficient to allow Jonathan comfortable accommodation for the journey. He had also been able to purchase a clean shirt and sufficient books to give credence to his once familiar alias as John Miller the bookseller.

He had been stopped and questioned, but as he rightly surmised, a traveller heading in the direction of Worcester excited considerably less suspicion than one going in the opposite direction. With his cropped hair and plain but respectable clothes, he did not need further disguise. To account for his black eye and lack of papers, he had concocted a story of being attacked and robbed by renegades from the battle.

He suppressed a shudder as he approached Sidbury Gate. The Commandery, now garrisoned by Parliament troops, lay on his right. Ahead the gate stood open, no longer impeded by the bodies of the dead who had lost their lives in their frantic efforts to gain the safety of the city. He wondered how many of his friends lay in the charnel pits: Kit Lovell and his idealistic brother, Daniel? Giles?

The soldiers on the gate accepted his tale and, two weeks after he had fled the town, he re-entered Worcester, hoping that he would not be recognized by the townspeople. He pulled the hat down low over his eyes and hunched over the saddle to disguise his height but no one cast a second glance at the plainly dressed man on the solid little horse.

He took a room at one of the inns on a side of town where he thought it most unlikely he would be known. With the company of one of his books and a decent bottle of wine, he took his meal in the parlour. After he had eaten he sat by the fire and tried to read.

The clatter of cavalry boots on the flags announced the arrival of a weary young lieutenant of horse who drew a chair up to the fire beside Jonathan to warm himself. Jonathan set down his book.

'Greetings, friend,' Jonathan said. 'May I buy you an ale? You look in sore need of one.'

The young man smiled gratefully. 'Aye, I have just ridden from London and I plan to go no further tonight.'

'Where are you bound?' Jonathan asked.

'My regiment is garrisoned near Kidderminster,' the boy said. 'I know I should be back there tonight but my horse can go no further.' He added with a noticeable tightening of his lips, 'I'll just have to face Major Prescott's wrath tomorrow.'

The breath stopped in Jonathan's throat. 'Prescott?'

The young man looked at him curiously. 'Aye, do you know him?'

Jonathan attempted to cover his slip. 'I am acquainted with a Nathaniel Prescott, is that the man?'

The officer shook his head. 'No. My commander is Major Stephen Prescott, and a hard man he is too.'

'Were you at the fight here?' Jonathan asked, changing the subject.

His companion nodded. 'Aye. It was a grim day, but God was with us. The Lord General calls it a crowning mercy.'

Crowning mercy indeed, Jonathan thought. Cromwell had fought a good battle that day.

'And what are you doing at Kidderminster?' he asked.

'Rounding up the stragglers,' the lieutenant said. 'I've just returned from escorting some prisoners to London for trial. The Earl of Derby among them,' he added with a note of pride.

Poor Derby, Jonathan thought. It would not be long before the Earl's head adorned London Bridge. Someone had to pay the price for the battle of Worcester.

'I hear that Charles Stuart still roams the countryside,' Jonathan ventured.

The boy nodded. 'Vanished into thin air, but we'll get him, sir, and he'll meet his father's fate.'

The grim determination on the soldier's face made Jonathan shiver.

'So, where did you say you were garrisoned?' he asked, returning to the subject of Stephen Prescott.

The young man leaned back in his chair and sipped his ale. 'We are billeted at a house which has the strange name of Seven Ways,' he said. 'The major says it used to be the home of a notorious family of malignants but the lady who is there now seems godly enough. I swear she must sleep with her Bible under her pillow. Her conduct of prayer meetings would make the regimental parson proud.'

Jonathan schooled his face to remain neutral, although his heart raced. He should have known that Prescott would go straight to Seven Ways in search of him and now Kate had Stephen Prescott under her roof. She could only be in the greatest danger.

The lieutenant continued, the ale loosening his tongue. 'If you ask me, the major's a bit sweet on her.'

Jonathan's unease doubled. 'The major has a partiality for such godly women?'

'Well I've not seen him look twice at a woman before but he seems in no hurry to leave.' The boy sniggered.

Jonathan summoned another ale for the young soldier and stood up. 'Well, my friend, I'll leave you to your ale. I wish you well with your commander in the morning.'

Alone in his room, Jonathan flung himself full length on the bed and stared at the ceiling. The enmity Stephen Prescott held for him extended to anyone connected with Jonathan Thornton. Five innocent men had already died for Jonathan's sins. Now Prescott's hatred threatened his family in a way it had never done before. More than that, the one person who mattered most to him in the world appeared to be the object of Prescott's attention. No amount of prayer meetings would help her if he were to discover her secret.

The people he cared most about in the world were in the gravest danger. He clenched his fists in impotent rage, although he could not have said whether his anger was directed at Prescott or himself.

He had no choice but to return to Seven Ways and finish this business with Prescott for all time, even at the cost of his own life.

CHAPTER 32

Not normally a man given to profanity, Jacob Howell swore volubly when he opened the door to his cottage and found Jonathan standing on his doorstep. Without waiting for an invitation, Jonathan stepped into the cottage, divested himself of his wet cloak and hat and stood in front of the fire. As steam rose from his damp clothes he smiled at his astonished bailiff.

'You look like you have seen a ghost, Howell.'

Before he closed the door, Jacob peered into the damp gloom of the autumn night. 'Where's your horse?'

Jonathan lifted the lid on the stew pot Howell had simmering over the fire.

'I've left her in the old quarry. She'll be safe enough there. Have you anything to eat? I'm starving.'

'You must be addled to come back now.' Jacob spooned the last of the stew he'd made for his supper into a trencher. 'The house is full of Roundheads.'

Jonathan took the proffered trencher and spoon and said

calmly, 'I know, and that is exactly why I've come back.' He sat down on a stool by the fire and stretched his legs out towards the fire.

'Now tell me everything that has happened?' he asked between mouthfuls. 'And why is the quarry full of livestock?'

Jacob resumed his chair and picked up his discarded pipe. He poked at the tobacco and took several sucks on the long stem before he said, 'That Colonel Price, he came by with an order to sequester the bulk of the harvest and the stock. I managed to get some of the best beasts away, but he drove off the rest and took most of the harvest, too.'

Jonathan set the spoon down on the trencher and sighed. 'Revenge is mine, saith the Lord.'

'Aye,' Jacob agreed, 'as if it weren't bad enough having that Prescott and his men up at the Hall.'

Jonathan looked up. 'What has Prescott been up to?'

Jacob gave his master a knowing look through narrowed eyes. 'You know this man?'

Jonathan nodded. 'Go on.'

Jacob frowned. 'Hard to say. Sometimes he's here and sometimes he's not. Been asking a lot of questions about you.'

Jacob sighed. ''Tis '45 all over again. You should've stayed away, sir. Mistress Ashley don't need you around to add to her woes.'

No, she did not need him to add to her woes, but he could not leave her alone to face whatever Prescott had planned.

He cleared his throat. 'How is she?'

'Poor lady,' Jacob said with feeling, 'beset all around she is, and having Lord Longley under the roof don't help.'

'Longley? Here?' Jonathan stared at his bailiff. 'How?'

'I don't rightly know how but they've got him well hidden. He's laid up with a twisted knee.'

'That's the best piece of news you've given me, Jacob.'

'Well he's not good for much,' Jacob conceded, 'and a terrible worry for the poor lady.'

'Can you get a message to him?'

Jacob shook his head. 'Maybe. Prescott always leaves a guard on the house. They're used to me coming and going, but it mayn't look right if I starts traipsing through the house. If you needs a message getting through to his Lordship, the lass, Ellen can be trusted.'

In the firelight, Jonathan caught the flush that had risen to the bailiff's thin cheeks at the mention of Ellen and shot him a quick smile. 'Sweet on her, are you, Jacob?'

Jacob coughed awkwardly. 'Not me, Sir Jonathan. Women bring naught but trouble in my experience.'

'You always were a poor liar, Jacob,' Jonathan said.

Jacob smiled a crooked, self-deprecating smile. 'She's a terrible, vexsome wench, that Ellen.'

Jonathan smiled. 'I would agree with that.' He sobered. 'Ellen can be trusted but make it clear that on no account is she to say anything to her mistress. I don't need Mistress Ashley to know I am here for the moment. She has enough on her mind.'

Jacob knocked out his pipe on the heel of his boot and as he refilled it he looked up at Jonathan with a sly look. 'If you don't mind me askin', sir, but it seems to me that you're more than a bit sweet on Mistress Ashley.'

A muscle twitched in Jonathan's cheek. 'More than a bit sweet,' he conceded.

'Then why don't you want her to know you're here?'

Jonathan ran a hand through his cropped hair. 'You said it yourself. I don't want to add to her worries, and I'd like to see what Prescott is up to before I decide my next move.'

'This Prescott, would he hurt her?'

'If he saw her as the way to get to me, yes, he would.'

Jacob shook his head. 'This is a bad business,' he said. 'So what are you going to do?'

'I don't know,' Jonathan conceded. 'I need time to think. Do you have a weapon of any kind, Jacob?'

Jacob indicated an old-fashioned musket propped up behind the door. 'Just that.'

'That's not much use to me. I need a pistol.'

Jacob rose to his feet and rifled in a large wooden chest. He produced a long bundle and handed it to Jonathan.

'This may be some help,' he said

Jonathan turned back the wrapping and revealed a sword. He pulled it from the scabbard and held it up to the light, recognising it as the serviceable weapon Jacob had carried in the late wars. Not a gentleman's weapon, but better than nothing.

'Needs cleaning and sharpening,' Jacob observed.

Jonathan nodded. 'It'll do well. Thank you, Jacob.'

Jacob surrendered his bed for the night, but Jonathan lay awake for a long time, staring at the ceiling. A house full of soldiers, Prescott, Giles, Kate... the thoughts jostled together in his tired mind. It was a tangle that only he could resolve.

The time had come to face his nemesis.

CHAPTER 33

*K*ate scoured the house looking for her errant son.
No one seemed to have seen him since luncheon
and the dark, drear evening was already closing in on them.

As she contemplated sending one of the servants to enquire at
the Knowles' farm, Essie Barlow appeared at the door to the
parlour.

'Beg pardon, ma'am,' the girl said, 'but Major Prescott's in the
library and he's asked to speak with you.'

'Damn the man,' she muttered to herself.

Since their encounter in the garden, his attitude toward her
had changed. Any pretence at sympathy had vanished and the
previous day he had insisted on yet another search, pulling the
furniture away from the wall and urging his troops to tear at the
wainscoting with increased ferocity.

He didn't find Giles. She and Nell had insisted he remains in
the priest hole while the soldiers were in the house. On days
when they were away, they let him out, but never further than the
study. With the strain of enforced confinement and the ever-

present danger of discovery, tempers within the household were fraying and it was little wonder Tom sought to escape the house when he could.

Leaving instructions with Essie to send a boy to Knowles' farm, she straightened her collar and attended on Major Prescott.

She found him in the library, standing in what had become a familiar pose, with his back to the fireplace.

'You look distracted, Mistress Ashley,' he remarked and for once his tone seemed genial and sympathetic.

'I am,' she said. 'My son is playing truant and after your mens' work yesterday, I am ill-disposed for pleasantries. What can I do for you, Major?'

He spread his hands in a conciliatory gesture. 'I was acting on orders, Mistress Ashley. As it is I have come to tell you that we've found new quarters in Kidderminster and will not be requiring your gracious hospitality any longer. I have sent my men on, and I plan to join them in the morning.'

Kate felt the breath leave her body with relief at this news.

'Well, that at least is good news,' she said, hoping her face did not reveal too much. 'I suppose it's too much to expect some remuneration for the feeding of your soldiers?'

'I am sure if the appropriate representations are made to Colonel Price you will be rewarded for your loyalty,' Prescott said.

As he spoke he left his position by the fireplace and crossed the floor as if he intended to leave the room but as he passed her he took her by the arm and drew her towards him.

Too startled to react, Kate stared at him.

'What are you doing? Let me go this instant or I will scream,' Kate protested.

He answered by pulling her into his arms and clapping a hand over her mouth.

'You will listen to what I have to say,' he whispered in her ear. 'You can make whatever representations you wish, but I'm sure that once Price learns the truth about where your loyalties lie, you may find the rewards are not what you expected.'

Releasing his hand from her mouth but still holding her arm, Prescott thrust a paper at her. With trembling fingers, she took it and read the few short words. It said simply. *'Long Barn after night-fall. Come alone. This ends tonight.'*

'You recognise the writing?'

Kate shook her head.

'I do and I know you for a liar. You've been hiding him all this time.'

'Who?'

'Don't play any more games with me, Mistress Ashley. Jonathan Thornton. This note comes from Thornton's hand.'

She looked up at him in disbelief. 'No,' she said. 'As God is my witness, I've not been hiding him.'

His eyes narrowed and his fingers tightened on her arm causing her to wince with the pain. 'You're Thornton's whore. I knew it as soon as I saw the ring that you wear around your neck. Now if you value your son's life, you will do as I say.'

He flung her away from him and Kate stumbled against a table, catching at it to prevent her fall.

She looked up at Prescott. 'Tom? What have you done to my son?'

Prescott's mouth curled in a parody of a smile. He glanced at the window and nodded. 'It's past nightfall. If you wish to see your son and your lover, I suggest you come quietly. We have no wish to alarm the household.'

Prescott pulled out one of the heavy cavalry pistols he wore in his belt and took her arm again, pressing the muzzle to her side.

Kate struggled to control her breathing as he guided her

towards the door. As Kate opened the door she almost bumped into Essie. Prescott moved in behind her and she felt the muzzle of the pistol press hard against her back.

'Oh mistress,' the girl said. 'I've sent one of the stableboys to Knowles' farm like you asked. Will Major Prescott be dining tonight?'

Essie glanced at the soldier who stood behind Kate. The pistol prodded her harder.

'No. He is just leaving,' Kate said, surprised at how calm she sounded. 'Thank you, Essie. Get back to your work and tell Lady Longley that I will not be long.'

The girl bobbed a curtsey and disappeared down the corridor.

Once outside, Prescott pushed her ahead of him. She tripped and stumbled along the uneven path that led to the Long Barn. The old building loomed, a dark silhouette on a slight rise. On a moonless night like tonight, Kate could almost believe the tales of it being haunted.

Prescott opened the door of the barn and pushed Kate inside.

'Thornton?' he called, but there came no reply from the gloom. 'Thornton? I have the woman. If you value her life, show yourself, now.'

The sound of tinder striking flint disturbed the silence. A light flickered in the dark and a man stepped out of the shadows, a drawn sword in his right hand and a lantern in his left. He hung the lantern on a nail in a post and turned to face Stephen Prescott.

'Jonathan.' Kate breathed.

He ignored her. His entire focus centred on the man who stood behind her.

'I thought I told you to come alone. This is between you and me,' he said.

'I thought you might like to see your strumpet before you die,' Prescott said.

His fingers tightened on her arm, twisting it behind her and forcing her to her knees. He put the pistol at her head and she gasped.

'I don't understand— '

'Let her go, Prescott,' Jonathan said. 'Kate knows nothing.'

'Really? You mean she doesn't know how you debauched my wife, turned her mind against me? She doesn't know how you killed her with your bastard?' He wrenched Kate's arm again, forcing her to look up at him. 'Mistress Ashley, let me tell you how Mary comes to me at night, wringing her hands and crying out for vengeance, begging my forgiveness. All for a bet, Mistress Ashley, all for a bet.'

Kate stared into a face contorted by bitterness and hatred that was beyond reason or logic. Her eyes flicked to her lover. He stood motionless, the sword balanced in his hand, his gaze still fixed on Stephen Prescott.

'You know that wasn't how it was, Prescott. Let the past go. Let Mary rest.'

Kate's breath came in shallow gasps. How could he sound so calm? The man holding her arm would think nothing of killing both of them.

Prescott shook his head. 'No. Mary will not rest until I have seen you dead.'

'Jonathan,' Kate cried out. 'For pity's sake! Where's Tom?'

Jonathan glanced at her and back at Prescott. 'He's not here, Kate. Where is he, Prescott?'

Prescott laughed. 'I don't have him.'

'You said —' Kate began.

'Ah, no, Mistress Ashley. It was you who said he was playing truant, I just chose to let you think I had him or you would not have come quite so willingly.'

'Prescott, this does not involve Kate. Let her go,' Jonathan said.

Prescott looked down at Kate. 'You'd be proud of dear Mistress Ashley, Thornton. A dissembler and a liar just like you — pretending to be a godly and virtuous widow while all the time she was your bedmate, your paramour.' Prescott let go of her arm and wrenched the chain from her neck. 'This,' he said, holding up the ring. 'When I saw this I knew you for what were. Thornton's whore.'

Without warning, he struck her across the face with the full force of his hand. Kate fell back in the hay, and the world dissolved into bright lights and then blackness.

JONATHAN GLANCED at the fallen woman and his hand tightened on his sword. She lay quite still, blood trickling from a cut lip.

'Rot in hell, Prescott,' he said between gritted teeth.

'Drop your sword Thornton,' Prescott replied, swinging the long muzzle of his pistol around to point at Kate's head.

Jonathan took a slow, shuddering breath as he weighed up the situation. At such a short range Prescott would not miss. He could kill Kate and turn the other pistol on Jonathan without blinking. They would both be dead by night's end and there was nothing to be done.

He had badly misjudged his opponent and Prescott had bettered him — for the moment. An old cavalry sword against a brace of pistols? What had he been thinking? That Prescott would fight a gentlemanly duel?

With as much contempt on his face as he could muster, he laid his sword on the ground at his feet.

'Now get down on your knees,' Prescott gestured with the weapon, grinning as Jonathan fell to his knees, his gaze fixed without blinking on the other man's face.

Prescott strutted over to Jonathan. Standing behind him, he gripped his left shoulder. Jonathan gritted his teeth, determined not to show pain as the fingers tightened on the wound that Prescott himself had inflicted.

'You should not have escaped me last year,' Prescott said. 'My men thought you must have been in league with the devil to have vanished into thin air but I know you are real enough and the person you were in league with was not the devil, for all she may yet prove to be a witch.'

Prescott paused and the grip tightened. 'It was her, wasn't it? The virtuous widow Ashley. It seems she has the power to make men disappear. I will have the greatest of pleasure in seeing her hang as a witch when I am done with you.'

As he spoke, Kate moved and groaned and started to pull herself up. Prescott's grip on Jonathan momentarily relaxed and Jonathan took advantage of the lapse. Lunging backwards with his right elbow, he hit Prescott in the knee, throwing the man off his balance and forcing him to release his grip.

Twisting, Jonathan jerked Prescott's legs from beneath him and both men fell to the ground. The pistol scudded into the hay beyond the reach of either of them.

Although Jonathan was the taller of the two by at least a head, Stephen Prescott was solidly and powerfully built and Jonathan knew he could not better him in hand-to-hand combat. Out of the corner of his eye, he saw Kate rise unsteadily to her feet, dashing the blood from her mouth with the back of her hand.

'Kate, the pistol,' Jonathan gasped.

She dropped to her knees, scrabbling in the hay for the elusive weapon.

'I have it,' she cried.

Her hand shook as she brought the heavy weapon up, pointing it at Prescott. As the muzzle wavered, Prescott broke Jonathan's hold and grabbed at her, catching her ankle and pulling her foot from underneath her. The pistol discharged, the ball striking the door of the barn as Kate fell backwards, striking her head on a post.

Jonathan let out a groan of rage and frustration as Prescott struggled to his feet, drawing his second pistol from his belt. It caught in his jacket and Prescott lost precious seconds freeing it.

In that instance, Jonathan dived toward his discarded sword. Freeing the weapon, Prescott drew the hammer back and fired.

Nothing happened.

In the breathless pause that followed, Jonathan's hand closed on his sword. Prescott lunged at him, bringing the butt of the pistol down like a club. It caught Jonathan on the forehead and he crumpled to the floor.

Above him, he dimly heard Prescott's heavy breathing and felt a boot in his ribs. He went still, feigning unconsciousness. Prescott needed time and concentration to reprime the pistols and Jonathan braced himself, coming to his feet with all the speed and agility he could muster, striking the pistol from Prescott's hand.

Prescott stumbled backwards, losing his footing and hitting the floor with a thud.

Blood from the cut on his forehead running down his face, Jonathan held the deadly, unrelenting point of the sword just below Stephen Prescott's left ear. He glanced across at Kate. She lay quite still where she had fallen. Only the faintest rise and fall of her breast indicated that she still lived.

'Get up, you bastard.'

Jonathan moved the sword to the underside of the man's throat, scoring a thin bloody line in the soft skin.

Prescott looked up at him without flinching and without fear.

'Get it over with,' he said with a twist of his mouth.

'I cannot think of a death that would be slow or painful enough to make amends for your work today.' Jonathan struggled to keep control of the anger in his voice.

Jonathan lifted the sword away and stepped back.

'Unlike you, I'll not kill a man in cold blood. Get up and let's finish this. Draw your sword.'

Prescott needed no further invitation. He rose to his feet and drew his sword, while Jonathan wiped the blood away from his eyes and shrugged off his jacket.

The two men faced each other in the faltering light of the lantern.

They circled, both summing up the other's ability. Jonathan knew without a doubt that he was the superior swordsman and Prescott had never been much of a swordsman. However, physically Prescott probably had the advantage. He had not suffered the privations of the last few weeks.

'She was telling the truth, Prescott,' Jonathan said. 'She's not been hiding me.'

Prescott's eyes narrowed. 'She's been hiding someone. Lying to me. Does she have another lover, Thornton?'

When Jonathan did not respond, Stephen Prescott laughed. 'You should have killed me while you had the chance' he said. 'It will give me the greatest pleasure in making your motherless bastard an orphan.'

Motherless bastard? Did he imply that the child had lived? Mary's child— his child?

This time his words had the desired effect. The point of Jonathan's sword wavered.

'What the hell do you mean?' he growled.

'Your bastard in Oxford. Old Woolnough tried to palm it off on me but I'd have no truck with it.' Prescott drew his lips back in a wolfish grin, clearly relishing this sudden rush of power.

'They told me the child was dead,' Jonathan found his voice.

'And why do you suppose they would say that? You put a cuckold's horns on my head, Thornton and brought shame to her family.'

Prescott lunged but Jonathan parried. Being taller, he had the advantage of reach and experience, but Prescott was equal to the challenge.

'You've been practising,' he noted with a deliberate note of sarcasm as he found himself parried again.

'I had good reason to,' Prescott replied. 'I thought— I hoped— we would meet again in these circumstances.'

'I don't believe for one minute you ever wanted to meet me over a sword. What death did you plan for me, Stephen? Hanged? No, you had that opportunity, didn't you? A nice drawn-out and grisly death perhaps? This must be a grave disappointment to you.'

Anger flashing from his eyes, Prescott lunged again. To Jonathan's surprise, the blade came within a whisker of his arm, slicing through his shirt sleeve. The two swords clashed, again and again, making sparks in the gloom of the barn.

Prescott managed to slip out from Jonathan's blade and he repositioned himself just out of reach. Jonathan dashed the blood from his face away with his sleeve. It was running into his eyes and he did not need to have his vision impeded.

Both men were tiring. The contest was proving more evenly matched than Jonathan had anticipated. His shoulder hurt like the devil from Prescott's earlier ill-treatment and the pain distracted him, but Prescott had begun making mistakes. Jonathan's superior swordsmanship and his lighter and more agile build had begun to tell on the dour cavalry officer.

Prescott backed off, his breath coming in short, sharp gasps and the sweat standing out on his forehead and running down his nose.

Panting heavily, Stephen Prescott said, 'I could have been a good husband to her.'

'She wanted more than a good husband, Stephen. Mary needed love. You don't know the meaning of the word.'

That had the effect he sought and with a cry of rage, Prescott lunged wildly. Jonathan saw his advantage and closed in for the kill. Their swords locked, and in a quick, practised motion, Jonathan flicked Prescott's sword from his hand. It went spinning into the hay and this time Jonathan did not waste the opportunity.

It should never have come to this, Jonathan thought as the sword, honed to a razor-sharp point pierced Prescott's heart.

For a moment Prescott tottered, staring at Jonathan in disbelief. Jonathan took a step back as Prescott's eyes glazed over, blood-stained flecks appearing in the corners of his mouth, and he crumpled into the hay. Jonathan stood over him, his sword lowered, panting heavily. The cold, blue eyes stared sightlessly into the dark recesses of the old building.

Am I really any better than him?

'You seem to have everything under control.' The voice came from the doorway.

Jonathan turned on his heel to see Giles Longley limping into the barn.

'Giles. Your timing is, as always, impeccable,' Jonathan remarked wryly.

Behind Giles, Jacob Howell stood in the shadows, his hands on his hips, scanning the scene with a shake of his head.

Giles limped over to the crumpled figure at Jonathan's feet. He bent and felt for a pulse. Finding none, he looked up at Jonathan's taut, strained face.

'This always was a bad business, Jonathan,' Giles said quietly.

'It's over now,' Jonathan said.

He threw his sword into the hay and turned away to where Kate lay crumpled like a child's broken toy. He knelt and took her in his arms. He held her close, stroking her bruised and bloodied face. At his touch, her eyes, blank and uncomprehending, flickered open and her body began to shake.

'Tom,' she muttered. 'He took Tom.'

'Tom?' Giles leaned over her. 'Tom's quite safe, Kate. He's been out with Peter Knowles all day and forgot the time. He came back this evening with the stable lad.'

'He said he had him.' Kate gave a strangled sob and closed her eyes.

'Hush. He would have said anything, Kate, if he thought it would get your co-operation.' Jonathan held her to him, kissing her gently as she sobbed.

Jonathan looked up at Giles. 'How do you come to be here?'

'Ellen told me this morning you were back. Then she came to me this evening, ranting some tale about Prescott having taken Kate off and we found this in the Lower Parlour.' He handed over the note Jonathan had left for Prescott in the dead of the night, propped up on a table in the soldier's quarters.

'I recognised your writing. God's death, what were you thinking?' The normally placid Giles blazed at him. 'Did you believe he would meekly walk up here and you would slug it out like gentlemen? You must have realised you were putting Kate into the gravest danger.'

Jonathan tensed. Giles was right, he hadn't thought it through.

'I had to end it, Giles.'

'And in doing so, you nearly destroyed us all.' He glared at his friend. 'Bravo, Thornton. Act without thought. Follow your heart. You don't change. Surely we could have dealt with this another way?'

Jonathan set Kate down and rose to his feet. He crossed to Prescott's body and stood looking down at the man's face.

'For ten years he has hunted me. He has murdered men in cold blood in my name. No, there was no other way this could have ended.'

CHAPTER 34

$\mathcal{N}$ ell met them in the courtyard, holding a lantern high as her gaze moved from one face to the other, her expression one of helpless bewilderment.

'What has happened here tonight?' Nell's voice cracked in distress.

Kate, lay in Jonathan's arms, limp and broken and barely conscious. Giles, supported by Jacob Howell, favoured his good leg, his face grey and drawn. Jonathan realised he presented the worst picture with his face and shirt covered in blood from the cut above his eye.

There would be time for explanations later — for now there were other priorities.

'Help me here, Nell. Kate must be put to bed and I don't think I can carry her much further.' He turned to Giles. 'You and Jacob wait for me in the parlour.'

Jonathan set Kate on her feet but her knees buckled and he had to catch her before she collapsed. Nell took Kate's arm around her shoulder and Jonathan steadied her on the other.

In Kate's bedchamber, Jonathan laid her gently on her bed, tenderly smoothing back the tangled hair from her face.

Jonathan looked up at his sister. 'Is Tom all right?'

Nell nodded. 'He's fine. We've put him to bed and Ellen gave him a stern talking to about staying out so late.' She caught his hand and looked into his face, her eyes hard. 'Is this Major Prescott's work? Did he hurt her?'

Jonathan stroked Kate's bruised cheek. How could he even begin to explain to his sister the tangled web of events that had begun ten years ago and had ended tonight?

'Why?' Nell sounded on the edge of tears. 'I don't understand, Jon. Tell me what happened?'

Jonathan ran a hand across his eyes. 'Not now, Nell. I'll tell you the whole story in the morning, I promise.'

She narrowed her eyes. 'Where is Prescott?'

He looked away, unable to face Nell's accusing gaze. 'Prescott is dead. Now, I am leaving Kate to you. Giles and I have unfinished business.'

Price came the next morning and it fell to Nell to deal with him. Crammed into the priest hole with Giles, Jonathan chafed with impatience. He hated hiding like a rat in a hole but they had no choice.

It seemed an age before Nell swung back the beam and the two men crawled out into the light.

Giles took a deep breath. 'If you'll excuse me, my knee hurts like the very devil. I will retire to the comfort of the bedchamber.'

He limped out leaving brother and sister alone together.

Jonathan stretched his stiff sore muscles and turned to face his sister.

'What did Price want?'

Nell crossed her arms and fixed her brother with a hard glare. 'He came to tell me that Major Prescott had been found dead on the side of the Kidderminster road this morning. They suspect it was the work of footpads. He was knifed. The weapon was found in the body and his purse is missing. He wanted to know when we had last seen him.'

'What did you tell him?'

'I told him that Major Prescott was here yesterday evening. He had come to advise us that his soldiers would no longer be occupying this house. I said he had left just after dark and that Kate had warned him of the dangers of travelling abroad after dark in these unsettled times.' She took a deep shuddering breath. 'None of that is true. You killed him didn't you, Jon?'

Jonathan swallowed and nodded. 'In self-defence, Nell.'

She shook her head. 'I don't doubt your word and it was clever to disguise the sword wound with the knife. I suppose they will bury him properly, not that I think that he will be greatly mourned. Certainly not by me but I will pray for his soul.'

Jonathan laid a hand on his sister's shoulder. 'You can pray for mine too.'

Her lips twitched in an unconvincing smile. 'You are constantly in my prayers, Jon.'

He walked across to the window and looked out at the sweep of the Thornton land.

Nell joined him. 'Jon?' she said softly. 'Go and rest. You are strung like a bow.'

He shook his head. 'Later, Nell.'

He couldn't tell his sister that every time he closed his eyes he saw only Prescott's face, contorted with hatred.

'I know what lay between you. Giles told me about your affair with Prescott's wife. Small wonder he hated you so much.' She laid a hand on his sleeve, compelling him to look down at her. 'Why did you do it?'

He took the hand, pressing it to his lips. 'My dear sister. It was another lifetime ago when I was a different person.' He sighed. 'Mary and I paid dearly for that affair and I'm only sorry to have had to involve any of you in my sorry business.'

Nell threw her arms around him and held him tight. 'I just hope that this is the end of it, Jonathan. For all of us."

As they parted, she asked. 'What happens now, Jon?'

Jonathan blew out a breath and looked up at the fine plaster ceiling, hoping for inspiration. 'I will return to France by the easiest route I can find.'

Nell sighed. 'That's not what I meant. What of Kate? You do love her, don't you?'

He looked away and nodded. He loved her as he had loved no woman before. A different, deeper, more abiding love than the youthful passion that he had for Mary.

'Will you take her with you?' Nell asked.

He swung his gaze back to his sister, unable to disguise his surprise at her suggestion. In the wild turmoil of the past months, the thought had not occurred to him. A life in exile with Kate by his side? Was that possible?

He remembered the grim reality of an exile's life, the hand-to-mouth existence of bad food and worse beds, and shook his head.

'Dearly as I would like to, Nell, what can I offer her? There is Tom to consider. We would hate each other within weeks.'

Nell cocked her head to one side and bit her lip. 'Well, that is her decision, but I think you owe it to her to make that choice.' She sighed. 'Now, I should go to her. Will you come with me?'

Jonathan shook his head. The sight of Kate's bruised face reminded him that he had failed her. Once more his hubris had caused hurt to someone he loved. He didn't know how he could ever face her again.

'If you want me, I will be in the library,' he said.

At the door, Nell cast him one last look before catching her skirts in her hand and leaving the room.

SOMEWHERE IN THE HOUSE, someone was singing. Kate lay quite still, straining her ears to catch the distant song as Nell bustled around the room. She wondered how anyone in the world could find such joy in life. It seemed all happiness she had ever known or ever dreamed of had been extinguished in the headlong events of the past few weeks.

Even turning her head hurt.

'Nell, can you bring me a mirror?'

Nell stopped folding clothes and straightened. 'Are you sure? I don't think—'

'A mirror… please.'

Nell sat on the bed and held up the mirror and Kate grimaced. The bruised and swollen face that looked back at her seemed almost unrecognisable. She touched the cut on her lip and tears started in her eyes as she remembered how close Prescott had come to killing her.

A gulping sob escaped and Nell laid the mirror down and took Kate's hand in hers.

'Ellen says there is no lasting damage,' Nell said, mistaking Kate's distress for concern over the physical scars.

Kate shook her head. A mistake. She winced.

'No,' she said. 'Not that. I can't see how it will ever be right again.'

'Tell me what happened in the barn, Kate?'

Kate closed her eyes, trying to make sense of the headlong events of the previous night but it only came to her in snatches. The storm broke and the pent-up emotions of the past year poured from her. She howled her fear and her despair into Nell's embrace, grateful for the comfort that only another woman could give her.

When she had no more tears to shed, Nell laid her down, wiping her ravaged face with a cold cloth.

In a voice thick with her tears, she asked the one question she didn't know the answer to. 'Prescott... Is he dead?'

Nell nodded. 'Yes.'

'And Jonathan?'

Nell's lips tightened. 'In the library. He's lost in a black mood. Giles says they come on sometimes. I've tried to talk to him. He blames himself for what happened to you, rightly so in my opinion.'

Kate turned her head to look out of the window. 'I don't blame him, Nell.'

'I'm not sure I agree with you. He has to face you and above all, he owes you a proper explanation and an apology.' Nell smiled and smoothed the hair away from Kate's forehead. 'He will come soon, I am sure of it.'

Kate closed her eyes, spent from the emotion. 'I wish I had your faith. He will go on blaming himself, Nell.'

And the Lord alone knew what the consequence of that would be.

CHAPTER 35

*J*onathan sat on the broad window ledge in the library, his long legs cramped into the window space, an unread book in his hand and a table with a half-empty bottle of wine at his elbow.

'God's death, it's like walking into the past, Thornton. You used to sit there sulking when your father had chastised you.'

Jonathan swung his gaze around to the doorway where Giles stood, leaning heavily on one of Sir Francis' stout sticks.

'What are you doing here?' he snarled.

'Escaping my wife. I've had weeks of being cooped up in a room filled with frills and furbelows. I need some male company.'

Giles helped himself to a glass of wine and pulled up a chair. Resting his bad leg on the window ledge, he stretched. 'God's blood, Jon, as dearly as I love my wife I am beginning to yearn for the freedom of France.

Jonathan cast him a sideways glance. 'And the freedom to choose your bed mate?'

Giles shrugged. 'Nell thinks she is with child again,' he said.

Jonathan raised an eyebrow. 'That should occupy her idle hours in your absence. Giles, I swear you just have to hang your hat on a nail and you get her with child. It's a miracle you don't have by-blows from here to Paris.'

Giles ignored the jibe. 'In your idle hours have you considered how best you and I are to escape this tangle?' he asked, changing the subject.

Jonathan shook his head. 'My only thought is to head for London. How about you?'

Giles shook his head and ruefully rubbed his knee. 'It'll be a few weeks yet before I can sit on a horse,' he said.

They lapsed into silence again. Jonathan poured them both another glass of wine from the rapidly diminishing bottle by his side.

'I've been wondering if Prescott was telling the truth?' he said at last.

'What about?' Giles asked, idly shuffling a stained and battered pack of cards.

'Prescott told me Mary's child still lived.'

Giles' hands stilled. 'Did he, by God? My dear Thornton, have you considered that under the circumstances he probably would have said anything if he thought it would put you off guard? He told Kate he had the boy, don't forget.'

'*Your motherless bastard*' — Prescott's words had reverberated in Jonathan's mind.

He had never been in a position to verify the facts about Mary's death. He'd had the news thirdhand from a mutual acquaintance. Mary and the child had died. Women died in childbirth along with their babies. But could it be possible that the child had lived, its existence deliberately concealed from him?

Jonathan swilled the wine in his glass. 'I have to know, Giles and there is only one way to find out.'

'You're surely not thinking of going to Oxford?' Giles asked, his eyes widening. 'You'd be mad. The Woolnoughs would turn you in as soon as you knocked on their door.'

'I am sure they would,' agreed Jonathan. 'You're quite right. It would be madness. Now, are you going to deal those cards?'

He swung his legs off the window ledge and cleared the table. Giles obligingly cut the pack.

'Bear in mind, old friend' — Jonathan placed a heavy emphasis on the last two words — 'I don't have a groat to my name.'

Giles waved his hand expansively. 'Neither do I but I am willing to add the debt to the ledger,' he said.

They played a hand before Giles remarked, 'When are you going to talk to Kate?'

He might just as well have dealt Jonathan a physical blow. The wine in Jonathan's glass slopped onto his hand.

He looked away. 'I don't know what to say to her.'

'Well, sorry might be a good start.'

He cast Giles a sharp glance. 'Sorry? The word is barely adequate to compensate for what she has endured for me. The best thing for both of us would be for me to walk away from this house and never return.'

Giles set his glass down on the table.

'You're running away again,' he snapped. 'You ran away from Mary Woolnough and now you're running away from Kate. You are entirely undeserving of the love of either of them.'

'Since when have you started lecturing me on how to treat women?' Jonathan sprang to his feet.

'Since I met Kate Ashley,' Giles retorted, his voice rising. 'Jonathan, that woman has lied for you, risked her honour and nearly died for you and now you are leaving her without so much as a word? How much more do you intend to hurt her? Good God, man, there are times I don't understand you.'

'Sweet Jesu, Giles.' Jonathan swore, running his fingers through his hair as he paced the floor of the library. 'What can I offer her? I have nothing — nothing at all. No home, no future, no money.'

When Giles spoke again it was in a low, controlled voice. 'Have you asked her what she thinks?'

Jonathan whirled around to face his friend. 'I know what she thinks. I saw it in her eyes. You're right. I've hurt her, Giles, and I will go on hurting her.'

'All right, end it then.' Giles said picking up his cards. 'But do her the courtesy of telling her to her face. She deserves that at least.'

Jonathan returned to his seat and they resumed their game in relative silence, disturbed only by the driving rain on the windowpanes. As the afternoon wore on, the warmth of the room and the wine took their toll on Giles and he slumbered, snoring sonorously, in his chair.

Jonathan pushed aside his chair and stood up. He crossed to the window and looked out at the moat. He opened his jacket and drew out the gold ring emblazoned with a leopard. He had found it on the floor of the barn the morning after the encounter with Prescott. The leopard's head glinted in the light and he closed his fingers over it again.

He had given it to Kate and it had betrayed her — HE had betrayed her.

He opened the window and, heedless of the sudden rush of cold air, he hurled the ring into the moat. It hit with a small plop, barely disturbing the surface of the water, and sank.

He watched the faint ripples dissipate and leaned on the window sill, his head lowered. He had behaved despicably. Giles was right. He had to speak to Kate, tell her to her face that for her sake alone, their relationship had ended on that night in the barn.

～

HE FOUND Kate in her bedchamber, huddled in a chair beside the fire, her feet drawn up underneath her, her arms around her knees. She wore only her nightgown with a woollen shawl draped over her shoulders, and her undressed hair hung limply around her face.

'Kate?'

She turned her face to look at him and his heart jolted. Her eyes were sunken and smudged with grey, and beneath the livid bruising he saw only utter weariness and indifference. He had done this to her. It didn't matter that it was not his hand that had struck the blow.

He knelt by her chair and took her battered face in his hands.

He forced a smile. 'We make a fine pair,' he said in a light tone.

She turned her face away from his hands. 'Don't, Jonathan.'

He dropped his hands. 'Kate...' he began but could go no further. He did not know what to say, how to assuage the hurt in those lovely grey eyes.

'I don't know how to make amends, Kate. Somehow simply apologising does not seem enough.'

She leaned her head back against the chair, her eyes brimming with unshed tears.

'It's not that, Jonathan,' she said in a voice that trembled. 'It's not what happened in Long Barn. It is the utter futility of clinging to hope where there is none. You'll be gone tomorrow or the next day or next week — it doesn't matter. I'll be left with nothing but memories. We were both fools to think that we could even dream. Our dreams ended last night.'

He sat back on his heels as if she had struck him. It was as if she had read his mind. He had come to say the same words to her and now all he wanted to do was to take her in his arms and tell her she was being a fool.

Her hands gripped the arms of her chair, the knuckles white and she had turned her face away from him.

'You're wrong, Kate. Nothing ended that night except a tortured and unhappy life,' he said.

She looked at him and her face twisted in anguish. 'But he hasn't gone, Jonathan. Every time I close my eyes, I see his face, hear his voice… feel the muzzle of his weapon and I know I am utterly powerless. Prescott will haunt me forever, Jonathan. I can't make him go away.'

The tears now streamed down her face, and she wrapped her arms tighter around her body, defying him.

He took a breath and straightened, still on his knees. Despite her rigid, defensive posture, he cupped her face in his hands, forcing her to look at him.

'Kate, Stephen Prescott is dead and the guilt for his death is my burden, not yours. Sometimes we have to learn to live with memories that we think are too horrible to bear. We have to learn to recognise them for what they are — ghosts from a past that no longer have the power to hurt us.'

She dashed his hands away. 'But I don't understand your ghosts, Jon. What did you do to cause Stephen Prescott to hate you so much? I have a right to know about Mary Prescott… I have earned that right.'

He drew a long breath and rose to his feet. 'I should have told you at the beginning, after the affair in York.'

He paced the length of the room before returning to her. He pulled up a stool and set it in front of her. Seating himself, he began.

'It goes back long before the war when Giles and I went to Oxford.' He paused, allowing a glimpse of memory to tug at the corners of his lips. 'As anyone in my family will tell you, probably has already told you, we weren't there to study. We learned to drink, to fight, to play cards and we learned the delights of women. If the war had not intervened I would probably look back and think those were the best days of my life. As it is…' He tailed off and glanced up at her. She regarded him without blinking, her face without expression.

'My mother blamed Giles for leading me astray but I don't think either of us needed much leading. Giles had the luck with cards and I had something of a reputation with women. Giles and our friends wagered no small amount that I could seduce the daughter of one our dons, a girl called Mary Woolnough.'

He swallowed, remembering that drunken evening. A tidy sum had been put on the table.

'The challenge lay in the fact that the Woolnoughs were Puritan, unusual in Oxford at the time, with the added challenge that Mary was betrothed to a young lawyer called Stephen Prescott.'

Kate gasped and put her hand to her mouth.

'It was despicable, Kate. Giles and our friends made it their business to distract Prescott. He was the son of a farrier and by dint of his hard work he had turned himself into a lawyer with a promising career. His weakness was that he was socially ambitious and a snob and it made him easy prey. He was pleased by the apparent patronage of the young bucks and they enjoyed cheating him at cards and getting him drunk to the point of insensibility. While Giles and the others diverted Prescott, I paid court to Mary.'

He swallowed and looked away into the depths of the fire, remembering Mary's heart-shaped face and brown eyes. So trusting, so easily flattered — so easily won. It hurt to recall that time but he had promised Kate the truth and if she despised him for it then that was all for the good.

'It was so easy. She was seventeen and innocent, impossibly pretty and had the sweetest nature, despite her ghastly family. She fell for me without much persuasion.'

'The Thornton charm can be quite irresistible,' Kate interrupted, her tone harsh and bitter.

He flinched and turned his gaze back on the fire, unable to face the scorn in her eyes. 'What I had not counted on was my own feelings. I told the others I had failed and paid up the bet. It was a price worth paying. I was in love with her and she with me. We met in secret but her grandmother found some letters I had written and her family was outraged.' He glanced up at Kate. 'Believe me when I say I had not seduced her to my bed. However, neither my family nor Mary's were willing to believe that. Letters were written to my father and I was summoned home in disgrace.'

He closed his eyes, remembering his father's wrath and his mother's tears. Looking back he could no longer be sure if their anger was directed at the nature of the relationship or the fact that they considered Mary Woolnough beneath them.

'I would have married her but my father banished me to London to redeem myself by becoming, of all things, a lawyer. I don't know what her family did to Mary but within months they had succeeded in marrying her to Prescott. Mercifully for the legal profession, the war broke out and when I returned to Oxford as an officer under Prince Rupert, I sought her out. She was living with her father and grandmother. She told me that Prescott, not surprisingly, had joined Parliament. Despite my yearning to see her, I thought I would do the honourable thing and not pursue the friendship anymore.'

Jonathan pushed back his sleeve and looked at the scar on his arm. 'I took this at Marston Moor. It made me useless for fighting for a while and I found myself back in Oxford kicking my heels until my wound was healed. I could have had the choice of any number of court beauties but I was bored and lonely and despite my best intentions I went looking for Mary again and we found each other again.'

He drew a sharp breath and looked at Kate. The hands that had gripped the arms of the chair now rested in her lap and the clear grey eyes rested on his face without expression.

'Nothing had changed, Kate. We still loved each other and she was trapped in a marriage to a man for whom she felt nothing.' He swallowed. Now came the hard part. 'This time there was nothing innocent in our relationship. Over the winter months, we stole as much time together as we could and we became lovers. What had begun as a foolish bet had become the dangerous game of adultery.' He closed his eyes. 'By the spring of '45, I had run out of excuses. I had to go back to the war.'

The breath stopped in his throat at the memory of the frightful scene with Mary that had followed that news. The anguish of that last meeting still cut his heart like the blade of a bright sword. 'Mary begged me to take her with me. She pleaded with me but I had no choice but to leave her in Oxford.'

'Why didn't you take her?' Kate asked.

Why indeed. The reasons had seemed so clear at the time.

'I couldn't have her trailing after me like a draggle-tailed camp follower. You've seen it, you know the life she would have led. She was not bred for that. She would have been at Naseby and you know the fate of the women in the King's baggage lines.'

Kate shook her head. 'No. What happened to them?'

'The women, Welsh, Irish and English, were raped, mutilated and turned out to die in the fields and the lanes. It was not a proud moment for the Lord's chosen. Surely you heard the stories, even in Yorkshire?'

Kate's eyes widened and she shuddered. 'I had no idea.' She paused. 'But you could have brought her here to Seven Ways?'

He laughed. 'Here? My mother would hardly countenance me installing my mistress, someone else's wife, under her roof. My mother called her a whore even before the war. As I saw it I had no choice but to leave Mary in Oxford, safe with her family, as a problem that I would sort out after the fighting ended.'

'And did you go back to Oxford?' Kate asked.

He shook his head. 'After Naseby, the war was all but lost. Rupert was sent west to hold Bristol, and as one of his officers, I went too. The west was ill-disposed to the King's forces. Goring and Grenville had seen to that,' he said angrily. 'After Rupert surrendered Bristol in September of that year, he went back to Oxford and was promptly cashiered by the King for cowardice. He had left me in the west to lend what little support I could to the lost cause. For a few months, I had some success leading raiding parties and harrying the tail of Fairfax's army, but my luck ran out. My men were tired, hungry and demoralized. Half of them had already deserted. One morning we ran straight into a regiment of Parliament horse. I had no choice. After putting up a token resistance I surrendered.'

He paused before taking a deep breath. 'It was my misfortune to fall into the hands of a man whose family had paid dearly for their allegiance to Parliament at the hands of Goring and his crew. He had no love for the King's men. He incarcerated us in the tower of an old church and left us there with no food and water for two days before he summoned me to his presence.'

Jonathan closed his eyes. He could still see the scene of that encounter so clearly — the tallow candles flickering on the table, the rancid smell of the two troopers who had escorted him and above everything else the hatred in the eyes of the two men who faced him; the colonel because he was a Royalist and Stephen Prescott because he was Jonathan Thornton.

'Is this the man?' the colonel had asked Prescott.

Prescott nodded, his eyes glittering in the light of the candle. 'I can confirm that this is Jonathan Thornton. He is responsible for the hanging of five of our men he had taken prisoner.'

'You lying bastard,' Jonathan spat. 'I've never hung prisoners.'

Prescott's lip twitched. 'Ah, but I have a witness, a personal account.'

Jonathan gave Prescott a contemptuous glare. 'And I bet you paid him well.'

The colonel thumped the table and rose to his feet. 'Be quiet. I've not given you leave to speak. Thornton, you will be taken to London for trial and tomorrow five of your men hang.' He glanced at Prescott. 'As we agreed, the prisoner is yours. I'll leave you now.'

'No.' Jonathan lunged forward as the colonel left the room. 'I've never hanged prisoners and I expect the same rights of war to be accorded to my men.'

But the door slammed shut, leaving him at the mercy of Stephen Prescott.

Prescott laughed, a cold mirthless laugh. 'Tomorrow, Thornton, you'll have the pleasure of watching your men die and know there is nothing you can do to prevent it.'

He crossed the floor towards Jonathan and struck him hard across the face with his heavy leather gauntlet. As Jonathan buckled against the troopers at the force of the blow, Prescott hit him again then seized him by the hair, forcing him to look into his face.

'This is for my wife, you bloody adulterer. You murdering whoreson.'

Blood ran from Jonathan's nose, and he could taste it in his mouth but he forced himself to meet Prescott's eyes. 'What do you mean?'

'You thought you could set cuckold's horns on my head, the

pair of you?' Prescott said. 'You have both paid the price. Mary is dead. Dead giving birth to your bastard.'

'Dead?' Jonathan groaned and his knees gave way.

'Dead and her bastard child with her. I knew the child couldn't be mine. I'd not lain with her the three years past. They tell me that on her death bed she called your name.'

Jonathan's knees gave way and he groaned aloud, sagging in the grip of his captors.

As Mary had pleaded with him, she must have known she carried his child. Why hadn't she told him?

Prescott hauled him up again but he had accomplished his end and Jonathan was too far gone in grief at Mary's death to care what happened to him anymore.

'She's rotting in hell where she deserves to be,' Prescott replied viciously. A cold smile spread across his face. 'And you're here with me. Hell may seem like a pleasant alternative.'

Prescott stood back and let the troopers finish what he had started. They stopped short of killing him, and when he came around he was back in the dank tower. As he looked around the dirty, anxious faces he wondered what he could say. Five of these innocent men would die for his folly. All he could do was pray for a miracle but there were no miracles and God had deserted them.

'Jonathan?'

Kate's voice brought him back to the present and he felt the weight of his past settling on his shoulders.

In slow, halting words he recounted that encounter with Prescott. As he spoke Kate leaned forward, taking his hands in hers.

'Prescott made my men draw straws.' Jonathan's hands tightened on Kate's. 'Cornet Williams took fifteen minutes to die, choked at the end of a badly tied knot. He was only seventeen.'

Far away from that scene, both in time and distance, Jonathan closed his eyes as he saw again so clearly the faces that had haunted his dreams from that day on. So many, many times he had played the episode through in his mind, wondering what he could have said or done that may have averted the ultimate tragedy of those five wasted lives.

'Prescott never took his eyes off me,' Jonathan concluded with a shuddering breath. 'He watched and he smiled. The same smile I saw as he raised his pistol against me in York.'

Of all the deaths he had witnessed in the bloody years of war, his brother and his father among them, the death of those five ragged, starving men had wrought the greatest change in the reckless young man who had stolen his grandfather's horse and ridden off to war.

Kate wrapped her arms around herself and shivered. 'Prescott had his chance. Why didn't he hang you when he could?'

'He wanted me to suffer. He wanted me to live with the knowledge that it was I who was responsible for the death of my men - my innocent men. On the road back to London to face my trial, I escaped and took ship for France as soon as I was able. The rest you know.'

He dared himself to look up and face the judgment in Kate's eyes but he saw only tears. Were the tears for him or for the ghosts of all the people he had wronged?

'I'm sorry, Kate. It's an unlovely tale but you deserved the truth about me,' he said.

'I'm glad you told me. I had no idea such things went on in the name of King or Parliament.'

He shook his head. 'David Ashley protected you well. Be thankful that you never saw the dark side of human nature.'

Until now, he thought. *Now through me, you have seen evil.*

'And you,' she said, 'you're a soldier too, just as capable of doing the acts of which you were accused.'

He looked her in the eye. 'Kate, I was young and I was arrogant but I pride myself on being a professional soldier. I never raised a hand against a woman or a child and, to my knowledge, no man under my command has ever done so.'

And lived to tell the tale, he may have added, but chose not to.

They sat in silence for a long time, He had given her the whole story. He had nothing more to say. Now he waited on her judgment.

She straightened and raised her right hand. She frowned and she touched his face, tracing the line of his cheekbone as if she were searching for ghosts.

They were there, they always would be — the frail wraith that was all that was left of his memory of Mary, the young Cornet and the four other soldiers who had died for that illicit love, and now, linking them all, the spectre of Stephen Prescott. But in telling her the story they seemed diminished, incapable of hurting him any longer.

All his words to Giles, all his resolve forgotten, he slid off the stool and knelt on the hearth before her. He took her hand in his and lowered his head, burying it in her skirts like a penitent seeking forgiveness.

'Jon,' she lowered her head to his. 'We can't change the past, but we can determine our future.'

He straightened and they both rose to their feet. Her eyes did not leave his face as he took her in his arms and held her close, almost crushing her.

'Kate, Kate,' he whispered into her disordered hair, saying the three words he had said to no woman since Mary. 'I love you, Kate. You're everything to me and even if I am gone tomorrow, that will not change.'

She whispered his name, her body melting in his embrace. Conscious of her bruises, he kissed her gently and with infinite tenderness, desperate to obliterate the dreadful memories of the last few weeks.

They stood together for a long time in silence, just holding each other.

Jonathan closed his eyes, breathing in the familiar scent of rosemary that was so intrinsically a part of this woman he loved so much. He looked down at her, smoothing the unruly hair from her face.

'Kate, would you marry me?' he whispered.

She looked up at him and smiled and his heart leapt at the warmth of that smile.

She laid her hand on his face and spoke in a calm, clear voice, more like the old Kate. 'Yes, my dearest love, I will marry you,' she said and paused. 'But only when you can stand beside me a free man.'

He stiffened, as desolation swept over him. He broke from her and walked across to the window, running his fingers through his hair. As he stood looking down at the moat, she came to stand by his side. Her fingers twisted into his and she squeezed his hand.

'It's not a woman's fancy, Jon. There is nothing I want more in this world than to call myself your wife, but one thing the past weeks have taught me is that I am more use to you and your family untrammelled by the Thornton name.'

He glanced down at her. The curse of the Thornton name, he thought.

He sighed. 'I've always been so sure of the rightness of the cause I fought for but I too have had plenty of time to think in the past weeks. God alone knows how tired I am of fighting and running. I don't want to see out my days in penury in some garret in Amsterdam or Paris in the name of a cause I can do nothing more for.' He shook his head. 'Kate, I don't know what to do.'

'Make your peace with Parliament?' Kate ventured.

He looked at her and sadly shook his head. 'There is the little matter of my death warrant. For me, there will be no peace with Parliament.'

'Maybe not right now,' Kate said, 'but memories fade.' She paused. 'There is another alternative. Take me with you.'

The poignant echo of Mary's pleas took Jonathan's breath.

'Would you leave Tom and your home and your family to follow me? Spend your life wondering where your next meal is coming from or where you will sleep the night? Dearest, that would kill our love surer than anything that has come between us before.' He took her hands and turned them over, kissing the palms. 'I will untie this hellish knot that is my life. I promise. Will you wait for me, Kate?'

She nodded. 'There will never be anyone else, Jonathan,' she said. 'I will wait for you, even if you find me stiff with rheumatics, making clothes for my grandchildren, I'll be waiting for you.'

He smiled at the thought. 'Picture us, my dearest, hobbling down the aisle together, exchanging recipes for rheumatic ointments at the altar.'

Kate leaned her head against him, laughing, and he wrapped his arms around her. They had to laugh, seize what happiness they could, to live only for this precious moment because to contemplate what was to come would be too painful.

CHAPTER 36

*K*ate woke to the gentle touch of lips on her forehead. She opened her eyes and looked up at the man she loved. He smiled down at her and bent his head to kiss her.

'Good morning, Mistress Ashley,' he whispered.

'Good morning, Sir Jonathan.' She smiled sleepily. 'What are you looking at?'

'You,' he said. 'I want to remember you like this.'

Memory jolted her into the present and she felt the pricking of tears behind her eyes. 'Today...' she said, unable to complete the sentence. Today he was leaving her.

'Shhh.' He kissed her again.

She reached up and her arms circled his neck, pulling him down towards her and they clung to each other as if relinquishing the bond between them would mark the irretrievable separation that had to occur.

So many words crowded Kate's mind, words of love and loneliness, hope and despair, but they would all remain unsaid. Everything they had to say to each other passed silently between them.

Jonathan kissed her hair and pulled away from her embrace.

'Dearest,' he said, 'it's time. I must be away.'

She nodded in bleak agreement. Any protest would be pointless. He had to go and she had to let him go. Another farewell; too many farewells.

He sat on the edge of the bed for a moment, and she knelt up behind him, wrapping her arms around his well-muscled shoulders, nuzzling his ear.

'Kate,' he protested. 'I have to get dressed.' He grabbed one of her hands and put it to his lips. 'Who would ever guess you were such a wanton,' he said, extricating himself from her arms.

She lay back on the bed and watched him dress, trying to hold this memory of him.

'Where will you go?' she asked at last.

He paused in lacing his shirt. 'London,' he said, 'and from there, the Hague. I will send word as soon as I reach safety. What about you?' he asked.

'As soon as Giles can travel, we will go north to Barton for the winter,' she said. 'Suzanne is with child again and I would like to be with her.'

'With child again?' Jonathan shook his head. 'I swear William must only have to take his boots off.'

Kate's hand moved involuntarily to her flat stomach, and she bit her lip, wondering if she may be carrying his child. While the thought filled her with dread, a small part of her cried out to have his child, to hold a part of him with her always.

The family gathered in the courtyard to see Jonathan on his way: Giles, still leaning heavily on a stick, stood beside Nell who held little Ann by the hand, and Kate, determined to hold herself together for the sake of the others and the servants who gathered in the doorway.

Jonathan gathered up the reins of Nell's old saddle horse that he was taking in exchange for Amber. Kate had told him to sell the horse in London, as it would give him sufficient money for a fare to the continent and a start to life as an exile.

'Wait.' Tom ran into the courtyard, clutching a filthy rag in an equally filthy hand.

Kate looked at her son with distaste. 'What do you have there, Tom?'

Tom unwrapped the bundle and held up the Order of St George that the King had given him on the night of the battle.

'Jonathan, can you give this back to the King?' the boy asked.

Jonathan took the precious George from the boy and shook his head. 'No. I think Giles should have custody of it,' he said.

'Why would it be any safer with me?' Giles enquired.

Jonathan shook his head. 'I just think it would be.'

Kate caught a conspiratorial look that passed between the two men and her heart skipped a beat. Surely Jonathan had nothing else planned that would put him further into danger?

'Do you have to go?' Tom asked Jonathan.

Jonathan nodded. 'I do, Tom. You know that.'

Tom grimaced. 'What will you do? Will you fight for Prince Rupert again?'

Jonathan pulled a face. 'I think not. When last I heard, the noble Prince had taken to the sea as commander of the King's navy, and I have no great desire to join Rupert on his aquatic adventures.'

'You will write and tell us your adventures, though?' Tom moved beside his mother and suffered her to put an arm around his shoulders.

'Of course.' Jonathan swung up into the saddle. He had become once again, John Miller, in a plain grey, woollen jacket and breeches beneath a dark cloak, his much-battered hat on his head. In his luggage, he carried Jacob Howell's short, serviceable sword, a pistol and sufficient books to cover his alias.

Kate crossed to the horse and he bent from the saddle to kiss her, a chaste public kiss on the cheek, not that anyone in the household would be in any doubt about the true nature of their relationship. They had abandoned any pretence in the few short days they had together.

'God speed,' Nell said and lifted her hand.

Jonathan looked down at Kate and smiled.

'Don't cry,' he said in a low voice.

'I'm not,' she lied, sniffing back the tears.

He straightened in the saddle and with one last wave, put his heels to the horse, riding out beneath the gatehouse without a backward glance.

CHAPTER 37

The last time Jonathan had seen Oxford, it had been the King's headquarters and the streets had thronged with soldiers and courtiers. It would take more than six years to obliterate the massive earthworks and other evidence of the important role the city had played during the war but superficially, at least, it seemed to have returned to its peaceful role as a place of learning.

Despite his promises of absolute honesty, he'd not told Kate of Prescott's revelation. He'd only confided his intentions of visiting Oxford to Giles and Giles had, quite rightly, tried to dissuade him from this venture — folly he had called it. But the thought that he may have a child yet living had played continually on Jonathan's mind until it had become a familiar tune.

He needed to discover the truth before he shared this last and greatest secret from his past.

Jonathan stabled his horse at an inn just outside the city wall and strolled unchallenged through the gates. Outwardly Oxford had become once more the pleasant, dreamy city of Jonathan's dissolute youth. Students in gowns, their heads bent against the cold, wet weather, mingled in the streets with the townspeople, just as they had done for hundreds of years.

The Woolnoughs' house in Turl Street had remained unaltered in the six years since he had last seen it. He almost expected to see Mary's face at the parlour window, watching the street for his arrival, but the lower windows were shuttered and the house looked cold and impenetrable.

The rain that had fallen persistently since he had left Seven Ways continued to fall on Oxford. The cold, autumnal drizzle penetrated his heavy cloak and ensured that the streets of the town were largely deserted. He gave the house one last look but dared not loiter. Instead, he slipped into a warm hostelry from which he could just see the house, bought himself an ale and waited.

The afternoon slipped by, and he had been considering abandoning his watch when he heard a familiar voice.

'Now then, do stop thy complaining. We're nearly home, see?'

Bet, Mary's loyal and devoted maidservant, had stopped just outside the door. Jonathan's heart lurched. Bet held a child by the hand. The child, too heavily bundled in a cloak for Jonathan to even see what sex it was, complained in a high, fretful voice.

The blood in his veins quickened and Jonathan picked up his hat and stepped outside the door just as Bet, pulling her unwilling charge by the hand, had started towards the Woolnough house.

'Bet.'

At the sound of his voice, the woman froze and then swung around sharply on her heel, her eyes wide and her mouth falling open. He put his finger to his lips to stall her from declaring his name for the world to hear.

'You,' she said. 'I never thought to see you again.'

He forced himself to look down at the child; a girl, he saw with a lurch of his heart. She looked up at him with bright, curious eyes— brown like Mary's.

She seemed about the right age. Could it be possible that Prescott had told him the truth and that this was indeed his daughter?

'Bet, I must talk to you,' he said. 'Can we meet?'

Bet considered a moment. 'I must get madam here home and in some dry clothes and see to Dame Judith. I could meet you in an hour, perhaps,' she said. 'Where?'

He hesitated. They needed privacy and somewhere dry.

'The church of St Michael. In an hour.'

Bet nodded. The church of St Michael had been the favourite meeting place for Jonathan and Mary and Bet had willingly aided and abetted her mistress in the first flowering of youthful love. Later, in the more deadly game of adultery, Bet had carried their notes and arranged their trysts.

She nodded and jerked the hand of the child, who had become bored with the conversation of adults and was poking an already damp foot at the puddles. 'Come on, madam, we best get you home afore your Grandam gives us both a telling off.' Jonathan watched them until the door of the Woolnough house slammed shut.

THE CHURCH of St Michael stood open and quiet. A few godly souls occupied the front pews, too intent on their prayers to notice the tall man who slipped quietly into a darkened pew to the rear of the church.

Jonathan removed his hat and knelt and lowered his head to his hands, grateful for the peace and the chance to make some amends with God.

It had long gone past the hour before Bet slipped in beside him with muttered apologies for her tardiness.

'You've not changed, Bet,' he said.

'You always did have a silver tongue.' She blushed and self-consciously patted the brown curls that strayed from beneath her cap. 'I can't say the same for you. I scarce recognised you in the street.'

It was not the time for idle gossip, so he came straight to the point.

'I've come about the child,' he said, adding, '...my child, I believe.'

Bet paled and sat back against the pew. 'How did you hear about her?' she said. 'Master and Dame Judith were dead set about you ever knowing.'

Hundreds of questions suddenly flooded into Jonathan's mind. He caught his breath and finally asked the one question that had haunted him for the last six years.

'Why didn't Mary tell me she was with child?'

Bet's cheerful face clouded over. 'Oh, Sir Jonathan, at the time you went, she wasn't sure and she didn't want to trap you into taking her with you.'

Agonised, Jonathan twisted his hat in his hand. 'I would never have left her to Prescott and that old harridan if I had known, or even suspected.'

Bet touched his arm sympathetically. 'It went ill with her. She couldn't hide the fact that the child could not have been her husband's but in the end, it wouldn't have changed anything. Like as not she'd still have died. She were just too small for child-bearing.'

Jonathan swallowed and looked up at a beautiful lily window that had survived the ravages of war. A representation of Mary in her blue robe, clutching a lily in her hand, the colours bright in the evening sun.

His mouth had gone dry. 'What's her name?' He forced himself to speak.

'Tabitha. Mistress Mary named her afore she died.'

'Tabitha.' He tried the name out. He brought his gaze back to Bet. 'What sort of life has she led?'

Bet sighed. 'She's led a lonely life, poor, motherless thing. There's only her great grandam left now… and me. I tell you the old lady is not long for the world, although she's going to her Lord kicking and screaming.'

'I can imagine,' Jonathan remarked grimly, remembering his last, unpleasant interview with the old woman during which he had been likened to Beelzebub.

'Can I see her, Bet?'

Bet stiffened and shook her head. 'Not while the old lady lives and breathes. She would call the soldiers as soon as she laid eyes on you.' Bet paused. 'I tell you what. Come tonight. When you see the light go out upstairs, knock twice on the kitchen door and I'll let you in.'

Jonathan smiled. Bet the schemer had not changed.

They parted at the church door. Jonathan took his evening meal before returning to the street to wait for Bet's signal. He lurked in the shadows in the cold for hours but when the tiny light in the upstairs window went out, it took him all his courage to knock on the door.

Through the kitchen window, he could see Bet setting the dough to rise for tomorrow's bread. Brushing the flour from her hands, she opened the door to him. 'Come in and warm yourself,' she said.

Although the rain had abated, it had been a long, cold wait and he accepted the offer of the fire.

'Is she here?' he asked, his voice tight with anticipation.

'Aye, upstairs in her bed asleep. I'll go and wake her.'

Jonathan caught Bet's arm as she stood to leave. 'You'll not wake the old lady?'

'Bless you, no. I've given her a sleeping draught that would fell an ox.' Bet winked.

Jonathan stood by the fire, every nerve in his body strung to breaking point. Even facing battle he had never felt so ill.

My daughter... Tabitha.

The name spun in his mind as it had done since he had spoken to Bet that afternoon. What could he say to her to make amends for an absence of so long?

It seemed an age before Bet returned, leading the child by her hand. Tabitha's long, dark hair cascaded from beneath her nightcap and she clutched a ragged dirty doll of sorts.

She yawned and rubbed her eyes, blinking sleepily in the light of the kitchen as she looked at the tall, strange man by the fireplace with the same curious gaze that she had used when they had met in the street.

Jonathan searched her face, taking in every detail. She had Mary's heart-shaped face but the hazel eyes and dark hair were his legacies. He did not doubt that Tabitha was indeed his child.

Bet laid a hand on the child's shoulder and said, 'Now, Mistress Tabitha, this is your father, Sir Jonathan Thornton.'

The child looked at her, then up at Jonathan. The sleep had gone from her eyes and they were bright as she scanned his face. She looked up at Bet, a frown puckering her forehead.

'Is he really my father?'

Jonathan, normally at ease with children, suddenly felt inadequate. He hunkered down, bringing himself to the level of the child and said softly, 'I am your father, Tabitha.'

Her reaction was not what he had imagined in the long wait to meet her. He had pictured shyness and disbelief but the small face contorted with anger and she flew at him, her fists flailing against his chest.

'I hate you, I hate you,' she screamed.

'Hush, child,' Bet scolded, twisting her hands in her apron. 'You'll wake your Grandam and there'll be hell to pay for both of us.'

Jonathan gently disengaged the small virago and held her at arm's length. She glared at him, her chest heaving and tears splashing on the flags of the kitchen floor.

'Shh,' he said, bringing his finger to his lips. 'Bet's right, your Grandam will punish us all if she sees me here.'

At the second mention of her great-grandmother, the child's sobs ceased and she stared, still gulping, into her father's eyes.

'Tabitha,' he said, making sure he held her gaze, 'why do you hate me?'

She hiccupped, and the rage in her face subsided to be replaced with fear. 'You're the devil. You killed my mother.'

'Is that what Grandam told you?' he asked.

She nodded.

Still holding her gaze he said, 'Do I look like the devil?' She shook her head, and he continued, 'Tabitha, I'm just an ordinary man and I loved your mother very much.'

She quivered with rage. 'I don't believe you.'

Bet interrupted. "Tis true, Mistress Tabitha, he did, and your mother loved him too.'

'Then why did you go away?' Tabitha challenged.

Jonathan tried to keep his voice even but he could hear the emotion at the edge of his words. 'I was a soldier, Tabitha. I had to go away to war.'

Tabitha looked from one adult to the other. Her face crumpled, and all the years of hurt and loneliness spilled out of her.

Clutching her doll, she ran out of the room. Jonathan made to follow her, but Bet's hand restrained him. He met her gaze, agonised and rendered helpless by the child's pain.

Bet shook her head. 'You must give her time, Sir Jonathan,' she said. 'Dame Judith's filled her 'ead with all sorts of stories about you. None of 'em good.'

'Devil take that woman,' said Jonathan with feeling, subsiding onto one of the kitchen stools. He flexed the fingers of his right hand, trying to imagine them circling Dame Judith's scrawny neck.

'Bet, what will become of her when Dame Judith dies?' he asked.

Bet shook her head. 'Dame Judith's the last of the family, save for a cousin who will inherit the house. I've already heard him say that he won't take responsibility for a motherless bastard child but he'll keep her if she earns her keep.'

Jonathan knew what meant. Tabitha would become a servant in her own mother's house. He ran his hand through his hair in despair and frustration. For now, cold and unloving as it might be, she did at least have a home, but without the protection of her grandmother what hope was there for an illegitimate child nobody wanted?

He stood up and walked slowly over to the kitchen door.

'What will you do?' Bet asked.

He turned and looked at her. 'I don't know, Bet. I need some time to think.'

He stumbled back to his lodgings through the dark, familiar streets of Oxford. His feet had turned to lead, and utter despair weighed on his shoulders.

Giles had been right; it had been madness to come here. He would have been better off never knowing about the child.

He shook off that unworthy thought as he flung himself onto

the bed and stared up at the ceiling beams. He could never live with himself if he abandoned his child again to such an uncertain future. He owed Mary and her daughter some atonement for the past.

But what could he do? Should he take her back to Seven Ways? Add another burden to Kate's woes or take her with him into exile?

The last thought almost made him laugh. He couldn't make a life for himself, let alone for a six-year-old girl.

The thought of his present parlous situation overwhelmed him, and for one of the few times in his twenty-eight years, alone in the concealing darkness of his inn room, tears gathered in the corners of his eyes and slid unchecked onto the none-too-clean bed covers.

CHAPTER 38

*H*is head heavy and dull with lack of sleep, Jonathan stood outside the neat house in Turl Street. He had faced the worst any foe in battle could throw at him and he had known real fear, but nothing in this world could fully prepare him for an interview with that fearsome termagant from his past, Dame Judith Woolnough.

Several times he had made to knock on the door but his courage had failed him. He paced the street heedless of the curious stares of the passersby and with a deep, steadying breath raised his hand to knock and froze.

A child's scream came from within the house.

The sound cut Jonathan to his heart and without further hesitation, he beat on the door.

Bet opened it, her face pale and strained.

'Oh, Sir Jonathan.' She grasped his hands. 'Miss Tabitha told her about your coming here. I've never seen her so angry. She'll kill the lass and then she'll start on me.'

Jonathan did not wait to hear more. From the parlour came

Tabitha's voice, choked with sobs, interspersed with the shrill, strident tones of her great-grandmother.

'Disobedient child.'

'Grandam, don't hit me.'

Thwack.

The unmistakable sound of a cane being applied with force on a solid object, followed by another scream.

Jonathan threw open the door of the parlour, his hand instinctively going to the hilt of his sword.

Dame Judith held the child by one arm her cane raised to strike the child, who she held by one arm.

She looked up and her mouth curled in an unlovely snarl. 'So it's true. You've come back.' She glanced at the sword. 'Would you seek to run me through, you whoreson Jonathan Thornton?'

With difficulty, Jonathan restrained himself from that temptation and lifted his hand away from the weapon. For all Bet's assurance that the old lady was not long for the world, she did not seem to have lost any of her vigour or spite.

'I've never yet taken my sword to a woman. Leave the child be,' he said in a low, quiet voice.

He took a step towards the woman and she released her grip on Tabitha, tossing her aside like a bundle of rags. She straightened to face him, her face twisted in hate.

'Why have you come?'

'Stephen Prescott sent me,' Jonathan replied.

At that name, her gaze wavered. 'Prescott? What dealings have you had with him? He was a good man.' She pointed a gnarled finger at him. 'You did him a grave wrong when you debauched his wife. I have prayed that he would seek you out and take his rightful vengeance.'

Jonathan returned her scornful gaze. He was no longer a

stripling boy in the flush of his first love and he had no wish to relive the confrontations of his past.

'Stephen Prescott is dead,' he said.

The old woman's mouth curled up in a cruel parody of a smile. 'And you killed him? Add murder to your sins, Jonathan Thornton. May your soul burn forever in the torments of hell.'

'Aye, it probably will.' His eyes narrowed. 'But if it does, yours will burn with mine. You bear as much responsibility for the past as I do.'

'I?' Her eyes widened. 'It was you who ravished my granddaughter and cuckolded her husband.'

'It was you who forced her into marriage with a man she did not love. I would have married her.'

As he took a step closer, she picked up the cane and brandished it threateningly at him.

'And do you plan to beat me as you have my daughter?' Jonathan said with icy composure.

He caught the cane as she brought it down in his direction. With an easy movement, he wrested it from her grip and broke it over his knee. He flung the pieces aside and stood facing Dame Judith.

'Tell me, what this child has done that you should treat her so?'

'She is a lying, deceitful Jezebel. The spawn of a whore and the devil. She must need be beaten to correct her wicked ways.' Dame Judith's voice cracked with the fury of her emotion.

Jonathan looked away from the woman to the child, who cowered on the floor sobbing into her hands.

'Come to me, Tabitha,' he said softly.

The child looked up at him from between her fingers and he held out his hand to her.

'Tabitha?' He smiled at her.

She rose unsteadily to her feet and stood looking from her

great-grandmother to him. Dame Judith had eyes only for Jonathan and if those eyes could have shot sparks of hell fire, they would have burned him to the quick, but she was just an old, unpleasant woman and she had no hold over him. Not any more.

Jonathan ignored the old woman and turned his full attention to Tabitha. Hesitantly she took a step toward him.

He knelt and held out his arms to her. Stumbling over her skirts, she ran across the room to him, falling into his arms. He held her close, feeling the warmth of her small, fragile body, stroking her hair — his daughter.

HIS daughter. He could never let her go again.

'Tabitha?' he whispered. 'Would you come with me?'

Tabitha looked up at him with large, fearful eyes. She glance at Bet, who cowered in the doorway, watching the scene in the parlour, her hands twisted in her apron.

'Dame Judith won't let me,' she said.

Jonathan shot a glance at the old lady. She seemed to have deflated, leaning on the table as if it was the only thing that kept her from sliding to the floor.

'It's not for Dame Judith to say,' he said.

'You take her from this house and I will set the soldiers after ye.' For all her frailty, Dame Judith's voice had lost none of its spite.

He nodded. 'Yes, you probably will,' he said, 'but it alters nothing. Tabitha is my daughter and she is coming with me.'

The old woman subsided into a chair. 'You'd take her from me?' she asked and for the first time, she sounded fretful and pleading. 'She's all I've got in the world. My little Tabby.'

Jonathan did not reply. Words were inadequate to express his repulsion for this woman whose mean spirit had shadowed the short life of her granddaughter and now seemed set to do the same to her great-granddaughter. It was too late for Dame Judith to play at being the loving grandmother.

'I've seen for myself how much you value the love of this child,' he said. He set Tabitha down and laid a hand on her hair. 'Go with Bet and pack your clothes,' he said. 'We will leave now.'

'Where are we going?' Tabitha's eyes shone with sudden hope.

Dear God, I have no idea, thought Jonathan. He forced himself to smile at the child. 'We'll know when we get there,' he said.

He stood up and looked at Bet. 'Dress her warmly.'

Bet glanced at the old woman who sat hunched and defeated in her chair. 'Sir Jonathan,' she said, 'she'll send for the soldiers, you can depend on't.'

'I'll be long gone, Bet. Now hurry.'

Bet disappeared upstairs, leading Tabitha by the hand. Dame Judith glared up at Jonathan like a predatory bird caught in a net from which it knows there is no escape. He looked away. He had nothing to say to her; she was beyond his contempt.

Bet returned with Tabitha dressed in a thick winter cloak. She clutched a small bundle and the raggedy doll he had seen her with the day before. She looked up at him and smiled and just for a moment he thought he could see a little of Tom in her.

'Are we going now?' she asked.

He nodded and Bet knelt beside her and made a pretence of fussing over her cloak. 'Now you be very brave and do everything your father tells you,' she said in a tear-choked voice. 'It'll be a grand adventure. Just remember your Bet loves you.'

The child threw her arms around Bet's neck. 'I love you too,' she said.

'Bet, would you come?' Jonathan asked impulsively.

The maid looked up at him then over at the old woman. 'No, thank 'ee, Sir Jonathan,' she said reluctantly. 'I can't leave her, not now.'

He nodded. 'Will you be all right?'

Bet smiled at him. 'Aye. She'll rant and rave but she knows I'm all she's got.'

'I can't leave her to raise the soldiers as soon as I have walked out the door.' He sighed. 'I have no choice but to lock you both in the cellar.' He stood back from the door and bowed mockingly. 'After you, ladies.'

Dame Judith laughed, a harsh, humourless cackle. She rose to her feet and hobbled towards him and her eyes, unrepentant, held his for a moment.

'Take your spawn and I wish you well of her. She'll bring you naught but grief. Born of tears she was.' She rounded on Bet. 'And as for you, you traitorous baggage, you'll be out by the evening.'

'Oh, you don't mean that,' Bet said. 'It's for the best and you know it. If you send me away, who'll put up with you?'

Jonathan gestured at the cellar door. 'In there, both of you.'

He waited until the old woman had descended the stone steps before catching Bet's eye. He held up the key and indicated that he would leave it where it could be reached under the door.

Bet nodded in silent agreement. She would ensure Jonathan a good head start. He shut the door and locked it, gently placing the key within reach. He returned to the parlour where Tabitha waited for him.

Jonathan held out his hand. Looking up at him with her trusting eyes, Tabitha placed her small hand in his.

CHAPTER 39

A gust of icy wind, laced with sleet, whipped through Jonathan's sodden cloak. He had wanted to put as many miles as he could between himself and Oxford and he had ridden hard for the morning. Although he had slowed the pace in the afternoon, as the drear evening closed in his horse shivered underneath him, head drooping in exhaustion as it plodded onwards.

His daughter lay limp and unresponsive in his arms. She had borne the long day with great fortitude and even chattered to him through the morning but now as night closed in her eyes had closed, the lashes dark on her damp, ashen cheeks.

The child whimpered and Jonathan held her closer.

'It's all right, just a little further,' he said.

London lay just a few miles away, tantalisingly within his grasp. It could wait. For now, he had a refuge closer at hand.

He looked up at the familiar gateposts and sighed. Beyond the open gates, a light burned in a downstairs room of the pleasant house that had been more nearly a home to him than Seven Ways had ever been.

Throwing himself on the mercy of this house would probably mean the end to any hope of reaching the continent, but he was beyond caring about himself. The child needed rest and shelter and here he could be assured she would get it. For Tabitha's sake, he had to take the risk.

He turned the weary horse into the forecourt of the familiar neat, half-timbered house that stood on the banks of the River Thames, just outside the village of Putney, only a few miles from London.

No one had heard him arrive and no groom came out to take his horse. He dismounted awkwardly and, hefting the child in his arms, he knocked on the door.

He stepped back as a small, portly man opened the door. Holding up his candle, the man peered out into the dark, cold night.

'Who's there at this hour?' he demanded of the darkness.

'It's me, Uncle.' Jonathan moved into the thin circle of light thrown by the candle.

Nathaniel Freeman thrust the candle upward and peered into the face beneath the dripping brim of the hat.

'My God,' he declared in surprise, a response that prompted a wry smile from Jonathan. 'Is this madness, boy?'

'Of a kind,' Jonathan said. 'We need shelter for the night.'

'We? What do you have there?' Freeman gestured at the bundle in Jonathan's arms.

'My daughter.'

'Your daughter? Come in, come in…'

His uncle stepped back to let him pass and followed him into the house, shutting the door behind him.

Knowing the house well, Jonathan headed for the well-lit study where he could see a fire burning in the hearth.

Freeman fussed in his wake. 'What's this about a daughter? I didn't know you had a daughter? Put her by the fire. That's it.'

'What's happening? Nathaniel? Who was that at the door?'

A plump, diminutive woman, dressed in a woollen robe pulled on over her nightgown, appeared at the door.

Jonathan looked up at her, and she gave a small squeal of pleasure, her hands going to her mouth.

'Surely not? Is that Jonathan? Oh, my dearest boy. What brings you here?'

Her husband frowned at her. 'No time, Hen. He says he has his daughter with him, and by the look of her, he's nearly killed the child.'

'His daughter? What daughter?' She came closer, her face crumpling with concern. 'The poor little lass.'

Jonathan laid the child down on the hearth beside a cheerfully crackling fire. He knelt beside Tabitha chafing her frozen hands, as his aunt took charge of the situation, summoning a maid for blankets, dry clothes and hot milk.

Tabitha's eyes, huge in her waxen face, flickered open and looked back at him. His heart lurched. The poor mite was too exhausted to even shiver. He cursed himself for his selfishness in pushing her through the day.

He summoned a smile. 'It's all right, Tabby. We are safe here. Aunt Henrietta will see to you and you'll have a warm bed for the night in no time.'

Tabitha didn't reply but her gaze flicked to Henrietta who knelt beside them.

Henrietta knelt beside Jonathan and took Tabitha in her arms. 'Come here, my sweet, let's get you out of those wet clothes.'

A maid appeared with blankets, hovering at her mistress's

elbow to take the abandoned garments. With practised efficiency, Henrietta stripped the child of her wet clothes, and as she pulled off the child's shift she gasped, recoiling in horror.

'Jonathan. What have you done to this poor child?'

Jonathan sat back on his heels staring at the wheals that covered the child's back and arms. The dark lines of the morning's beating overlaid bruises of varying colour shades.

The old woman must have been in a habit of regularly beating the child. Jonathan stood and dashed his hand against the panelling in his anger and frustration, half regretting he had not taken his sword to the vile old woman.

'That was not my doing, Aunt. Her great-grandmother...' He tailed off. No words were adequate to describe Dame Judith Woolnough. 'I took her from that witch this morning.'

'Oh, poor darling. Only a monster would treat a child so.' Henrietta held the child close to her, rocking her. 'No one will hurt you again, my sweet.'

Nathaniel laid a hand on Jonathan's shoulder.

'You're done in, Jon. Sit down and let Hen see to the child.'

Jonathan sank into a chair as Henrietta wrapped Tabitha in the blankets and forced some warm milk into the child's unresponsive mouth.

Thomas poured Jonathan a brandy. 'Perhaps you'd better tell the story, lad?' he suggested.

Jonathan took a sip of the excellent brandy, feeling the warmth slide like fire into his frozen bones.

'She's Mary Woolnough's daughter,' he said at last.

His aunt and uncle looked at him and he saw the shock in their eyes. They both knew the early part of the unrequited love affair but not the sad epilogue.

'I thought that was all over long before the war,' Henrietta said.

Jonathan shook his head. 'We met again in Oxford during the war. Only then it was adultery.'

He caught his aunt's disapproving look and took another swig of the brandy as he continued, 'I'm not proud of what I did, Aunt, but believe when I say Mary didn't tell me she was with child when I left Oxford. I'd never have let it come to this had I known. I only learned much later that Mary and the child had died in childbirth. That was hard enough.'

'And you're certain this is Mary's child?' Nathaniel asked, always the lawyer.

'Tabitha,' Jonathan said. 'Her name is Tabitha. I learned only recently that the child lived and resolved to seek her out. I found her living with Mary's grandmother, Dame Judith Woolnough.'

'Ah, yes. I recall that it was Dame Judith who sought to break your relationship with Mary,' Nathaniel said.

Jonathan closed his eyes. 'It was such a long time ago,' he said. 'Mary has been dead these six years past.'

Nathaniel sat back with a lawyer's impassive face and looked thoughtfully at his nephew. 'And you are sure she is your daughter?'

Jonathan leaned forward. 'Yes, Uncle, I'm sure,' he said.

'Nat,' his wife scolded. 'You just have to take one look at the mite to see she is a Thornton.' Henrietta stood up with the child in her arms. 'I think it's time for one young lady to go to bed,' she said. 'She has had more than enough adventures for one day.'

Jonathan took Tabitha from his aunt. 'I'll take her, Aunt Hen.'

'Jon, you're soaked to the bone and in need of food yourself,' his aunt protested.

'I can wait,' he said. 'Come little lass, it is time you were in bed.'

He lifted Tabitha in his arms, ignoring the scream of protest from his shoulder and followed Henrietta up the stairs. He was gratified to see a freshly made fire in the hearth and a warm brick in the bed. As all her clothes were soaked through, Henrietta found an old shirt of Nathaniel's to use as a makeshift nightdress and Jonathan laid the child in the bed and pulled the covers tight over her.

'Where's Lucy?' she asked.

'Lucy?'

A look of distress crossed her face. 'My dolly,' she said. 'Mama made her for me before she died.'

Jonathan reached into his jacket and pulled out the disreputable object he had rescued from a puddle earlier in the day. Fortunately, the warmth of his body had dried the doll. He straightened the doll's limbs and skirts, which had been made with such love by the child's mother.

The thought of Mary's small hands, lovingly plying a needle to make this toy for her unborn child, brought a fresh stab of pain. He tucked the doll into the bed beside the child and she drew it to her, snuggling down in the big, warm bed.

'Close your eyes, kitten,' he said.

A small hand crept out from under the covers and found his hand. 'I used to dream about you,' she said. 'Bet said you were very brave and handsome. I thought one day you would come for me but you never did.'

'But I have now,' he said, his voice choked with regret.

'Promise me you won't go away again?' she asked.

At that moment Jonathan would have promised her the moon if she had asked for it but that was one promise he couldn't make. He bent and kissed her. She tightened her grip on his hand and he sat without moving, still holding her small hand, long after she had fallen asleep.

This small wonder. My daughter.

Conscious of his own damp and weary state, he tucked her hand beneath the bedclothes and stood up. He smoothed the dark hair away from her forehead and gently kissed her again.

'I could never leave you again,' he whispered. 'Not willingly.'

Downstairs, Henrietta and Nathaniel sat by the fire, their heads together engaged in earnest conversation. Jonathan leaned against the door. It occurred to him that even after thirty years of marriage and the death of their son, they were as close to each other as young lovers. He hoped, prayed, that one day someone would say that of Kate and him.

'She is asleep. You can send for the soldiers now.'

Nathaniel rose to his feet and stood facing Jonathan, his back to the fire. 'Why would I do that?' He paused, his eyes searching his nephew's face. 'I take it you were part of that affray at Worcester?'

Jonathan nodded.

'Come and sit down and Henrietta will fetch you some supper. You are done in, Jon.'

He stumbled into a chair by the fire.

'I'm not sending for the guard and if ever I'm asked, I've not seen you for ten years,' Nathaniel said. 'You are quite safe here, Jon.'

Jonathan lowered his head. 'Thank you.'

Nathaniel poured him another brandy. In his current state of exhaustion, he would be foxed before he could even make his bed. Henrietta set a bowl of soup and fresh bread down on a table but he was almost too weary to eat.

'You know they've still not caught Charles Stuart?' Nathaniel said.

Jonathan tried to keep his face impassive. 'God grant they never do,' he said. 'England will never survive the judicial murder of another King.'

Nathaniel wisely changed the subject. 'How are things at

Seven Ways?'

'I've told Kate to write to you again. I know you helped her before. That man Price has been causing trouble again and she had a troop of Parliament horse billeted on her for several weeks without recompense.'

Nathaniel nodded. 'I'll see what I can do. I've yet to meet Kate, but I knew David Ashley.'

Jonathan shook his head. 'I didn't know that.'

'He was a member of the Long Parliament. A good man. Poor Katherine cannot owe any thanks to your grandfather for saddling her with Seven Ways.'

'No,' Jonathan agreed. 'It's been a heavy burden.'

'Still, she seems to have taken it on. Brave woman.'

Jonathan nodded. 'She's an extraordinary woman.'

Jonathan caught the glance between his aunt and uncle, but let it pass without comment from him.

'How is Nell?' Henrietta asked.

'I believe Nell is with child.' Jonathan passed on the small snippet of family gossip.

'How?' Henrietta asked ingenuously.

Jonathan looked at him and laughed. 'The usual way I presume, Aunt,' he said, then added, 'Giles was hardly likely to miss an opportunity to see his wife once he was as close as Worcester.'

Nathaniel nodded. 'Ah, Lord Longley. I presumed him still in France. He was at Worcester too?'

Jonathan nodded.

'Where is he now? Is he all right?' Henrietta asked.

'He's safe,' Jonathan said.

Henrietta looked at Jonathan and leaned forward, placing a hand on his arm. 'You're exhausted, Jon,' she said. 'Go and rest and we will talk in the morning.'

CHAPTER 40

ith the infinite capacity of youth for speedy recovery, not only was Tabitha up, but she was playing on the floor of the parlour with Henrietta's little dog when Jonathan went in search of her the following morning.

A smile lit her face and she rushed up to him and took his hand.

'Is this where we are going to live, Father?' she asked. 'It's a lovely house and everyone is so nice.'

Jonathan picked her up and smiled. 'Well I'm glad to see you looking so bright this morning,' he said, ignoring her question. 'What's the dog's name?'

'Pippin,' Tabitha replied.

Henrietta came in with some flowers from the garden.

'You should have woken me,' he said.

Henrietta shrugged off the reproof. 'Nathaniel has gone to town but he will be back later. He said you were to go nowhere until he has spoken with you. Now, you probably want to break your fast?'

An obliging maid brought a tray loaded with a substantial breakfast and, while Jonathan ate, Henrietta sat with Tabitha on the window seat, showing her a complicated game involving winding string around fingers. Tabitha giggled as she succeeded in mastering the correct moves and Jonathan watched on, fascinated that the unhappy child of just two days ago could so suddenly blossom.

The rain had passed and the sun broke through the heavy clouds. Henrietta suggested a walk by the river and Jonathan and his aunt strolled through the fine garden with Tabitha.

'I know someone who would love this garden,' he said, his fingers brushing the fragrant lavender bushes.

Henrietta tucked her hand into the crook of his arm. 'Someone special?' she asked.

He looked down towards the river. 'Someone very special,' he admitted.

'Let me guess... Kate Ashley?' Henrietta enquired.

Jonathan looked down at his aunt. 'Am I that transparent?'

'Of course you are, dear boy. Don't forget, of all your family, I pride myself that I probably know you the best.'

Jonathan patted her hand affectionately. 'You flatter yourself, Aunt. It has been ten years.'

'And you think you're so very different?'

He looked at her with a half smile. 'I thought I was. I have lived a hundred years in the last ten... seen things... done things, no man should ever do.'

Henrietta shook her head. 'Not a day goes by when I don't think of my own dear boy — but enough of yesterday. Now you have slept on your problems, have you any thoughts as to what you are going to do with your daughter?'

They stopped on the terrace to watch Tabitha throwing a stick for the dog.

He shrugged. 'What can I do? I have no choice but to take her with me to Holland, Aunt. I can't send her to Seven Ways at the moment. Her great-grandmother will probably look for her there and Kate — Kate has responsibility enough without another mouth to feed.'

'Does she know about the child?'

He shook his head.

'I see,' Henrietta pressed her lips together. 'Jon, be sensible, you've not a penny to your name. How can you possibly expect to give the child a decent home in Holland or France?'

She had asked the question that he had been turning over and over for the last two days. He hefted a heartfelt sigh. 'I don't know, Aunt Hen. God help me, I do not know.'

Henrietta stopped and took both his hands, forcing him to look at her. 'Jonathan, please don't take this the wrong way, but Nathaniel and I lay awake for hours talking last night and we both agree.' Her gaze held his. 'Jon, leave her with us. She can stay here until you have an alternative to offer her, whether that is with Kate Ashley or…', she shrugged, '…something else.'

She had given him the answer, the perfect answer. The Freemans were offering Tabitha a much needed sanctuary. More than that, she would have for the first time a loving, comfortable home. Perfect except for one thing — he would not share it.

A physical pain wrapped around his chest and he looked away.

Henrietta mistook his hesitation and squeezed his hands. 'Jon, you must see that it is the only solution until you have sorted out your life.'

He forced a smile. 'You're right, Hen, and I thank you both for the offer. It's one I cannot refuse but how can I tell her?'

Before Henrietta could reply, they were interrupted by Tabitha herself, flying across the grass, her skirts billowing out.

'Father, father, come and see, there are ducks.'

Father. How could one simple word carry a world of meaning?

He bent to gather her in his arms as she flew toward him.

How can I leave her when I have only just found her?

Henrietta excused herself, leaving Jonathan alone with this daughter he hardly knew. They admired the ducks and he swung Tabitha onto his shoulders as he walked slowly back to the house.

'Do you like this house, kitten?' he asked.

'Oh yes, it's lovely,' she said. 'Is it yours?'

He set her down on a low garden wall and sat down beside her. 'It's not my house, Tabitha. I don't have a home,' he admitted.

'Nowhere?'

'My family lives in a lovely old house called Seven Ways. A long way from here.'

She frowned. 'That's a funny name.'

He smiled. 'It's a funny house.'

Tabitha swung her legs, kicking her heels against the wall. 'Do I..?' she began. 'Do you have any other boys or girls?'

Despite himself, Jonathan smiled, remembering a similar conversation with Tom. 'No, I don't, but there is a lady who lives at Seven Ways. I hope to marry her one day. She has a boy who is a little older than you, called Tom. He's your cousin.'

'What's a cousin?' Tabitha asked.

Jonathan explained about cousins and told her about her aunt Eleanor and little Ann and the new baby.

'So I do have a family?' Tabitha ventured at last. 'Grandam said I had no one left to love me or take care of me when she died.'

Jonathan flexed his fingers at the thought of Judith Woolnough.

Tabitha looked up at him, her eyes wide and bright. 'When am I going to see them?' she asked.

'Sometime soon, I hope,' Jonathan said.

Now he knew Tabitha was safe and cared for, he would write

to Kate and explain the situation as soon as he reached France. Quite how he would explain the appearance of a hitherto unknown daughter defeated him for the moment.

'What's this lady's name? The one you're going to marry,' Tabitha asked.

'Mistress Ashley.'

Tabitha frowned. 'So when you and Mistress Ashley get married, she'll be my mother?'

Jonathan considered that question for a moment, as he untangled the complexity of family relationships.

'Of course she will be,' he said.

Tabitha contemplated the ground for a moment. 'Is she kind?' she asked in a small voice.

A rush of pity for this child who had only known kindness from one person in her whole life swamped Jonathan.

'Very kind,' he said.

That seemed to satisfy Tabitha. She straightened and looked up at him. 'So when are you going to get married?' she demanded.

Jonathan took Tabitha's little hand in his. 'Not for a little while.' He steadied his nerves. 'I have to go a long way away, kitten. If I don't the soldiers will come and put me in prison.'

'Did Grandam send the soldiers after you because you took me?' Tabitha's voice shook.

'No. It's nothing to do with you,' said Jonathan. 'I am a soldier and I fought in a big battle. We lost and I need to hide somewhere safe for a little while.' He paused. 'Tell me, Tabitha, do you like Aunt Henrietta and Uncle Nathaniel?'

She nodded. 'Very much.'

Jonathan took his courage in both hands and said, 'Where I am going, kitten, I can't take you with me.' Her eyes widened and she opened her mouth but before she could protest, he put his finger to her lips. 'Hush and hear me out. You are going to stay here with Aunt Hen and Uncle Nat until it is safe for me to come home.'

'You promised.' Her wail cut him to the very core.

'I know, Tabby, but I have to go and I have no money and nowhere for us to live. Where I am going I can't take you with me. Here you will have a warm bed and someone to love you and I promise no one will beat you. Aunt Hen wants you to stay very much. She has never had a little girl of her own.'

She looked at him, her face crumpled with pain. 'You promised you wouldn't go away again.' With a strangled sob she flung herself off the wall and ran into the house.

Jonathan sat with his head in his hands, listening to the sound of her retreating footsteps and hearing again her mother's plea. *Take me with you. Please take me with you.*

Oh, Mary, why didn't you tell me you were with child? I would have taken you away. I would have left you at Seven Ways and Tabitha would have grown up there... Why...?

He raised his head and stared despondently at the river, gliding by on its timeless and ceaseless course to the sea.

For all her angry words, surely his mother would have grown to love Mary and once she held her granddaughter all would have been forgiven? Perhaps at Seven Ways, Mary would not have died? How different things could have been?

Every life he touched he seemed to hurt: Mary, Tabitha, Kate and even Stephen Prescott.

'Deep in thought, Jonathan?' His uncle's voice made him start and he came to his feet, composing his face to greet Nathaniel Freeman.

Nathaniel waved him back down. 'Sit, sit... we need to talk.'

The two men sat for a long moment in silence broken by Nathaniel at last. 'Henrietta says you have agreed to our suggestion of leaving the lass here?'

'I am grateful and it is the perfect solution. Unfortunately, Tabitha doesn't seem to agree with the idea.'

Nathaniel nodded. 'Well you can hardly blame her for that, but give her time and she'll get used to it. You will promise to write regularly to the lass?'

'If you don't feel that would compromise you, Uncle?' Jonathan said with a wry smile. 'I am conscious of your position. A friend and adviser to Oliver Cromwell should hardly be seen to be sheltering the children of known delinquents.'

Nathaniel pursed his lips. 'My family connections with notorious delinquents are no secret. No, we would like to have her here. Makes up for our own sadnesses. Hen needs someone to love and fuss over. You know what she's like.'

'The debt I owe to you can never really be repaid, Nathaniel,' Jonathan said with genuine feeling.

His uncle shrugged. 'We've always done what we felt was right,' he said.

'Nathaniel.' Jonathan broke the silence that had fallen between them again. 'Tell me honestly, what would happen to me if I came openly back to England? Made my peace?'

Nathaniel frowned. 'I think you already know the answer to that, Jonathan. Memories are long and your part in the second war has not been forgotten. I think at best you could expect a lengthy stay in the Tower. At worst— '

He didn't have to say it. Death.

Jonathan sighed. 'Then I'm trapped, Nathaniel. Trapped between a life spent in exile and an uncertain future if I return.'

Nathaniel nodded. 'That about sums it up. Although I will tell you something in confidence,' he said. 'I don't think many more will die for the King's cause. Derby probably, and a few of the other senior officers, but as for the rest of the poor wretches, possibly release or sent to the colonies as bondsmen.' He paused and turned to look directly at Jonathan. 'If you take my counsel, lad, wait till this latest business is just a memory and then I will see what can be done.'

'But that could be a year or so,' Jonathan said bitterly.

'It's the best advice I can give in the circumstances.' Nathaniel stood up. 'For now, Jonathan, I suggest you find a boat to France. And take this to speed you on your way.' Nathaniel dropped a small purse of coins into Jonathan's hand.

Jonathan looked up at the lawyer. 'Thank you, Uncle. It's more than I deserve. I'll be gone within the hour.'

After Nathaniel left him, he sat looking across the garden, thinking of Kate and a peaceful life of hearth and home that seemed to be forever denied him. Just as he decided the time had gone to be on his way, he felt a small hand on his shoulder and turned to see Tabitha, her eyes red from crying, with Henrietta behind her.

'Father,' she said. 'I'll stay here if you promise to write often. I can't read but Aunt Henrietta says she'll teach me and I'll learn how to write too. So I can write you letters.'

Jonathan took her in his arms, burying his face in her soft, dark hair. She smelled of soap and rose water. 'You dear child,' he whispered. 'Of course, I'll write when I can and I promise I will come back as soon as I am able.'

'And you'll marry Mistress Ashley and we'll all go to live at Seven Ways?' Tabitha's voice was muffled by his coat.

He smiled. 'That is what I want more than anything else in the world, Tabby.' He disengaged her and held her by the forearms, studying the small, heart-shaped face. 'Wait for me. Promise?'

She nodded and he rose to his feet. He held his daughter's small hand in his as they walked back up to the house together.

CHAPTER 41

*J*onathan stood in the shadows pondering the size of the boat on which he had bought a passage to Dieppe. It looked depressingly small and he silently prayed that the crossing would not be unduly rough.

He'd got a good price for the horse and with the money, Nathaniel had given him, for the first time in weeks he felt some prospect of a reasonable start to life in exile again.

The general buzz of activity around the small vessel indicated that sailing would not be long off so he stepped forward to take his place.

The master of the vessel surveyed him. 'There y'are. I was beginnin' to think you weren't coming.'

'When do we sail?'

The master looked up and down the wharves, an anxious frown on his face. 'Tide's on the turn. A few minutes, no more.'

Jonathan tossed his satchel containing his few books and clean linen down into the boat where it was deftly caught by one of the crew. He made to grasp the ladder to step down but as he did so the master grabbed his arm.

'I need no assistance,' he began to say but the look in the man's eyes gave him a warning and he twisted around to see soldiers, some six of them in the command of an officer in a leather coat and orange sash, running down the docks towards them.

'I have him,' the master shouted exultantly, tightening his grip.

Jonathan tried to shake his arm free of the master as the soldiers reached them. The officer stood panting, drawing his pistol from his belt and levelling it at Jonathan.

'What is the meaning of this?' Jonathan protested, wrenching himself free of the man's grip. 'I'm a bookseller and I've appointments on the continent to buy books. Who can you possibly think I am?'

'You tell us,' the officer responded with heavy sarcasm.

'I've told you. I'm a bookseller. My name is John Miller. Search my bag if you like. You'll find naught but books in it,' Jonathan replied, trying to keep his voice calm and steady. 'We will miss the tide if you do not desist.'

'If you're a bookseller, why do you carry a sword?' the officer cast a pointed glance at the serviceable sword Jonathan carried on a leather baldric.

Jonathan's gaze flicked around the circle of soldiers who surrounded him, their swords drawn and spread his hands. 'Gentlemen, these are dangerous times. I carry it purely for self-defence.'

'I tell you, he's Charles Stuart,' the master of the boat insisted. 'I want that reward.'

Jonathan turned to the man who still held his arm in a vice-like grip.

If the situation were not so serious, it could be considered laughable, he thought. This surely could not happen to him twice? Not now he was so close to escape.

He shook his arm free and gathered his fraying nerves as he addressed the officer. 'My good sir, I assure you, I most certainly am not Charles Stuart. Here are my papers.'

He handed over the papers, including letters of introduction to mythical booksellers in Amsterdam, purchased that afternoon from a forger in Fleet Street, recommended by his uncle.

The officer handed his weapon to his sergeant and squinted at the papers in the dim light of the ship's lantern.

'These look genuine enough,' he admitted, 'but in the circumstances. I have to insist you come with us.'

'I'm not going anywhere with you. My papers are in order and I've appointments in The Hague that must be kept.' Jonathan tried to keep the edge of panic out of his voice.

The officer dropped any pretence of cordiality and reclaimed his pistol. He advanced on Jonathan, the weapon levelled. 'You'll come with us, sir. Your journey must be delayed while we verify the truth of these papers.'

Jonathan threw his head back in a gesture of despair and frustration. He'd not spent the last five weeks on the run to be taken at the last minute.

His choice was simple: go with this man and try and bluff his way out or throw caution to the wind and fight for his freedom.

He narrowed his eyes as he weighed up the situation. The soldiers stood between him and the water. If he could fight his way through to the edge of the dock, he could always swim for it. One last reckless act, one last gesture of defiance; he did not intend to be taken without a fight.

With a swift movement that took the officer unawares, he knocked the pistol from his hand. Before any of the soldiers could react he had drawn his sword. For what seemed an eternity the soldiers eyed him until one, more daring than the rest, lunged forward. He took a sword point to the arm as a reward for his audacity and fell to the ground with a shriek of agony.

That goaded the others to action. As a body, they advanced on Jonathan. In the fast, furious fight that followed two more soldiers fell back, nursing painful but not fatal wounds. Jonathan felt his arm tiring with the old, heavy sword. Sweat poured down his face and he seemed no closer to the water.

'Put up your sword.'

He turned on his heel and once more faced the officer's weapon. At such a close range, the officer could not miss.

Panting from the exertion, he looked back at the remaining soldiers and conceded defeat. His sword fell to the ground with a clatter as he raised his hands in surrender. The officer advanced cautiously, placing the muzzle of his pistol under Jonathan's chin.

'Now, I'll ask you again,' he said. 'Are you Charles Stuart?'

Jonathan laughed. 'No, I'm not Charles Stuart. I assure you, sir, were you to meet him, you would see at once that I bear no resemblance to the King.'

'Charles Stuart is no King in this country,' the officer said with obvious contempt. 'So, if you are not Charles Stuart, then who are you?'

Jonathan's eyes flashed. 'If you don't know then I am damned if I'll tell you. Find out for yourself.'

'I tell you, he's the King. I claim the reward.' The master of the boat jumped up and down in impotent fury.

'YOU'VE DONE WELL, CAPTAIN.'

The speaker was a man of early middle age dressed in a dark suit and plain linen collar and cuffs, who had entered the room with Jonathan's captor. They had manacled him and brought him to one of the buildings in the old palace of Whitehall.

'The man refuses to tell us who he is. Do you think he could be Charles Stuart?' the young officer asked.

The newcomer smiled. 'Oh no. I hate to disappoint you. He most certainly is not Charles Stuart, but he is a most elusive quarry for whom we have been searching for quite some years. You have snared Sir Jonathan Thornton.'

He drew up a chair on the opposite side of the table to Jonathan and leaned forward.

Do you remember me, Thornton? We met a long time ago before the war when your family had some hope of turning you into a lawyer.' He turned to the officer. 'We have Sir Jonathan to thank for the London Trained Bands, Captain. He did a fine job with them. Pity he turned for the King.'

Jonathan raised his head to look at the man and recognition hit him. His master had shared chambers with this man. "John Thurloe. Yes, I remember you. What are you going to do with me?'

'Probably what you could expect, Thornton.' He pulled a paper from his jacket and handed it to the young officer. 'Convey Colonel Thornton with all speed to the Tower, Captain.'

Jonathan ran a tongue over his dry lips. 'What then, Thurloe?'

A thin smile lifted Thurloe's moustache. 'I need to lose you for a little while, Thornton before we make any decisions about your future.'

'What do you mean by that?'

John Thurloe smiled. 'Exactly what I said. As far as the world is concerned, the bookseller John Miller will be held indefinitely in the Tower of London for selling seditious pamphlets.'

'Did we not fight a war to ensure there could be no imprisonment without trial?' Jonathan demanded.

Thurloe raised an eyebrow. 'Oh, is that what it was about?' He leaned forward again. 'No one knows I have you and I will ensure you have no way of alerting any of your friends, if you have any, to your predicament. You'll not be seeing the light of day for some time.'

Jonathan abandoned all pretence at bravado. 'Thurloe, I am Colonel Jonathan Thornton of His Majesty's Lifeguard. I fought at Worcester and I demand my rights as a prisoner of war.'

Thurloe shook his head. 'I don't care whether your name is Charles Stuart, John Miller or Jonathan Thornton, you will be conveyed to the Tower of London forthwith. You are to neither receive nor to send any messages and you are to remain manacled hand and foot for the duration of your incarceration.'

With a nod to the officer, Thurloe left the room.

IT WAS NOT until the heavy iron-studded door had slammed shut that the full enormity of his position hit Jonathan. The walls of the dank room somewhere in the heart of the Tower of London closed around him and as despair washed over him, he slid down the wall to the floor. Ignoring the clank of the two feet of chain on his manacles, he pushed his hair out of his eyes and surveyed his accommodation.

The small room contained only a narrow bed with a couple of threadbare blankets, a small table, a stool and the ubiquitous bucket. His few possessions, his sword and what little money he had were all gone. He had no way of ameliorating his condition and even if he had, there seemed to be no chance of any request being heeded.

He bowed his head on his manacled wrists and wondered at the severity of his treatment. In the greater order of things, he represented no great prize. Surely he was only a minor player in the drama? So why this solitary confinement in the Tower?

Whatever position John Thurloe held in the new regime, he was powerful enough to ensure that Jonathan Thornton disappeared from the face of the earth.

He sighed and looked up at the damp, mildewed walls and the small window set high in the wall that admitted neither light nor air to any great effect. This time he was well and truly caught, and escape would require nothing short of a miracle.

CHAPTER 42

BARTON, YORKSHIRE DECEMBER, 1651

*I*s it really only seven months since I left Barton for Seven Ways, Kate wondered. A whole life seemed to have passed her by in those few short months.

In contrast to Kate's life, nothing in Yorkshire seemed to have changed except Suzanne's shape with another bairn due any day.

Kate had used the need to return to Yorkshire for Suzanne's confinement as the solution to getting Giles away from Seven Ways and they had travelled north with Giles disguised as Nell's maid.

He had not taken well to the plan and even Kate had to admit that things had come to a pretty pass when Giles Longley, the most debonair of cavaliers, had to escape England dressed in petticoats.

Happily, their journey had been uneventful, marred only by one unfortunate incident when a drunken tapster had taken a fancy to the strapping 'Gillian'. He had been rewarded by a hefty right hook and was probably still nursing a broken jaw.

Now at Barton, with his knee healed and disguised, with more dignity, as William's servant, the time had come for Giles to leave. William had agreed to take him to Hull and put him aboard a ship of wool bound for the continent, posing as William's agent to the merchants in Amsterdam.

Kate stood beside her sister at the window overlooking the courtyard where Giles and Nell were engaged in a long and passionate farewell.

'Is he faithful to his wife?' Suzanne asked suddenly.

'Not for a moment,' Kate replied. 'He'll be seeking out company as soon as he arrives at The Hague, I wager.'

'I know a rogue when I see one,' Suzanne said. 'Poor Eleanor.'

'I think Nell understands,' Kate said. 'I do not doubt that Giles loves her but she told me once that Giles was a man who loved women and Jonathan was a man whom women loved.'

Her sister gave her a quick sideways glance. 'And Jonathan. Is he safe?'

Kate's lips tightened. 'I've heard nothing. It's nearly six weeks since he left and I had expected some word by now.' She forced herself to smile. 'But he's no letter writer. I can only assume that no news is good news and he is safe on the continent. Giles has promised to send word as soon as he arrives in Amsterdam.'

Suzanne straightened her aching back as she turned away from the window. Kate caught the grimace on her sister's face.

'Is it close?' she asked

Suzanne nodded. 'Tonight perhaps,' she said as she lowered herself into her chair beside the cheerful fire that burned in the hearth.

Kate glanced out of the window. Giles had mounted the sturdy little horse, William provided and Nell was waving her husband off while dabbing decorously at her eyes with a lace-edged kerchief. By contrast to Suzanne, Nell's slender figure still betrayed no sign of the child she carried.

By next summer Nell would have a baby to hold and ease the pain of her separation from Giles. Kate had nothing of Jonathan except memories of snatched moments of intimacy. Even the ring he had given her had disappeared on the night it had betrayed her.

For no logical reason, she envied her friend. Her disappointment at finding she was not with child after Jonathan's departure had taken her completely by surprise. She surely had not wanted to explain a bastard child to the curious world?

'What are you thinking?' Suzanne's voice startled her out of her strange reverie.

Kate joined her sister beside the fire. 'It's strange, Suzanne, but you and Nell are both with child and I feel...' she sighed, '...I feel lonely. I long to hold a baby in my arms again, to share that joy of new life.'

'You're being sentimental, Kate.' Ever pragmatic, Suzanne shifted uncomfortably in her chair. 'You're welcome to this ponderous belly and the pain of childbirth. I've told William that this is it. No more children for me.' Suzanne winced and tightened her lips.

'Shall I send for the midwife?'

Suzanne shook her head. 'It will be some hours yet.' She smiled at her sister and held out her hand. 'If it's a girl I shall call her Katherine,' she said.

Suzanne reached out and took Kate's hand. 'You don't belong here anymore,' she said.

Kate looked up. 'What do you mean?'

'I've been watching you since you returned and you have a restlessness about you. Seven Ways holds your heart now, Kate.'

Kate squeezed her sister's fingers, the tears pricking the back of her eyes. Suzanne, who knew her so well, was right. Seven Ways did hold her heart.

Seven Ways meant Jonathan and as soon as the roads allowed

she would return and begin to build a life that would, she hoped, one day include Jonathan Thornton. If only she had word from him...

She rose to her feet and walked over to the window, looking out over the now deserted courtyard. A chill ran down her spine and she shivered.

Where are you, Jonathan?

CHAPTER 43

LONDON MARCH, 1652

*T*he lawyer, Nathaniel Freeman, bowed low over the hand Kate held out to him.

'Mistress Ashley, this is an unexpected pleasure.' he said, indicating a chair and resuming his place behind his vast table, covered with neatly arranged stacks of paper.

Kate smiled at the lawyer as she arranged her skirts. There were formalities to be concluded before she could get to the real reason for her visit.

'I must thank you, Master Freeman, for all you have done for us in the past months. We have received the promised compensation for our troubles after the affray at Worcester and, with God's blessing, have weathered the winter.'

'I am glad to hear it. We have intended to pay a visit to Seven Ways when the weather improved, but as you know the winter proved harsh and of course,' he waved a hand at his desk, 'the press of work.'

'I quite understand,' Kate said.

She looked down at the velvet mask she held in her hands. She had already asked so much of this man and had rehearsed what she had planned to say but now the words escaped her.

'Master Freeman, I have come to ask one more favour of you.'

He sat back and pressed his fingertips together. He wore a lawyer's inscrutable mask and she wondered how he would react to her question.

'My dear, Mistress Ashley, whatever is in my power.'

Kate gathered her courage and brought her gaze up to look the man in the eye. 'I am looking for Jonathan Thornton,' she said.

No flicker of emotion crossed the man's face and her nerve faltered.

'Jonathan? A known malignant, a wanted man? What is Jonathan Thornton to you?' he asked.

Kate hesitated a moment. 'He is everything to me.' Taking a deep, steadying breath she raised her eyes and met his gaze without blinking. 'You have been good to us and I'll not lie to you. I hid him after the battle at Worcester and saw him safely on his way by early October. He intended to make his way to London and from here to the Continent but to the best of my knowledge he never gained the Continent.'

Nathaniel Freeman's mask wavered and she saw a momentary uncertainty in the line of his mouth.

'How do you know?' he said.

'I know he would have sent word, had he reached safety. However poor a correspondent he may be, he gave me his word but I did not become truly concerned until Nell received this letter from her husband.'

Kate handed him a much folded, crumpled and stained letter.

'Nell received this scarcely two weeks ago. Lord Longley wrote it shortly after Christmas, nearly three months after Jonathan left us.'

Nathaniel put on a pair of glasses and peered at Giles' impatient scrawl, reading aloud:

Dear Heart, God knows if this will reach you but I pray that it does for you will know that I have reached Amsterdam safely. The knee has mended well but we are a sad and sorry crew, so many friends lost or imprisoned. While I do not wish to alarm you or Kate, I hold great fear for Jonathan of whom there has been no word. I have made extensive enquires in other likely places he may well have turned up, Holland, France and Spain and the like but there is no sighting or word of him. Perhaps he has decided to turn to the New World and we will hear shortly of his doings in Barbados or Virginia? Few know better than I his aptitude for turning up where least expected. I hope that perhaps by the time this letter reaches you one or other of us may have some better news. My love as always to you and Ann and the new baby. Keep yourself well and give Kate my warmest regards. Yr Loving husband, Giles L.

'He has vanished,' Kate said, a note of desperation rising in her voice. 'I have been in London nearly a week. Every day my man has been down on the docks but all to no avail. If any of the boatmen know anything they will not tell me and so I have come to you.'

Nathaniel Freeman laid the letter on the table and regarded her from over the top of his eyeglasses. 'They would not talk to strangers, Mistress Ashley. You need to know the right people to ask.'

She sat forward eagerly. 'Please, can you tell me where I should look, who I should ask?'

Nathaniel took off his glasses and pinched the bridge of his nose. 'You should have come to me sooner.' He sighed and replaced the spectacles. 'Or I should have come to you. Firstly please let me put your mind to rest on at least one count. Jonathan reached London. He came to us and we helped him on his way.'

She stared at him, relief and puzzlement clouding her mind. 'Why did he come to you?'

The man's glance flicked the door and he leaned forward lowering his voice. 'He had his reasons. I must confess my wife and myself have shared your concerns, Mistress Ashley. We too have been troubled over the lack of word from Jonathan.'

Kate too leaned forward and said in a lowered voice. 'If he did indeed take a boat to France, is it possible the boat was lost in the crossing?'

Freeman's lips tightened and he shook his head. 'I would have heard.' He sat back. 'Let us not think the worst. Leave your enquiries with me for now and I will see what can be discovered.'

Tears of gratitude sprang into Kate's eyes as she felt the weight of concern being lifted from her shoulders. 'Thank you, Master Freeman. In a world gone mad with hate and revenge, it is reassuring to know that we are not entirely without friends. I am so grateful he sought you out. I am staying at the White Swan at Southwark. Please send me word as soon as you have discovered something.'

She dashed the betraying tears away and rose to her feet, turning for the door.

'Mistress Ashley, there is perhaps one favour you can do for me?'

Kate turned back as he stood up. 'Please, whatever is in my power,' she said.

'You are to return to your inn, pack your belongings, and my wife will be expecting you at our home in Putney by supper.'

'I cannot intrude on your hospitality,' Kate protested.

'Nonsense.' The lawyer waved his hand, 'Henrietta would be mortified if she thought you were staying in an inn when we have a large house with guest chambers to spare.'

He came out from behind the desk and leaned one hand on the

door to prevent her from leaving. 'One last thing,' he said, lowering his voice again. 'I am aware that my nephew was in the habit of travelling under aliases. You would not happen to know what name he is likely to have used?'

'I only know of one,' Kate replied without hesitation. 'John Miller, a bookseller.'

Nathaniel smiled. 'I do not recall in Jonathan's short career as a law clerk that the boy had any great enthusiasm for books, but many years have passed and perhaps that is a taste that has matured. Please do not fret, Mistress Ashley. I promise I will make the necessary enquiries and I may even have something to report by this evening.'

'THIS MASTER FREEMAN must be well thought of,' Ellen commented as they turned in at the gates of the handsome red brick house, constructed in the style popular at the turn of the century.

Unlike the shabby and downtrodden Seven Ways, the house and grounds surrounding it wore an air of comfortable prosperity.

As Dickon helped Kate dismount, a woman who could only be Henrietta Freeman flew down the front steps with a light step that belied her solid appearance.

'My poor, dear girl,' she exclaimed, taking Kate's hands, 'what you have been through. You should have come to us before now. Please call me Aunt Hen, everyone does.'

Kate managed a smile. 'It's kind of you to take me in like this, Mistress Freeman... Aunt... Hen.'

'Nonsense, my dear,' she said. 'You are family. Nathaniel and I seem to have been looking after stray Thorntons all our lives. One more makes no difference.'

Henrietta took her arm and guided her into a warm, well-polished parlour while Ellen and the luggage were directed upstairs. A cup of mulled ale and some cakes awaited her arrival and Kate was seated in a comfortable, well-cushioned chair.

'Now you must tell me all about yourself,' Henrietta said, seating herself down and helping herself to a cake. 'You have a son, I believe?'

'Thomas.'

'Is he with you?'

'No, I have sent him to school in Worcester. Since I returned to Seven Ways last month, I felt he needed the companionship of boys his age and to continue his education.'

'You must miss him.'

Kate's lips tightened and, with a betraying wobble in her voice, she replied, 'We have never really been apart before and I confess I miss him terribly but...' She reached for another cake. It had been a hard winter in the north and food had been plain and frugal. 'I cannot hold him to my side forever.'

'And Nell. How is my dear Nell? Jonathan told me she was with child.'

Kate looked up sharply at the mention of Jonathan's name. 'Nell is suffering most terribly,' she said. 'She has been constantly sick and it shows no sign of abating even though her pregnancy is now well advanced. However, the baby seems to be growing well and little Ann is looking forward to having a sibling.'

They were silent a moment. Henrietta's hands twisted in her lap and she tightened her lips as if summoning her courage. 'Nathaniel has told me your concerns about Jonathan. We too had been expecting some news from him. Poor correspondent though he is, he is not a man to break his promises. If he gave his word that he would write then he would have done so.'

'That is why I'm so anxious,' Kate confessed. 'I am certain some ill has befallen him.' She looked away to hide the betraying tears. 'I know he must be in some terrible trouble or worse, he could be dead and we have no way of knowing.'

'Love can sometimes be a powerful medium,' Henrietta said and, seeing the alarm in Kate's face, smiled. 'It's all right, my dear. Jonathan has confided his feelings for you and even if he hadn't, it was written in his eyes whenever he spoke of you.'

Kate looked away. She could no longer disguise the tears that slid down her cheek. All her rigid self-control began to crumble and encircled in Henrietta's motherly arms, Kate gave way. The months of strain poured out in an uncontrolled torrent while Henrietta stroked her hair and muttered soothingly.

Too exhausted to face supper, Kate allowed herself to be put to bed as if she were a small child, with a hot brick at her feet. She turned her hot cheek on the cool linen of Henrietta's best bed and closed her eyes, drifting into a deep, dreamless sleep.

Kate woke in the morning feeling better than she had done for months. Having the support of the Freemans shared the burden she had been carrying for so many months. They seemed as concerned as she about Jonathan and it comforted her to know someone else cared as much for him.

Ellen brought her breakfast and after she dressed she went in search of her hostess.

The faltering notes of a virginal guided her towards the parlour. She pushed the door open and to her surprise saw a young girl seated at the instrument, her ankles crossed and her forehead puckered in concentration. A small black and white spaniel that had been asleep at her feet leapt up and bounded over to Kate, jumping up in excitement, as young dogs are prone to do.

Its mistress stopped playing and clapped her hands. 'Oliver. Bad dog. Come here.'

Reluctantly the puppy abandoned Kate and slunk back to the child who left the stool and executed a neat curtsy.

'Good morning,' she said.

'I'm sorry to interrupt your practice,' Kate said, 'but I was looking for Mistress Freeman.'

'Aunt Hen is in the kitchen, I think,' replied the child. 'Who are you?'

As she spoke the child flicked back a lock of dark brown hair that had escaped her neat, white cap. Kate stood quite still, her heart catching in her throat. A simple, common gesture but in its way, oddly telling. The child had to be a Thornton, a Freeman grandchild perhaps.

'I'm Mistress Ashley,' she replied.

The girl frowned and something that appeared to be recognition crossed the girl's face. 'Are you the lady who is going to marry my father?'

The world tipped on its axis as Kate stared at the child.

'Your father?'

'Yes, he told me he was going to marry a lovely lady called Mistress Ashley who has a boy called Tom. He is my cousin. Is he here?'

Kate shook her head. 'No, Thomas is at school,' she said.

A look of disappointment crossed the child's face and Kate took a breath and asked, 'What is your name, child?'

'My name is Tabitha.'

Kate forced a smile and crossed to the virginals. 'Tabitha is a pretty name,' she said. 'Are you Tabitha Freeman?'

The girl cocked her head to one side. 'Well I used to be called Woolnough,' she said, 'but Aunt Hen says it is proper I be called Tabitha Thornton. I think Tabitha Thornton sounds better don't you?'

Kate nodded, her throat constricting as the truth of this child's identity began to dawn on her. Tabitha Thornton... Jonathan's daughter? But he'd said nothing about a daughter—

'What are you playing?' she asked. 'It was very pretty.'

The girl's face lit up. 'Shall I play it for you?'

'Please do.' Kate sank onto an aged darkened oak settle beside the fire. She needed time to think.

The girl's fingers moved with a precocious surety over the notes. Watching the intent little face, Kate knew without a shadow of a doubt that this indeed was Mary Woolnough's daughter, the child of her adulterous affair with Jonathan.

'You wouldn't think that the child had never seen music before she came here.' Henrietta's voice came from the door, as Tabitha brought her rendition to a firm end. 'Her music teacher says she has a natural talent,' Henrietta continued, crossing to the child and placing her hands affectionately on her shoulders

Any number of questions filled Kate's head but she could not bring herself to articulate any of them.

Henrietta patted the child. 'Run along, my dear. You can practice later. Mistress Ashley and I must talk.'

Tabitha bobbed a hasty curtsy and, freed from the tedium of practice, skipped from the room with Oliver at her heels.

'Nathaniel gave her the puppy for Christmas,' Henrietta said, seating herself next to Kate on the settle. 'She said it was the first present anyone had ever given her. She called him Oliver after Oliver Cromwell dined here.'

Kate scarcely heard Henrietta's prattle.

Are you the lady who is going to marry my father?' My father.

'He told me the child was dead,' she blurted out, her voice choked between tears and anger. 'And all the time she has been here? Why did he lie to me?'

Henrietta patted her arm. 'He didn't lie to you, Kate. Tabitha has only been with us since Jonathan brought her here in October last year. He told us that he had only recently discovered the child was alive and he went to look for her in Oxford after he left you. She was in the care of her great-grandmother. The poor child had been ill-used. When he brought her to us she bore the marks of a terrible beating. You should have seen the little mite. He could not have left her.'

'He could have brought her to me?'

Tears of hurt pricked the back of her eyes. She would have taken the child to her heart, kept her safe and loved until her father came back to them both.

Henrietta shook her head. 'He felt he had brought enough trouble upon you and to return to Seven Ways presented too much of a danger. We agreed to take care of her until it was safe for her to go to Seven Ways. He intended to write and tell you. Of course, we had thought to hear from him before now so we have waited. When he saw you yesterday, Nathaniel thought you had come to fetch her but then you said he was missing.' The woman's face crumpled. 'Oh dear, I do hope the boy is safe.'

Kate frowned, still trying to understand the enormity of Tabitha's existence. 'How? How did he find her? He would not have willingly risked going to Oxford, where he is known unless he knew she was there.'

Henrietta shook her head. 'He wouldn't tell me, but for some reason, the knowledge that she existed had come to him only recently.'

A memory, so painful that Kate had willed herself to obliterate it, came flooding back and she saw Long Barn again and the two shadowy figures circling each other and heard their voices, low and menacing.

'Prescott told him,' she whispered more to herself than to Henrietta. 'All the time the child lived.'

'Sorry, dear, I didn't hear that.' Henrietta leaned towards her. 'My hearing is not what it was.'

Kate recovered herself. Now she understood. 'But why didn't the grandmother send soldiers to Seven Ways? If that had happened, I would have known.'

Henrietta shook her head. 'Nathaniel made inquiries in Oxford. The old lady took ill with apoplexy shortly after her encounter with Jonathan.'

'Is she dead?'

'I don't believe so, but she deserves no sympathy, Kate. Her treatment of the child was appalling. The child is here now and safe...' She smiled. 'And loved.' Henrietta's smile faded. 'Nathaniel and I have grown very fond of her but not a day goes by when she does not remind us of Jonathan's promise to write to her. It breaks the child's heart. What can we tell her?'

'He would not break that promise unless he had to. Unless—'

She couldn't say it— *Unless he was dead.*

The two women looked at each other, their fear written in their eyes.

Henrietta grasped Kate's hands and said urgently, 'All we can do is pray that Nathaniel can find her father.'

CHAPTER 44

A sharp jab in the ribs pulled Jonathan from a fitful sleep back to reality. He cursed and pulled his cloak and the rough, threadbare blanket closer around him.

'You've company.'

The turnkey jabbed him again and Jonathan forced himself to straighten up. The mere act of moving caused him to cough. He put a hand to his chest as if the touch would stop the pain but he knew it would not. The cough had been getting steadily worse and the movement of his arm irritated the suppurating sores on his wrists where the manacles had rubbed.

'In you go,' the turnkey said.

The wavering light of a lantern appeared at the door. Jonathan blinked, the light obscuring the visitor.

'Dear God. Is that you, Jonathan?' His breath caught at the sound of the familiar voice.

'Nathaniel? Are you a vision?'

'No, lad, I'm real enough.'

Nathaniel Freeman gave a curt order to the turnkey to leave

them. Jonathan swung his legs to the floor as he heard the chink of coins and the door closed leaving them alone together.

Nathaniel set the lantern down on the small table and sat on the rickety stool. He peered at Jonathan's face.

'Christ,' he blasphemed. 'What have they done to you, boy? Have you been tortured?'

Jonathan gave an ironic snort of laughter. 'They've done nothing to me, Uncle Absolutely nothing. Just left me here to rot.' The chains clanked as he swept his hand around the small room.

Nathaniel lifted the length of heavy chain. 'Have you been manacled the whole time?'

'Yes. How did you find me?'

'Something of an educated guess. Do you know John Thurloe?'

Jonathan frowned. 'Yes, he's the bastard that put me here. Said he wanted to lose me. Cursed if I know why. He's not been back to tell me the reason. I was beginning to fear that this time I would remain lost.'

'Thurloe has a particular interest in the security of the realm. I can only guess that he thinks he may have a use for you, and this little interlude is to make you more receptive to his proposal.'

'How long have I been here? I've lost count?'

'It's March the fifteenth.'

'Sweet Jesus. It's been five months? How—'Jonathan's effort to speak dissolved in a coughing fit.

Nathaniel reached for the jug of fetid water on the table and poured it into the cup, handing it to his nephew.

'How long have you had that cough?'

Jonathan drank the water and raised his head, shaking back the tangled hair. 'A few weeks. I don't know. It's been getting worse. How did you find me?'

'Your Kate Ashley came to me because she was concerned that you had disappeared. It didn't take me long to discover you had been taken on the night you were going to leave England. I made a few discreet enquiries with Thurloe's clerk and found he was holding a prisoner by the name of John Miller, a bookseller being held for selling seditious pamphlets. I thought that might be you.'

Jonathan felt his pulse quicken.

'Kate is here? In London?'

'Staying with Henrietta and me. I've not told her anything yet. I needed to be sure that you were at least alive.'

'Barely.'

'Nonsense. You always had a capacity for overdramatising.'

Nathaniel's familiar, pragmatic voice brought a smile to Jonathan's mouth.

'And Tabitha?' he asked.

Nathaniel chuckled. 'You wouldn't recognise her, Jon. A different child.'

Jonathan closed his eyes. 'But I failed her again. I promised I would write.' The cold hand of utter despair closed over his heart. 'I couldn't even send you word. They have me guarded closer than a nun in a cloister in here.'

Nathaniel laid a hand on his shoulder. 'Jon, you're alive. That's all we need to know. Now I need to get you out of here.' He jerked his head around at the sound of heavy footsteps outside in the corridor.'

Nathaniel stood up. 'I must go. Thurloe won't know I've been. The turnkey has been well paid, and he'll see you have some modicum of comfort until I can secure your release. Promise me you won't die in the next twenty-four hours and I'll see what I can do. A little more patience, lad. John Thurloe is not an easy man to get around.'

The door creaked open and the turnkey appeared in the doorway. 'Time's up. Got word himself is coming, and he'll be none too pleased to find you here, Master Freeman.'

The door slammed behind Nathaniel, and for the first time in the six months of his captivity, Jonathan allowed himself a small glimmer of hope.

He leaned back against the wall and drew his knees up to his chest, wrapping cloak and blanket tightly around him. The cold, grey walls closed in on him and he shut his eyes, forcing his mind to turn away from his present predicament to Seven Ways and the memory of Kate standing by the gate, her hair dishevelled and her face flushed from a day at the harvest, smiling up at him— loving him.

The image that had sustained him every day since the key had turned on his imprisonment.

JONATHAN'S second visitor for the day arrived within the hour. Feigning sleep, Jonathan watched from half-closed eyes as the door creaked open to reveal a man standing in the doorway, a kerchief pressed to his nose.

'He's not well, sir,' the turnkey said. 'I reckon as he'll be lucky to see out the month.'

'I see. Why was I not informed of his condition earlier?'

'You said —' the turnkey began but a wave of the man's hand cut his protestations short.

'Wake him.'

The turnkey moved to the bed and prodded Jonathan. Jonathan, his breath rattling in his chest, pulled himself into a sitting position and pushed the hair away from his eyes to face the man responsible for his misery.

Forearmed by Nathaniel's visit, he gathered his scattered wits and prepared for battle.

'Turnkey, remove those manacles,' Thurloe said.

The turnkey obeyed, removing the ankle chains as well. Jonathan had not been expecting that one act of compassion. It was probably intended to make him profoundly grateful to this man. All part of the game Thurloe was playing with him.

'Leave us,' Thurloe commanded and the door shut behind the turnkey.

'Stand up, Thornton.'

Not without difficulty, Jonathan complied with the order. The movement brought on a bout of coughing and he found he had to lean against the wall to keep himself upright.

Thurloe looked him up and down and Jonathan wondered what Thurloe saw behind the filthy, bearded prisoner. A man whom he had broken? A man who could be made to see reason?

'Are you ready to talk with me, Thornton?'

'What do you want of me, Thurloe?'

Thurloe smiled. 'You are the singular possessor of attributes that could be of great value to me.'

'I have nothing of value.'

'Ah, but you do. To begin, you have no family, no ties.'

'Not quite true,' Jonathan said. 'I have a sister who cares for me.'

Thurloe shrugged. 'Secondly, you have no money.'

That at least was correct.

'And thirdly you are a close personal friend of Charles Stuart, who you will no doubt be relieved to hear made his way back to France like a whipped dog.'

Jonathan closed his eyes. The King was safe.

He summoned his strength. 'So?'

'I am prepared to offer you your freedom.'

'And in return?' Jonathan asked, already guessing at the answer.

'Information,' Thurloe replied. 'I can arrange your plausible escape from your present predicament. Your friends in Paris will of course greet you with open arms and there you will be in an ideal position to provide me with regular information of use to the Commonwealth.'

Jonathan gave a hollow laugh. 'Why don't you just say the word "spy" and be done with it?'

'Very well, I want you to spy for me. Direct enough?' Thurloe looked around the cell. 'You must admit that at this point you have nothing to lose.'

'Only my life.' Jonathan coughed again.

'Do sit down, Thornton. Your health is obviously of some concern. Had I known you were ill I would have—'

'Done what? Absolutely nothing, Thurloe. Be honest. It makes little difference to you whether I live or die.' Jonathan subsided onto the cot. 'No doubt there are plenty of others within these walls willing to take your offer.'

The act of talking was straining his physical reserves. What had his uncle said? He had to play for time. 'What is to prevent me from taking your offer of freedom and then withdrawing my co-operation once I was beyond your reach?'

Thurloe's eyes narrowed. 'My reach is long, Colonel. I already have agents in the exiled court. Information can be easily verified, and if you are found to be playing me false... accidents can be arranged.'

Jonathan rose to his feet again and paced the short distance to the opposite wall before turning to face the Secretary of State.

'Master Thurloe, I'd not be lying if I said that in my present circumstances, your offer is not extremely tempting but' — he paused for breath — 'in this world, I serve two masters, the lawful King of England and my conscience. I can't be loyal to both if I have sold my soul to you.'

Thurloe turned to face him. 'I take no offence at the analogy,

Colonel Thornton. Indeed it's refreshing that, despite your present condition, you still feel that way. There are others, as you rightly observe, who would not be quite so obstinate. I think you are a fool, so think about it. The offer remains open. A simple yes, and in a few days, a comfortable bed in Paris and money in your purse —' He crossed to the door and banged loudly. 'Turnkey.'

'And if I do not change my mind?' Jonathan asked, leaning against the damp, mildewed wall.

Thurloe turned to look at him once more. 'You will be dead within a week or so, with no intervention from me. Good day to you, Thornton.'

Jonathan slid down the wall as the door slammed shut.

'Damn you, Thurloe. Damn you to hell,' he shouted at the impervious oaken door and solid stone walls.

His only hope now rested with Nathaniel Freeman.

CHAPTER 45

'I have found him, Kate,' Nathaniel Freeman said as he laid his hat and gloves down on the table.

Kate stared up at him, the words coming out in a desperate rush. 'Where is he?'

'In the Tower. As we feared he was taken prisoner just as he was to board a boat for the continent.'

'Six months. He has been a prisoner six months and no word? Why—'

'Circumstances prevented him,' the lawyer replied.

'Circumstances? What circumstances?'

'He quite simply did not have the ability to send a message.'

'Oh really, Nathaniel.' Henrietta put in. 'Turnkeys are notorious for lining their pockets. It surely would not have taken much to get a message to you?'

The lawyer's mouth set in a hard line. 'He could not.'

Kate regarded the lawyer, sensing the evasion in his eyes and fought down the impulse to question him further. There would be time later to hear the whole tale.

'Can I see him?' Kate asked.

Nathaniel withdrew a paper from his jacket. 'Better than that, Kate. I have an order releasing him into house arrest, into my custody.'

'How...?' Kate asked, scarcely able to breathe.

Nathaniel shook his head. 'Let's just say I had words with Master Thurloe. I persuaded him that we had not fought a war to see innocent men die in prison without a fair trial.'

'And he just agreed to let him go?'

'I threatened to go to Cromwell. I like to think our new Lord Protector has some compassion and I am certain if he knew how Thurloe was using his power, he would be less than pleased.'

'You took a terrible risk,' Henrietta said.

Freeman's lips compressed. 'He was quick to remind me of my loyalties, Hen,' he said. 'It's done. I've ordered the coach and will go straight to the Tower.'

Kate laid a hand on his sleeve. 'Thank you. This is a debt we can never repay you.'

The lawyer put his hand over hers. 'Kate, you must prepare yourself. He is seriously unwell.'

Kate's happiness evaporated. 'Unwell? What do you mean?'

The lawyer swallowed. 'A lung fever, I fear. Another few days and I would have been too late.'

Kate put her hand to her throat. Lung fever could kill the strongest man. She took a step back and felt Henrietta's reassuring hand on her shoulder.

'There is no time to lose then,' Henrietta said. 'Go Nathaniel.'

'I'll fetch my cloak.' Kate turned for the door.

'No,' said the lawyer in a tone that brooked no opposition. 'It's no place for you.'

Kate turned back to face him. 'I'm not easily upset.'

'No, Kate. I will not waste time arguing with you. Make whatever preparations you think are needed and we shall return within the next hour or so.'

Picking up his hat and gloves, Nathaniel Freeman left the parlour.

~

THE FREEMAN COACH turned in through the gates of the house long after it had gone dark. Kate seized the lantern she had ready by the door and ran out into the cold night air, with Henrietta and Ellen hard on her heels.

Dickon jumped down from the box and opened the door and for a brief, horrible moment Kate thought it had all been a terrible mistake and she found herself unable to move. Surely the ragged, filthy ruffian Dickon had to lift from the coach was someone else? The sturdy groom put one arm around the man, steadying him and the man lifted his head.

'Kate? Is that you?'

Her heart shattered into a thousand pieces at the sound of his voice and the wretched state he was in. She gave a choking sob and thrust the lantern she held at Ellen and ran to him with tears running down her face unheeded.

Dickon relinquished his hold and she took him in her arms. 'My dearest love,' she said. 'You're safe now.'

'I never thought to see you again—'

His legs gave way and together they sank to the ground, disturbing the neatly raked gravel. Kate smoothed back the tangled hair from his forehead that burned to her touch. His eyes, bright with fever, held hers and his breathing came in short, painful rasps. Was it possible they were too late?

From the door of the house came a wail. Kate looked up and saw Tabitha, clad only in her nightgown, standing on the step with her hands to her mouth.

'He's dead.' The girl's eyes grew wider and her face paler. 'It's all my fault.'

She turned and ran.

'You leave 'im to Mistress Freeman and me,' Ellen said, placing her hand on Kate's shoulder. 'Go and see to the child. You're more use to her than you are to him. You'll just get in't way.'

Ellen was right. There was nothing practical she could do for Jonathan. She surrendered him to Ellen and his aunt and went after Tabitha.

The child had retreated to her bedchamber and huddled on the bed with a wriggling Oliver in her arms. Kate laid her hand on the child's rigid back.

'Tabitha, he's not dead,' she said softly. 'He's very ill but he's not dead.'

Tabitha pressed her face into Oliver's side, her shoulders heaving with the wracking sobs. Kate took the child in her arms, allowing Oliver to wriggle free. He sat on the floor looking up as Kate rocked the stiff, unresponsive child.

'It's all my fault that they put him in prison and now he's going to die.' Tabitha's voice sounded muffled against Kate's bodice.

'Nonsense,' said Kate. 'It's nothing to do with you, Tabitha. My dear, he was in prison because he fought for the King, not because he took you away.'

Tabitha looked up at Kate and fresh tears welled in her hazel eyes. 'Dame Judith said I was wicked and God would punish me for my father's sins.'

Kate's lips tightened. If Dame Judith had finally departed this earth, Kate sincerely hoped that she was rotting in hell.

'Tabitha,' she smoothed the child's hair, 'you're not wicked and God forgives. He does not punish.'

Tabitha looked at her unblinkingly, as if weighing up the truth of what Kate said. There was so much of Jonathan in her expression that Kate almost wept.

'Would God listen if I prayed hard?' the child whispered.

Relieved, Kate replied, 'Of course, he will, my dear. Come, we'll both pray.'

Tabitha swallowed the last of her sobs and clapped her hands together. She closed her eyes, her lips moving in silent, fervent prayer.

Kate found the words and in them the comfort she needed for herself.

At her *Amen*, Tabitha gave a last, shuddering sigh and opened her eyes.

'Will you look after him?' she asked.

Kate nodded. 'And when he is well, we'll all go to Seven Ways and you can meet your cousins.'

Tabitha nodded, forlornly sniffing.

'Tom can teach you to ride a horse. And your Aunt Nell will have a new baby soon. So much to look forward to. Now climb into bed and go to sleep and we'll see how your father is in the morning.'

Kate fetched the warm bricks from the fireplace, wrapped them in flannel and tucked them into the bed. Tabitha crawled underneath the sheets, and Kate tucked her in. Tabitha's pale, disembodied face looked at her from the pillow.

'Please don't go,' she pleaded.

Kate thought of Jonathan, who needed her and looked down at his daughter, who at this moment needed her more.

'I won't go,' she said. 'Close your eyes and I will tell you a story.'

She sat with the child until she slept before making her way to the chamber where Henrietta had put Jonathan.

The flickering light of the candles and the fire barely illuminated the dark, panelled room. Kate stood beside the large, carved oak bed and looked down at the almost unrecognisable face of her lover, propped high on the bolsters. If it had not been for the agonised breathing, Jonathan could have been dead.

Henrietta and Ellen had done a masterly job in cleaning him up. The beard had gone and they'd cropped his hair short, giving his gaunt face the look of a carved stone saint. Even after he had been shot in York, he had never looked like this. The months of incarceration and deprivation had robbed him of all his light and strength.

She sat down beside him and picked up his hand, cold fear clawing at her. The sleeve of his nightshirt fell back, revealing a neat, white bandage around his wrist. Kate looked up questioningly at Henrietta, who stood on the other side of the bed.

'Nathaniel told me that he had been manacled,' Henrietta said softly, barely keeping the disgust out of her voice.

'For all that time?' Kate asked.

Henrietta nodded.

Kate leaned over him and whispered his name. His eyes opened and recognition flickered like a candle in the dulled depths. The corners of his mouth curled in a smile and he tried to speak but the effort started the coughing. Kate held him, feeling his body, once so hard, now wasted and frail beneath the nightshirt. She laid him back on the pillows and tried to summon a reassuring smile.

'Where...have you been?' he whispered at last. Every word seemed to be a physical effort.

'Seeing to your daughter. She seems to think this is God's punishment for your past sins.'

'Perhaps it is,' Jonathan muttered. A crooked smile flitted across his face. 'Ellen's already started pouring her potions...

down me. I think… I think she's the only person I know who can make death seem like a pleasant alternative.'

'Would you rather I sent for the doctors?' Henrietta interposed. 'Perhaps he should be bled?' The last remark was addressed in a low voice to Ellen, who had entered the room carrying a tray covered with a cloth.

'It'd kill him,' Ellen said.

Jonathan rasped. 'No doctors, Hen. Ellen… may be a witch but I trust her.' He looked at Kate and stretched out his hand to her. She took it and his fingers tightened on hers.

'Tabitha,' he said, his voice now so faint that she had to strain to hear him. 'If… if anything happens to me… promise me you will look after her?'

There was such urgency in his face that tears pricked Kate's eyes. Was it possible after everything they had been through that he could die?

'Kate?'

'I promise,' she said between stiff lips.

The grip on her hand relaxed and for an awful moment, she thought she had lost him. His eyes were closed but the rattle of his laboured breathing showed he still lived.

She leaned over and bent her head, resting her forehead on his. 'You are not going to die,' she whispered.

If he heard her, he gave no sign.

CHAPTER 46

abitha sat, as she had done for the past week, at the top of the staircase, her elbows on her knees and her chin cupped in her hands, Oliver by her side. The dog looked up hopefully when he saw Kate coming up the stairs, his bottom waggling in anticipation of a walk or more cheerful company.

'Tabitha,' Kate said, 'it's cold out here. Go and play your music in the parlour where it's warm.'

She shook her head. 'When can I see him?'

'We've talked about this. When he's a little stronger.' The child's face fell and a thought occurred to Kate. 'If you leave the parlour door open, we will hear you playing the virginals. Your father would like that.'

'Would he?' Tabitha's face brightened and she scurried down the stairs with Oliver bounding beside her.

Kate waited until she entered the parlour, propping the door open as she did. The first uncertain notes from the virginals rose up the stairs as Kate opened the bedroom door.

'Do you hear that?' she asked.

The man propped high on the bed turned his head toward the door.

'That is your daughter.' Kate answered his unspoken question.

'Mary...her mother...had a rare gift for music.' Jonathan's voice was faint and hoarse. 'Her father...would not allow her to have lessons. He thought music...music was the work of the devil but she sang...'

She crossed to the bed and sat down beside him. He reached up and touched her face, tracing the dark circles under her eyes.

'You look... very tired, Kate. Is that my... fault?'

Her fierce battle to keep him alive had made for several long, sleepless nights but he had got through the worst of the fever and the hope that he may make a full recovery compensated for her exhaustion.

She smiled and took his hand. Turning it over, she kissed the palm and held it to her cheek. He would live, and at this moment she cared for nothing else. Still holding his hand in hers, they listened in silence as the gentle and erratic notes of the virginals drifted in through the open door.

'Why didn't you tell me about Tabitha if you knew about her before you left Seven Ways?' she asked.

'I couldn't... be sure. Prescott could have been lying.' He coughed, a deep, rattling cough and it took a long few moments before he could compose himself again. 'I'm... sorry, Kate. I never meant... to deceive you. I intended to... write and tell you once I reached Holland but... my life is full of... good intentions and bad mistakes.'

'She's your daughter and she should live in your home. We shall take her back to Seven Ways and if I can go some of the way to giving her the love her mother never could.'

'Kate… Kate, you're crying.' He reached up and brushed away the offending tears.

She caught his hand, twining his fingers in hers and pressing it to her cheek.

'Don't leave me again, Jonathan.'

'My dearest…dearest, Kate. I will never willingly leave you again. You have my word on that.'

'Willingly? Is that a promise you can keep? Surely that is for those Fates, spinning out our lives in Whitehall to decide.'

His lips tightened and he nodded. 'You're right, Kate. It's…it's not a promise I can keep.' He glanced at the open door. The music had stopped and the house was silent once more. 'I would like to see Tabitha.'

She brushed a lock of hair from his forehead. Even wasted and gaunt, sallow with spent fever, he still presented a considerably less fearsome aspect than he had on the night Nathaniel had brought him home.

She smiled and bent over to kiss him.

'I'll fetch her. I know she is anxious to see you.'

She found Tabitha kneeling on the window seat in the parlour, looking out at the driving rain.

'Your father liked your music,' Kate said.

The girl spun around to face Kate. 'Did he?'

Kate held out her hand. 'He wants to see you. Come with me.'

Tabitha took Kate's hand, holding it tightly as they approached the door to the sick room. As Kate put her hand to the door catch, the child hung back. Kate squeezed her hand reassuringly.

'It will be all right, Tabitha. He's been very ill but he's getting better.'

Jonathan turned his head towards the door as they entered. 'Tabitha.' He smiled and held out his hand.

With a strangled cry, Tabitha leapt onto the bed and buried

her face in his bad shoulder. He winced but did not attempt to dislodge her. Instead, his arms tightened around the child, holding her as she wept.

Kate turned and slipped from the room. There was no place for her at this moment.

CHAPTER 47

*J*onathan had the peculiar feeling of being watched. He opened his eyes and almost jumped in alarm.

Three small faces regarded him solemnly from the foot of the bed. He pulled himself up against the bolster and ran his gaze down the line that comprised, in order of height and age, Thomas Ashley, Tabitha Thornton and Ann Longley.

'You look terrible,' Tom said.

Jonathan ran a rueful hand over his unshaven chin and up through the closely cropped hair.

'I'm certain I do,' he said, surprised at how weak his voice still sounded to his ears after three long weeks. 'What are you doing here?'

'Nan and I came with Aunt Nell,' Tom said, 'but they,' he indicated the door, 'wouldn't tell us anything so we thought we'd see you for ourselves.'

'Are you going to be all right, Uncle Jon?' Ann asked.

Jonathan forced a smile. 'I believe so,' he said.

'I picked these for you.' Ann held up a small bunch of wilting spring flowers, no doubt picked from Henrietta's garden.

'Why did you let them catch you?' Tom's eyes were bright and his tone held a note of accusation as if it had been Jonathan's choice to fall into John Thurloe's hands.

'Some fool mistook me for the King and there were too many of them,' Jonathan said.

'The King?' Tom scoffed. 'You don't look anything like the King.'

'How do you know what the King looks like?' Tabitha demanded.

'I met him.' Thomas straightened and the two girls stared up at him with new respect.

The door opened and Nell glided in.

'How did you children get in here? I thought we told you.'

'It's all right, Nell,' Jonathan said. 'They're fine. Ann brought me flowers. Can you put them in water?'

Nell took the flowers from her daughter and shooed the children in the direction of the door.

Tom stuck his head around the door frame. 'Can we play chess?'

'Perhaps tomorrow,' Jonathan said as Nell closed the door behind them.

His sister stood by the door, regarding her brother with her hands on his hips. Jonathan in turn studied his sister. Kate had told him that the baby would be coming soon.

'Did you come from Seven Ways in that condition?'

She sniffed. 'The coach still has wheels. I wasn't going to sit on my hands in Worcestershire when my only living relative was so intent on dying.'

'Sorry, you came all this way for nothing.' Jonathan smiled.

'Complete waste of time,' Nell agreed.

She walked over to the bed and with a sigh sat down on the chair beside him, easing her aching back.

'However, I think this child will be born in London,' she said. 'I can't see me making it back to Seven Ways. Quite the family reunion, isn't it?'

'You've met my daughter?'

Nell smiled. 'I have. No denying her parentage, is there? She and Tom seem to be getting on very well.'

'Are they? That's good, isn't it?'

'I think so,' Nell said. 'Now would you like the gossip?'

'Giles is safe?'

'Giles is in Amsterdam. You know the King made it back to Paris safely?'

Jonathan nodded. 'Did he get the George back?'

'Giles delivered it personally. Did Kate tell you how we got Giles away?'

Jonathan lay back against the bolsters and let his sister talk about the sojourn in Yorkshire and the trivialities of life at Seven Ways. Her voice drifted over him and just for a few brief moments, he allowed himself to hope that the unfortunate circumstances of his recent detention might finally end his fugitive life and there might yet still be a future here for him in England.

CHAPTER 48

Kate sat by the window of the parlour, pretending to be intent on the smock she was sewing for Nell's baby. Out of the corner of her eye, she was watching with some amusement, the game of chess being waged between her son and Jonathan.

She wondered if Jonathan deliberately pretended to be losing, lulling his opponent into a false sense of superiority, before apparently turning the tables.

'Ha,' Tom declared. 'Check.'

Jonathan narrowed his eyes and squinted thoughtfully at the board. As he lifted his knight to make his move, the door to the parlour opened and Henrietta entered, making way for a dark-haired man of middle height.

Jonathan rose slowly to his feet, still holding the chess piece. What little colour he had regained, drained from his face and something about Henrietta's tight mouth and deferential manner left her in no doubt that the visitor could be none other than John Thurloe.

'Thornton.' The man inclined his head. 'I must say you look somewhat improved since our last meeting.'

'Master Thurloe,' Jonathan responded, setting the knight back on the board with deliberate care.

'Checkmate, Tom,' he said, without even looking at the board.

Kate's pulse quickened. Nathaniel Freeman had warned them to expect a visit from Cromwell's Secretary of State now Jonathan had recovered and his arrival could mean only one thing— Thurloe intended to revoke the house arrest and return Jonathan to the Tower to face trial and possibly death.

She remembered the times the Roundhead soldiers had pulled Seven Ways apart looking for Jonathan and thought she had been afraid then but now she knew real fear. She set her sewing aside and crossed the yawning expanse of floor to stand beside Jonathan.

'Have you come to take him away?' she demanded, determined not to let the man see her fear.

Thurloe looked her up and down. 'I beg your pardon, Mistress. I do not believe we are acquainted.'

'Ashley. Katherine Ashley,' Kate replied.

Thurloe raised an interested eyebrow. 'I know that name. Are you kin to David Ashley of Yorkshire?'

'I am.'

Thurloe nodded, 'I knew him from his days in Parliament. A fine man and loyal to our cause.' Thurloe bowed towards her. He looked from Kate to Jonathan. 'But what is the connection with the Thornton family?'

'David Ashley's wife was a Thornton,' Jonathan replied.

Thurloe's face betrayed nothing. 'I see. Well, it's a pleasure to make your acquaintance, Mistress Ashley.' Thurloe made a deprecatory gesture. 'But if you would excuse me, madam, I have business with Sir Jonathan.'

Kate did not move.

Jonathan put his arm around Kate's shoulder, drawing her close to him. 'Whatever you have to say to me, Master Thurloe can be discussed in Mistress Ashley's presence.'

Henrietta beckoned to Tom. 'Come, Tom, let us leave these people to talk.'

Tom pushed his stool back and stood up. 'Have you come to take Jonathan away again?'

A muscle twitched in Thurloe's cheek. 'You are very direct, young man. I have come merely to talk.'

'Leave us, Tom,' Jonathan said.

Tom scowled at the Secretary of State as he gave him a half-hearted bow before leaving the room, closing the door behind himself and Henrietta.

'Forgive me if I sit, Master Thurloe,' Jonathan resumed his chair. 'I find I tend to tire somewhat easily.' He waited for a beat before he asked, 'So, as Tom just asked, have you come to return me to the Tower? If so, you have come extremely badly prepared. I see no escort for such a dangerous prisoner as myself.'

Thurloe smiled. 'And I see no guard on the door. You surprise me, Thornton, I would have thought you may have seized the chance to escape.'

'Aside from the fact that I am barely out of my sick bed, I have no heart for flight, Master Thurloe.' His eyes narrowed. 'Let's not waste time. What is my fate to be?'

Thurloe regarded him for a moment before he spoke. 'You are fortunate in your friends. Through the direct intercession of your uncle with our Lord Protector and the Council, I have come to offer you your freedom, on one condition, you undertake never again to take up arms against the lawful government of the Commonwealth of England and swear the Solemn Oath and Covenant.'

Thurloe reached into his jacket and handed a paper to Jonathan.

Jonathan read the document and handed it to Kate. It was not long but the closely written words danced and blurred before her eyes and it took an effort to process what she was reading.

As she handed it back to him, she read the question in his eyes. Surely he did not need her to supply the answer? His King had sworn the Oath and he could do it as well. It meant nothing. Just a few words on a piece of paper, nothing more.

'Do you give that undertaking?' Thurloe said.

Jonathan drew a deep breath. 'Yes, I give that undertaking.'

He stood and walked over to the small table where an inkstand and pen stood. He laid the paper out and scratched his signature on the bottom.

As he turned to hand the signed paper to Thurloe, a black and white spaniel pushed its way through the door, hotly pursued by its small owner, who burst into the parlour with cries of 'Oliver, bad dog. Come here.'

Tabitha pulled up short and stared at her father's guest. 'I'm sorry, Father,' she said.

'Master Thurloe, my daughter Tabitha.'

Remembering her manners, Tabitha curtsied politely. Jonathan smiled and held out his hand to her.

'Come here, Tabitha. Master Thurloe is a very important man with some very good news. Has just told me that I do not have to go back to prison.'

A smile lit Tabitha's face and she looked from her father to John Thurloe. 'Thank you,' she said and Thurloe cleared his throat. She looked back at her father. 'May I tell Aunt Hen and Aunt Nell and Tom and Ann?' she asked.

He nodded. 'Take Oliver,' he reminded her as she turned to flee.

Tabitha scooped up the dog in her arms and skipped from the room.

'It seems you do not know as much about me as you thought you did, Master Thurloe,' Jonathan said as he handed the Secretary of State the paper that would give his freedom.

Thurloe smiled and shook his head. 'Apparently not. What will you do now you are a free man?'

Jonathan considered a moment. 'I do not consider that is any business of yours, Thurloe. You will have more pressing matters of State to concern you than the fate of one spent Royalist.'

Thurloe narrowed his eyes. 'On the contrary. I may have badly misjudged you once but my thought is that while domesticity may suit for a while,' — he shot a glance at Kate— 'it will begin to pall and you will yearn for the old days when you rode roughshod over the forces of Parliament. You were a master at the agent's craft, my friend and you will miss those times.'

'What is your meaning?' Jonathan asked.

Thurloe stood and picked up his hat and gloves. 'I am saying that leaving your politics aside, England could still use those talents. We have enemies other than Charles Stuart.'

Kate caught her breath.

Jonathan regarded Cromwell's master of spies and rose to his feet. 'I am weary of war and weary of the games that go with war. You're a clever man and you will always find others prepared to take your gold but not I.' His tone dripped ice and a lesser man than Thurloe would have quailed. 'I'll not forget or forgive how ill you dealt with me, John Thurloe. You have what you came for, please leave.'

Thurloe inclined his head. 'It seems we must part on those terms. I will bid you a good day, Thornton.' He turned to Kate and swept a bow. 'Mistress Ashley. It seems we were mistaken in our judgment of you too. I wish you both happiness.'

They stood side by side without speaking until they heard the front door close and the wheels of Thurloe's coach crunch on the gravel.

Kate let out an audible breath and Jonathan turned from her and walked over to the window. He stood staring out at the garden, his mouth set in a hard line.

'You understand what it was I signed?'

'You told me you could never swear the Solemn Oath and Covenant. To do so was a heavy undertaking.' Kate said.

He turned and held out his arms. She ran to him and he caught her lifting her off her feet with a sudden strength she would have doubted he possessed ten minutes earlier.

'I don't care anymore, Kate,' he said and the corners of his mouth lifted. 'For you, my lovely lady and for my daughter, it is an undertaking I make willingly.'

He set her down and took her hands in his. His eyes glittered. 'You may recall a promise you once made me. If it pleases you, now I am a free man, will you wed me?'

Kate took his face in her hands. 'Oh yes, my dearest love, as soon as it can be arranged.'

He drew her into his arms and they kissed, as if for the first time. No longer with the urgent passion of secrecy but the long, slow promise of the new life they would build together.

THE END

AUTHOR'S NOTE

The Thornton and Ashley families are entirely fictional but they move around the people and events of their times. The battle of Worcester is among the last battles ever fought on English soil and the reminders of that time are still very much to be found around that lovely city. The story of Charles II's unsuccessful attempt to regain his throne and his flight from the battle of Worcester has been the subject of many books, both fact and fiction. It is a tale so full of near misses and unbelievable courage that no mere fiction writer could ever have imagined it.

'Seven Ways' itself bears a very close resemblance both in appearance and location to Harvington Hall near Kidderminster in Worcestershire, a place that held a special significance to my grandfather, who took great pleasure in showing me all the priest holes--including the one in the study that is much as described. However, unlike many old houses in that part of Worcestershire, there is no recorded history of the fleeing Charles II taking refuge there.

The song 'Here Dwells a Pretty Maid' is taken from *Songs and Marches of the Roundheads and Cavaliers* by Lewis Winstock.

THANK YOU

Thank you for reading BY THE SWORD.
If you enjoyed this story, I would love you to leave a review or a
rating on your favourite review site or bookstore.

AND YOU ARE INVITED TO SIGN UP TO ALISON'S
NEWSLETTER
for FREE READS and VIP Exclusives, including contests,
giveaways and advance notice of pre-orders.
www.alisonstuart.com

www.alisonstuart.com

THE KING'S MAN

THE GUARDIANS OF THE CROWN BOOK 2

*Y**ou first met Kit Lovell playing cards with Giles Longley in a grubby inn in Perth and left him alone and wounded on the battlefield of Worcester. THE KING'S MAN continues Kit's story into the dark days of the Interregnum when all hope of a restoration of the monarchy seemed just a dream.*

LONDON *1654: As England languishes in the grip of the reign of Oliver Cromwell, there are those who plot to restore the King.*

Fleeing her old life, Thamsine Granville has nothing left to lose. Alone and friendless, the desperate act of throwing a brick at the coach of Oliver Cromwell could well mean her death. Only the act of a stranger saves her.

Kit Lovell is one of the King's men, a disillusioned Royalist who passes his time cheating at cards, living off his wealthy and attractive mistress, and plotting the death of Oliver Cromwell.

Far from the bored, benevolent rescuer that he seems, Kit

plunges Thamsine into his world of espionage and betrayal – a world that has no room for falling in love.

Torn between Thamsine and loyalty to his master and King, Kit's carefully constructed web of lies begins to unravel and to save Thamsine he must make one last desperate gamble – the cost of which might be his life.

~

THE KING'S MAN
CHAPTER ONE
LONDON, FEBRUARY 1654

THAMSINE GRANVILLE HAD NOT BEGUN the day with the intention of killing Oliver Cromwell.

Around her a jovial crowd pressed against the barricades, determined to enjoy the spectacle of the Lord Protector's ride in state to dine with the Lord Mayor of London. The bells of London, silenced for so many years, rang out, and above her, the flags of the City Guilds flapped in the chill wind.

But from across the road, she had been seen and recognised. A triumphant smile crossed her nemesis's handsome face and he raised his hand to his hat, doffing it as he bowed. He mouthed her name and started to push his way towards the barricade.

Thamsine swallowed, her mouth dry with fear. She only had a few moments to make good her escape, but the press of people to her rear hemmed her in, pushing her towards the barriers.

A roar went up from the crowd as the coach bearing Cromwell approached. As it drew closer, the Lord Protector, clad in a reddish-coloured suit embroidered with gold, inclined his head to acknowledge the cheers of the crowd with all the aplomb of a man born to such a station. She could see no trace of the simple farmer he had once professed to be.

Thamsine's heart beat a rapid tattoo as she stooped and gathered up the broken piece of brick at her feet. Oliver Cromwell, Lord Protector, the false King, was about to become Thamsine Granville's unwitting protector.

Oblivious to his fate, Cromwell smiled, his right hand raised in a parody of benediction as if forgiving them their sins. At the sight of his face, solid and pudding-like, framed by the open window of the carriage, she raised her arm and threw with all the strength that she could muster.

The brickbat hit the body of the coach barely inches from the open window. She got a brief impression of surprise on her intended victim's face. The coach stopped, the horses rising in their traces, whinnying in alarm. The crowd, stunned into silence, held its collective breath, every eye fixed on the ugly graze on the coach's paintwork where the brickbat had struck.

A roar of approbation went up, but Thamsine Granville had disappeared. In the instant her fingers uncurled from the missile, someone had grabbed her from behind. Strong fingers dug into her arm and drove her with force through the crowd that parted before them like the Red Sea.

The world roared in Thamsine's ears. She was only dimly aware of a commotion in the press around her. Soldiers yelled and a woman screamed but all she felt was utter despair. Despite her reckless act, somehow *he* had reached her.

Her captor thrust her down a dark, noisome alley. It was all going to end here, she thought.

Her knees buckled and she could feel herself slipping into unconsciousness, only to be drawn back by a sharp, agonising tug on her arm as it was cruelly and expertly bent behind her.

'Don't faint. Don't you dare faint. Now, unless you want to end your life on a gibbet on Tower Hill, you will co-operate fully in what we are about to do,' he said.

She didn't recognise the voice, and her senses sprang back. She nearly screamed with relief. It wasn't *him* but her relief was short-lived as he turned her to face him, pushing her back against the wall and pinioning her arms at her side.

She closed her eyes as his body pressed against her and she braced herself for the blow or whatever punishment or unspeakable act was coming her way.

She did not expect to be kissed, firmly and expertly.

Her instinctive reaction was to resist, but with her arms and her head immobilised she was reduced to trying to kick her assailant. He responded by placing a booted foot on her instep. She gave a muffled yelp of pain.

'Who's down there, then?'

A voice from the entrance to the alleyway caused her assailant to break off, allowing Thamsine the luxury of taking a deep breath. The fingers holding her arm tightened, digging into her flesh. It was a warning not to move, not to make another sound.

The soldier gave a ribald whistle. 'Got yourself a tasty piece, then?'

In the shadows, she saw her assailant turn his head towards the soldier. 'Now then, sergeant. Can't a man get a bit of privacy around here?' he said in a low and well-modulated voice, with an unusual undertone to the accent that she could not place.

'What's her charge?' The soldier said.

Thamsine shifted, determined to protest the insinuation, but the firm and painful pressure on her upper left arm deepened and she kept her peace.

'My dear sir, there are some pleasures beyond price.'

'We're looking for a woman.' The soldier's voice became

clipped and businesslike. 'Just tried to kill the Lord Protector. Has she come this way?'

'I doubt I would have noticed. I have been otherwise occupied these minutes past.'

Thamsine squirmed in the tight grasp. The easy, lascivious intonation of his voice made her want to slap him. He may well have saved her life but his intentions seemed far from honourable.

'Good day to you, sir. I wish you the joy of it.'

'He's gone.' Her rescuer removed his boot from her foot and stepped back, although he maintained his hold on her arm.

Thamsine found her voice. 'Let me go. You're hurting me.'

'Hurting you? Is that gratitude for saving you from the gibbet?'

He released her and she straightened, rubbing at the place where his fingers had pressed. In the gloom of the alley, it was hard to make out his appearance, and he wore a wide-brimmed hat that hid his face, but she could see that he was clean-shaven, his hair, dark and rough-cut, skimming an immaculate, white collar.

'Maybe I didn't want saving.'

He waved at the entrance to the alleyway. 'Very well. No doubt you can catch up with the good sergeant if that's what you wish.'

To her embarrassment, she started to tremble with cold, fright, and with delayed shock, as the audacity and foolishness of what she had done began to sink in.

She had tried to kill the Lord Protector. Men had hanged for less.

In her desperate bid to escape the greater threat, she had given no thought to what penalty she may have had to pay had she been apprehended.

She looked up at her rescuer. She owed this man thanks for her deliverance, but the words stuck in her throat.

'You do realise what you just did?' he asked.

She nodded.

'May I ask why?'

'Because I wanted him dead,' she said, without much conviction in her voice. It was not the Lord Protector she had wanted dead.

'Well, I'm sure there are plenty who would share the sentiment, but hurling brickbats at a coach is hardly the best way to accomplish that end.'

She drew herself up to her full height. 'And what do you care?'

'I don't,' he answered. 'I have enough problems of my own without rescuing dim-witted whores who choose to hurl objects at the Lord Protector.'

'I'm not a whore.'

He touched his mouth. 'Well, you certainly kiss like one.'

She raised her hand to give the impudent cad a good slap, but he caught her wrist. 'Now, now, mistress. I apologise for calling you a whore. Perhaps you prefer 'failed assassin'?'

He let her wrist go and her arm fell to her side.

'I have nothing more to say to you, sir,' she said, gathering what remained of her pride. 'Thank you for saving my neck from the gibbet. I bid you good day.'

He did not attempt to stop her, standing aside to let her pass. As she did so, he bowed. 'Good fortune to you, mistress.'

She gave him what she hoped was a withering glance and stepped back onto the street. It seemed unnatural that the crowd had resumed its normal bustle. Soldiers mingled with the passers-by, occasionally stopping a person to question them.

Thamsine, in her threadbare cloak and patched and faded dress, attracted no attention. With dragging footsteps, she traced the familiar way to the dreary, rodent-infested hovel on the outskirts of Blackfriars where she had lodged for the last few months.

The smell of cooking coming from the shops and homes she passed made her stomach growl in protest. She had not eaten since the previous day, and even that had been no more than a morsel of stale bread and a thin broth bought with her last coin.

If she wanted to eat, if she wanted to keep a roof over her head, she had only one choice.

The man who had rescued her had called her a whore and she, with her last shred of dignity, had denied it. She could never deny it again. She had sold everything worth selling and now she had only one thing left.

A couple of streets away from her lodging, she stopped in a boarded-up doorway. She loosed her hair and shook it out. With shaking fingers she unlaced her bodice a little way, displaying a hint of her almost-flat chest. She hitched one side of her skirt to show what she hoped was a tantalising glimpse of ankle above the cracked shoes. It was not, she thought, a very alluring picture, but it would have to do.

She took a deep breath and stepped back into the street, tossing her cloak back over her shoulders and adopting the hip-swinging saunter she had observed others of her newly adopted profession use.

Prospective customers should be in no doubt as to what trade she was plying. They would not see how her heart hammered against her ribs and her stomach had become a hard ball of fear and self-loathing. The part of her that still remembered who she was and where she had come from hoped and prayed that the men who frequented the dismal streets of Blackfriars would pass her by without a second glance.

A hand grabbed her shoulder and she gave a small yelp of alarm as she turned to face the man who had accosted her. A bearded face scrutinised her closely, his fingers digging painfully into her wrist.

'What's yer charge?' His breath smelt as if it came directly from the pits of a Hell charged with rotten teeth, onion and stale wine.

Her eyes widened. 'Charge?'

'For your body.' One hand slid down her bodice and the other caught her arm with such ferocity that she cried out in pain and pulled back.

His fingers tightened, drawing her towards him.

'Half a crown,' she said. Her attempt at bravado sounded pathetic even to her ears.

He gave a guffaw of laughter. 'Half a crown for a tight, skinny little arse like yours? Sixpence is all you'll get and count yourself lucky!'

Sixpence would buy a wedge of stale bread and thin broth.

Thamsine nodded.

'Got somewhere to go?'

The thought of plying her trade in the pathetic room that had been her lodgings for the past month horrified her more than the thought of what she was about to do. She shook her head.

'Never mind. Down 'ere will do as good as any.'

Propelling Thamsine by the arm, he thrust her down a filthy alley. A small part of Thamsine's brain registered the irony that it was the second time in one day a man had dragged her down just such a laneway. This time the intention was real and there would be no escaping the consequences.

He pushed her up against the slimy wall and his mouth clamped onto hers, his beard rasping her skin. His tongue, hard and insistent, penetrated her mouth, thrusting inside her while his spare hand grappled with her skirts.

She felt his hand on her thigh. His vile, stinking breath, the taste of him, the insistent probing of his tongue began to suffocate her. Nausea rose in her throat and she tried to twist away but he held her too close. Her struggles were as useless as a reed against the wind.

He leered at her. 'You're a tight little bitch. I reckon you need a bit of softening up.'

The blow came with such ferocity that she fell sideways, her head ringing, her world exploding into a thousand different-coloured lights. Hard fingers closed on her arm, hauling her to her feet.

'Don't hit me. I'll do whatever you want.'

Her plea went unregarded and she sensed rather than saw the shadow of his hand ready to strike. She closed her eyes and with the last of her strength, she braced herself.

The blow did not come.

Instead, the man gave a strangled cry and released her arm, causing her to fall to her knees in the stinking mire. She cowered away, covering her face with her hands as her client said 'Oi! What's yer game! There'll be plenty left for you,'

'Leave the lady be.'

At the sound of the familiar voice, Thamsine felt tears prick the back of her eyes. For the second time in the day, the stranger had come to her rescue, completing her humiliation.

'Lady ... ?'

The sound of a fist on bone cut short the scoffing voice. A heavy body fell to the ground beside her. Through her fingers, she saw the man rise and heard the sound of feet scuffling and the grunts of a struggle in progress. Someone spat at the ground by her feet.

'Take her! She's yours if you want her that bad, but you'll get no joy from her. Not worth a farthing.'

'Get out of here!' The words were followed by the rattle of a sword loosened in the scabbard followed by the clatter of running feet and then silence.

A hand touched her shoulder. 'Let's see the damage.'

'I can't,' she mumbled into her hands.

'Come on, lass, he fetched you a mighty wallop. You weren't much to look at before. I doubt your appearance has been much improved by his handiwork.'

She screwed her eyes tightly shut as he pried her hands away from her face and gave a low whistle. With surprising gentleness, his fingers probed along her right cheekbone. She flinched.

'You've the makings of a truly spectacular black eye but I don't think anything's broken. Now, open your eyes and look at me! I'm not going to hurt you.'

With a supreme effort, she obeyed. Her saviour had crouched in front of her and surveyed her with his grey-green eyes. Nice eyes, she thought, with the lines of humour crinkling at the corners. But she saw no humour in them now, only pity, and pity was the last thing on Earth she wanted.

The shame overwhelmed her and the last of her rigid self-control evaporated. She lowered her head to her knees and began to weep, slow, silent sobs that wracked her thin body.

He made no move towards her; just let her cry until there was no more misery to expend. With a supreme effort, she choked back her misery, wiping her eyes on the sleeve of her dress and forcing herself to look at the man who still crouched before her.

He had a sharp, clever face dominated by a nose that was slightly too long and a mouth that curled as if about to break into a smile.

His hat had fallen to the ground during the scuffle with the bearded man and a cowlick of dark hair fell over his eyes. He pushed it back and reached out a finger, curling a lock of her hair in a gesture that was more paternal than sexual.

He shook his head. 'You'll be dead by week's end if you persist in this chosen vocation,' he said. 'Whoever you are, you're no whore by nature or, I warrant, necessity.'

'You're wrong. I've no choice,' she mumbled.

She wiped the back of her hand across lips that felt bruised and swollen. The vile taste of the man who had violated her rose in her mouth. She leaned away and retched onto the revolting cobbles.

Her rescuer picked up his hat and stood up, fastidiously brushing the mud from the brim. She expected to see him walk away but he remained standing, looking down at her.

'Go away,' she said.

She lowered her head, her hands hanging limply between her knees. She could debase herself no further.

'When did you last eat?'

She looked up at him. 'Yesterday.'

'Come.' He held out a hand to her. 'At least permit me to buy you a decent meal. Take a moment to tidy yourself.'

With an effort she pulled herself to her feet, declining his proffered hand. He strolled to the end of the lane and stood with his back turned as she re-laced her bodice and straightened her skirt, grateful for the time to collect her scattered thoughts. Her head still rang from the blow and she put her fingers to her face, tentatively exploring the bruising.

Taking a deep breath, she addressed his back in a stiff, formal voice. 'I thank you for your assistance, sir, but I beg you, leave me. I'm not fit company for you.'

He turned to face her. 'I'll be the judge of that.' A slow, sardonic smile crossed his face. 'It may be that I'm not fit company for you.'

She regarded him through narrowed eyes. 'Who are you? How

do you come to be here? Were you following me?' The questions rushed out.

'As to the first, my name is Christopher Lovell, although my friends call me Kit.' He swept her a bow. 'Your servant, ma'am. As to the second and third questions … yes, I admit I was following you.'

'Why?'

'I was concerned for you.'

'Concerned for me?'

He cocked his head to one side. 'Are you so far lost that you don't recognise genuine concern when you see it?'

It had been so long since anyone showed her any kindness that she viewed it with suspicion.

'You don't know me, sir. You know nothing about me.' She brought her chin up and met his gaze.

'True, but I've seen your like before. Unless I'm gravely mistaken, you are like me, the flotsam of war, one of the survivors. We're what is left when our friends and our family have nobly sacrificed their fortunes and their lives for a lost cause. I am right, am I not, Mistress … ?'

'Granville,' Thamsine said, too tired to lie. 'Thamsine Granville.'

Her teeth began to chatter and she drew her inadequate cloak tightly around her. It afforded little protection from the biting cold.

His fingers tugged at the cords of his cloak and he swung it around her shoulders. It settled on her thin frame, still warm from his body and Thamsine pulled it close around her.

He hunched his shoulders against the sudden chill and gave a deep, indrawn breath. 'Mistress Granville, it's cold and we've both had a trying day. I meant what I said about a meal.'

She looked down at the toe of her scuffed and leaking shoe.

There seemed little point in any more displays of stubborn pride. For the first time in weeks, she had the prospect of warmth and food. Only a fool would decline, and God alone knew she had already played the fool enough times in one day. There may be a price to pay but at least this Kit Lovell presented a more attractive prospect than her previous 'client'.

She raised her face and met his eyes. She inclined her head as if accepting an invitation to dance and he smiled and crooked his arm.

'Mistress Granville?'

She accepted his arm and he drew her close, shielding her from the icy wind that blew down the narrow streets. Through the sturdy cloth of his jacket, his muscles tensed at her touch and he placed a gloved hand over her cold, dirty fingers. The simple gesture permeated her icy bones, thawing the cold places of her soul.

~

CHAPTER TWO

Kit threw open the door to the busy taproom of The Ship Inn. Beside him, Thamsine pulled his cloak tightly across her thin body as she surveyed the crowd. He put an arm around her and began to guide her towards his usual table. The woman within the circle of his arm had no more substance to her slender frame than a sparrow and she trembled like a trapped bird as he led her to a secluded corner of the taproom.

She subsided onto a stool with her back to the wall, her eyes darting around the room. The sister of the publican, a young woman with a riot of blonde curls falling from beneath a disreputable cap bounded forward, hooking her arm into his and beaming up at him.

'Cap'n Lovell! We didn't expect to see you out so soon!' May's gaze switched to Thamsine and the smile disappeared. 'Got company I see.'

Kit suppressed a smile at the jealous suspicion in her voice.

'A friend of mine, May,' he replied. 'Now, a slice of pie and a jug of ale would be appreciated.'

May sniffed and disappeared into the kitchens.

'What did she mean when she said she didn't expect to see you "out so soon"?' Thamsine asked.

Kit smiled. 'I have spent the last couple of months in the Clink. A small misunderstanding concerning a horse. Now happily resolved,' he added

Thamsine's eyes widened. 'You've been in prison?'

He shrugged. 'I'm often in prison. It's an occupational hazard. Ah, here come the girls with our food.'

May was accompanied by her twin. May and Nan were identical in nearly all respects, although Nan was slightly taller with a warier, more knowing expression on her face and a sharper tongue in her head.

The girls slapped the food and drink down in front of Thamsine. May gave her one last, baleful glance before tending to the demands of another customer. Nan stood behind Kit running her fingers through his hair and, he had no doubt, casting Thamsine a proprietorial and suspicious look as she did so, before returning to the kitchen.

'They seem to regard you as their private property,' Thamsine observed. 'Is this pie safe to eat?'

Kit laughed. 'Those two girls have the biggest hearts in London.'

'And the widest legs, I wouldn't mind betting,' she observed, her eyes on May, who flirted outrageously with a bearded man by the fireplace.

'You are hardly in a position to cast stones on that count, Mistress Granville,' Kit reminded her. 'Now eat before it goes cold. I'll warrant it's the best pie you'll have tasted for some little while.'

Kit picked up the pot of ale and took a deep draught as he regarded the woman who sat opposite him, demolishing the pie with all the grace and elegance of the roughest soldier he had ever known.

Thamsine Granville, if that was her real name, appeared to be an educated and intelligent woman. Even if properly nourished she would still have been considered too thin for beauty. However, beneath the grime, she had an arresting face with high cheekbones and large brown eyes. Her mouth was wide and mobile. Her long nose curved slightly upwards. A strong nose on an interesting face. In the right circumstances, he thought, Thamsine Granville would not go unnoticed.

He finished his ale and poured himself another one. His reasons for going to her aid, not once but twice, went beyond altruism. True, her haunted eyes had touched something within him. He, more than anyone, knew what it was to be balanced on the edge, as this woman seemed to be. However, he also recognised that she could be useful; a card to be played when the time was right.

In the meantime, it seemed he was stuck with her.

He pushed his platter, with his serving of pie, across to her. She looked up at him and he inclined his head. After a momentary hesitation, she polished it off, wiping the last of the gravy up with a piece of bread. When she had done, she set aside the shining platters, taking a deep draught of ale from her tankard.

'You have some colour in your cheeks again. Do you feel better?' Kit remarked, refilling her cup.

She nodded. 'Better than I have for months. Thank you, Master Lovell, or is that Captain Lovell?'

He waved his hand. 'Kit. I think after what you and I have been through today, we can dispense with formalities. May I call you Thamsine? That is your name?'

She hesitated for a moment and nodded. 'It is.'

He leaned forward. 'Well, Thamsine Granville, as I have saved your life twice today, I think it is time to claim some form of reward.'

Her eyes widened and her cheeks coloured. Her lips parted slightly and she swallowed. 'Do you have a room we could go to? I have no wish to try another alley and no coin to pay you.'

Kit stared at her. Did she think that after everything she had been through that day, he wanted her body? The idea was preposterous. Anyway, why would he want this scrawny, dirty scrap of womanhood when Lucy waited for him in her warm, comfortable house in Holborn?

Without thinking, he laughed out loud. 'My dear Thamsine, did you think I meant that sort of payment?'

The colour in her cheeks darkened and she looked away. 'I have nothing else.'

His smile faded at the misery on her face. 'I'm sorry. I shouldn't have laughed. I'm not so mean-minded as to demand such a recompense.' The smile crept back onto his face. 'Anyway, I prefer my women with a bit more meat on them. No, Mistress Granville, all I request by way of reward is your story.'

She looked at him, her eyes widening. 'My story?'

He nodded. 'I would like to know how the gently born Thamsine Granville came to be trying her hand at whoring in the streets of London. Oh yes – with a bit of attempted assassination on the side.'

'How do you know I was gently born?'

Your voice, your demeanour, everything about you.

'A guess, nothing more. Let us start with a simple question. Where are you from?'

She took a deep breath, her gaze flitting to a space above his head. 'You've been very good to me, Master Lovell, but you owe me no more kindness. You must have a wife and a home to go to.'

'Neither. I told you I am like you, flotsam adrift on the streets of London. I have all night to hear your tale if that's what it takes.'

He refilled both their cups and sat back, crossing his arms and stretching out his legs as if in anticipation of the tale that would follow.

Thamsine's eyes darted around the crowded taproom. Was she seeking inspiration or an escape route?

Kit tried again. 'All I wish to know, Thamsine Granville, is what has brought you to this impasse?'

'Captain Lovell.' She returned her gaze to him. This time her eyes were steady. 'What has brought me to my present position is of no interest or concern to you. I have no wish to confide my story in anyone, whatever the debt I owe them. Suffice to say that I have lost everything in the world I hold dear and what little I brought with me to London has been either stolen or sold. I have nothing of interest or value.'

'So you're reduced to selling yourself?'

The blunt words caused a flush to rise again to her pale cheeks. She looked away, resting her chin on her hand and he thought he could detect the glint of tears on her eyelashes.

He tried again. 'What did you hope to achieve by killing the Lord Protector?'

This time what little colour she had drained from her cheeks as she stared at him. 'Kill the Lord Protector? I didn't mean ... I would never ... '

She recollected herself and looked down at her cup and this time a tear dropped from her lashes into the dregs of the ale.

Kit leaned forward. 'Whatever your intention, you only missed him by inches. You could hang if they caught you. If you are intent on assassinating Cromwell, you won't kill him with brick-bats, Mistress Granville.' He lowered his voice, 'There are better ways to kill a king.'

She looked up. 'Is that what brings you to London?'

He laughed and sat back, taking a draught of ale. 'Me? No, Thamsine. All that brings me to London is the pretty face of my mistress and the promise of some lucrative games of cards. I'm done with soldiering and conspiracies. As far as I'm concerned Cromwell is welcome to England.' He spread his hands in a gesture of hopelessness. 'Like you, I've lost everything. Some would say that the only thing I have left is my honour and, believe me, even that is a poor commodity.'

She tilted her head, her gaze scrutinising his face. 'And Where are you from, Captain Lovell?'

He raised a finger. 'Ah, now, the arrangement was that you told me your story, not that I tell you mine.'

'There is something in the way you speak. Your accent ... '

'My accent?'

'It's not quite ... English.'

Kit raised his ale in a mock salute. 'How very perceptive of you, Mistress Granville. You're quite right. My mother was French and by dint of my parents' unhappy marital arrangements, I didn't learn a word of English until I was eight. The accent has never quite left me. My friends tell me it only becomes noticeable when I'm in my cups.' Kit looked into the depths of his tankard. 'Obviously, I've reached that point. Now you've elicited far more information from me than I have from you so, in fairness, I must insist that I hold your answers in credit for another time.'

She rose to her feet. 'Thank you for your kindness. Now I must leave you to return to the arms of your pretty mistress, who is, no doubt, wondering where you are.'

He regarded her for a moment. 'And where would you be going?'

She glanced at the window, where snow now tumbled softly against the heavy glass, and before she could answer he raised a hand. 'I've not gone to all the trouble of pulling you out of the gutter just to send you back out there on a cold, February night. The landlord of this establishment, Jem Marsh, is a friend of mine. He'll give you lodging.'

She frowned. 'As we may have already established, I've no means of paying for this meal let alone lodging.'

'Can you cook?'

'No.'

'Wash dishes?'

She paused. 'I suppose so.'

'Make beds?'

A smile lifted the corners of her mouth. 'As long as I'm not expected to lie in them.'

Kit stood up and beckoned May. She sauntered over to the table and he put an arm around her waist, drawing her in towards him. 'May, my dear. Can you fetch your brother for me?'

May's mouth drooped. 'That all?'

'That's all.' He released her and gave her a playful slap on the rump. The girl squealed and with a coquettish glance over her shoulder to him disappeared into the kitchen.

Wiping his hands on a grubby apron, Jem Marsh appeared at the kitchen door and lumbered over to the table. The badly tied patch over his left eye didn't quite disguise the ugly scar that ran from his temple to his cheekbone. Out of the corner of his eye, Kit saw Thamsine recoil as he loomed over them. What Jem Marsh lacked in looks he made up for in his good nature.

'Well, Cap'n Lovell. The girls said you were out of the Clink. You must have the luck of the Devil. I thought you was locked away for a goodly time.'

'Mercifully, Jem, that little misunderstanding was resolved. Now, old friend, I have a favour to ask of you.'

'Anything, as long as 'tis legal.' The big man laughed.

Kit indicated Thamsine. 'This is my friend, Thamsine Granville. Mistress Granville is a lady, who through the vicissitudes of fortune with which we are all familiar, finds herself in somewhat dire circumstances. Thamsine this is my old sergeant, Jem Marsh.'

Jem looks Thamsine up and down. 'She doesn't look much like a lady.'

'Well she is, and she needs some work, Jem, to pay for lodgings and food.'

'What's she good at?'

Kit gave Thamsine a quick, appraising look and said, 'Not much that is useful, but I'll warrant she's a quick learner.'

Doubt creased Jem's brow and he cast a glance at Thamsine.

'You wouldn't want to work here, love.'

'I have little choice, Master Marsh.' Thamsine looked up at him.

'Jem to me friends, miss.' He scratched his head. 'Well if you've a mind to it and can manage a few rough sorts, I'll take you on Capn' Lovell's recommendation.' He tapped his patch and in a lowered voice, added, 'If you've a mind to making a few shillings on the side, I'm willing to turn a blind eye, lady or no.'

'No,' Thamsine said, the colour staining her cheeks as she caught his meaning. 'I've no need of those sorts of shillings. I am happy to serve drinks, sweep floors, wash dishes, anything, Master Marsh.'

Jem shrugged. 'You can doss in with the girls. You met my sisters, Nan and May? Nan's got a bit of a tongue in her head but she don't mean much by it. You won't mind, will you, girls?' he bellowed across the room.

Nan and May poked their heads out of the kitchen. 'Mind what?' Nan asked.

'This here's Cap'n Lovell's friend, Thamsine. She's coming to work for us. You don't mind her dossing down with you?'

The ensuing pause indicated that neither girl thought this arrangement particularly satisfactory.

'Just as long as she's the open-minded sort,' May said at last.

'Good. That's settled.' Kit drained his cup and rose to his feet. 'Now, if you'll excuse me, Thamsine, I have an appointment to be kept.'

'Will I see you again?' Thamsine clutched his sleeve.

He looked down at the small, cold, chapped hand and put his hand over it, squeezing the fingers. 'My friends and I meet here regularly for a drink and a game of cards. You will probably see me tomorrow night.'

She released her grip on his arm and straightened. A small smile caught at the corners of her mouth. 'Good night, Captain Lovell, and thank you.'

He inclined his head. 'Until next time, Thamsine. Keep her away from brickbats, Jem.'

The big man frowned. 'Brickbats?'

Thamsine stared at Kit, the alarm shining in her eyes.

'Doesn't matter,' Kit said and winked at her. 'Until tomorrow.'

'Private parlour?' Jem asked.

Kit nodded, shrugging his cloak across his shoulders. As he opened the door on a flurry of snow, he turned to look back.

Thamsine had turned to face the Marsh twins, who regarded her with such intensity that she looked like a moth trapped in a flame, her wings singeing under their gaze.

'So, m'lady, fancy yourself as a taproom wench, do you?' Nan flung a grimy apron at Thamsine. 'Well, you can start with washing the platters.'

Kit smiled and shut the door.

~

KIT WALKED through the snow-driven streets to High Holborn where Lucy Talbot, the widow of the late Martin Talbot, wine merchant, had a small, comfortable dwelling above what used to be the wine shop.

'Kit!'

He barely had time to shut the door against the snow as Lucy hurled herself down the stairs and into his arms, covering his face with kisses.

'Where have you been?' she cried, repeating the phrase between kisses.

He disengaged her, allowing himself the luxury of one last, lingering kiss. 'Lucy, dearest, I'm cold and wet and longing for the warmth of your fire.'

She fumbled at the sodden knot on his cloak, pulling the wet garment from his shoulders and abandoning it in a soggy pile on the floor. Kit retrieved it and, carrying it before him, followed Lucy upstairs into the warmth of her parlour. He flung the cloak over the back of a chair to dry, together with his hat and gloves. He gave the dispirited feather in his new hat a regretful glance, setting it down to take the glass of wine that Lucy offered him.

He held up the fine glass, his fingers ridiculously large for the slender, twisted stem, and swirled the ruby contents, watching the play of light from the candles through the liquid before taking a deep draught of the excellent vintage. He silently thanked the good fortune that had thrown him in the path of a wealthy wine merchant's widow.

Lucy traced a finger across his brow and down his nose. Her touch sent lightning bolts of desire shooting through his body.

'You haven't answered my question,' Lucy pouted. 'Where have you been these last weeks?'

'Ah!' Kit set the glass down and took a seat by the fire, stretching out his long legs to dry the damp boots. He took Lucy's small hand and drew her down onto his lap. 'I have a confession, Mistress Mouse.'

'What confession?' she asked.

'I've been in the Clink.'

'Again!' Lucy squeaked with indignation and thumped him firmly in the chest. 'What over this time?'

'The small matter of a horse.'

'A horse is not a small matter!'

'Well, no, it was quite a large horse.'

'And who paid your debts this time?' Her lip curled in derision.

'The matter was settled amicably.'

'Cards, I wager!' she spat at him. ', Kit Lovell, you are incorrigible.'

'But you must admit you missed me,' he wheedled, curling his mistress's blonde locks around his finger.

'Not for a moment!' she protested without conviction, her head tilting backward as his fingers strayed to the soft part of her throat, tracing a line down to the top of the bodice.

He replaced his finger with his mouth, blowing soft butterfly kisses on her clean, soft, white skin, while his fingers grappled with the knot on her bodice laces. She moaned as his kisses dropped lower and his hand fought with the layers of skirts and petticoats, finding its way up past the wool of her stockings to the smooth skin of her upper thigh and heaven where he could lose himself.

As he fumbled with his belt, Lucy took advantage of the distraction and with a shriek of laughter, gathered up her skirts and ran from the room. He caught her on the staircase and together they slithered and tripped up the stairs to the warmth and comfort of Lucy's large tester bed.

FOR MORE INFORMATION *and to purchase THE KING'S MAN click HERE...*